To Sandra,

Best wishes.

Sheena Macleod.

Reign of the Marionettes

1673 –1684

Restoration London

Sheena Macleod

Text copyright © 2016 Sheena Macleod
All rights reserved.

First Print Edition 2016 Dark Ink Press
www.darkink-press.com

ISBN-13 978-0998480121
ISBN 0998480126

Cover design by Michelle Azru

Printed in the United States of America

For my family.

Cast of Characters

Main Characters

Earl of Castlemaine, Roger Palmer. Powis' cousin. Husband of Barbara Palmer, former first mistress of King Charles II.

Mrs Cellier, Elizabeth. Midwife to the Catholic nobility, writer, and almoner.

King Charles II, Charles Stuart. King of England, Scotland and Ireland. His Queen, **Catherine of Braganza**. No legitimate children.

Edward Coleman, Secretary to Mary Beatrice. *Mrs Coleman*, his wife.

Elizabeth Herbert, married to William, *Earl of Powis* - Aide to King Charles II. Their children - *Mary, Frances, Anne, William, Lucy and Winifred*.

Titus Oates, Anglican priest. Mother, *Lucy*, a midwife. Father, *Reverend Samuel Oates*.

Earl of Shaftesbury, Anthony Ashley Cooper. Leader of the opposition. His wife, *Margaret*, and grandson, *Anthony*.

Duke of York, James Stuart. Charles II's heir. Future King. Married Anne Hyde and had two daughters (*Mary* - future Queen. *Anne* - future Queen.) Married second, *Mary Beatrice* - Maria Beatrice d'Este of Modena. Future Queen Consort.

Secondary Characters

Baron Arundell **(of Wardour)**, Thomas. Catholic Lord, impeached in the Popish Plot.

William Bedloe, letter carrier for Catholics and Jesuits. His wife, *Anna*.

Duke of Buckingham, George Villiers. Politician and poet.

Earl of Danby, Thomas Osborne. Lord Treasurer.

Thomas Dangerfield, alias of Thomas Willoughby. Conspirator.

Sir Edmund Berry Godfrey, Magistrate. Justice of the Peace and Timber Merchant.

Louise de Kérouaille, French mistress of Charles II.

Duke of Monmouth, James Scott. Eldest illegitimate son of Charles II and his mistress, Lucy Walter.

Sir William Scroggs, Lord Chief Justice.

Viscount Stafford, William Howard. His wife, *Mary,* and sons, *Henry and John.* Catholic Lord, impeached in the Popish Plot.

Doctor Israel Tonge, Anglican Devine.

Minor characters

Sir Richard Barker, Physician, and his coachman, *Butler.*

Paul Barillon, French Ambassador.

Baron Belasyse, John. Catholic Lord, impeached in the Popish Plot.

Henry Berry, porter in Queen Catherine's chapel at Somerset House.

Father Berry, Jesuit Priest.

Sir Robert Clayton, Lord Mayor of London.

Claude La Colombière, Sacred Heart Missionary in Mary Beatrice's household.

Mr Cooper, friend of Miles Prance and the Earl of Shaftesbury.

Henry Coventry, Secretary of State. Northern Department 1672 -1674, Southern Department 1674- 1680.

John Dryden, literary critic, playwright, Poet Laureate.

Stephen Dugdale, accuser.

Father John Fenwick, Jesuit Priest. John Caldwell. London agent for St Omer.

Father John Gavan, Jesuit Priest

Father Saint Germain, alias of Dr. Burnet. Jesuit Priest. Mary Beatrice's confessor.

Sir Henry Goodricke, Member of Parliament.

Robert Green, cushion-man in Queen Catherine's chapel at Somerset House.

John Grove, Jesuit lay-brother.

Marquess of Halifax, Sir George Savile. Politician and writer.

Father William Harcourt, alias of Father William Barrow. Jesuit.

Lawrence Hill, servant at Queen Catherine's chapel, Somerset House.

Father William Ireland, Jesuit Priest. His sister, Anne Ireland.

Judge Jeffreys, George. Baron.

Sir Leoline Jenkins, Secretary of State.

Frances Jenks, linen draper.

Sarah Jennings, one of Mary Beatrice's ladies.

Henriette de Kérouaille, sister of Louise. Married to a relative of Powis; the **Earl of Pembroke,** Philip Herbert.

Jack Ketch, hangman.

Christopher Kirkby, held a position in the Royal Laboratory.

Sir Roger L'Estrange, press censor.

Doctor Lloyd, preached at Godfrey's funeral.

John Locke, philosopher and physician. Father of Classical Liberalism.

Luzancy, Frenchman. Claimed to be a converted Protestant.

Matthew Medbourne, actor and playwright.

Father Edward Mico, alias Hervey and Baines. Jesuit Priest.

Father William Morgan, Priest. Friend of Elizabeth and Powis.

Duke of Norfolk, Henry Howard. Arundel House. His long-term mistress and then his wife, *Jane Bickerton.*

Thomas Otway, playwright and poet.

William Parker, Schoolmaster at Hastings, and his father, **Captain Parker**.

Baron Petre, William. Catholic Lord, impeached in the Popish Plot.

Father Petrie, York's confessor. Privy Council member.

Thomas Pickering, Benedictine Monk in Queen Catherine's chapel.

Miles Prance, silversmith occasionally employed by Queen Catherine.

Earl of Rochester, John Wilmot. Poet, satirist, wit and libertine. His wife, *Elizabeth Malet*.

Earl of Salisbury, James Cecil. Privy Council member.

Catherine Sedley, one of Mary Beatrice's Ladies. York's mistress.

William Smith, Schoolmaster.

Father Richard Strange, Jesuit. Provincial of the Society of Jesus.

Father Anthony Turner, Jesuit Priest.

Sir George Wakeman, physician to Queen Catherine of Braganza.

Sir William Waller, Middlesex Justice of the Peace.

Baron Wharton, Thomas. Anglican nobleman and politician.

Father Whitbread, Provincial of St Omer. Jesuit Priest.

Sir Joseph Williamson, Secretary of State - Northern Department.

Reign of the Marionettes

PROLOGUE

Smithfield, London - 27th January 1556

With a lace-gloved hand, she pulled back the black silk curtain of the mourning-coach and looked out across the Elms. The morning had dawned clear, but a fine mist rose from the ground, making it appear as though she watched through a veil of fine gossamer threads.

A long row of black mourning-coaches lined the length of the grassy mound, containing the families of the condemned. The hot breath from their horses, mingled with the cold air, sending swirls of smoke upwards.

Letting the curtain drop, she stared ahead. The intense rage she felt would not abate. She sat straight-backed and fingered her rosary and prayed for release. Nothing soothed the hatred she felt towards her family. She spent her days, and part of her nights, on her knees in her chapel praying for an end to her torment.

She blamed her father's whore. For, like Eve in Eden she'd tempted her father to vice with her body.

The roars of the crowd grew louder, and she pulled back the curtain again and peered out. Three ragged Protestants were dragged forward and placed individually into empty wooden tar barrels and chained to stakes. When they were in position, faggots and loose straw and tinder were stuffed around each barrel.

As a silk-robed priest held up a gold cross and addressed the condemned, the crowd remained silent. When not even one heretic would renounce their Protestant faith, gunpowder was placed around the barrels, and the faggots lit. When flames crept up to engulf the dissenters, their moans mingled with the silent screams erupting inside her head. The carnage that had been her life flashed before her eyes and played out once again.

Her father, King Henry VIII, and his whore, Anne Boleyn, were dead, but the legacy of their lust lived on through her. Her own child - the son who never was - hovered on the horizon of her thoughts, looking down at her with doleful eyes and calling to her, "Mama, Mama."

The courts had condemned near two hundred heretics. But, no matter how many Protestants they destroyed her soul called out for more. The sound of their screams and the stench of their seared flesh seeped into her soul temporarily feeding her desire for justice for her mother. She took comfort in knowing that none of their deaths was her doing; it was the law of the land.

A ragged boy ran alongside the coach, fleeing the pitiful sounds of the Protestants now writhing at the stakes. He stopped, turned and looked at her window.

As the boy's eyes met hers and fear flooded through them, he screamed and fled, shouting, "It's Queen Mary!"

His words faded into the distance, but his voice echoed in her head, "It's Murdering Mary."

SHEENA MACLEOD

Part One: The Barren Queen

December 1673 - December 1674

'I am definitely the best king in England at the moment.'

King Charles II

(Said during the restoration negotiations)

CHAPTER ONE

The Cavalcade

Grey clouds formed over London, casting dark shadows across the river entrance to Whitehall Palace. In the dimming light, Elizabeth stepped through a double door, set high on the crumbling facade of the palace wall. As she weaved her way through the throng of courtiers gathering on the cobbled courtyard, their accusing faces turned towards her.

Keeping her head down, she pulled her fur-lined cloak tight against the biting air and quickened her steps. Her thoughts filled with concern for her family. At forty, she'd already spent a lifetime glancing behind her, looking for danger. A surge of fear, tinged with excitement coursed through her. Could the approaching cavalcade bring them greater freedom? She dared not even think it. All she could do now was wait and hope.

Reaching the stone balustrade, overlooking the privy stairs, Elizabeth stopped and gazed out in surprise. All along the riverbank bonfires blazed into life and flames lit up the darkening sky. It was as if half of London had come to watch the procession of gilded barges sail up the Thames. The left bank of the river had transformed into a teeming mass, and shouts of, "No papists!" rang from the milling throng.

"*Meu amigo*, Baroness Powis."

A smile formed on Elizabeth's face. She hadn't heard Queen Catherine approach, and she turned around. Her smile faded. Since they'd last met a few days before, Catherine's olive-tinted skin had paled, and dark shadows had formed beneath her eyes.

She curtsied. "Your Majesty."

Linking into Elizabeth's arm, Queen Catherine leant towards her. "So many ears, always they are listening," she whispered and gestured for her ladies to stand back.

Understanding, Elizabeth drew closer to the Queen's tiny frame. "And fingers, pointing. Do they really believe I helped arrange this marriage?" She touched Catherine's arm. "But, dear God, it must be harder for you."

Catherine waved a hand, ending further discussion of the matter.

Taking in the group of gossiping courtiers beside them, Elizabeth nodded her agreement.

"Ah! No fireworks," Catherine said in her accented English and inclined her head.

Elizabeth followed the Queen's gaze and echoed her sentiments. "Tut, tut. Such a poor welcome. But few will consider the arrival of a Catholic bride as a cause for celebration."

"Ah, but they hid it better when I came from Portugal. It filled me with false hope," Catherine said with sadness in her voice.

Recalling the Queen's arrival, eleven years earlier, Elizabeth smiled. "What a blessed welcome you received. The minstrels, the fireworks –"

Loud cries of 'No Popery' sprung from the riverside, interrupting Elizabeth. The cries turned to roars as a group of men held up an effigy of the Pope and thrust it into a raging bonfire. Sparks scattered and streams of smoke swirled into the cold air. Cats, stuffed into the Pope's belly, screamed as they fled to safety.

Elizabeth reeled back and gripped Catherine's arm. "God's truth."

With a trembling hand, Elizabeth fingered the strand of pearls around her neck. *Hail Mary, full of grace. Keep my family safe.* Beside her, Queen Catherine lifted a gloved hand and worried at her own rope of pearls.

"They're here," a voice yelled, and an almighty roar sprang from the crowd.

Excitement coursed through Elizabeth, and she leaned across the balustrade and watched the first barge sail into view. The Modena standard flapped above its stern as if urging the cavalcade to return to Italy. A drummer in a red coat crouched in the front, beating time to the dip of the oars. Rat-a-tat. Rat-a-tat. Behind the drummer, the Duke of York and his new bride, Mary Beatrice, sat under a red canopy and waved to the crowd.

Barge after barge followed behind, carrying the bride's retinue and possessions. As the cavalcade progressed through the murky water, shadows from Elizabeth's past resurfaced in her mind. Her throat tightened. Did this retinue bring with them calm waters or a raging sea? As the oars ploughed into the murky depths, leaving furrows of uncertainty in their wake, Elizabeth doubted whether prayers would be enough to protect her family.

Church bells rang out, drawing her back to the moment. Queen Catherine stared towards her husband's barge, and Elizabeth saw the deep longing in the Queen's eyes. Impatient with waiting, King Charles had set out to look for the cavalcade's approach. The Royal barge now turned in a wide arc, rocked on the current and sailed into dock. Mooring ropes were thrown from it onto the landing stage.

Charles leapt ashore, and the crowd's roars turned to cheers. Two horse guards, swords drawn, moved over beside him. Charles paced impatiently back and forth in front of them, his eyes fixed on the first gilded barge. Elizabeth's gaze moved beyond him, scanning the faces still disembarking, searching for her own husband.

When Powis jumped ashore, Elizabeth drew in her breath with delight. Though he was forty-eight and his jowls had slackened, she still saw the young man she had married twenty years before. She hadn't seen him all day – Charles had kept the entire Court busy preparing for the arrival of the royal bride. Her eyes followed Powis' movements until he disappeared into the throng surrounding the King.

When James of York's new wife stepped out from under the crimson canopy, and down onto the landing stage, the crowd surged forward and roared, "Papist whore, go home!"

Angling their pikes, guards pushed the crowd back. Elizabeth let out a moan of fear and covered her mouth with her hand.

Charles strode over to York and his wife, a frown further furrowing the lines already etched onto his swarthy face. Stopping in front of Mary Beatrice, he pulled off his wide-brimmed hat and bowed low before her. His dark periwig and lace cravat and cuffs billowed in the downdraught. Charles linked his arm into Mary Beatrice's and walked her up the privy stairs. Holding his head high, he smiled at the crowd and, with his usual long strides, marched towards the palace entrance. In an effort to keep up, Mary Beatrice hurried along beside him.

Followed closely by her ladies, Queen Catherine walked over to join her husband. Elizabeth made to follow but stopped, entranced by the sight of Mary Beatrice. Swamped by the large retinue clustering around her, the girl appeared terrified. Her hair and eyes, peeping out from the hood of a blue cloak, were as black as jet, and full red lips formed a stark contrast to her pale face. She looks no more than a child, Elizabeth thought. Like a summer bloom transplanted into a winter garden, this fifteen-year-old had been plucked from her homeland and brought to a country that didn't want her.

When Mary Beatrice disappeared from view, Elizabeth turned to follow Queen Catherine into the Palace. Beside her, Anthony Ashley Cooper, the Earl of Shaftesbury, reached for his walking sticks resting against the balustrade and winced from the effort. Without thinking, Elizabeth reached for them.

Brushing her arm aside, Shaftesbury raised his hooked nose in the air. "I'm not an invalid. I can manage."

Elizabeth shook her head at him and bit back a nasty retort. What an insufferable man he was, but she saw no point in getting on the wrong side of his temper. "Ah! My Lord Shaftesbury," she said with all the enthusiasm she could muster. "I'm gladdened to hear it. Then perhaps you could escort me inside, for my feet are frozen from standing here."

The coldness between them broken, Shaftesbury laughed, and they joined the throng threading their way through the maze of corridors, towards the Great Hall. The clip-clop of Shaftesbury's high-heeled shoes echoed off the stone floor.

"It's not just because she's Catholic. My objection," he said and his thin lips formed into a smile. "I've got nothing against Catholics. You know that?"

Elizabeth nodded. What Shaftesbury said was true enough, but her husband, Baron Powis, didn't trust him. "So why are you so against York marrying Mary Beatrice?" Puzzled, she turned to look at him and almost bumped into a man thrusting his word-sheet towards them. She stepped around the ballad seller.

"What good is a Parliament that's not consulted?" Shaftesbury said. "We cannot tolerate decisions being made without our say. If we do, what then? Your husband will know this."

Was he hoping to draw Powis over to his point of view, through her? It was hard to tell with Shaftesbury. "But, none of this is Mary Beatrice's fault," Elizabeth said. "And she can provide us with our much-needed heir."

Shaftesbury glowered at her. "Your hope, Elizabeth, is my greatest fear."

Elizabeth took her position beside the other royals and nobles, waiting to meet Mary Beatrice. Trumpets sounded, and Charles escorted the new Duchess of York into the Great Hall and along the long line.

The Queen's tiny frame diminished further, as she reached up and hugged her new sister-in-law. York's daughters by his first wife, Anne and Mary, giggled and blushed as they greeted their stepmother, who was only a few years older than themselves.

When her turn arrived, Elizabeth dropped to her knees. Mary Beatrice extended a hand to her, palm down. As Elizabeth bent to kiss it, the ring given by James of York to mark the marriage took her by surprise. The large ruby was far too heavy for such a delicate hand to carry. Was this an omen, she wondered? Would this girl secure a Catholic heir or, as had happened to Queen Catherine, would the burden prove too great?

CHAPTER TWO

Cold Comfort

Later that evening, after a feast in the Great Hall, servants cleared the long, wooden tables and scraped them back along the stone floor to make room for dancing. Musicians gathered on a stage at the front, setting up their instruments, and liveried servants carried in pitchers of ale and wine, and plates of sweetmeats and dried fruit.

Elizabeth linked into her husband's arm. They'd dined together, but Powis was now deep in conversation with his cousin, the Earl of Castlemaine; about the divide within Parliament over York's marriage. The collective hum of voices surrounding Elizabeth built to a loud babble. She had never acquired a taste for Court life and longed to return home. She pushed tighter into Powis' arm.

Powis bent down and whispered in his strong Welsh accent, "Will this day never end? As soon as the dancing begins, we will leave."

Stretching up, Elizabeth kissed his cheek and relished the familiar rasp of his face. "I should go and talk to Queen Catherine . . . Before we go."

She excused herself and hurried across the Great Hall. She didn't belong here. Like actors in some gaudy pageant, courtiers roamed around vying for applause. Whores in the latest gowns and glittering jewels fawned over the nobility. Claiming their space in the arena, wits moved around in their frills and mock smiles, looking for someone, anyone, to impress. Elizabeth frowned. Taking centre stage, and surrounded by laughing courtiers, King Charles petted the spaniel on his lap and the mistress on his knee.

A strangled sob caught Elizabeth's attention, and she turned to see Mary Beatrice running behind a screen. The girl's tear-stained face looked back and then disappeared, a swirl of pale blue silk trailing behind her.

Elizabeth looked towards Mary Beatrice's retinue. It took them a moment to realise the girl had gone. Their heads turned, eyes searching. "Maria Beatrice! Where is Maria Beatrice?" they called.

Guards drew their swords. Bodies quickly dispersed, searching the huge hall, calling her name, *"Principessa." "Duchessa." "Maria Beatrice."*

Reaching the screen, Elizabeth hesitated. She should turn back, tell them where Mary Beatrice had gone but, as a fellow Catholic, she wanted to find her first and offer her some small comfort. She ducked behind the screen and entered a chamber.

Picking up the hem of her gown, Elizabeth hurried down a stone staircase, past the Great Kitchen, and on towards the Thames. She shivered. Even for December it was bitter, and she rubbed her arms. Green slime clung to the bottom of the stone walls, and a putrid stench from the river polluted the stairwell.

A sound echoed upwards, like a child sobbing for its mother. Elizabeth lifted a candle from a wall sconce, and its brightness illuminated the dark space. The sobs guided her steps, and she followed them towards a small passage at the side of the staircase. Was this how she had once cried for her mother? She tried to remember, but nothing came. Her throat constricted, she had been too young. The only image she held of her mother was of a portrait, surrounded by a large gilt frame. Elizabeth moved further into the darkness.

A muffled sob caused her to stop and look around. Breathless, she bent down and moved under the stairwell, wax dripped onto her hand. Amongst abandoned relics of the old religion, stripped bare of anything of value, she found Mary Beatrice huddled in a corner – crouched on the ground, with her arms grasped around her knees, and her head bent, rocking back and forth.

The girl looked up, her dark eyes wide with fear, her face streaked with tears. Long dark hair trailed over her shoulders and wet tendrils clung to her face.

Hunkering down, Elizabeth reached out a hand to help her up.

Mary Beatrice drew back, staring. Silver threads, in her blue satin gown, glittered in the flickering candlelight. "Your name; I cannot remember your name," she said, between ragged breaths.

Elizabeth laid the candle on an upturned stool and, with great difficulty, for she was no longer as slim as she once was, sat down. She put her arm around Mary Beatrice's shoulders and pulled her close. The smell of jasmine and spirit of musk on the girl's skin reminded her of her eldest daughter.

"Hush, hush, child. Hush, hush," Elizabeth said as if comforting one of her own children. "All will be well." Despite the chill of the passage, sweat coursed down the girl's neck. "You'll catch a fever if you stay here. What will you do then, confined to your bedchamber, your ladies fussing around? No, 'tis better you stay well."

Placing her head on Elizabeth's shoulder, Mary Beatrice shuddered. Elizabeth cradled her in her arms and rocked her as any mother would.

Mary Beatrice babbled in Italian.

Elizabeth shook her head. "English . . . In English, please."

"*Che so*, but my English, it is not so good."

"Then you must practice, for I speak no Italian, and we have to talk."

"Why me? Why choose me? He has already been married. I beg them . . . take my aunt!"

"Hush now. One day you will be Queen and your aunt will not." Elizabeth recalled Shaftesbury's words. Holy Mother of God, she couldn't bring herself to tell this girl she'd been selected *because* she was Catholic and the Protestants in Parliament had not agreed to it. God help her.

"I refuse. I say no." A frown creased the girl's brow. "But the Pope . . . he commands me. He say I am doing a great service for Catholics."

"And you are. Your mama will have explained. We cannot practice the true religion here."

"*Si*, and for that, I agree. But I had never heard of James, Duke of York. I did not know where London was. Then strangers arrive. They tell me I have to marry a man – Blessed Mother . . . A man of forty. His face . . . it frightens me."

Elizabeth sighed. "Yes, York is old and scarred, but he's your husband, and you'll grow to love him."

Mary Beatrice squealed. "Never! It is not possible."

"Shush, you say that now but you'll soon grow fond of him. Once you have children –"

"No! No *bambino*! I am to become a nun. I have prepared for this . . . It is to be my life. It is what I want."

15

Mary Beatrice sobbed, and Elizabeth held her close. As an Italian princess, this girl would never have been allowed to enter into any convent. In truth, if it hadn't been York, it would have been some other foreign royal. At least York was kind hearted and seemed to adore her.

"It's God's will," Elizabeth said. "There are many ways to serve Him. Let us pray He guides you in your task. Now come, your ladies will be searching for you. We should head back before they come here." Standing up, Elizabeth dusted herself down and helped Mary Beatrice to her feet. She picked up the candle, and they made their way back along the stone passage.

Mary Beatrice stiffened. "The people here say I am Catholic whore. But, I am not a whore. They shout, 'Look, it is the Pope's daughter.' My *papi, he* died when I am four years."

Elizabeth thought of her own father. Though he'd lived through her childhood, he may as well have died. He'd spent most of that time imprisoned in the Tower, in exile abroad, or in Ireland with his new wife and family. "Dear child. I pray your burden grows lighter. When people get to know you, things will improve."

When they arrived back in the Great Hall, the girl broke away and ran towards her Italian ladies. Their arms enfolded her. "Maria Beatrice is here," one of them called out.

The band struck up for a minuet, and Elizabeth went in search of Powis. She would call on Mary Beatrice tomorrow, to see how she had settled. She couldn't imagine being forced to marry someone she didn't know or care for. The very thought made her shudder. She glanced back to see Mary Beatrice surrounded by her retinue. They were the closest thing she had to Modena. Elizabeth knew well the feeling of longing for home. Thanks be to God, her own family were going home to Wales next week and wouldn't be returning to London until Parliament opened again in the new year.

Scanning the room for Queen Catherine, Elizabeth observed the vast array of servants scurrying around like an army of ants. Barrows, filled to overflowing with wood, were brought to a young boy who fed the fuel into the hungry flames. Wax dripped from wall sconces, and the smell of oil seeped from lanterns suspended from pulleys attached to the ceiling. Two young boys, no older than Elizabeth's nine-year-old son, heaved a basket of candles, tapers and oil between them, replacing those that burned out. Elizabeth sighed. Throughout the palace, a vast army worked to keep the great wheel of Court life turning, *and* she had to play her part.

She halted. A small group of Protestant Lords was engaged in a heated debate. Over the music and background noise, she'd heard Mary Beatrice's name and recognised Shaftesbury's voice. Turning her back to them, she looked out the window.

"The people won't tolerate having a Catholic heir foisted upon them. We should have been consulted. Continue to push within Parliament. York must divorce her. Give him no other option," Shaftesbury said.

"And Charles must divorce his Barren Queen and marry a Protestant. One who *can* birth a male heir. It has never been more vital than now," one of the other Lords added.

"We could arrange for the Barren Queen to be secretly shipped to the colonies and have Charles divorce her for desertion," Shaftesbury said and roared with laughter. "Come, let's find Buckingham and see what he says."

As the Protestant Lords passed behind her, Elizabeth looked out at the moonless sky. Powis had been right not to trust Shaftesbury.

CHAPTER THREE

Giving Pearls to Pigs

Seated behind his desk, in the study of his London townhouse, the Earl of Shaftesbury sank back and lifted his glass. Firelight reflected off the ruby red liquid. Sipping the claret, he relished its fine flavour. The tapestry of tastes, of wild berries, plum and spices, spread warmth into his belly and settled his racing thoughts.

It wasn't his dismissal as Lord Chancellor that plagued him. He had risen many times before, and no doubt would remain a key figure in Parliament. He'd only said what the majority of other Lords whispered amongst themselves about the growing Catholic influence at Court. He would be damned before he apologised for that.

Shaftesbury searched through the papers on his desk and found the tract he'd been working on earlier. Three weeks had passed since Mary Beatrice's arrival in London, and he was no further forward in having her removed. Laying down his glass, he lifted a quill pen and dipped it into a silver inkwell. What argument could he present? Damnation! No words came. Was he fighting a lost cause? Though the other Protestant Lords muttered about York's marriage, they seemed unwilling to do anything about it. He stretched his leg, and his foot kicked against something on the floor.

Bending down, Shaftesbury pulled out a small replica of one of the King's yachts from under the desk. Anthony must have left it when he'd been playing there earlier. His grandson had returned home, but this was his favourite toy, and he would be missing it. Pushing aside the broadsheets, pamphlets and letters littering his desk, he gently laid the yacht in their place.

He lifted his glass, and once again savoured the claret's succulent flavour. The clock on the mantle chimed out the hour of eight, and a dog barked outside on the Strand. He closed his eyes. In two months his grandson would turn three. Could he get a working model of the King's yacht made for him? Would Anthony like that, or some toy soldiers perhaps? A knock came on the door, and Shaftesbury opened his eyes.

His butler entered and bowed. "The Duke of Buckingham has arrived and wishes to speak with you, my lord."

Buckingham rarely called, and never at such a late hour. Intrigued, Shaftesbury said, "Show him straight in." He lifted his grandson's toy yacht. "Wait! Wait one moment. Send someone to return this to young Anthony. Do it straight away and make sure he gets it *tonight*."

When Buckingham hurried into the room, Shaftesbury reached for his stick. Standing up, he winced as a sharp pain shot through his side. Taking in the deep lines etched across Buckingham's brow, he waited until the butler closed the door before addressing him.

"What ails you? You look like death. Has something happened?" Shaftesbury turned and poured a generous glass of wine from the decanter on his desk. Holding it out to Buckingham, he continued to take in his distressed state. "Drink this."

Buckingham, who had paced the length of the room with his hands behind his back, turned and strode back. Taking the glass, he downed the contents in one swallow. "You ask what has happened. God's truth, I don't know where to start. Damn Charles as the son of a Papist." Removing his long dark periwig, styled in the fashion set by the King, he threw it to the ground. "Blood and wounds, he'd sell his soul to Hell."

Coming around the desk, Shaftesbury looked up at him. "I've never seen you so angry. I cannot help unless you tell me what's wrong." Buckingham had forever been like a brother to the King. What new falling out could have taken place between them? No doubt it would be over some woman.

Buckingham grimaced and roared as if in pain. "We've been deceived. Nay, we've been duped."

Startled, Shaftesbury leant over to steady himself on the edge of the desk. "Duped! What are you saying?"

"My sister tried to warn me, but my vanity led me to believe otherwise." Buckingham shook his head, shifting the loose flesh of his double chin and drooping jowls. "I wouldn't believe Charles would do this. Damn him. Today I received new information about the matter."

Buckingham pulled his sword from its scabbard and raised it above his head. The diamonds in the sword's hilt glittered in the candlelight, and the luminance of the many pearls stood out in stark contrast. "As a devoted Protestant, I'd never assist anything promoting Catholicism. Charles knows this." Buckingham cast the sword aside. "Never again will I wear this. I gave my life's work to purchase *these* pearls."

"But . . . you were given that sword by King Louis, as a token of thanks for negotiating the treaty against the Dutch." Shaftesbury reflected on Buckingham's words. Duped, but how? It seemed to be related to the war negotiations with France. But . . . promoting Catholics.

Whatever was Buckingham talking about? He shook his head. As a fellow member of Charles' Cabal for war, he'd also helped with these negotiations. "What new intelligence might this be?"

"While we, as the Protestant members of his Cabal, were arranging the war treaty with France, Charles and the Catholic members were negotiating a separate treaty behind our backs."

"Nay!" Shaftesbury called out in disbelief. The treaty was signed four years before. Since then, though the war continued, the Cabal had been disbanded. "This cannot be right. You negotiated the treaty yourself. We all signed it." He collapsed back into his chair and let out a loud exhalation. "Pish! Is this true?"

Buckingham nodded. "According to information I received."

"Is your source reliable?"

"As good as any . . . He had already informed Orange in Holland."

Shaftesbury held his hands to his face, as if in prayer. A candle on the desk spluttered and died. He opened a drawer and took out another. With a shaking hand, he placed its wick against a lit candle and replaced the extinguished one. "Do you think there's any truth to this?"

"Without a doubt but we can't prove it. The documents relating to the Treaty are held in France. We have no evidence."

"Tell me about this other treaty."

"In it, Charles promised to support the French in their war against the Dutch. In return, he received funds to enable him to rule independently of Parliament."

Bile rose in Shaftesbury's throat. "Nay! Now we know how Charles can prorogue whenever *he* wants. Hah! He receives his money from France. He has no need to open Parliament to receive those revenues agreed by us. It makes sense now. What else?"

"The remainder was as the treaty we signed. God damn him. Apart from an additional clause saying he'd help re-establish the Roman Catholic Church in England." Buckingham fixed his gaze on Shaftesbury. "When he had achieved this, he would convert to Rome."

Ignoring the pain in his side, Shaftesbury jumped up. "What? It said what? How can this be?"

Shaftesbury poured two glasses of claret and handed one to Buckingham. "I've always doubted the Stuarts' allegiance to the Anglican Church and suspected their loyalty lay with Rome. Charles is promoting religious tolerance. Add this to the rumours of his brother's conversion and it could explain my dismissal for challenging their marriages to Catholics."

Buckingham gave a hollow laugh and laid his glass down. "God's truth, we can't speak out about any of this, for we've no evidence to support these claims."

A large piece of coal shifted in the grate, tempering its warm glow. Shaftesbury went over and placed a log from the hearth on top. The dry wood flared into life, and flames licked up the chimney. The soot at the back caught and reddened sparks appeared and disappeared, like soldiers marching to war. The Civil War remained fresh in Shaftesbury's mind. Could he change allegiance again?

He'd been lucky after Charles' restoration, luckier than most Parliamentarians. Though he'd been accepted back into the Royalist camp, he'd retained the old Republican vision. *For one and for all*, he'd believed. He still did. Nobody should work and then go without so a king could live well.

Shaftesbury shook his head. "I can't abide to watch the growing cost of maintaining the Royal Court," he said, still watching the sparks appear and disappear. "All that money wasted. Think of the ships and commerce it could fund. One of Charles' mistresses' jewels alone could pay for the repair of all the naval ships sitting full of holes in dock."

He'd allied himself to Cromwell during the Civil War but what difference had it made? The common people remained without a voice. Shaftesbury watched until the sparks burned out then sat down at his desk. "How *can* we keep this information to ourselves? Our people have a right to know."

Buckingham picked up his periwig and put it back on. "If the public hear of this it would lead to another bloody civil war. We have no choice but to contain it."

"What are we to do? Parliament opens in less than two weeks."

"Unless Charles prorogues . . . To prevent us debating York's marriage again."

Shaftesbury picked up the abandoned sword and studied the diamonds and pearls on it. "Jesus said, 'Do not throw your pearls to pigs.' I gave my heart freely to Charles, and he deceived me." He looked up. "I'll arrange for this sword to be buried."

CHAPTER FOUR

If Wishes Were Horses

Elizabeth found Powis standing alone in their terraced garden in Wales. The ground and shrubbery glittered white with frost, and wisps of mist billowed from his mouth, where his breath hit the cold air. It was as if the view held him so transfixed he couldn't turn away.

Linking into his arm, Elizabeth looked up at their home, Powis Castle, set high on the rocky ridge sloping towards her. The morning light dulled the natural glow of the gritstone, turning the walls and turreted tower a mellow red. "I could stand here all day looking at this view, but it won't get us to London."

"Is it time?" Powis asked.

Elizabeth inclined her head towards him. "If we are to reach Lincoln's Inn Fields before nightfall tomorrow, then yes, we must leave soon." In three days time, Powis would attend the opening of Parliament. He would also resume his duties as an aide to King Charles. "The carriages are readied and waiting."

They walked towards the courtyard. The slow stride of his long boots, crunching on gravel and frozen leaves, matched her hesitant steps. Recalling the conversation she'd overheard between Shaftesbury and the other Protestant Lords, about the Queen and Mary Beatrice, Elizabeth shivered. "Trouble is brewing for Catholics again. I can feel it."

"But few talk openly about such matters, and you should follow their example."

"Instead, they whisper about bad omens – the war, the plague, the Great Fire."

"Bad omens?" Powis said. "Pish! It has nothing to do with omens. This is about men seeking power. Disputes lead to changes in power –"

"And loyalties," she added. Stretching up, she kissed Powis' cheek. "Take care, my love. It's becoming harder to know who to trust." She breathed in the pungent aroma of wood smoke and the fresh, sweet smell of pine and sighed. "What a contrast life is here, from the constant bustle and stench of London –"

A wail interrupted their conversation. "Mama!"

Elizabeth turned to see their four-year-old daughter running across the courtyard.

"Mama, *am* I coming with you and Papa? William said I'm to stay behind," Lucy called out between ragged breaths.

Pulling away from Powis, Elizabeth took Lucy's outstretched gloved hand. "Don't mind him. Of course you're coming with us." She frowned at nine-year-old William, who leant out the window of the middle carriage. Four black horses whinnied and stamped their feet in front of it. Their luggage had been strapped onto the third carriage, which also carried provisions and clothes for the long journey.

Powis walked on, but Elizabeth stopped to take Winifred, their fourteen-month-old baby, while the nurse climbed into the first carriage. Once the nurse had settled into her seat, Elizabeth handed Winifred back and helped Lucy inside.

Lifting the skirt of her woollen dress, Elizabeth stepped into the middle carriage. William and seven-year-old Anne would travel with Father Morgan, a family friend. "Rest when you can and keep covered," she said, as she wrapped a woollen rug around Anne's lap. "It's a bitter day."

"When will we stop for food?" William asked and nudged Anne, while wriggling to tuck a rug under his legs.

Anne yelled and rubbed her arm, padded beneath a thick cloak. "Mama, he hit me."

"Settle down or I'll have Father Morgan test you on your catechisms . . . all of them." Elizabeth said and raised an eyebrow.

"My pleasure," Father Morgan said and, with exaggerated movements, pulled a basket out from under his seat and held it up. "Refreshments . . . for children who travel in silence."

Elizabeth smiled and turned towards the door. She had no doubt the elderly priest would keep a watchful eye over William and Anne. She hesitated. "Remember children . . . when we reach England, there must be no talk of Mass. Safe journey. I'll see you when we rest the horses."

She found Mary and Frances on the front steps, saying goodbye to their father. Powis hugged them both and made them promise to write long letters.

Tears formed in Elizabeth's eyes, at bidding farewell to her eldest daughters. "You should come to London. In a month perhaps?" She rubbed her gloved hands together. "Think of all the new gowns you're missing. This season's three-quarter sleeves would suit you both –"

Mary grimaced. "Mama, I'm a twenty-year-old widow, not a young debutante."

"Nay, Elizabeth. I'll not have our daughters anywhere near Court,"

Powis said and strode to the waiting carriage.

Elizabeth stared after him. He'd misunderstood her intentions. She would rather lie down in front of a fast moving carriage than let her daughters mix with any of the drunken, adulterous, pox-ridden libertines who frequented Court. But, there were many good men in London. They were not all wastrels. After all, she'd found Powis.

At last, the carriages ambled out of the courtyard and made their way along the track towards the castle gates. Pulling a travelling blanket around her, Elizabeth prayed. *Let this journey be uneventful*. They passed under a tunnel formed from birch and rowan trees, and the familiar sight of holly and hazel growing around their bases filled her with delight. Emerging from the tunnel, she settled back and resigned herself to the long journey ahead.

She fell asleep to the sound of the nurse reciting a nursery rhyme to Lucy. "If wishes were horses, beggars would ride," the nurse chanted.

Before reaching Oxford, they stopped at a coaching inn. Apart from patches of mud the roads had remained clear. After settling the children for the night, Elizabeth dined with Powis. They ate generous portions of mutton stew and bread and remained seated at the wooden table. They often used the inn, and she'd grown accustomed to its stark furnishings and bleak decor. After the constant clatter of the carriage the relative silence soothed her.

The other diners looked like fellow travellers, dust-covered and tired. A young minister sitting alone caught Elizabeth's attention, and she tried not to stare.

"Bring me blaady pottage and a jug of small ale," the minister roared to the landlord in a brash, strange voice. "Now," he slurred. As he spoke, his huge chin bobbed, making it appear as if his mouth sat in the middle of his face. He wore clerical robes, and a Bible lay open in front of him. The minister lifted his small sunken eyes and caught her watching.

Elizabeth turned away. Something about the way he had looked at her filled her with dread. She thought of her children asleep upstairs and shuddered. Though she'd set off with reluctance, she now longed to reach London. And, she wanted to talk with Mary Beatrice. "I'm delighted Mary Beatrice is with child. I pray she delivers a male heir. If she does our children could worship freely and not have to live their lives in fear as we have. I'll call on her," she said, as her excitement grew. "If only Frances had come with us, I could have taken her. They are similar —"

"I've already told you to keep our daughters away from Court." Powis glared at her. "Why must you insist on disregarding my wishes?"

Elizabeth stared back at him. "But, you know I agree with you. I only meant that Frances could visit her in her apartments," she replied in a hesitant voice. This was the second time today he'd misunderstood her intentions, and it rankled. "What harm is there in it?"

"What harm?" Powis raised his eyebrows. "Frances or Mary need only to be seen at Court to catch the eye of some wastrel. Why do you think I asked them to stay behind? Hmm!"

Stunned, Elizabeth shook her head. "You *asked* Frances and Mary to remain?"

"I won't risk their names appearing in some broadsheet, linked with some rake. Or have some bawdy joke printed, hinting at some wit's desire for them. Nay, it's too easy to turn an innocent girl's head with false words of passion and desire. I won't let it happen to *my* daughters."

Elizabeth gasped and gripped his hand. "But they're my daughters too, and I want them close. Why now?" She would always keep a watchful eye over them. How could he think otherwise? She'd been three-years-old when her own mother died, and wanted her children to have the close bond she'd been denied. "You should have discussed this with me. Why didn't you?"

Powis leaned closer. "It's hard to explain."

"Well, try." Elizabeth loosened her grip on his hand.

"Mary Beatrice likes you. What would you say if she asked for Frances as one of her Ladies?"

"Such a request would be an honour."

"How many royal mistresses belonged to York's first wife's retinue?"

Elizabeth winced. "Oh! Powis, I didn't think. By God, I couldn't refuse."

"Then you'll let the matter rest?"

Understanding dawned, but Powis' reasoning made her more uncertain about the ways of Court. What else had she failed to grasp? "And what about you? It's fashionable to keep a mistress. I know those who don't are ridiculed."

"It's the mode and no crime."

Elizabeth pulled back her hand. "Dear God."

Powis snorted with laughter. "Pish. Do you really think the gossips would leave me alone? Everything at Court's the subject of gossip. It's what they do best . . . slaughtering the truth." He became serious. "But, I do agree with you about Mary Beatrice. Let us pray she births a male heir. Our children's futures depend upon it."

During the night, Elizabeth awoke with a start. Bathed in sweat, darkness enveloped her, and it took a moment to realise where she was. A nightmare had invaded her dreams. The King, York and members of the Court were hunting. Dogs raced ahead, chasing their quarry. But . . .

it was her husband who ran from them through the wood. She called out to tell them it was Powis, but no sound came. She tried to run after them but her legs wouldn't move. A soundless scream froze in her throat, waking her.

The hunt had seemed real. She reached out and touched Powis. Reassured he was safe, she snuggled into his back and fell into a fitful sleep.

They set off at first light, stopping just after one o'clock to graze the horses. Before leaving again, the nurse took Lucy and Winifred and put them into makeshift beds in the third carriage. Stretching out, Powis laid his sword beside him and fell asleep within minutes. Elizabeth pulled one of Behn's plays out of her travel-bag, and sat back and resumed reading 'The Forc'd Marriage.'

Just before five o'clock the carriages clattered into London. Elizabeth laid her book down and pulled aside the green velvet curtain. In the half-light, she watched the familiar landscapes passing. A strong wind blew, buffeting the trees. It was as if they were dancing and she improvised a tune to match. A sight from her past flashed unbidden before her eyes. Royalists dangling from trees, priests in cassocks suspended beside them. The decaying bodies hung from ropes around their necks. The Civil War had ended, and they'd been placed there as a stark warning to others.

She pulled back and blinked to block out the recollection. Turning around, she prised open a velvet panel. Taking out her rosary, she whispered, "In the name of the Father, the Son and the Holy Spirit. Hail Mary, full of grace, protect my family." Then, she placed the rosary back into the small space.

Her movements woke Powis. Sitting up, he yawned and stretched his arms. "God's truth, I'm in need of a wash. Are we near?"

"We've just crossed the bridge."

He nodded and donned his rust-coloured long jacket and then his brown periwig. "Will he open Parliament, or won't he? Hmm!"

Elizabeth chewed on her bottom lip. "I say he will. Most definitely."

He raised his eyebrows.

Powis' reaction made Elizabeth hesitate, but she was confident in her reasoning. "England's at war. The war needs to be funded. Charles will open Parliament asking for funds for the Navy . . . And himself, of course."

Powis turned and looked out the window. A muscle twitched in his jaw.

She stared at him. What was he keeping from her?

When the carriage drew to a halt, Powis stepped out and strapped his long-bladed sword onto his belt.

Sitting alone, Elizabeth watched his retreating back and wondered what new troubles awaited them.

CHAPTER FIVE

Rumours

Powis hurried into the Stone Gallery of Whitehall Palace, removed his hat and shook the snow off. The soft flurries, falling for the past two days over London, had grown heavier. Slush dripped from his silver-buckled boots and formed a muddy puddle at his feet.

The whitewashed arched-gallery stretched forty feet wide. Windows, placed at intervals down one side, filtered in dull light through the grime. On the opposite side, laughing courtiers lounged on two faded red velvet settees. A sour stench of stale wine and body odour surrounded the group, who were no doubt remnants from the Court revelries of the night before. A young woman lay asleep across the laps of two of the courtiers, her arms and legs spread out and a breast exposed. Beside them, a courtier with his wig askew, turned hazy eyes towards Powis as he passed.

Powis looked above the weary revellers, at a marble statue perched on a plinth extending from the wall, and grimaced at the black coating of dust.

All around him, cloaked figures scurried through the gallery, either arriving or heading out of the palace. The chatter of their raised voices echoed off the stone walls. Powis nodded his acknowledgement to the few faces he recognised.

Continuing up a flight of stone stairs, he made his way towards the Long Gallery. At the Guards' Chamber, he unstrapped his sword and handed it over to a liveried guard. A week had passed since he had returned from Wales, but it felt longer. He stifled a yawn. Parliament had opened as planned. As he had anticipated, the session had not gone well for the King.

Stopping in the Lords' chamber, he removed his cloak, hung it on a peg, and placed his hat beside it. A log fire blazed in the grate and, as he passed, he held his hands towards its welcome heat. The stench of stale periwigs filled the small room. Three Protestant Lords sat at a circular oak table. Picking up a decanter of claret from the table, Powis poured a good measure into a glass. He lifted down a spaniel, asleep on a tapestry-backed chair. Drawing in the chair, he joined the Lords.

After taking a sip of claret, Powis held a hand to his mouth and yawned. He wanted to close his eyes. He'd barely slept since the opening of Parliament, and Elizabeth had hounded him to find out what had transpired at the end of the last session.

"Ah, Powis! Are you here to see the King as well? Is there a conclave on? You're the third Papist to pass through here," the youngest of the Lords said, and the others laughed.

Though they couldn't ask him outright, these Protestant Lords wanted to know why Charles had called his trusted Catholic Lords and advisors together. Powis chuckled. Did they really think to find out from him? He raised his glass. "Be reassured my Lords, it's not another of our Catholic plots. Hah! Do you not have enough false ones already without fabricating more? By God's hooks, your stories will keep me entertained for years to come."

"But it cuts deeper than that," another of the Lords said and pushed a pile of pamphlets towards Powis. At over six feet tall, the man's shoulders stooped.

Powis pushed them back. "Of course I've seen these pathetic attempts by the Dutch to fuel hatred in England against Catholics and the King. We were at war. Surely you're not fooled by these lies."

The youngest Lord picked up one of the leaflets. "Whether or no you consider Orange an enemy, the public no longer fear him. How does that bode for you as a Catholic?"

Powis glared at him. He wouldn't be drawn by the implied threat against his family. "Orange is painting a portrait of himself as a heroic Protestant, ending a Papal conspiracy in England. An image no less, fed by him in the hope that it's swallowed up whole by gullible men . . . like yourselves. God's truth, 'tis war propaganda, designed to turn us against each other."

The third Lord sneered. "Pish! Be that as it may. But taken together, events that have transpired recently raise doubts. You cannot deny this. If it's true Charles made a treaty with France, then this constitutes a Papal alliance. This could lead us into another bloody Civil War."

Powis shook his head. "That's why we're all sworn to secrecy. The war is over. The peace treaty is being signed as we speak. The issue is finished with –"

The tall Lord interrupted him. "Nay! Not if it affects us directly. The talk within the corridors is filled with concerns that Charles intends to govern without a Parliament. He makes no secret of his belief in his Divine Right to rule without *our* interference. Thanks to Shaftesbury and Buckingham, we now have good reason to suspect France is providing him with the funds to achieve this. What do you know of his alliance with France?"

Powis gulped the last of his wine and stood. Rubbing his hands down his breeches, to remove the dog hair they'd picked up, he made to leave. On reaching the door he turned. "You'd do well to remember that during his opening address the King denied making any *secret* treaty with France. To state otherwise is treasonable talk and I want no part of it."

As he walked the corridors, heading for the King's private chambers, Powis couldn't fathom why Buckingham had leaked the notion of a secret treaty during session. Had it been intentional? Though it had been said during a heated argument, and Buckingham had immediately backtracked, the rumour had spread faster than the Great Fire. Pish! Powis would rather it hadn't happened. The King had now dismissed both Shaftesbury *and* Buckingham. No doubt, this would not be the end of the matter.

Powis nodded to the liveried guards. After checking he wasn't carrying any weapons, a guard opened one of the double doors into the privy chamber and closed it behind Powis. Standing in Charles' inner sanctum, Powis glanced around and took in the worried faces surrounding the King.

William Chiffinch, Page of the Backstairs and Keeper of the Cabinet Closet, hurried over and escorted him over to Charles, who stood beside a fire filled high with blazing coal. A novel lay open on a small table beside him. A book on pendulums lay beside it, handwritten notes jutting from the pages. Clocks from Charles' precious collection sat along the mantelpiece, their beats forming a constant hum.

Charles towered over Powis' medium frame. Dressed in a loose flowing white shirt and black breeches, a black periwig hung past Charles' shoulders, and a frown accentuated the deep lines etched onto his face.

Three matching red velvet settees had been pulled around the fire. James of York sat on one. He wore a dark blue jacket, trimmed with gold braid, and sported a light brown periwig. His sullen face was weather-beaten and scarred by smallpox. York's sixty-year-old secretary, Thomas Howard, Lord Viscount Stafford, sat at his side.

Powis bowed. "Your Majesty."

Indicating Powis should sit, Charles remained standing.

Powis nodded to his cousin, the Earl of Castlemaine, and sat beside him.

Rubbing at his thin moustache, Charles stared down at his brother, York. Charles' dark eyes blazed. "Odd's fish. Let's get on with this business," he said and sat on the empty settee.

Lost in thought, Charles adjusted himself to allow a spaniel to snuggle in beside him. He stretched out his long legs and glared at York. "Well Jamie, once again you've brought us together to sort out your affairs. Pray tell me you've had a change of heart?"

A few years ago, York had confirmed to those present, and a few trusted friends and family, that he had converted to Rome. Apart from Charles they were all Catholics, and worked together to keep his conversion secret and ensure he could practice his faith in private.

"Nay, I'll not renounce my f-f-faith. I will not be f-f-forced to sign it," York replied, with his usual stammer.

Charles blew out his cheeks and exhaled. "No one's asking you to abide by the damn thing. Just sign the Test oath and be done with it. You can do as you please afterwards."

"I have thought about it," York said. "And I've decided to resign from my position as Lord High Admiral."

Powis' throat constricted and his body stiffened, as he fought to conceal his rising fear. As an aide to the King, he should support him in this matter. But how could *he*, a practising Catholic, advise York to deny his faith? He couldn't bring himself to do it.

Charles' face paled. He pulled off his periwig and rubbed his hands over his shaven head. "Nay, I will not approve this, Jamie. You're placing us in danger. Rumours of your conversion are widespread. Odd's fish, this will be viewed as the confirmation people seek."

"It's God's will. Have some trust in me . . . brother. I'll remain discreet," York replied.

Castlemaine rubbed his hands together. "Your marriage has set rumours aflame."

Filled with concern for his family, Powis sat forward. If York refused to sign the Test Act, swearing his allegiance to the Anglican Church, it could confirm his religious stance and ignite further hostility towards Catholics.

"I will not divorce Mary Beatrice." York tilted his head. "They know she is with child. And, all they have is their suspicions. I'll give them no proof."

Charles raised his eyebrows. "Then you'll attend Anglican services again, Jamie?"

"God's truth, yes! Yes, I will!" York replied. "But remember, Shaftesbury's also petitioning for you to divorce your Catholic Queen. Are you to do his bidding?"

"So be it, Jamie. I'll approve your resignation." Charles glared at him. "You've always been stubborn, and I doubt you'll ever change your nature."

Powis stared at Charles in disbelief. If the public learned that he knew his brother was a practising Catholic, they could turn against him, just as they had against his father. When Charles died, York would succeed him. How would England tolerate a Catholic King? "It's becoming harder to keep your conversion secret," he said to York. "The Protestant Lords are becoming more direct in their questions about your faith. For the safety of us all, this must be contained."

"I understand what you say, but I won't have the likes of Shaftesbury and Buckingham telling *me* what to do." York folded his arms and glared at Charles.

A sense of foreboding swept through Powis and settled in the pit of his belly. Rumour of Charles' deception of the Protestant members of his Cabal had been leaked during session. How would the Lords now respond to hearing of another deception, this time involving them all?

Charles stood and walked over to a window. Powis followed him and gazed out at the darkening snow-filled sky. "I don't trust Shaftesbury," he whispered. "I don't know what he'll do next."

"Odd's fish," Charles replied and his voice wavered. "As sure as there is a God in heaven, he'll use my brother's resignation to further his cause against me."

Powis opened his mouth to reassure Charles that Shaftesbury loved him and would cause him no harm. He closed it again. The lie wouldn't come.

CHAPTER SIX

Beer Street

The flurries of snow had intensified into a blizzard that brought London to a standstill. Thick drifts still lined the roads and walkways, but paths had been cleared, and the capital's inhabitants once again made their way around.

Shaftesbury stepped down from his carriage in Fleet Street. Famished, he made for the Olde Cheshire Cheese Tavern to dine. Today, he used both his walking sticks and needed them. Fearing he might slip on the icy path, he kept his eyes fixed on the ground until he was safely inside.

Having secured an empty table, Shaftesbury studied the board and ordered hare hashed with fresh bread from a serving girl. When the meal arrived, the claret in the stew tempted him, and he called for a jug. He needed to shed his Royalist wine-drinking ways, and take on the ale-drinking habit of the Country Party he'd now aligned himself with.

When his stableboy had informed him earlier that the roads around Westminster had been cleared, Shaftesbury had set off at once for the House of Lords. Pacing the corridors, he'd listened in on the gossip and had been relieved to hear that many members supported Buckingham for leaking the rumour of Charles' secret treaty with France.

Though satisfied with his morning's endeavours, Charles' deception still consumed Shaftesbury. What else had Charles kept from him? He took a deep breath, to steady his racing thoughts. There had been no need to deceive him. He'd been loyal. His frustration mounted, and he gulped the last of the claret. He savoured its excellent flavour but resisted the temptation to call for more.

Leaving the Olde Cheshire Cheese Tavern, Shaftesbury made along Fleet Street towards its junction with Chancery Lane. There, he struggled up a flight of stairs to the King's Head Tavern. He signalled to William Mart, the proprietor, who rushed over and escorted him to one of the booths at the back. The accompanying noise of raised voices, mixed with laughter, was both a pleasure and a comfort to his ears.

"I'll have ale," Shaftesbury informed Mart and joined a table where his friends and political allies were seated. Letting out a sigh, he leant his walking sticks against the table and settled onto the wooden bench. Like himself, Buckingham and Halifax were Protestants and held seats in the House of Lords. Both sported long dark periwigs and white frilled cravats, and their wide-brimmed feathered hats lay beside them on the coarse woven tablecloth. As a jest, they referred to themselves and their supporters as the 'King's Head Club', after the tavern.

"Ah, my friends," Shaftesbury said with mock tenderness. "It must be all of four hours since I last saw your arses. I swear I see more of yours than I do my own wife's."

"Hmm. Now that I do believe," Buckingham said and, shifting a young serving girl from his knee, sent her off with a pat to her rump. He lifted his eyebrows at Shaftesbury. "I have intelligence from a source that there's a certain, um . . . lady, receiving your attentions. I've heard it said you've bedded more whores than the King."

After accepting the tankard from the proprietor, Shaftesbury looked over at him and smirked. "Humph! Such slanderous talk against me . . . and uttered by a notorious rake!"

"Well, now you're both notorious. And you really should mind your manners towards Old Rowley," Halifax said.

Shaftesbury frowned. "He duped us. If Buckingham hadn't uncovered Charles' bloody secret alliance with France, we'd all still be in the dark. Louis will want Charles to rule without our interference. That much is obvious."

"Make no mistake," Buckingham added. "Louis is paying him to rule without a Parliament."

"Matters are more serious than we thought. We need to put a stop to this," Halifax said.

Buckingham nodded. "What else is he deceiving us about? If he has aligned with France, then most likely he intends to turn England into a Catholic state. Be warned, all Protestants would then need to sign an oath, swearing their allegiance to the bloody Pope."

"All the while I considered myself Charles' trusted advisor, he'd been lying to me." Shaftesbury frowned and stood up. In desperate need to empty a now full bladder, he made his way to the folding screen at the back of the tavern.

He cursed his slow progress, and stumbled in his haste. He glanced around, but no one had observed him. "Pish, so what if they had," he muttered.

A sense of relief flooded through him as he urinated into the pot. No, he would not forgive Charles for deceiving him. He was perhaps weak of body, but Shaftesbury's mind and will were strong. He would prove himself a formidable opponent to Charles and *his* belief that he had a divine right to rule without Parliament's interference. Well, interfere he would and as often as bloody possible.

Making his way back from the urinal, the fug of tobacco smoke hit Shaftesbury, and he relaxed and breathed in its deep aroma. He called out to Mart for more ale.

Halifax held up a hand and beckoned him back over. "Shaftesbury, come and settle down. Buckingham's relating a story."

"A story from Buckingham is a story indeed. Please do not interrupt, let him proceed," Shaftesbury rhymed. Laying down his walking sticks, he reached out to receive a pewter tankard from the proprietor.

"Methinks my wanton hours I see, and passing by they turn and laugh at me," Buckingham rhymed back, causing Shaftesbury to roar with laughter.

"Oh, do get on with it Buckingham. Just start again," Halifax said and rubbed at his thin moustache.

A grin spread across Buckingham's face. "Very well, as I was explaining, Otway lives opposite Dryden. One morning Otway called on him, only to be told he was dining with Pembroke. At the same time, the following morning Otway arrived at Dryden's house again, to be informed this time that he was dining with me, which in truth he was.

"'Well,' the frustrated Otway exclaimed, 'The Devil he is', and pulling a piece of white chalk out from his jacket he wrote on Dryden's door: *Here lives Dryden, poet and wit.* Reading this on his return, Dryden wrote under it: *Written by Otway, opposite.*

"Dryden then sent his manservant to invite Otway to dine with him the following morning. When Otway arrived and saw the line added to the door, he stormed off; informing Dryden he could keep his wit and his meal."

Halifax stretched out his hands, palms up. "Is that it?"

"What a pointless story," Shaftesbury said.

"I could have written a better rhyme myself," Halifax said, adding a mocking laugh.

"Ah, but it's the moral of the story that's important, not the story per se." A smile lit up Buckingham's face.

"Do explain," Halifax said. "After two ales I think my brain's quite fuddled. I can't see any moral within that tale."

Caught up in the merriment of the moment, Shaftesbury banged his tankard on the table and shouted, "Here! Here!"

Buckingham leant back and laced his hands behind his head. "Just like Otway, we're frustrated and disgruntled."

"Ah, I have it now. We're to use chalk to write our message on the door of the Lords," Halifax said and roared with laughter.

Like a candle lit in a dark room, Shaftesbury realised the significance of what Buckingham had said. "Ha, ha. Nay," he said. "We will not walk away disgruntled. Otway lost out to Dryden. But we will deliver our message again and again, and in as many ways as we can until it's received. We'll formalise our opposition against the Crown, and together we'll push our points until they are acknowledged. Buckingham, you are a bloody genius."

"How should we proceed with the issue of York and the succession? Mary Beatrice being with child adds urgency to the matter. There's no doubt the child will be raised a Catholic." Halifax's eyes glanced around the table. "York will dance to France's tune, and it will spell the end of Parliament and the Protestant faith."

"Let the people decide," Buckingham replied. "We denounce York as a Catholic and discredit him as the rightful successor. As there are already rumours he has converted, our task should be easy."

"And then what?" Shaftesbury had heard such plans discussed before but nothing came of them. Until now he'd pushed for religious tolerance, but both Parliament and the Protestant religion had to be preserved. To retain them, York had to be removed from the succession. If denouncing Catholics achieved this, so be it.

"We promote Monmouth as the rightful heir," Buckingham said.

Shaftesbury sat up and took a swallow of ale. He liked the idea and saw how it could further their cause. As a Protestant, Monmouth would never align with France, or do the French King's bidding. Also, with a malleable king, Parliament would survive. A shiver of excitement ran through his belly. "Monmouth's vain. He prefers to think of himself as a wronged successor rather than the King's eldest bastard. I'll befriend him and tell him of our support for him as the rightful heir. Together we'll nurture and promote his aspirations."

"Nay, let me befriend Monmouth and bring him in as a member of the Kings Head Club," Buckingham said and laughed. "Shaftesbury, you focus on an anti-Catholic attack within the Lords. Halifax and I will support you. Push the boundaries. Present as many provocative bills as possible."

As he considered this, Shaftesbury's eyes closed. He smiled as he acknowledged the implication that he would lead the assault. *Let the game commence. Parliament versus the Crown.* He'd do whatever it took to win. He opened his eyes. "Agreed . . . Halifax, can you work to increase the club's membership?"

"I'll draw in the younger Lords," Halifax said. "We can discuss and agree with them on the issues up for debate in the Lords."

Shaftesbury nodded. There was no turning back now. He'd shaken off his Royalist ties. These men were now his allies. He lowered his voice, "And our 'private' discussions can take place elsewhere." He raised his tankard aloft. "To Beer Street."

"To Beer Street," his colleagues replied in chorus.

CHAPTER SEVEN

Just Rewards

Elizabeth hurried down the great staircase of her London home and made for the dining room. She had said her goodnights to the children, and smiled at Lucy's solemn approach to her prayers. God's truth, she was only four-years-old and already pious. She opened the door and gasped. A host of candles lit up the room and glittered off the glassware and porcelain.

All day she'd flitted back and forth between the kitchen and dining room, adding little finishing touches to the large table, now set for a party of eight. Flames from a log fire added a warm glow to the oak-panelled room.

"Oh, it looks lovely," she said to Lowry, the housekeeper, who was busy arranging fruit in a bowl on a large oak dresser. Elizabeth straightened the floral arrangement of spring flowers and vines, forming the centrepiece, and tutted at the limp state of the tulips. The ferocious and relentless blizzards that swept the country until March had left her with a poor choice from the garden.

"Everything's in order, my lady," Lowry said and stood beside Elizabeth. "But your guests will be here in less than an hour. If you don't mind me saying, unless you go attend to yourself they'll find you checking the position of their cutlery when they arrive."

Elizabeth laughed. She looked forward to celebrating her husband's elevation to Earl with their closest friends, and was still smiling when she reached her bedchamber. Shaftesbury and Buckingham's disloyalty had resulted in Charles noticing Powis' loyalty. Their decline had led to his rise in favour.

Beth, her lady's maid, chattered as she washed Elizabeth with a cloth soaked in rosewater, then helped her into a new cobalt blue gown. When she had finished, Beth reached into her own bosom and retrieved the pearl necklace Powis had given Elizabeth on their wedding day.

"Warmed as you like em', m' lady." Beth said and fastened the single strand of pearls into place. Elizabeth's thick brown hair flowed with natural curls. Beth pinned the front back to the crown and left the rest tumbling down Elizabeth's neck. After surveying herself in the mirror, Elizabeth nodded her approval.

As Elizabeth laughed with Powis and their friends, her worry about the preparations disappeared. Covered dishes were brought in and laid on the vast sideboard, ready to be passed around. The smell of roasted meats, boiled vegetables and rich spices filled the room.

A servant placed a large roasted goose, stuffed with apples and cloves, in front of Powis. He carved some slices from the breast and pushed the platter to his right. "This is the latest trend copied *a la mode* from France. We thought we'd try it out on you tonight," he said, and passed on a steaming dish of apple sauce.

"Apart from a few small scraps no one else wanted, the dish of venison reaching me a few moments ago was empty," Edward Coleman said and smiled over at Elizabeth. Warming to the theme, he continued. "In my capacity as Secretary to Mary Beatrice, I recently returned from

France, where I rather reluctantly developed a taste for cold soup. On one occasion at Court I was placed at the end of a long table, and watched the slow progress of a steaming urn of soup making its way towards me. It got enticingly close, and I'd started to salivate at the thought of getting some before the steam settled. Then, I noticed to my horror that the old dowager duchess sitting a few seats away had fallen asleep, and the urn had halted in front of her.

"You know what the French Court is like about etiquette? Well it wouldn't have been polite to wake the duchess, or to pass the soup on ahead of her. The meal had come to a halt, and no one was sure what to do about it. Almost all the men at the table had commanded troops, but this had them flummoxed. After a good ten minutes, a young priest sitting next to the duchess dropped his purse. On the pretext of bending to retrieve it, he nudged her awake, but by that time . . . the soup was cold." Coleman held up his hands in exaggerated despair, and the room filled with laughter.

"Sounds like my school days." Powis laid his fork down and wiped tears of mirth from his eyes.

Elizabeth looked at Coleman and raised her eyebrows. She thought he fasted too often and needed a good meal. "Eat up Coleman, before your food gets cold."

"Very clever Elizabeth . . . As always, I may add," Coleman said.

When the plates had been cleared and more wine poured, William Howard - Viscount Stafford - eased his chair back. At sixty-three, he was by far the oldest member of the company. He refused to wear a periwig, and his thin receding grey hair sat on his shoulders. His dark, kind eyes roamed the room, and he rubbed at his thin moustache. At a pause in the hum of conversation, he stood and rapped a fork against his glass. "Let us all raise our glasses to our host and good friend, William Herbert. The First Earl of Powis. Baron no more!"

Around the table glasses clinked, and cries of 'Earl of Powis' echoed around the room. Powis smiled in acknowledgement, rose to his feet and bowed. "King Charles enjoys rewarding his loyal supporters, and I've received just such an honour. I thank His Majesty, for granting me an earldom. To the King."

Cries of 'God bless the King,' rang out.

Turning towards her, Powis raised his glass. "To my wife, Countess Elizabeth Herbert."

Elizabeth gazed at him with open admiration. Kissing the rim of her glass, she raised it towards him. As the guests talked amongst themselves, she watched Powis' cousin, Rodger Palmer, seated across the table. What would she have done without him? He'd always been there for her and Powis during their difficult times. In her opinion, he didn't merit the harsh treatment he received from his wife. Created Earl of Castlemaine thirteen years earlier, his conferment had been an affront rather than an honour. In their first year of marriage, his wife, Barbara Villiers, became the King's mistress. It had been clear to all that his earldom had been given as payment for his wife's service in the King's bed. Despite this insult, Castlemaine remained dignified and loyal to the King.

Reluctant to raise the issue of Castlemaine's earldom, Elizabeth addressed Philip Herbert, the newly created Earl of Pembroke. "Powis and I were saddened to hear of your brother's death."

"Half-brother, dearest Elizabeth," Pembroke said and frowned. "The best thing William ever did was pass his title over to me. Sorry, but I never much liked him. Too stuffy and boring by far."

"Good gracious. But . . . he was so young, only twenty-two," Elizabeth said and stared at Pembroke in surprise.

Pembroke emptied his full glass in one swallow. "Don't misunderstand me. It was very unfortunate . . . for him. But I have to admit, becoming an earl is very fortunate . . . for me."

"I knew him as MP for Glamorgan, and liked him well enough," Powis said.

Stafford pointed his glass towards Pembroke. "I liked him a lot better than that rascally devil, your grandfather. A supposed opponent of the new model army. Pah! When they marched into London he soon changed his mind. He made himself a laughing stock over it."

"Of course," Pembroke sneered. "Many say I'm like Grandfather, but they underestimate me. I'm not weak."

Pembroke's fiancée, Henrietta de Kérouaille, looked bemused. At twenty-four, she was considered one of the beauties at Court. Elizabeth had reservations about the match. From what she'd seen of Pembroke's impulsive and arrogant nature, she very much doubted the marriage would be a happy one. She hoped, for Henrietta's sake, to be proved wrong. Ever since his brother's death, Pembroke spent too much time drinking at Court. She would ask Powis to talk to him.

Catching her gaze, Stafford leant towards her. "It's a pity neither have their parents close to guide them, for I'm sure they'll need it."

"Indeed they will," Elizabeth said. "And how are your own children?"

Before Stafford could reply, Henrietta announced: "Our marriage promises to be the event of the season."

She's so unlike her sister, Louise, Elizabeth thought. While she liked them both well enough, she couldn't abide that Louise was the King's mistress. It was unfair of her to take this out on Henrietta, but she couldn't help herself. Last week, Mary Beatrice had miscarried, and Shaftesbury had pressed again within Parliament for York to divorce her. Dear God, if the child had lived. Despite the devastating news, Elizabeth held firm to her hope of a Catholic succession – Mary Beatrice would be big-bellied again soon.

"It's the talk of the Court," Elizabeth said and took a sip of wine. "And how is your sister's child?"

A smile lit up Henrietta's face. "Charles Lennox will soon celebrate his second birthday. Charles dotes on him," she said in her charming accentuated English.

Pembroke refilled his glass. "Henrietta, the child's Charles' youngest bastard, he's no more to him than that."

A red flush spread up Henrietta's neck. "Oh dear, Philip. *Non.* Do not say that."

"His eleventh acknowledged one at that," Pembroke said. "Or is it his fifteenth? God alone knows. Old Rowley, Charles' stallion, produced many a fine colt and, because of his vigour, the name stuck to Charles himself. But . . . two years without another bastard, is it time to put Old Rowley out to pasture?" Pembroke gave out a raucous laugh, gulped the content of his glass and refilled it.

Henrietta's face turned a deep shade of red.

Elizabeth glared at Pembroke. She would definitely have Powis speak to him about his behaviour.

Clicking open a small silver box, Castlemaine retrieved a pinch of snuff. "The stench of periwigs never gets any sweeter. Thank God for snuff to make it more bearable."

Once the other guests had been escorted out, Elizabeth joined Powis and Edward Coleman in the earl's study. Coleman had asked to speak with them in private.

She checked to ensure the windows were closed. "You never know who might be skulking about. It's better to be overcautious, than risk being overheard."

Coleman sat beside the fire. "Mmm. They pay good money for even the smallest grain of information that brings down a Catholic. They're targeting Jesuits, but in such a climate we all need to be cautious," he said and turned the conversation to his main concern. "I'm trying to raise some money . . . so Charles can keep Parliament prorogued. My visit to France paved the way for further negotiation, but in all honesty, I'm not certain of success."

Taken aback, Elizabeth looked at Powis, who stood behind the desk, pouring sherris sack into two glasses. Like most Catholics, they also wanted to keep Parliament from voting to restrict them further, but to set up against them? No, she couldn't do it. To do so would place her family in danger. "If Charles needs foreign aid, his ambassadors can ask for it," she said and sat down.

Powis handed Coleman a glass. "Why are you taking this upon yourself? You shouldn't meddle in such matters."

Taking the sherris sack, Coleman sipped it. "I'm not meddling. It's my duty to York. The path to religious toleration within England lies with the King's financial independence from Parliament. Surely you can both see that."

"Whether I agree, or no, you're no longer York's secretary. Leave Stafford to fulfil that duty now," Powis said and sat down.

Coleman shook his head. "We can't put all our hopes into Mary Beatrice birthing a male heir. She didn't even come to term with this one. What if she also proves barren?"

"Nonsense!" Elizabeth exclaimed. "It's early, there is plenty of time. No, leave matters be."

"I can't," Coleman said. "It's becoming harder to keep York's conversion secret. If this is confirmed his position will be jeopardised. Parliament will side with the Bishops against a Catholic inheriting the Crown."

Elizabeth pondered this. "Not necessarily. There are many Catholics within Parliament."

"Yes, but for how long?" Coleman said.

"Then focus your efforts on keeping York's conversion quiet," Powis said and set his glass down on the low table.

Elizabeth had lost everything once and had no desire to flee abroad again. She had a bad feeling about Coleman interfering in matters that were not his concern. "I don't like what you're doing either. Leave matters be."

"I have to keep trying. There's no other way," Coleman said and stood up.

"If you believe that, then your thinking is limited. Of course there's other ways." Powis rose from the chair and faced him. "I know Charles has already told you to leave things be. Why do you think he removed you as York's secretary?"

Coleman paled and a muscle on his face twitched. "Be that as it may, I'm only serving York's interests."

Powis shook his head. "Are you sure it's not your own interests?"

"By God's good name, how can you even think that?"

If Coleman was telling the truth, then Elizabeth couldn't fathom why he continued to persist in this matter. Her concern for him grew.

"Then you're risking both your position and your life . . . for York?"

Powis replied.

"Nay, for the sake of the Catholic faith," Coleman said. "Without funds Charles will bow to Parliament's demands to restrict Catholics even further. We may even be forced out of England. I can't let that happen."

Powis shook his head. "Leave others to fight this out."

A coach drew up outside, and Coleman looked out the window. "My wife's waiting up for me. I'll bid you good night."

Powis grasped Coleman's arm. "I don't know what York's asked you to do, but I want no part in it. Shaftesbury's gathering support against the Crown. He'll view any attack on Parliament as an attack against himself. Have a care, my friend."

CHAPTER EIGHT

Bar Sinister

Shaftesbury entered Wills Coffee House in Covent Garden, with Buckingham, and handed over his penny at the door. The bitter smell of burning beans replaced the sour stench from the street, and Shaftesbury inhaled the fresh aroma. Conversations and laughter spilled through the large room.

The benches were filled almost to capacity, as people came in seeking company and the latest gossip. Shaftesbury glanced around looking for somewhere to sit, and secured seats at a wooden table when a group rose to leave. The door banging closed behind them added to the din.

They both ordered a dish of coffee from the serving boy, who had hurried over with pipes and tobacco.

Filling a pipe, Shaftesbury peered over at a table around which were seated about a dozen of the King's courtiers. Tobacco smoke wafted upwards forming a fug above their heads, and laughter emanated from the table. A stab of regret pierced Shaftesbury. He could no longer join them. He frowned and laid the unlit pipe back down. With Charles' betrayal still fresh in his memory, the courtier's joviality served as a lance to an open wound. He lifted one of the leaflets scattered around the table. "I'll be damned before I apologise to Charles."

Buckingham waved a hand. "You'll be damned if you even think of apologising. You've too many followers looking for you to lead them against the Crown. For Parliament's sake, you cannot abandon us. You sound as though you miss him."

Never again would Shaftesbury be on friendly terms with the King and he regretted it. He shook his head and scanned the leaflet advertising some play. "I don't."

Buckingham snorted. "God's nails, you miss the power. Be assured, as leader of the opposition against the Crown, you'll have all the power you desire and more."

A boy placed their coffee on the table, saving Shaftesbury from having to reply.

Buckingham reached into the pocket of his topcoat and retrieved a letter addressed to one of his French spies. He handed it to the boy. "Anything for me?"

"Nay, my lord. Nor for you, my Lord Shaftesbury. Mayhap later?" the boy said and gathered up the used dishes.

When the boy left, Buckingham shrugged his shoulders. "I know Charles better than anyone. His greatest fear is of another Civil War. He may well want to rule without Parliament, but will do nothing to bring this about. Of that, I can assure you."

"That's all very well, but if York becomes King, can you say the same?" Shaftesbury said. "This Queen will never birth an heir, but Mary

Beatrice likely will. We may as well accept York will inherit the Crown. A return to Queen Mary's Catholic tyranny –" He paused, and the leaflet slipped from his hand and fluttered to the floor. The King's eldest bastard son, James Scott, Duke of Monmouth, had entered with John Wilmot, the Earl of Rochester. Shaftesbury waved them over.

Monmouth turned around and looked at Rochester, who in turn, beamed at Shaftesbury and strode over. Monmouth looked hesitant but followed him.

Holding up his hands, Rochester uttered a raucous laugh. "By God's own truth, don't drink that piss or you'll sober up before you know it. Bloody stuff doesn't agree with me. It dilutes the wine in my body."

For months now, Shaftesbury had been looking for a way to draw Monmouth into his circle, but the means had not arisen . . . until now. Excitement coursed through him, and his hands trembled. He picked up his stick and stood. "Rochester, Monmouth, pray join us," he said, indicating the vacant seats at the table.

Rochester collapsed onto the bench opposite him.

Looking around, Monmouth's gaze fixed on to the table filled with laughing Royalists. Shaftesbury sensed Monmouth's reluctance to join his company and directed his attention to Rochester. Realising he wasn't the focus of his attention, Monmouth sat down.

Both Rochester and Monmouth were renowned for their handsome looks, and each was as rakish as the other. While Monmouth's features were pretty and soft, Rochester's were chiselled and rugged. The King's eldest bastard, Monmouth, was twenty-six, Rochester twenty-eight. Both were married and had young children. They sported long periwigs and velvet coats. Monmouth also wore a blue velvet sash over his shoulder, displaying the Stuart crest. Sliced across the crest lay a black line, the baton sinister, denoting his illegitimacy.

"And from which whores' beds have you dragged your arses?" Buckingham asked.

Shaftesbury sat back down and snorted. "I'll be damned. They can't have been very good if you jumped out of them at this early hour. Why it's not yet three o'clock."

"In the Devil's name." Rochester stared at each of them. His dark eyes bright with amusement. "You found us out. Our senses lead to our pleasures . . . and our pleasures lead us back to our senses. How else can it be?" He slapped a hand across his thigh and hooted.

Monmouth leant forward. "Rochester, have you given my father any more of your verses to read?" Laughter erupted around the table. Rochester had inadvertently given Charles a bawdy poem which he'd written about him, one he wasn't meant to see.

Shaftesbury smiled at Monmouth, both to acknowledge his wit and to draw him in.

Feigning offence, Rochester jumped up and lifted his arms. "I gave it in error, and he was confused, someone must have played me a trick. Twas' a game verse and he gave me game chase, but 'twas only an ode to his prick –"

Buckingham leapt up and continued the ditty. "For it does not stand as proud as it once did, a fact he would rather have kept hidden. But Rochester's here to tell the tale, and no doubt will once again do his bidding."

Flushed from their performance, they both bowed and sat down to a round of applause.

Monmouth laughed and relaxed back.

"You must learn to leave the King's prick alone," Buckingham said and roared with laughter.

Rochester smirked. He'd been banished from Court yet again, for smashing the King's phallic glass sundials in a drunken brawl. "I am disinclined to believe anything without personal experience of it. That way I can make up my own mind, rather than relying on the word of another," he said and set off to amuse another table with his wit.

While Buckingham chatted with Monmouth, Shaftesbury sipped the bitter coffee and contemplated how he should proceed with the issue of York. Though no one would confirm it, he remained certain York had converted. He couldn't envisage England surviving a Catholic King, who would dance to France's tune. Parliament wouldn't survive it, nor would the Protestant faith. He would cut off York's support and have all Catholics barred from sitting in Parliament. He'd already given a speech, resulting in the barring of all non-Resident Catholics from coming within ten miles of London. But, it wasn't enough. He wanted more.

Shaftesbury leant over to Monmouth and lowered his voice. "You have many supporters who believe you are the true heir, the next King James." He traced the line of Monmouth's baton sinister with his index finger. "We intend to push within the Lords for your father to acknowledge you as his true son and heir."

Monmouth's face paled as he stared, first at him and then at Buckingham.

Lowering his voice further, Shaftesbury said, "Trust no one else with this. But, if you wish to meet some of your supporters and speak freely with them, come to the King's Head Tavern with Buckingham tonight."

That evening, Shaftesbury lifted his tankard and raised it towards Monmouth. "To our future King, James II of England and Ireland and James VII of Scotland, all say aye."

A flush of pleasure spread up Monmouth's neck. As Shaftesbury had anticipated, Monmouth was responding to the adulation being heaped upon him by the members of the King's Head Club. Shaftesbury smiled.

"And a brave soldier . . . or so the ladies say," Buckingham added, and laughter erupted around the table. "I stayed with your father during his time in The Hague and met your mother. You're his very likeness."

Shaftesbury was pleased Buckingham had raised the subject of Lucy Walters. To all accounts, she had had many lovers and was of no consequence to Charles after their affair ended, but a rumour persisted that they'd married. He didn't know whether they had. Charles always denied it, and Lucy herself was long dead from the pox.

"Mother told me she married Father. Why would she lie?" Monmouth said.

Shaftesbury leant towards him. "No reason at all. You've been denied your rightful place. Wrongfully stamped a bastard and denied your position as The Prince of Wales. Nay, 'tis not right. A great wrong has been done, and we want to put it right. You have vast support amongst our members."

Touching his Bar Sinister, Monmouth smiled. "No one else chooses to believe me. I say it suits their purpose. But how will *you* change their minds?"

"By giving these doubters proof," Shaftesbury replied. "The rumour of the marriage certificate being held in a black box is widespread. If the certificate does indeed exist, we'll find it and present it as conclusive evidence of your legitimacy."

"But how?" Monmouth said. "Nothing would give me greater pleasure than to find it. But I've searched many times for this box. I've greater access than anyone to father's private papers. I can assure you it's not amongst them."

"Then someone else is holding it." Shaftesbury doubted the certificate existed, but Monmouth wanted to believe it did, and that was what mattered. Whether it was found or not was neither here nor there to him. "We'll fuel the rumour of its existence and push to have you acknowledged as the rightful heir. It would also help us in our quest if we could confirm your uncle's conversion to Rome. Do you know anything of this?"

His question unsettled Monmouth, who dropped eye contact and glanced around.

Shaftesbury continued, "The public seeks a Protestant king. Think about it, and if you've any news on this matter, it will be used to your advantage."

As if sensing Monmouth's discomfort, Buckingham changed the topic. "How's your wife? Is she still in Scotland?" he said and called out to the landlord for more ale.

Monmouth grimaced. "Aye, and thanks be to God for that, for I cannot abide her company."

"To a new queen as well, then?" Shaftesbury held up his tankard again. He would continue to nurture Monmouth to do their bidding. Now he had been brought over to their side, he would do whatever it took to keep him there.

CHAPTER NINE

The Warning

To Elizabeth, Winifred's wails sounded like a cacophony of crows, and she rubbed at her throbbing temples.

"You best be off m'Lady. I'll see to this little one." The children's nurse said and reached out to lift Winifred up. Winifred screamed and clung tighter to the bottom of Elizabeth's winter cloak. The nurse looked at Elizabeth and raised her eyebrows.

Elizabeth knew she should pick her daughter up, hand her to the nurse and be on her way. But she couldn't leave Winifred screaming like this. She chewed her bottom lip, contemplating what to do. Her two-year-old had developed a will of her own. It was time for Winifred to rest but she didn't want to go. Elizabeth glanced at the hall clock. She'd arranged to visit her friend, Mrs Cellier, at three o'clock and would be late if she didn't leave.

When the nurse tried to prise her fingers from Elizabeth's cloak, Winifred kicked out and screamed. Crouching down, her face level with Winifred's, Elizabeth looked into her daughter's tear-filled eyes. "All right, settle down. Mama will carry you to the nursery."

Winifred released her fingers and held up her chubby arms. She wore a blue silk dress, matching the colour and style of Elizabeth's.

None of the other children had been so difficult, Elizabeth concluded as she returned from the nursery, and her feet traced the route towards the carriage. Was she spending too much time with Winifred?

Once outside, she walked at a brisk pace and held her hood over her hair. It was another cold, wet November and she yearned for sunshine. Before stepping into the carriage, she stopped and admired the crown entwined with leaves that had been added above the family crest, to signify Powis' status as an Earl.

When the carriage swished out of Lincoln's Inn Fields, Elizabeth yawned and sank back into the leather seat. Mary Beatrice had miscarried five months into her pregnancy, a boy. But she was with child again, and Elizabeth prayed this one would come to term. If she birthed a Catholic heir then her own children's futures would be secured. Elizabeth crossed herself and said a silent prayer.

The carriage turned out onto Great Queen Street, heading east towards St. Clement Danes on the Strand. With a gloved hand, she pulled the green velvet curtains aside, and watched the rain splatter off the weathered cobbles and run in rivulets down the side of the road.

She peered back when a group of beggars descended on the carriage behind, which had halted on its way out of the Fields. She watched the rain-bedraggled urchins jump up and shout to the occupants. "A penny! Spare a penny. Please, m' Lord, m' Lady. A penny for summit' to eat." A girl, of about six, carried a baby in a bundle of rags.

Elizabeth pulled her thick cloak around her body and frowned. The Fields were infested with vagrants. Most of the men had disabled their legs, so they could beg for alms – claiming to be maimed soldiers.

Grateful she'd been spared such an assault, she closed the curtain.

As the carriage splashed along on the short journey, she scanned the packages covering the seat opposite. As instructed, Cook had prepared generous food parcels. The other parcels contained family cast-offs and donations from friends. Each bundle contained clothes for either a man, woman or child. A penny lay hidden in each of the women's bundles.

Outside Mrs Cellier's townhouse, the carriage drew to a sudden halt, jolting Elizabeth forward. Mrs Cellier's husband, a French merchant, spent months abroad – buying spices, coffee, cocoa and fine silks. Her children were married, leaving her free to pursue her interests. Over the years, she'd built up a reputation as a skilled and discreet midwife and played a key part in the lives of many notable Catholics, including herself and Mary Beatrice. She also provided services above and beyond that of midwife, and it was to secure one of her 'other' services that Elizabeth called.

She pulled her hood up and stepped out of the carriage, and the midwife hurried towards her. Linking into Elizabeth's arm, Mrs Cellier ushered her out of the rain. As they climbed the front steps, the bells of Saint Clements Danes pealed out the hour. Entering the cluttered hall, Elizabeth removed her wet cloak and handed it to the housekeeper. She smoothed down the folds of her dress and followed Mrs Cellier through to the breakfast room.

The large room functioned as a workspace. Parcels and pamphlets filled the table. Copies of the London Gazette were stacked on a hard-backed chair, and the oak desk overflowed with midwifery books, notes and reports. As usual, the midwife offered no apology for the clutter that was a necessary part of her life. Elizabeth had employed her many years before, to collect and distribute alms to Catholics imprisoned in

REIGN OF THE MARIONETTES

Newgate.

Getting straight down to business, they cleared a space on the table and spread the twice-weekly broadsheet in front of them. Together they scanned the pages for news of any Catholics admitted to Newgate and in need of their help.

"Good, only one admission on the debtors' side, my lady." Mrs Cellier pointed to the section in the Gazette where the name was listed.

Elizabeth chewed her bottom lip as she read the listing. "God bless him. I know of this family. He has a wife and young children." She turned away from the table.

"I expect the poor souls will have gone in with him." Mrs Cellier pushed a strand of brown hair off her weather-beaten face. "Newgate's harder on the little 'uns. They can't thrive in such harsh conditions. The parcels you've brought will ease their burden." Calling out to her housekeeper to bring refreshments, she moved her small frame over to a chair and beckoned to Elizabeth to sit on the chair beside her.

Elizabeth considered what life in Newgate might be like for this family. Everything had to be bought from the keeper, including rooms, food and bedding. The midwife had seen more than most the conditions they lived in, and she had described the open typhus sores – which people called gaol fever – the stink of rotting flesh and the delirious moans from lice-infested bodies wrapped in filthy rags. Elizabeth couldn't imagine her own family suffering in such dreadful circumstances. "It's preposterous," she said. "Debtors paying for their stay and their clothes taken if they can't. It makes no sense."

"I know, but it's the way of the world. Believe me, if it wasn't for the keeper making a fast penny, they would have even less. But there's much we can do to help them –" Mrs Cellier turned to acknowledge the maid, who carried in a tray containing two cups of steaming hot chocolate.

"Can it ever be enough?" Elizabeth replied with concern in her voice.

The maid set the tray down onto a small lacquered table in front of them, gave a brief curtsey, and left.

Picking up a cup, Mrs Cellier held it between her hands. She bent forward and lowered her voice. "I received my reading from Bridgefield yesterday."

Elizabeth grimaced and lifted the other cup. She'd no time for astrologers and didn't understand the midwife's obsession with them. "Bridgefield! What did he tell you this time?"

Mrs Cellier held up a hand. "Don't dismiss him. What he told me was most interesting."

"I'm listening." This wasn't the first time Elizabeth had endured the midwife relating one of Bridgefield's readings. Though they were interesting enough, she didn't think it right to meddle with ones' destiny. She smiled. "A new amour, perhaps, but you're a married woman." To her third husband, she reminded herself and looked at Mrs Cellier with wonder.

Mrs Cellier laughed. "What! Hear me out before you pass judgement. Let me show you what he made for me." She searched through a pile of papers on the chair beside her. Clearing a space on the lacquered table, she rolled out Bridgefield's chart.

Elizabeth studied the strange diagram in the centre of the page. Meaningless lines, shapes and names covered a strange figure. It was the first time she'd seen anything like it and frowned. "You can read this?"

"No. Not at all, but Bridgefield can."

"What does it mean?" Elizabeth bent over the paper.

"Too much to recount in the time we have. But there's something that concerns me, more than the rest. It's something that threatens a senior member of State and the peace and stability of England."

"England?" Elizabeth wanted to dismiss this as nonsense, but couldn't help feeling alarmed.

Mrs Cellier flapped a hand over the chart. "Bridgefield is also concerned by this. At first, he seemed reluctant to tell me what it meant, or give me the chart. But, I'd paid three guineas for it, so he couldn't refuse."

"But why would these things appear in your chart . . . England?"

"He said nothing would happen yet, but it's showing in my chart because the events leading up to it are moving into place. It's most strange."

"Did he say anything else? It all sounds rather vague. This could refer to anything . . . at anytime."

"Oh, yes, there's more. Let me show you." Mrs Cellier pointed to one of the shapes on the chart. "This figure is Aries. In this position it represents England."

Elizabeth nodded.

"My recall of the meaning of these positions is imperfect, but I'll try to remember," Mrs Cellier said. "In Cromwell's chart, Mars in Aries, in opposition to Saturn in Libra, showed him as a threat to the State and to England. Their positions in this chart are similar."

Though the words meant nothing to Elizabeth, the meaning was clear enough. "Dear God in heaven, not another Cromwell, another Civil War." A strange sense of foreboding swept through her and settled in the pit of her belly.

"No, this is something quite different." Mrs Cellier waved a hand to dismiss her fears. "The position of the planets at the time of Cromwell's birth led to these events. The planets are in a different position here. Bridgefield was quite certain about this, and described an Arian ascendant. A man with vaunting ambition and cruel tyranny . . . A man who will infiltrate our Church and threaten the State."

Shaken by what she'd heard, Elizabeth tried to make sense of it. "Do you mean the Catholic Church? But why would such things show in your chart? Did Bridgefield say? Oh! Mrs Cellier, what's this about?"

Mrs Cellier shrugged her shoulders. "It's all very strange. But look here. Do you see how the diagram is split into sections? Bridgefield said my role in this is seen in the Northern hemisphere. It appears that regardless of my own will or desire, these events will be thrust upon me. 'Tis all very strange. And, look here, at the position of Jupiter. When it's in this position it represents someone with a large mole."

"I don't like this at all. You should refrain from consulting him again." Though she'd started out certain there was no substance to such readings, Elizabeth felt unnerved by what she'd heard – A senior member of State? Someone infiltrating the Catholic Church? What was this about? Fearing it concerned York's conversion, she changed the conversation. "Have you been to see Mary Beatrice yet?"

"Of course. Though she miscarried her first, she's young and should bear this one easily enough," the midwife said and rolled up the chart.

"She talks of nothing else and quizzes me endlessly." Elizabeth smiled at the memory. "She's so innocent in these matters. But at sixteen, so was I."

"God willing, she'll birth many more. Yes, such innocence doesn't last long."

Elizabeth frowned. "I'm concerned for Mary Beatrice. She's perplexed by the public's reaction."

"Times are difficult. But, she's kind and people will soon come to realise it."

"I hope you're right. I pray for her every day."

"She's fortunate to have your friendship and guidance.

When she made ready to leave, Elizabeth hugged Mrs Cellier and handed her a shilling, plus a penny to give to the keeper of Newgate, so he might turn a blind eye to her activities there.

On the journey home, Elizabeth chewed her bottom lip. What had Mrs Cellier said about her astrological reading? Someone infiltrating the Catholic Church. What could this person possibly uncover?

CHAPTER TEN

The Power of the Preacher

An autumn wind howled through Hastings, snapping twigs from bare branches and setting them free. It whipped against Titus Oates' back, like an unseen hand pushing him towards All Saints Church. To shield his face from the rain, Titus kept his wide-brimmed hat pulled down, and his head bowed.

Limping up the steep gravel path, Titus called out to a family, making their way to the afternoon service, "Miserable day."

The adults nodded their agreement and stopped to let him pass. "Good afternoon," the father called back, pulling his two young children clear of Titus' path.

Titus lifted his cane in thanks and strode ahead. Rain splattered off the large arched porch and dripped down to form a muddy puddle around the entrance. Continuing past, he entered through the door leading into the vestry. He shook out his coat and hat, hung them on a peg and removed his sermon from an inside pocket. After laying the papers on a chair, he donned his clerical robes.

Eager to see how many people had turned up to hear his sermon, he peered out from behind the vestry door. His heart soared. At least a hundred parishioners sat huddled in their pews. The smell of damp clothes and stale periwigs hung in the air, and he inhaled the pungent aroma.

When the church bell stopped pealing, Titus swaggered through the chancel, stepped up to the pulpit, looked around and beamed. Determined to prove himself, he'd spent many hours preparing this sermon.

He swallowed and took a deep intake of breath. "The Laard Gaad," he said in a loud brassy voice.

Laughter erupted from somewhere in the pews. Drawing his breath through his teeth, he glared around the congregation, seeking out the perpetrator. A dull light flowed through the stained glass windows, creating a dismal pallor on the faces staring up at him. In contrast, a bright halo of light surrounded him, arising from the host of burning candles he'd asked to have positioned around the altar. No matter how hard he tried to pronounce the letter 'O' it came out as a series of A's, like a lamb bleating. He had similar problems with the other vowels.

Titus stretched to his full height and stared in the direction of the culprits. Observing their fine clothes, he sneered. As a young boy, he'd been ridiculed – he heard again children laughing at his words, and saw others skipping behind him, bleating like lambs. On becoming a minister, such taunts had stopped. This was as it should be, and he had no compunction in reminding his father's parishioners of this; regardless of who they were.

Raising his voice, he pointed around the now cowed congregation. "Sinners, you must repent. You must pray for faith and attend to what *He* says," he boomed in his afflicted manner. In tandem with his words his large chin bobbed against his chest.

No one laughed.

"You," he roared and banged a large fist onto the pulpit. He didn't care the culprits were landed gentry. "You must pray that the bountiful and liberal Lord bestows his Spirit . . . on sinners." He paused and glared at the congregation, who now attended to his every word.

His father, Reverend Oates, sat in the front pew, peering up. His mother, Lucy, sat next to him, a pained look on her face. Titus' hands clenched. They'd witnessed this attempt to mock him. Well, he'd show these parishioners he wasn't someone to be laughed at.

His heart quickened – he had everyone's attention now. He leant forward over the pulpit. The power of his words surged out of him and resonated throughout the large building, like the ringing of a loud warning bell.

"Lest you forget, let me remind you," he bellowed and smacked his lips together as if savouring a tasty morsel. "It is *God* who speaks these words to you, not I. Laugh again while *He* speaks and be prepared to feel His wrath. The Lord's an *ass* if he lets you off with treating me like this. Be assured, it will be too late to repent when your maggot-ridden bodies lie rotting in the soil. Now, let us pray for the salvation of your souls."

After Reverend Oates had seen his parishioners out, Titus walked with him towards the church gate. His mother had left as soon as the service had finished. The rain had stopped, but the clouds remained dark. Turning towards his father, Titus waited for him to congratulate him on his sermon, but the Reverend strode on ahead in silence. Titus frowned and followed him down the steep gravel path. "Blaady hypocrite," he said under his breath.

When they came out of the gate, a white-haired man hurried towards them. Titus tipped his hat back, puzzling as to who this stranger might be.

The stranger moved from one foot to the other and stared wide eyed at Reverend Oates. "Papists burned down my church. It is well known they started the Great Fire to burn us out. Take heed to what I say, for I've heard Papists are plotting against us again. We have to stop them before we're all murdered. I heard all Protestants are to be massacred. They'll make candles from our grease and burn them in their altars. Pray to God we are spared."

Reverend Oates laid a hand on the stranger's arm. "We can discuss these concerns when we meet in London."

As if he hadn't heard him, the man continued. "York married a Catholic. I heard talk York himself had converted and –"

Reverend Oates flushed. "Titus, let me introduce you to Doctor Israel Tonge, former Rector of St. Michael's. Tonge this is my son, Titus."

Before Titus could comment, Reverend Oates turned away. "Come Titus. It's too cold to stand here. Our meal awaits us." His long coat billowed behind him as he marched ahead of Titus.

Titus' bow-legged gait prevented him from walking with any great speed, but he swung his cane and limped after his father. Glancing back at the small man with his long unkempt white hair, he sniggered. "Is he insane? Did he say that the Duke of York's a blaady Papist?"

Looking up at the imposing, grey stone church, Titus snorted. Some parishioner had mocked him, but he'd gained the upper hand. He'd proved he wasn't a man to be ridiculed. His father should be proud, not disdainful. But, he would show him. One day his father would marvel at his achievements. He couldn't wait for that moment to arrive. Swinging his cane, he visualised preaching to his own congregation. He imagined their rapt faces as his words stabbed into their hard hearts, converting them back to the true path of God. "Not like that imposter," he muttered and stared at his father's back.

Try as he might, Titus couldn't recall his father ever praising him. Thumping his cane onto the ground, he followed his father along the High Street. "Blaady parishioners."

His father slowed, enabling him to catch up. "Be quiet Titus and get yourself home," he said through clenched teeth. "Angry or no, how dare you call the Lord an ass, this day will not soon be forgotten in Hastings."

On reaching home, Titus followed Reverend Oates through the front door. In the hallway, his father stopped and spun around. "You always were a snotty-nosed fool, a dunce of the first order. Your mother felt sorry for you because you took convulsions and thought you wouldn't survive. Well, survive you did and to my cost. Damn you to Hell."

If he had somewhere else to go, Titus would leave this festering sore and never return. On receiving the position at Bobbing in Kent, he thought he'd left here for good, but circumstances had brought him back. He coloured as he recalled his dismissal. "Damn those liars for speaking out against me," he muttered and stormed to his room.

Later that evening, after a satisfying meal, Titus reclined on a chair beside the fire in the small parlour, a Latin textbook open on his knee. The wind howled outside, setting the windows rattling in their frames and sending billows of smoke from the fire into the room. The smell of boiled beef and damp clothes hung in the air. His mother sat on a chair beside him, reading her Bible. His father sat opposite them.

Titus threw aside the Latin text. "I can't make any sense of this."

"Hardly surprising since you haven't even grasped the rudiments of Latin," Reverend Oates said. "Perhaps if you'd studied your books instead of drinking and cheating your way through every college you were sent to?"

In no mood to argue with his father, Titus tapped his cane against his nose but said nothing.

His mother stopped reading and looked over at her husband and then at him.

Raising his eyebrows at his wife, the Reverend sighed. "No doubt you'll try and appease that snotty nosed fool. Leave him be. God himself couldn't teach *him* Latin."

She smiled at Titus. "You always were different, Titus. Indeed, I was just thinking about the day you were born. I swear you caused me more birth pains than the other three put together."

Reverend Oates gave her an icy glare. "I'll finish your tale for you, shall I, wife? His birth could have killed you –"

"Leave maather be," Titus called out. "Leave us both be."

"Or what?" Reverend Oates shouted and raised a fist. "As you well know, your mother struggled to sleep when big-bellied with you, and when she did, she dreamt she carried the child of the *Devil*."

Titus sucked air through his teeth but remained seated.

His mother jumped up from the chair and hurried towards the door. Holding the handle, she stopped. "It's no wonder he's so troubled," she called out, her voice wavering.

Titus rubbed his hands over his face. He had to control his rising anger. If he reacted, his father wouldn't hesitate to throw him out.

"This is your final warning, Titus. Speak to me again like that and you'll leave this house for good."

Titus smirked. He'd been right; his father was trying to provoke his anger. Well, he wouldn't blaady satisfy him.

Reverend Oates loosened his shirt collar. "I've spent years trying to build my reputation here, and am not about to let you destroy my efforts." He stroked his chin. "Who can I ask to take you on this time, eh? I've scanned my memory, but can think of no one I haven't already asked." He turned to his wife. "I've warned you time and again to stop coddling him. Since the day he was born you've given in to his every whim. Why won't you listen?"

"He has more of your nature than mine," Lucy said and glowered at her husband. "Perhaps if *you* had been here more often to discipline him," she snapped. "I have to go out . . . a woman nearing birth. Don't wait up for me, husband. I'll be late home."

Reverend Oates sank back into the chair and closed his eyes.

Titus glared at him. Though his father's hair was white and had receded almost to his crown, he still thought himself handsome. God alone knew how many bastards he'd produced while travelling the country as a young Anabaptist minister. Titus had heard the gossip about him, many times. The idea of throwing this back in his father's face appealed to him, but he was wary.

He sat on the chair beside him. "Faather . . . I'm sorry. I didn't mean to speak harshly to you. I rely on your help, but I deserve my own church."

Reverend Oates opened his eyes. Clasping his hands together, he stared at Titus. "Tell me . . . how can I help you, if you get yourself expelled from each and every position I obtain for you? Hmm? No time at all has passed between you starting at Bobbing and returning here. What were you expelled for this time? You never did tell me. Hmm. What was it? Perhaps I can refresh your memory. Was it theft, again? Drunkenness, perhaps?" He lowered his voice. "Or was it for sodomy?"

Lifting his walking stick, Titus made to get up.

Reverend Oates roared at him, "If you think you're going off to get drunk in some alehouse, think again! Now leave me be."

Titus jumped up and sneered. "You always mention my failings but never my successes. I completed my Orders. I'm an Anglican minister now." He slammed the door behind him. Standing in the hall, Titus rubbed at the mole on his brow. If he were ever to be free of his father, he had to find another position, and soon.

The following morning at breakfast, Titus had no appetite for the fish on his plate. "How common the parishioners of Hastings are," he said to his mother.

Reverend Oates rose from his chair, causing Titus to look up at him. Rocking back on his heels, his father stretched to his full height. "You seem as tired of my parishioners as they are of you, Titus. I think you should leave here for a while. Let things settle down. I had planned on attending some meetings in London, but you will go instead. Let London suffer you for a while."

"London," his mother said and beamed. "Why Titus, you've never spent time there. It's a wonderful idea. You might even meet someone looking for a curate."

Titus liked the idea of going to London. Perhaps his mother was right. And, it would get him away from here.

His father shook his head in despair. "Take that foolish grin off your face, Titus. No, I don't think you're worthy of it, but . . . needs must. The magistrate, Captain Parker, is causing endless bloody trouble for me. Your behaviour yesterday will no doubt bring him to my door again. So, London it is? And while you're there, perhaps you could give some thought as to how to keep Captain Parker away from my affairs."

Deep in thought, Titus peered at his father. Giving a loud sigh, he nodded.

Part Two: Stalemate

1675

'The world's a wood, in which all lose their way,
Though by a different path, each goes astray.'

George Villiers, Duke of Buckingham

CHAPTER ELEVEN

Confessions

Winter had set in with a vengeance, and Christmas and New Year had passed in a flurry of activity for Elizabeth. Family life had once again returned to normal at 66 Lincoln's Inn Fields. In the hallway, Elizabeth yawned and fastened her warmest cloak. They had to be discreet in carrying out their religious devotions and had waited until dark before leaving for Mass. Her heart quickened. They could face imprisonment if caught. She pushed the thought away.

"It's freezing outside. Should we leave Winifred?" she asked Powis.

Hearing her name, Winifred looked up and shook her head. "Mama, no," she whined.

Elizabeth immediately realised her mistake and shrugged at Powis. If she left Winifred behind now, she would cause a scene. Weighing up her options, she decided they were better to take her. She bent down. "Hush, hush. Don't fret. Mama just thought it a little too chilling for you to go outside. Of course, you'll come with us."

"William put your hood up. You'll catch a fever," she chided in exasperation. Beside her, Anne hopped around trying to pull her gloves on. William drew away from Elizabeth and hurried over to help Anne.

"I'm quite able to put them on myself. Leave me be." Anne scowled at William.

Elizabeth looked at Powis and rolled her eyes. She saw in her daughter the growing independence of an eleven-year-old. The long-case clock chimed out the hour of six, and it resounded throughout the great hallway. With a stern look, she addressed them. "We must leave soon, or there's no point going at all." They could not be late. "Winifred, hold Papa's hand."

Powis lifted Winifred into his arms and chucked her under the chin. "Is there a bear inside that furry hood?" he asked his two-year-old daughter. It was nearing her bedtime, and she was fretful and restless.

Her blue eyes widened, and she stared at him. "No, Papa. Look . . . 'tis me, Winfred."

"So it is!" he exclaimed in mock surprise. "Phew, I'm glad it's not a bear. I would have had to fight it off," he said and kissed her forehead.

Winifred giggled and wrapped her arms tighter around him.

To keep Winifred occupied, he took her over to the painting of Powis Castle. The gilt-framed picture hung at the bottom of the oak staircase. Two candles, placed in sconces above it, illumined their family home. Powis' brow furrowed. His family had lost everything after the Civil War, and he lived in fear of it happening again. As a known Royalist, his father had fled abroad, and their family home had been gifted to a Cromwell supporter.

He crossed himself and said a prayer of thanks to Charles for returning it to his father. "We'll return in the spring, perhaps for a month . . . maybe two. Do you remember being there?" he asked Winifred, who laughed and pointed to the painting.

Powis turned to Elizabeth, who fussed around Lucy. "Are we all ready?"

"At last, yes. Remember children remain silent until we get there."

Stepping out of the front door, a bitter wind assaulted Elizabeth. Powis carried Winifred, his arms wrapped around her to keep her warm. William walked by his father's side.

Elizabeth shivered and put her arms around Lucy and Anne, and drew them closer. Yesterday, another Jesuit priest had been caught preaching in public and been thrust into Newgate. Concerned for the elderly priest's health in such freezing weather, Elizabeth had arranged for Mrs Cellier to take food and blankets in to him. Dear God, he'd only been preaching his religion. Apart from praying for his safe-keeping, she could do nothing else to help him.

They remained silent as they walked together along the western side of Lincoln's Inn Fields. The frost-laden branches of bare trees glistened in the pale moonlight that lit their way, illuminating a rough path through the undergrowth. A lone carriage passed outside the wall, the horses' hooves slipping on the icy cobbled road.

Keeping her footsteps quiet, Elizabeth continued until they arrived at the gloomy archway which led out onto Duke Street. Next to it stood the Sardinian Chapel, where they were heading. Like many Catholics living in London, they'd resorted to using the chapels of Foreign Ambassadors. Those chapels tended to be left alone because they were for the use of foreign dignitaries.

Coming to a halt, Elizabeth huddled together with Powis and the children, to check if they were being watched or followed. The wind howled around them, and the breath from their warm mouths blew upwards in soft billowing clouds.

A rustling sound startled her, and she touched Powis' arm. He had heard it too and returned her touch. They moved back into the archway.

Elizabeth nestled Lucy into her body and shielded her face with her gloved hand, then she pulled the other children tight into her. Powis moved in front of them, shielding their bodies with his own. She listened. Hearing the sound again, Elizabeth shivered and rested her head on Powis' shoulder. She remained still and attentive.

Elizabeth shivered again. Five days ago, Mary Beatrice had birthed a daughter, Catherine Laura. But, Mary Beatrice was young, and sons would surely follow. Perhaps now Shaftesbury would stop pushing for York to divorce her. She would also say a prayer tonight for Mary Beatrice and Catherine Laura. Hearing the sound of a branch breaking, Elizabeth lifted her head from Powis' shoulder and whispered, "We need to turn back."

Powis nodded, and they moved out of the archway. Elizabeth could make out the shapes of people heading towards the door leading into the chapel. It looked like two adults and a child. In the distance, a dog growled and bayed, as if alerted to something. Then, a continuous low pitched barking started.

Elizabeth lifted Lucy and, pulling Anne with her other hand, started running. Powis ran beside her with Winifred in his arms, William beside him. Behind her, the dog continued to bark, and indiscriminate shouts started. A woman screamed, and a child wailed, "Mama! Papa!"

She willed herself to keep going, the breath caught in her throat and she dragged Anne along. It was dark, and she stumbled. Powis caught her before she fell and pointed to the road. Elizabeth nodded, though a safer option, it was too dark to go back through the undergrowth. The pale moonlight lit their way along the rough road. Winifred wailed, but there was no time to comfort her.

Glancing back, Elizabeth could see that they had not been followed and slowed her pace. Powis slowed beside her. As they hurried towards the safety of home, Elizabeth clutched her pearl necklace and prayed.

CHAPTER TWELVE

Allegations

Titus entered The Bull Tavern in Great Queen Street, London, looking for some supper. As he pushed through the crowd milling in the hallway, someone tapped his shoulder. Stopping, he turned and stared at a face he didn't recognise.

"Titus? Titus Oates?" the stranger asked.

"Yaas . . . that's me," he said and tapped his nose with the tip of his cane.

"I apologise if I startled you. I'm Sir Richard Barker, a good friend of your father. Come, let us dine together."

Titus recognised Barker's name as that of his father's patron. Curious, he nodded and followed him into the tap-room. The noise of scraping benches and raised voices made it difficult to converse. The room smelled of tobacco and boiled meat.

"Ah, there's Israel Tonge, let us join him," Barker said and strode to one of the booths.

Following behind, Titus took in the high quality of Barker's topcoat and hat. Titus sat on a bench and recognised Israel Tonge, seated on the other side of the wooden table, as the stranger he had seen outside his father's church in Hastings. He looked to be in his fifties, and Titus remembered his long white hair.

Barker sat down. "Tonge, you've met Reverend Oates' son, Titus, have you not?" he said and signalled to the proprietor for service.

Tonge, who had already been served, peered over at Titus and nodded. A pile of pamphlets lay beside a bowl of soup. He pointed to the papers and said, "My work."

"As a divine, Tonge's work must be encouraged. He lodges with me here in London," Barker said and turned to address the proprietor, who'd arrived to take his order of potage, bread and ale, for himself and Titus.

Tonge launched into an account of his latest pamphlet outlining Jesuit activities in London.

Titus stared at the bedraggled man and tried to follow what he said.

"Catholics started the Great Fire . . . to kill Protestants," Tonge said in a gentle, refined voice. "I was settling into my first position as Rector at St Mary Staining. I'd moved my wife and son into our new home. Then *my* church was burned in their fire. Everything destroyed! All I'd worked for burned to the ground by Papists. Now, visions come to me as dreams, and I write them down and sell them to others. I also read and translate Jesuit writings. Barker has been my saviour, and I'm indebted to him. There's another conspiracy afoot by the Jesuits. I'm gathering intelligence on it," Tonge explained between mouthfuls of thick soup.

"Conspiracy, you say?" Like everyone else in England, Titus had heard the rumour that the Great Fire had been started by Catholics to return England to Rome.

Tonge lowered his voice almost to a whisper. "Yes, to replace the King with his brother, the Duke of York. York has converted to Rome, and his new wife is the Pope's daughter. With our barren Queen, these Catholics will inherit the throne."

Titus had never heard such treasonable talk before and glanced at Barker.

Barker nodded. "These are difficult times. The common people won't tolerate a return to tyranny, but no more discussion of this here."

"I'll send you my book on the burnings at Smithfield," Tonge said. "The new model army has been infiltrated by Catholics. Did I tell you I was once a schoolmaster?"

Titus couldn't keep up with Tonge's conversation and latched on to the one thing he did understand. "I also have an interest in becoming a schoolmaster. I'm waiting to hear about a position in Hastings. I've some irons in the fire concerning the matter," he said in a loud brassy voice. He'd never considered the idea until now, but it had struck him that if he had such a position then perhaps Barker might sponsor him.

By the time he made ready to leave the Bull Tavern, Titus had accepted Barker's invitation to call on him the next time he was in London.

On the Tuesday following Easter Sunday, Titus tidied himself up, donned his clerical robes and pulled on a large-brimmed black hat. Picking up his cane, he set out to pay a visit to the Mayor of Hastings. The sun shone from a cloudless sky, and he whistled a merry tune. The visit to London had restored his sagging spirits, and he hadn't argued with his father since returning, three weeks before. Indeed, his father had helped him work on a plan to secure a schoolmaster's position.

Arriving at the Mayor's lodgings, Titus wiped sweat from his hands and knocked. When the housekeeper opened the oak door, he removed his hat. "I humbly beg your pardon. My name is Titus Oates. Is the Mayor at home? Is he able to see me?" he asked in a timid voice. "Something dreadful has happened, and I urgently need to speak to him about it."

The housekeeper ushered Titus into a small room, attached to the Mayor's office. "Wait here a moment." Her eyes darted around, as if unsure what to do. "I'll see if the Mayor's free to receive you." She knocked on the office door and disappeared inside.

A few minutes later, the Mayor opened the door and ushered Titus in. Indicating that he should sit on a chair beside his desk, the Mayor instructed his housekeeper to bring refreshments.

The Mayor addressed him. "Oates, is it?"

Titus licked his lips and sighed. "Yes, Your Worship. I'm Titus Oates, curate of All Saints Church, where my father is Rector."

"I know of the Upper Church and your father," the Mayor said and sat down.

Startled by a tap on the door, Titus let out a sigh of relief when the housekeeper entered, carrying a tray containing two small tankards of ale. Placing it on the desk, she nodded and left the room.

"What brings you to see me?" the Mayor asked and handed him one of the tankards.

Accepting the ale, Titus said, "Your Worship, I've been very troubled, and seek your help."

Raising a bushy eyebrow the Mayor nodded to him to continue.

"Something shocking has happened. 'Tis too terrible even to speak of," Titus said in a confidential tone. "Your Worship, on Tuesday past, at seven o'clock in the evening, I returned to my fathers' church to collect papers I'd left in the vestry following the afternoon service. On entering All Saints Church, I discovered something dreadful happening in the south porch. There, I saw young William Parker, the schoolmaster, committing an unnatural act with a young, distressed male child."

The Mayor laid his ale down. "William Parker! What are you saying?"

"Yes, Your Worship. I didn't know what to do. I returned home and finding my father in his study, I told him what I'd seen. Father returned with me to the church, to confront him. But when we got there, Parker and the boy had gone. I resolved to bring this to your attention. With your knowledge of such matters, I believed you would know what to do."

The Mayor's brows furrowed. "I'm deeply troubled by the allegations you've placed before me. Indeed, I'm aghast. Knowing William Parker's reputation as a good and law abiding teacher, I find it hard to believe what I have heard. These are severe allegations to bring against a family of good standing within the community. Sodomy is a crime punishable by death – and such accusations shouldn't be made lightly. Yet you . . . a rector's son, seem definite about the identity of the offender and the nature of the act you witnessed."

Sweat trickled down Titus' back. "I heard sobbing, like that of a young child. This is what led me to look in the south porch."

The Mayor winced. Scraping his wooden chair back, he stood. He steepled his hands together, as if in prayer, and tapped them against his mouth. Turning his attention back to Titus, he let out a deep sigh. "As confused as I am by these allegations, I feel compelled to take them seriously and will act immediately."

Titus held back a smile as he lifted his cane and left the Mayor's office. Once outside, he made for the nearest tavern. By the time he arrived home, the news had been received – Young William Parker, the schoolmaster, had been arrested and would appear at the next court session at Hastings gaol. Jubilant, Titus decided to visit the Mayor again tomorrow. This time with allegations that Parker's father, Captain Parker, had uttered treasonable and seditious talk. These were also serious charges to make – if found guilty, Captain Parker would be drawn to Tyburn, hanged and quartered.

On the morning of young Parkers' trial, Titus rose early and donned his clerical robe, long coat and black hat. A chill wind blew, and he pulled his coat tight around him. Accompanied by his father, he made his way to George Street, where he entered the courtroom at 9 am.

In a confident and buoyant mood, Titus couldn't wait to retell his story to the jurors of Hastings. Pleased by how things had progressed, he was filled with anticipation that the mastership of the local school was there for his taking. His father had accompanied him as a witness, to verify the truth of his account. Nothing could go wrong.

The trials commenced in the wood-panelled courtroom adjoining the gaol. William Parker was called second. Titus shivered with delight as a warder escorted Parker into the room and instructed him to stand at 'the bar'. Titus watched in fascination as the warder positioned a mirrored reflector above the Bar and adjusted it to ensure the light from the window reflected onto Parker's face. The warder then placed a sounding board over Parker's head.

Seated across from Parker, the Mayor presided over the proceedings. The jurors sat in a stall to Parker's right. On his left sat Reverend Oates and nine men and women, whom Titus suspected had come to feed on the court proceedings against one of their schoolmasters.

As the court clerk read out the charges, Titus' heart quickened.

"William Parker, of the Schoolhouse, here in Hastings, you are accused of committing a hideous and unnatural offence against a young male child, in the South Porch of All Saints Church. Titus Oates, give the details of your charge to the court."

Brimming with excitement, Titus stood. Under oath, he repeated what he'd told the Mayor. When he finished, his father swore to the absolute truth of everything Titus had said.

William Parker wasn't put on oath – he was expected to prove his innocence. The judge asked him to state his defence of the charges brought against him.

"Thank you, Your Honour. Titus Oates, you say you saw me in All Saints Church at seven o'clock on the evening of the fourth of April. Are you quite definite it was me you saw on that date and at that time?"

"Yes, I'm most definite," Titus said, and a flush of excitement spread over his face. "I'm certain because the papers I retrieved had the date of the sermon on them, and 'twas the fourth. I went for them after my evening meal which finished at 6.45pm. My father will verify this."

"Yes," Reverend Oates replied. "What my son says is true. I'm also clear regarding the date and time I accompanied him to my church."

Titus' stomach lurched when young Parker proceeded to call, one by one, six respected parents of children at his school who'd been in his company at a Gaudy day dinner at his home, over half a mile away from the church, on that very evening. It was as if all the air had left Titus' body, and he reeled as he listened to each parent testify that young Parker had never left the room for the duration of the meal, which had lasted from six until after eight pm.

When Parker called three stone masons who testified they'd been working inside all Saints Church at the time in question and hadn't heard or seen anything amiss that evening, not even Titus or his father arriving, Titus trembled.

When the Mayor asked Titus why he couldn't identify or produce the boy in question, tears sprang to his eyes and he blustered his way through an answer that belied the existence of the child at all. "He may have moved on. An orphan, perhaps? Or an urchin?"

The Mayor's eyes darkened and his face flushed a livid red, as he summarised the allegations as a complete fabrication from start to finish. The jurors huddled together for a few moments before presenting their verdict . . . "Not guilty."

Loud cries of approval erupted around the courtroom. Titus jumped up and scanned the room, looking for a way out. Perspiration beaded on his brow, and he wiped it off with the back of his hand. His breath quickened, and he slumped back down onto the seat.

"Silence!" The Mayor bellowed. "William Parker, I apologise for bringing you here today. It is my opinion that you, a respected member of this community, have been subjected to a great injustice. The case against you is dismissed."

Parker nodded. "Thank you, Your Honour. I wish to raise a case of my own. I've been subjected to gross lies against me and publicly slandered. I desire to raise a claim for one thousand pounds in damages, against Titus Oates."

At ten am, Titus and his father, with heads bowed low, left Hastings gaol and made their way home in shocked silence.

Later, Titus skulked in his bedroom. He'd stormed there after seeing his mother standing at the kitchen window, smiling out at the bonfires glowing throughout Hastings to celebrate William Parker's dismissal. Although it had been over an hour since his mother and father had supped, his mother had made no move to bring his meal up to him.

In June, Titus appeared in court again concerning his charge that Parker's father, Captain Parker, had uttered treasonable and seditious talk. Fearful of repeating the same mistakes he'd made at young Parker's trial, Titus avoided giving any specific details. As a result, he stumbled over his testimony and hesitated when asked where and when events had taken place. When it became apparent he had nothing to support his allegation, the Mayor charged Titus with perjury, and bound him over to appear at the next court session.

Titus faced being thrown into gaol for perjury *and* paying a thousand pounds in damages. Furious, he strode from the court. By the time he arrived home, he was close to tears. Left with no other option, he decided to leave Hastings. Heading to his room, he packed clerical robes and a prayer book into a bag. From there, he went to the pantry, wrapped large slices of cold meat and bread in a muslin cloth and placed them in the bag.

As he came out the pantry, his mother entered the kitchen. "What are you doing?"

"That blaady Mayor, the Parkers must be paying him to lie about me. Blaady perjury, 'tis all nonsense." Grabbing his mother's arm, Titus threw her to the ground. "Pish. How dare he accuse *me* of lying?"

Lucy drew her arms around her head and tried to scuttle away. "Desist, Titus. Please don't do this, again. I will help you, just let me up . . . Please," she begged between sobs.

"Help me! When have you ever helped me?"

Lucy raised herself from the ground and, still on her knees, moved towards the door. Titus lunged forward and kicked the door closed in front of her.

Kneeling down, Titus pushed his face into hers. He needed money, and his mother was the only one likely to give it to him. If he missed this chance, he might not get another. "Give me some money and I'll be gone from your sight . . . maather. I need to get away from here. Now give me some money!"

"Yes! Yes, Titus. I'll give you what money I have. Look! Here's a pound I saved. Take it." Pulling the coin from her apron pocket, she held it out. "It's all I have. *I swear* . . . I've no more to give you."

Titus snatched the money from her hand. "Don't tell *him* you gave me this." Grabbing his bag, hat and walking cane, he stormed out the house and banged the door behind him.

Without any destination in mind, Titus walked until it grew dark. He stayed on the coastal road to Portsmouth. At a secluded place off the main track, he stopped for the night. He ate a small portion of bread and meat and stuffed the rest into the bag. Too tired to walk any further, he lay down under a hedge, pulled his dust-covered coat around him and fell asleep.

When a thump hit his back, Titus awoke and screamed. He rolled over and received another kick. Opening his eyes, he saw a hefty youth towering over him. The youth grabbed Titus' bag, spilt the contents to the ground and rifled through them. Finding nothing of value, he kicked Titus again, forced him to stand, and searched through his pockets.

Titus cursed his cane, lying redundant amongst the long grass. Still groggy from sleep, he surveyed his attacker and concluded he was strong. The youth looked dirt-**encrusted**, his clothes were threadbare and he stank. An opportunist beggar, most likely.

On finding no money, the youth picked up the muslin cloth containing the bread and meat, and stuffed it under his arm. Then, without warning, he raised his other arm and landed a mighty blow to Titus' face and took off through the forest.

As soon as it grew light, Titus continued along the coastal road, arriving at Spithead before nightfall the following evening. He prodded his eyebrow with a dirt-encrusted finger. Little damage had been done, apart from a small lump. Having eaten nothing since the attack, Titus' belly rumbled. He smiled, as he recalled the clean clerical robes in his bag and the pound secreted in his hat. He yawned, picked up his cane and set off to find somewhere to eat and clean himself up.

He booked into a tavern, bought a shave, washed his hands and changed into his clean clerical robes, dumped the dirty ones, and ate a large bowl of fresh mussels with chunks of warm bread. Remaining at the table, Titus listened to the conversations around him. From what he could gather, a small fleet was in dock. What he found more interesting was the talk at the next table, of the Adventure, a Royal Navy vessel under the command of Sir Richard Rooth.

Keeping his back to the gossiping sailors, Titus edged nearer. From what he could hear, the Adventure was bound for Tangiers, to deliver the new Governor. The ship was moored and ready to leave as soon as the Governor arrived. Titus listened a while longer, gleaning as much information as possible, then set off in search of the 'Adventure'.

Waiting in line to enrol for work, Titus hoped he wasn't too late. The bustle and noise around him increased the sense of adventure. Women stood on the dock, seeing their husbands or sons off. Whores peddled their wares, and young boys sold pies from trays slung around their necks. Titus had never seen anything like it. Before he realised it, he was at the front of the line, and he stepped up to the clerk.

"Name, age and position," the bewigged clerk shouted, pointing an ink-stained finger at him.

"Titus Oates, twenty-nine . . . erm', chaplain."

Fortune was shining on Titus, and he secured the post of naval chaplain. The ship would set sail for Tangiers in the morning. Excitement coursed through him, and his sleep that night was filled with visions of the adventures which surely lay ahead.

At five o'clock the following morning, Titus joined the line again, to report for boarding.

CHAPTER THIRTEEN

The King's Birthday

Early in the evening of the twenty-ninth of May, Elizabeth linked into Mary Beatrice's arm and hurried along the stone corridors of St James's Palace. As Mary Beatrice skipped along beside her, it reminded Elizabeth of the vast difference in their ages. Reaching Mary Beatrice's apartments they slipped into a small ante-chamber and collapsed together onto a blue velvet settee.

Elizabeth held a hand to her head. "Your ladies will be looking for you." She gasped for a breath. "They'll blame me."

Throwing off her travelling cloak, Mary Beatrice picked up a small silk embroidered cushion and held it to her chest. "Pah! They know I am here. I tell them I have toothache, and you will attend to it. I tell them, remain at Palace Whitehall a little longer, and they seemed happy to oblige. Ah! This is one of the few places I can find peace." She laid the cushion aside and removed the pins from her long jet-black hair. "Thank you for coming with me. I count you as my dear friend, my *amica cara.*"

Elizabeth shook her head. "Join in with the others, have fun. Don't feign toothache so you can withdraw here."

"Shoosh!" Mary Beatrice stood up. "Help me out my gown and hand me a robe *per favore*. I cannot get comfortable when trussed up like a fowl."

Once Mary Beatrice had been settled into her long silk robe, Elizabeth sat beside her.

"Ah, this is so peaceful. It was an especially tiresome evening." Mary Beatrice rested her head on Elizabeth's shoulder. "All of them clamouring to pay birthday tributes to Charles and vying to outsmart each other. It was quite dreadful, with the wits striving to be at their wittiest, and the whores trying to outdo each other, and all of them *prostitute*."

Elizabeth thought Mary Beatrice was isolating herself from the courtiers. She felt deeply for her and was bemused by her indifference. "But, you must learn to stay for the entertainments. How else will those at Court get to know you?"

Mary Beatrice grimaced. "Unlike most others the tables bore me."

"Yes. I feel the same." Elizabeth was reluctant to force the issue, but Mary Beatrice was too young to understand she needed allies at Court. "Such extravagance and the losses are of no concern. I would be aghast. How can they do it?"

Mary Beatrice sat up. "I have watched them borrow hundreds to stay in a game only to lose it on the turn of the next hand, and all of them they have massive debts."

"The newest craze is for basset. It has taken a hold."

"It will never take hold of me. Yet, I am told to play because it's fashionable . . . and vulgar not to! Do you really wonder I do not stay?"

Elizabeth shook her head and sat in silence for a few minutes. "I was thinking about the day we met. It seems only yesterday I found you under the stairwell. You looked so young and . . . sad."

Mary Beatrice smiled. "When I first met James, I thought him old and ugly. I cried when told I am to marry a man of forty years. I cried when I arrive here, and for more than a week after I cry when I see him. His skin looked frightful. Only later I learn it is scars from smallpox. I was fluent in Italian and French, but my English it was not so good. His stammer made it difficult for me to understand. Everything seemed s – s – so f– f– frightening."

Elizabeth giggled and smacked Mary Beatrice's hand, in playful reprimand.

"*Che so*, but I was in a new country and all alone." Mary Beatrice shrugged her shoulders.

Elizabeth was surprised Mary Beatrice now accepted her fate. Or did she? "But you feel different now?"

"Oh, yes. I soon grew fond of James. He's kind and understanding, and we talk about many things."

"Do you really feel fond of him?"

"You seem surprised. But, yes. Yes, I do. How can I say it?" Mary Beatrice raised her hands. "He makes me feel . . . safe, *sicuro*. Many say he is a bore, but it is to my liking. I am blessed to have such a caring husband."

Elizabeth nodded. "Yes, I understand that, but something is concerning you. I hear it in your voice. What is it?"

Mary Beatrice hesitated before replying. "What I cannot countenance *amica cara,* is his mistress. It's loathsome to me they have four *bambini.* And the youngest not even one year. He tells me he is ending this. Ha! I believe him. Then she births another bambino. Pah! Of course they still bed together. The nursery is filled with his and his brother's bastards. It's unjust Elizabeth, ingiusto."

As Mary Beatrice talked, Elizabeth studied the sixteen-year-old Italian girl. She could already see the noble and voluptuous woman she would become. A fair complexion provided a stunning contrast to her jet-black hair. Her dark, lustrous, hooded eyes and full mouth, gave her a sensual appearance. Why did York have to distress her? Surely he had all a husband could want in a wife. His mistress, Arabella Churchill, was plain and as small as a child. Elizabeth saw the pain etched on her friend's face, but didn't know how to comfort her. She could never endure Powis taking a mistress. "It must be worse than death itself. But, what can we do?"

"Oh *amica cara*, I try to stay strong but am filled with fear," Mary Beatrice sobbed. "Catherine Laura is four-months, yet she is frail. Only last year I birth my stillborn son. I still dream about it, and am afraid something will happen to my precious daughter."

"Do not torment yourself. Let things take their course." Elizabeth could see Mary Beatrice was borne down with worries. She needed to enjoy herself, not fret away her youth like this.

Mary Beatrice reached over and gripped Elizabeth's hand. "*Amica cara*, I think I'm with *bambino* again. Let us pray it's the healthy boy we seek. It's early, not yet two months, but the signs, they are there."

"Congratulations. I wish you good health." Elizabeth's spirits lifted. So this is why she wanted to talk in private. This one could well be the male heir they needed. "Catherine Laura's a cherub. It's good she wasn't a boy, for you'll keep her longer by your side."

Mary Beatrice pulled her hands back and ran them through her hair. "I know you are right, but tonight . . . watching Queen Catherine sit by, as Louise de Kérouaille and Nell Gwynn vied for her husband's attention. It made my belly turn." She dropped her voice almost to a whisper. "She truly does love him you know, she told me. It broke Catherine's heart when she discovered she had to share her husband's love with many others."

Mary Beatrice raised her voice again. "Charles' whores fawn over him and accept present after present, while Catherine asks for so little. The earrings Louise wore today cost eight thousand pounds. Can you believe it? A *small* gift from Charles, Pah! If you see how she touched them whenever Catherine came near. It made my blood spill over. Dearest Catherine has resigned herself to having no *bambino*. I have watched her in the royal nursery, hugging and playing with her husband's bastards."

"I've witnessed this myself," Elizabeth said. Would Powis be wondering where she was? She should return to Whitehall Palace, but didn't want to leave Mary Beatrice in low spirits. Where were her ladies; they should have arrived by now? Elizabeth made to stand.

As if suddenly remembering something, Mary Beatrice jumped up and hurried over to a small bureau. Startled from her thoughts, Elizabeth sat back down.

"There is a reason I need to speak without my ladies hearing." Mary Beatrice glanced at the door. "Do you remember Edward Coleman visiting Paris last year?" Mary Beatrice bent down and unlocked the bottom drawer. Searching through the contents, she pulled out some papers and brought them over.

Elizabeth was taken aback by the question. Her friend, Edward Coleman was Mary Beatrice's secretary. He'd been in Paris for four months, and had arrived back in February. "Yes. Why? Whatever's the matter?"

"I found these among my papers." Mary Beatrice handed the top sheet to her. "I do not know what to do."

As Elizabeth read the letter, her hands shook.

February I, 1675.

Throckmorton,

You know that when the Duke becomes master of our affairs, the King of France will have reason to promise him all he desires. How shall we get this revengeful Parliament dissolved? By the help of three hundred thousand pounds. The Duke, by the dissolution of Parliament, will be all-powerful.

Your most humble and most obedient servant,

Edward Coleman

Elizabeth handed the letter back and went over to the fire burning in the grate. She held her hands towards it. She'd been aware for some time about Edward Coleman's negotiations with France. He had travelled to Paris to meet with a Jesuit Father, King Louis' confessor. Coleman had only made the journey because Throckmorton had given him a letter from the Jesuit, pledging King Louis' support for York.

"Do you think he intended to send this letter?" Elizabeth asked. "On his return from Paris, Coleman told Powis his negotiations there had been unsuccessful. But, dear God, this letter indicates he was still pursuing the matter."

"I think it already has been sent. This must be a copy." Mary Beatrice handed her another letter.

With shaking hands, Elizabeth read it. Her mouth opened in surprise; a reply, dated three weeks after the first letter, from Throckmorton, informing Coleman that King Louis had broken off all negotiations with Charles, and would no longer be providing funds to him, or to York. "Powis urged Coleman not to meddle in such matters. Have you shown these letters to anyone?"

"Though there is nothing there to confirm it, I'm fearful my husband instructed Coleman in his actions." Mary Beatrice shook her head. "If Charles learns of these negotiations he will be incensed. The first letter talks of James as King, after Charles' death. This is high treason. I am afraid for my husband, and for my child. Oh, Elizabeth, what should I do?"

Elizabeth gripped Mary Beatrice's arms. "You must ask Charles to remove Coleman as your secretary. Invent a reason. Do this as soon as possible. There's nothing in these letters to prove York was aware of Coleman's true intentions in Paris. In this instance, Coleman's meddling has come to nothing. If it had, we would have had to speak out. Let us pray no one else finds out about these letters. For your own protection, you must burn them." She pointed to the fire. "Do it now, and tell no one else about this."

CHAPTER FOURTEEN

Intentions

Shaftesbury flushed with pleasure. "Well, what do you think?" he asked John Locke. Looking down over Locke's shoulder, Shaftesbury rubbed his shaven head and surveyed the pages held in his friend's hand. With Locke's help, he'd just completed 'A Letter from a Person of Quality to his Friend in the Country', a pamphlet denouncing Danby's Bill.

Locke finished reading the final draft of the lengthy pamphlet and swept back his thinning hair which fell to his shoulders. "It's excellent, quite excellent. It goes straight to the crux of the matter and is sure to cause a stir."

They were in the small dining room of Shaftesbury's London Townhouse, where they'd remained after a late breakfast of eggs and coffee. The noise of carriages passing along the street carried into the room through an open window. Sweat beaded down Shaftesbury's face and neck. It promised to be another hot August day.

"God's truth, it's good to have you back again," Shaftesbury said.

"It's good to be back," Locke said, and his deep-set eyes sparkled. "France is fascinating, but there's an intolerance of Protestantism beneath the surface of much that's said and done there." A Protestant himself, he shook his head.

Sitting down at the dining table beside him, Shaftesbury considered what he had said. "Can we rely on King Louis' support to get rid of Danby then?" He trusted Locke's opinion. Nine years before, he'd developed a liver abscess. In excruciating pain, and in fear for his life, he sought treatment in Oxford and had a tube fitted to drain the abscess. There he met Locke, who added a copper tap to enable permanent drainage. The treatment worked, and he'd invited Locke to move into his home and act as his personal physician and aide. Locke, who at this time needed employment, readily accepted.

"I would say we already have it." Locke smiled, accentuating the slight protrusion of his lower lip. "As you know, Louis pays well for words and even better for actions. Anyone furthering the cause of Rome in England is now amply rewarded. Many members of parliament have felt the generosity of his purse, and others beside."

Shaftesbury raised his brows. "Tell me more."

"I met Coleman in France. I believe he's now the proud owner of a fancy berlin coach."

"Coleman? Edward Coleman, York's past secretary?"

"The very same man. I'm not sure why, but his presence there aroused my suspicion. Let's leave the remainder of this discussion for later. I'll tell you more then." Locke pointed to the pamphlet.

Lifting the 'Letter' from the oak table, Shaftesbury paced the room with the sheaves in his hand. He experienced a strange mixture of elation and fear at disclosing Parliamentary business. "So, when should we distribute . . . this?" he said and held the paper aloft. He was having second thoughts. He was uncertain what kind of response it would receive from the other Lords, and . . . who was or was not working for

King Louis.

The 'Letter' proposed that the Lord Treasurer, Danby, was conspiring to exclude the monarchy and the Bishops from Parliamentary Law. It detailed debates from the House of Lords, outlining Shaftesbury's arguments in opposition to Danby. Danby's 'Test Act', preventing anyone from altering the government of the Anglican Church, was presented as one example of Danby's attempts to free the Bishops from Parliamentary control. Shaftesbury had selected every word with care. He had to stop Danby from destroying what had been hard won; the voice of the people.

Locke took a moment before replying. "No one's ever published and circulated debates from Parliament before. I'm not sure how it will be received. There may well be an outcry if you do, and the fine content of this paper will be lost in the storm. Why don't you have it printed, and then as a first step distribute it abroad . . . to test reaction?"

"Mmm. Good idea. And you're right. It's not the time to publish this here. We need to focus on Danby." A few weeks before, Danby had signed a paper, drawn up by the Bishops for the King, advising him to enforce the existing laws against Catholics, and have them banished from Court.

Shaftesbury tapped the sheaves against the table. "I've no doubt that Danby intends to turn England into an absolute monarchy. Everything he's done since becoming Lord Treasurer confirms this. What infuriates me most is his attempt to restrict anyone else from changing anything. It's imperative that he's stopped, now."

Shaftesbury picked up his walking sticks. "Come . . . let us walk down to the river. It's a glorious day."

As Shaftesbury and Locke walked along a gravel path through the orchard, they continued their discussion. "Never before have I seen you so angry or so focused," Locke said. "Your swiftness in activating the opposition against Danby left me breathless. And to think you're collaborating with York, of all people, over this."

"York reached out to me. As it will remove all Catholics from positions of authority, he's also set against Danby's Test Act." Shaftesbury smiled. "For the time being we've drawn a truce . . . of sorts. I agreed to work with him to bring Danby down. I've no doubt the truce will be short lived."

Laughing together, they sat on a bench at the riverside. The smell of apples from the orchard mixed with the scent of the abundant trees and wild flowers surrounding them. Shaftesbury breathed in the pleasant aroma and relaxed. The river view always calmed him.

"There's rumour of Louis declaring, 'I am the State.' Is there any truth to this?" Shaftesbury asked, assuming Locke would have learned something of affairs in France during his visit.

Locke shrugged. "Whether it's true or not, Louis makes no secret of governing France by divine rule. The main purpose of his grand Court is to divert the nobility from political concerns. He rules without their interference."

"Charles seeks to emulate him but lacks the means. But, he has no need for concern. Parliament will never rule against him. His Restoration Parliament is filled with his supporters." Shaftesbury peered across the river. "Hmm! How will Charles react to this pamphlet . . . and my next move?"

"Next move? Tell me more. You have me intrigued."

Shaftesbury placed his arms behind his head and looked up at the clear blue sky. A sky filled with promise. "I won't allow Parliament to be destroyed. Aside from many others, young Anthony's future as a member of the Lords is at stake here. Nay, the current situation cannot continue, and I intend to put matters right. The only way to preserve the Lords is to have Charles' Restoration Parliament removed and replaced with a new Parliament. I've given this matter much thought, and now is the time to strike. Can I count on your support?"

"I'll help in any way I can. You know that. Leader of the opposition, you say? Against the Crown? Dear God, if anyone can do this, you can. I take it you mean a new Parliament that would do your bidding? But, how do you intend to approach this?"

"By stirring matters between the Lords and the Commons, of course. I'll give Charles no option but to disband Parliament." Shaftesbury chuckled. "It pleases me that he will understand what I'm doing, but will be unable to stop me."

"God's breath, yes." Locke ran his hands through his hair. "Things are already fraught between the Lords and the Commons. Parliamentary business has all but ground to a halt. Damn it. This is the perfect time."

Shaftesbury smirked. "Having stirred things, I'll then give my first speech as leader of the opposition. I intend proposing a motion calling for new elections, asking for the current Parliament to be disbanded and a new one formed. One which will function as it should, for the benefit of the people, not pandering to Charles' will. I'll make the members see this and that restricting the power of the nobility is part of a wider plot by Charles to remove Parliament altogether and rule through an army. If a king has divine rights, then he is not answerable to our laws. This will form my starting point."

"You realise Charles will view this as a declaration of war against him? Supporters or no, you'll make many enemies." Locke paused. "I'll help you draft your speech. Let's start it straight away." He made to stand.

"Grandpapa."

Shaftesbury looked up and smiled. Little Anthony ran towards him, carrying his new replica boat. Shaftesbury's wife, Margaret, hurried along behind him.

"Can we sail it, Grandpapa?" Anthony yelled and threw himself into Shaftesbury's open arms.

CHAPTER FIFTEEN

Tyburn Fair

On a warm August morning, Elizabeth and Powis travelled in Edward Coleman's new, open-topped, berlin coach. Opposite them sat Coleman and his wife. The sky held the promise of sunshine. As always, when a hanging took place, today had been declared a holiday. As the coach rattled along the rutted road towards Tyburn, Elizabeth stared out at the throngs of people from all walks of life. They all headed in the same direction, the vast majority on foot. They looked merry, and some already seemed drunk.

Turning to Edward Coleman, Elizabeth took in the melancholic expression etched onto his face. He looked older than his thirty-nine years. His sunken eyes and lean withered appearance reflected the repeated fasts he enforced upon himself. His black periwig made his face appear even paler by contrast. Pleased by this image, Coleman thought it made him look like a devout priest. She shook her head and hoped for all their sakes that he'd stopped meddling in York's affairs.

Despite her concerns, Elizabeth settled back, determined to enjoy the day. As they neared Tyburn, side shows grew in abundance, and vendors tried to coax the coppers from the pockets of passers-by. The sense of exhilaration, emanating from the eager crowd, helped brighten Elizabeth's dark spirits.

"Hmm, this is indeed comfortable," Powis said. "It's the first time I've ridden in one of these new-style coaches. It's strange not to be jostled about with every pitch and turn of the road. I do like it."

Coleman flushed. "Yes, the springs make a vast difference. These coaches are all the rage in France."

"Everyone of means in Rome uses them now," Elizabeth said. "Or so Father Howard informed me in his last letter. He also told me he's to be made a Cardinal."

"Howard, a Cardinal," Coleman said. "That's good news indeed for the Catholic cause here in England. Hmm! He still has great influence at Court."

"Look at the dresses these young ladies are wearing . . . such pretty colours." Mrs Coleman pointed towards a group of giggling women.

Elizabeth frowned. "Tut, tut. I swear the bust-line is becoming more revealing with each season." She was pleased by the change of topic. She hadn't liked Coleman's reference to Howard's influence at Court. Howard acted as Apostolic Vicariate, a form of missionary for the Roman Catholic Church. Elizabeth's dead sister, Anne, had been married to his brother.

As Elizabeth chatted to Mrs Coleman and took in the sights, the coachman, perched above the front wheels, manoeuvred a route through the growing crowd. The closer they got to Tyburn, the thicker the crowd grew, and it became harder for the coach to move along at a steady pace.

"Eee up . . . Out the way . . . Move along . . . Watch where you step," the coachman cried out to those veering into his path.

The shouts of vendors lining the route enhanced the carnival atmosphere. This was accentuated by the whistles, laughter and squeals accompanying them on their slow journey. A pleasant breeze blew, and Elizabeth breathed in the sweet aroma of pastries and meats carried in the air.

"Everyone's having such fun," Mrs Coleman said. "Perhaps we too should have come on foot."

Coleman gave out a rasping laugh. "My dear, the journey's almost three miles long. You've asked *me* to pass you a book sitting inches from your hand. Indeed, since we married I've never known you to walk more than three yards without protesting."

The others, including Mrs Coleman, laughed at this observation. Elizabeth continued to giggle and held a gloved hand to her mouth. She glanced at Powis, who seemed to be enjoying the outing, and settled back as they neared their destination.

When they reached Tyburn Brook a faint chill descended over Elizabeth, as the coach passed under a row of elms growing along its pleasant banks. She was impressed by the coach and wondered how much it had cost. Where had Edward Coleman found the money for such a grand one? Afraid to implicate Powis, she hadn't told him about the letters Mary Beatrice had found amongst her papers. When she'd broached Coleman and warned him again about interfering in state affairs, he swore that the negotiations in Paris had come to nothing and this had been the end of the matter. She had no choice but believe him. And, Throckmorton's reply did confirm that King Louis had refused to negotiate any further with him.

The coach drew to a sudden halt, shaking Elizabeth from her reverie. Alighting with the others, she moved forward with them, looking for their seats. Powis had booked the best ones at the front, in the Mother

Proctor pews. They cost more but were considered worthwhile, in hearing the condemned's last speeches and listening to their words of remorse. Though not to her taste, it also afforded the best view of the hangings.

As they jostled through a wall of bodies, a foul-smelling, toothless woman, selling a broadsheet containing the charges against the condemned, approached them. Pulling coins from his purse, Powis bought four copies, one for each of them to read while they waited for these wretches to arrive.

With no more than a passing glance they moved beyond the mourning coaches, containing the families of the condemned. Settling herself into the pew next to Mrs Coleman, Elizabeth looked over at the gallows. The first prisoner had not yet arrived, and Jack Ketch, the hangman, waited astride the triple tree, smoking his pipe.

"We've not been to a good hanging in a while," Coleman said. "There's a large crowd gathering." It had been almost a year since they'd last been to Tyburn.

Powis glanced around. "Not as large as last time, there must have been at least twenty-thousand to see the German Princess do the 'Tyburn jig'."

Coleman let out a snort of laughter and reached past Powis, to take a pie from Mrs Coleman. "Despite it being a cold January day, it was amongst the best hangings I ever attended. I wouldn't have missed it for anything. The sheer audacity of that woman."

"The city of London was too small a stage for her to act upon," Powis said and took a bite from a cold mutton pie.

"I just thank God I never met her. She cuckolded so many men out of their fortunes. Not that there was any chance of her showing interest in me," Coleman said.

"Ha!" Elizabeth exclaimed. "And to think she returned from transportation without anyone knowing she had even escaped, let alone returned to London."

Coleman laughed. "I kept the broadsheet. It makes interesting reading."

The sound of drums and flutes filled the air, signalling the arrival of the first cart.

"Who do we have first?" Powis held the broadsheet between them.

"It's a common thief. A young woman by the name of Anne Jurejon," Elizabeth said. Looking up, she watched a homing pigeon taking flight and shifted forward to get a better view of the cart which drew up. It was followed by a retinue of soldiers, which in turn was followed by the woman's friends and family, and finally by the Fyfe band. Around two hundred people, who had followed the cart from Newgate, clambered towards the stands looking for a space to watch the proceedings.

Jack Ketch jumped down from the scaffold and joined the woman on the cart. Anne Jurejon wore a bright green dress and a red cloak. Her bedraggled hair was tied up onto her head and pushed under a black hat with a red feather on it. Her cheeks were rouged a deep red and her lips lined with scarlet.

"She has dressed in her best finery." Coleman smirked. "Another poor attempt to make a good impression on the crowd. All in the misguided hope people will call out for her to be reprieved. Even if the rope broke the call wouldn't come from me, she's a common thief."

Elizabeth shook her head at Coleman, but joined in with the roars of, 'Hats off,' 'Hats off,' that had erupted as soon as Ketch had stepped onto the cart. She turned to Mrs Coleman and smiled. Just as it should, the carnival atmosphere was building to a crescendo. She watched as another homing pigeon swooped into the air, winging the announcement back to Newgate that the next prisoner, Amos Child, a pickpocket, had arrived safely at Tyburn.

Jack Ketch held up his hand, and the crowd fell silent. The young woman stepped forward, an imploring look in her red-rimmed eyes. She smiled in what looked more like a grimace, revealing a row of even pearl-white teeth. She might even have looked pretty had the circumstances not been so bleak.

Tears streamed down Anne Jurejon's face, streaking the rouge. "I'm innocent. I never meant to take anything of m' Lady's –"

Coleman placed his hands around his mouth and shouted. "Pish! You all claim innocence."

"You should ask His forgiveness for your sins, not add to them through more lies. Repent now," Powis called out.

Their yells joined the taunts and jeers, hurtled by the larger crowd.

The young girl's eyes widened. Urine dripped from under her skirt and puddled at her feet.

Unable to look, Elizabeth re-read the broadsheet outlining her charge and confession. Anne Jurejon, a lady's maid, had been accused of stealing jewellery from her mistress and passing it to her lover to sell. At her trial, it had been determined that they'd intended to use the money from the spoils to set up house together away from London. The man concerned had escaped capture and had taken the money with him. Elizabeth couldn't help but feel angry towards him, for leaving this young woman to take the consequences for his actions.

She whispered a prayer. "Mother of God, accept Anne Jurejon's soul into heaven." She called out, "Repent for your sins before it's too late.

Pray for forgiveness. Confess all."

The girl's family jostled to the front and threw themselves down before the scaffold. Their cries for mercy filled the air.

Jack Ketch stepped forward and placed a blindfold over the girl's eyes. With gentle but swift movements he pulled the rope over her neck and positioned the knot to the left. Without hesitating, he jumped off the cart, and it took off, leaving the young woman dangling in the empty space, her legs kicking.

Elizabeth lowered her eyes, but it could not block out the sight rising in her mind; of the girl's head lolling, her hat askew, her eyes bulging, her tongue protruding and swelling, her arms reaching for the rope, and her feet scrabbling to find leverage in the space where once had stood her only means of support. As her eldest daughter's face replaced Anne Jurejon's, Elizabeth shivered and blanked it out.

When the body was cut down, Elizabeth lifted her head to see the crowd flocking towards the executioner. Like crows pecking over a dead carcass, they pushed forward looking for a piece of rope or a gaudy bit of material from Anne Jurejon's clothes; as if by holding on to the last threads of her life they could somehow save their own. She turned away. Their frenzy turned her belly.

On returning home that evening, Coleman recalled Elizabeth saying that Father Howard was to be made Cardinal. At his desk, and feeling better about himself for doing it, he penned a letter.

Father Howard,

We desire your most gracious help in difficulties

affecting Catholics in England. If he can be freed from these difficulties, James, Duke of York, will be esteemed.

And the King himself, who has vast influence, will re-establish York as Lord High Admiral, and put the management of all trade into his hands.

We have great designs, and supported with the power of your friends, we have no doubt that we will succeed; to the utter ruin of the Protestant party.

Your most humble servant,

Edward   Coleman

CHAPTER SIXTEEN

Angelica Root and Wintergreen

"No, no! Not my precious *bambino*. Not my Catherine Laura. Tell me it's not true," Mary Beatrice demanded of Doctor Wakeman, between sobs. She reached her arms out in supplication to him. "Dear God in heaven, help me."

Elizabeth stroked Mary Beatrice's hair back from her face and signalled with her eyes that she wanted to speak with the Queen's physician, Doctor Wakeman. "Mary Beatrice, my heart breaks for your loss. I'll leave you one moment so your ladies can attend to you."

Outside the bedchamber, she urged Doctor Wakeman to put Mary Beatrice under stronger sedation; her nine-month-old daughter, Catherine Laura, had died during the night from convulsions.

Elizabeth walked the long, cold corridors of St James's Palace, heading for York's apartment. Summer had moved into autumn, and a carpet of dead leaves shrouded the grounds outside the window. A stunned silence had fallen over the Royal Court, and courtiers and servants bowed their heads as she passed in her black gown. Elizabeth fingered her pearl necklace and prayed. *Dear God, do not let Mary Beatrice suffer further. Keep safe the child she is carrying.*

Four days later, Powis and Castlemaine stepped out of Powis' carriage in Queen Street. They made their way along Cloak Lane and headed towards the General Post Office. They had been sent there as a matter of urgency by James of York.

"There is no point in speculating," Castlemaine said as they entered. "But, York has me intrigued."

Powis nodded. "I was instructed to tell no-one. I hope it's not more trouble. I could well do without it."

Castlemaine handed over the pass York had given him, to a clerk at the desk. The young man disappeared through a door at the back. He returned a good ten minutes later and beckoned them through.

Exchanging questioning glances with Castlemaine, Powis shrugged his shoulders and followed the clerk up a flight of stairs and along a maze of corridors. Even for October it was cold, and the place smelled of mildew and damp paper. It was the first time Powis had been up here. The sheer size of the building surprised him. It looked smaller from the outside.

The clerk stopped at a wooden door and knocked. He ushered them in and, without entering himself, closed the door behind them.

Seated behind a large desk, Henry Coventry looked up. "Ah! Good. You've arrived."

Powis paled and glanced at Castlemaine. As Secretary of State for the Southern Department, Coventry acted as spymaster. He was also Shaftesbury's brother-in-law. Dear God, what now? His belly lurched, and he drew in a sharp breath.

Coventry raised a hand and signalled for them to come over. A large circular box, sectioned with drawers, sat on the desk. "Let's get this sorry business attended too," he said in a hushed voice. As he spoke, he pushed the box around with ink-stained fingers and, opening one of the drawers, pulled a letter out.

Powis sagged, he felt as if his legs would give out beneath him. He searched his memory but couldn't think of any of his correspondence that could have been intercepted. He glanced at Castlemaine, but he appeared calm. Powis licked his lips and looked back at Coventry.

Coventry handed the letter to Castlemaine, who held it so Powis could also read it. "God's breath," Powis said and sucked air between his teeth. "English naval intelligence . . . sent abroad. What does this mean?" He read on. "Coleman wrote this?"

Castlemaine handed the letter back to Coventry, who refolded it. "The man's foolishness knows no bounds," Coventry said and replaced York's seal onto the letter, by dripping candle wax under it and pressing it down. "This is one letter that will not be sent. Corresponding abroad using York's seal, *without his permission*, leaking naval intelligence, will Coleman never learn? But, what is said with the tongue cannot be taken back by the teeth. This intelligence must be contained.

"As Lord High Admiral, resigned or no, York is still responsible for *all* naval matters. Any leaks in intelligence *will* be tracked back to him. York is still reeling from the death of his daughter and needs no more woe. Coleman will be dismissed forthwith as Mary Beatrice's secretary, a situation that suits her well. I want you both to keep a close watch over Edward Coleman. He must cease all correspondence related to state matters and, on no account must he use York's seal again. York's safety must be your main concern."

As soon as she received the message that Mary Beatrice's pains had started, Elizabeth set out for St James's Palace. The messenger asked her to hurry. Though she plied him with questions, he provided her with no answers. During the short carriage ride, Elizabeth prayed. *Mother of God, look over this dear child and deliver her of a healthy boy.* When she'd visited Mary Beatrice yesterday, she had looked pale and tired. Less than three weeks had passed since Catherine Laura's sudden death.

By the time Elizabeth arrived in the birthing chamber, it had already filled with family, dignitaries and attendants. The heat of the room hit Elizabeth, and her face flushed. Queen Catherine sat on a hardback chair, inlaid with rich French tapestries. York's daughters, Ann and Mary, stood at the foot of the bed. Their faces looked pale. Foreign dignitaries lined one wall, the representatives from Italy standing at the front.

Squeezing her way through the throng, Elizabeth moved down the side of the room and stopped with her back against the wall, behind Viscount Stafford's wife's chair. Mary's thin hair was slicked with sweat, and she mopped beads of perspiration from her brow. Elizabeth bent down and whispered, "Thanks be to God. I am on time to witness the birth."

Mary looked up and nodded. Elizabeth had not seen much of her and Stafford since he had raised the toast to celebrate Powis' earldom.

Elizabeth's eyes were drawn towards the bed. It was five weeks too early, and things were happening fast. She cursed herself for not being with Mary Beatrice when her pains had started. She winced at the thought of the indignity her dear friend must be experiencing.

Mary Beatrice tried to climb from the bed, but three aides held her down. She screamed out in protest and pleaded with them to let her walk about.

It was against the law to own a rosary, so Elizabeth touched her pearl necklace. *Dear God in heaven, grant her the strength to see this birth through. Safely deliver this dear child.*

Stretching up on her toes, Elizabeth was relieved to see Mrs Cellier tending to Mary Beatrice. The doctors stood back to allow the midwife room to work. To their side, three cradle rockers wearing identical white linen and lace dresses, stood behind a wooden cradle bedecked with white and yellow ribbons. Three wet nurses stood behind them.

Baskets, filled with herbs and spices, sat at the foot of the bed and the scent of myrrh, cinnamon and mint, mixed with the sour body odour filling the room. The fire was stoked, to raise the temperature in readiness for the birth. Sweat coursed over Mary Beatrice, and tendrils of long black hair were slicked tight against her face. A lace-frilled white nightgown clung to her body. A few weeks before, at her seventeenth birthday celebration, Mary Beatrice had rubbed her swollen belly and smiled over at Elizabeth.

When Mary Beatrice screamed out in torment, Mrs Cellier rubbed oil, mixed with angelica root and wintergreen, onto her swollen belly. The same mixture had helped ease Elizabeth's own agony during Winifred's birth.

The heat of the room made Elizabeth giddy. Sweat trickled down her back. She gripped onto the back of Mary's chair for support. How much more pain could Mary Beatrice endure? She itched to comfort her in some way. Her mouth became dry, and she feared she might faint. It was too much to bear. Wiping her brow with the back of a hand, she felt beads of sweat trickling from her forehead.

Excusing herself to Mary, she exited the room. Once outside the chamber she felt cooler.

Mary Beatrice had entered the last stages of labour. What if it was another stillbirth? Or, God forbid, not a boy? Sitting down on a high-backed wooden settle, outside the door of the bedchamber, she took deep breaths and tried to calm her racing thoughts. Apart from grief over Catherine Laura's death, Mary Beatrice had been well throughout this pregnancy. The room had just been overcrowded and overheated.

Feeling cooler, Elizabeth stood, wiped her hands down the skirt of her dress and returned to the chamber. Once again, she stood behind Mary's chair.

After a few minutes, of pushing and stopping, Mary Beatrice gave an almighty grunt and the head of a child appeared amidst gasps from the room. "Thanks be to God," Elizabeth whispered to Mary.

Moments later the room buzzed with activity. Elizabeth craned forward. A small white blanket lay on the bottom of the bed, and when the body of the child emerged, Mrs Cellier wrapped it into this and rushed from the room.

Elizabeth's heart raced, and she glanced at the confused faces around her.

"A boy child," one of the doctors announced . . . "Stillborn."

A shiver coursed through Elizabeth, leaving her trembling. Why had God deserted the True Faith? How much further could they be tested?

As Mary Beatrice let out the first piercing scream, Elizabeth rushed over and, without thought for hierarchy or etiquette, cradled her in her arms. The racking sobs, emerging from deep within her friend, tore at her heart. Holding her close to her chest, Elizabeth stroked Mary Beatrice's hair. Rocking her friend back and forward in her arms, she whispered, "I know child. I know."

Around the room, heads huddled together. Mary Beatrice had not provided a male heir. Elizabeth stiffened. Few of them would be mourning the loss of this dear child.

CHAPTER SEVENTEEN

Storm Brewing

In the early evening of the fifth of November, Elizabeth sat beside Powis on a settee and watched as the children crowded around the window of the withdrawing room, overlooking Lincoln's Inn Fields. As they stared out at the darkening sky, the children chattered amongst themselves about the vast bonfire about to be lit.

On seeing the excitement on their faces, an immense pleasure flowed through Elizabeth. Though this wasn't a celebration they participated in, the children enjoyed watching the bonfire. Thankfully, the hatred towards Catholics refuelled by the Catholic plot to blow up Parliament had now abated.

The unrest, caused by York's marriage to a Catholic, also seemed to be settling. The deaths and stillbirths of Mary Beatrice and York's children were regarded by many as a sign that they would never produce a Catholic heir. And, although tension still simmered throughout London, her family could go about their business as they had done before Mary Beatrice's arrival. Even the members of Parliament now seemed reluctant to pursue any new anti-Catholic legislation with any vigour.

Elizabeth leant her head on Powis' shoulder. "I hope there will be some fireworks for them to see this year."

"God's truth, I'd forgotten about last year's disaster." Powis smiled. "That dreadful storm . . . They had no chance of igniting the fireworks."

"The bonfire was sodden. 'Tis a wonder they succeeded in setting light to it at all. Perhaps they used some of Guido Fawkes' gunpowder," Elizabeth said and chuckled.

"Listen to the bells. Do you hear them?" Lucy called out.

Church bells had rung on and off all day, announcing the annual celebration of the failed Catholic plot. As soon as it had begun to grow dark, people had started gathering around the unlit bonfire.

Elizabeth looked over at Lucy. "Yes, we hear them."

"The bonfire's huge this year," William announced.

"Yes, the fire is huge," Elizabeth said and smiled up at Powis.

At that very moment, the bonfire was lit, amidst roars and cheers of, 'Gunpowder, treason and plot'. Powis helped Elizabeth blow out the candles, to see better what was happening outside, and they joined the children.

Huddled close to the window, Elizabeth watched the flames leaping up and illuminating Lincoln's Inn Fields outside and sending multi-coloured sparks scattering into the dark sky.

The children shrieked with delight.

"Ooh, look, look!" Anne shouted as a firework exploded into the night sky.

"And another!" William called out and lifted Winifred up to see them.

As if mesmerised, they watched a group of children using sticks to retrieve blackened chestnuts they had thrown into the fire.

Elizabeth peered out the window. What of the urchins who regularly ran after her carriage, begging coins? Were they eating chestnuts? She didn't like to think of them out there hungry and cold.

Picking up a taper, Elizabeth relit the candles and sat back on the settee beside Powis. Together they watched the children, who would remain at the window until the fire burned itself out.

A week later, Edward Coleman pulled the hood of his woollen cloak over his head and hurried to the bank of the Thames. A small boat tied to the jetty rocked against the side of the river. The oarsman nodded on his approach. Coleman's eyes had grown accustomed to the moonlight, and he raised a hand in acknowledgement.

He turned and made his way along the side of the river. Keeping his steps quiet, he stayed in the shadows until he reached a boathouse. He glanced around to make sure no one had followed him and slipped inside. The foul stench of the river filled the wooden shed. He listened above the sound of the lapping water but heard nothing untoward. Remaining in the shadows, he let out an owl-like sound. "Whoo!"

On hearing the call returned Coleman stepped forward, and a dark hooded figure moved towards him. He grasped Father Saint Germain by the upper arm and held a finger of his free hand to his lips, indicating that he should remain silent. "We must hurry, the boat is waiting," Coleman whispered.

Slipping his thick travelling cloak and long periwig off, Coleman handed them to the Jesuit Priest, who put them on. At the same time, Coleman donned Germain's thin cloak.

Coleman pressed a pouch of silver coins into the priest's hand. "Did anyone try to follow you from the Chapel?"

The Jesuit priest shook his head. Beads of perspiration ran down his temples. "You know I didn't do anything?"

"Whether you did or no, a search will now be underway for you. God be with you." Coleman pulled his hood up and escorted the priest over to the small boat waiting to take him to a larger boat bound for France. If caught, Father Saint Germain would be thrust into Newgate to await his fate.

At their approach, the oarsman stood up and helped the shaking Jesuit priest step down into the boat. Remaining in the shadows, Coleman watched until the boat carrying Father Saint Germain moved off. He let out a deep sigh of relief. He would keep his actions here tonight from Powis. Though they were firm friends, Powis had already made his position clear.

The evening was bitter, and Coleman shivered under his newly acquired thin cloak as he made his way back up the steep stone stairway towards Whitehall Palace. He had done what he had been asked to do.

The following morning, Powis sat in the House of Lords. While he waited for the session to begin, he pondered his son's education. Now almost ten, William needed to be prepared for college. Powis wanted him to receive a good Catholic education, but such tutoring was banned in England. One option was to send him to a Catholic college abroad. Although this too was against the law, many did it.

Powis startled when Sir Henry Goodricke raised his large figure from the bench and rapped his heel hard against the floor several times. Intrigued by Goodricke's agitated manner, and the attendance of a colleague on his feet by his side, Powis gave him his full attention.

Goodricke scratched beneath his high-combed, dark periwig and then straightened it. Rubbing on his small moustache, he addressed the attentive House. "Last night, here in London, an outrageous assault was perpetrated by a Jesuit. This assault was upon a common man who had converted from the Roman Catholic Church."

Alarm coursed through Powis, and he sat forward. He was eager to hear Goodricke's account, and joined the series of shushes in response to the interruptions and questions elicited by the news of the assault. "Silence!" he called out.

Goodricke continued. "Last night in the Chapel at the Savoy, a Frenchman by the name of Luzancy, preached a scathing sermon against Rome. When he finished and made his way out of the Chapel, he was accosted and under peril of his life from a dagger . . . was *forced* to retract all he had said in his sermon. He was then *made* to sign a recantation of his Protestant faith."

Powis shivered as he absorbed the implications of what Goodricke had said. Questions from the floor, in response to this perceived outrage, were silenced by calls of "*Order! Silence!*" and Goodricke was urged to continue.

"The person responsible was Dr Burnet . . . also known as Father Saint Germain. A Jesuit from the Duchess of York's household."

As the House erupted into a frenzy of protests and enraged comments, Powis' world collapsed around him, and he sank back in the seat. The outbursts circulating throughout the room echoed in his head.

"No Papists!"

"This goes beyond all precedent."

"It's an outrage."

"To persuade with force."

"I've never heard the likes of this before."

"It's a most damnable assault."

"No Papists!"

Powis took a deep inhalation of breath and the words circulating around him gradually came back into focus.

The Secretary of State for the Northern Department, Sir Joseph Williamson, stood up. "Order! Order! I assure the House that an inquiry is underway. The King has involved himself in this matter. Luzancy will be re-examined by the Privy Council today. A warrant has been issued to arrest Father Saint Germain, but it seems he has already fled."

After a short and heated debate, the House moved for a warrant to be issued to search for and apprehend *all* Jesuits and priests within London.

During dinner that evening, Elizabeth discussed Luzancy's story with Powis and Castlemaine.

Powis remained shaken by Goodricke's announcement, and Elizabeth was concerned for him. "Where's Luzancy now?" she asked.

"He's been taken into royal protection," Powis said and toyed with the food on his plate.

Castlemaine nodded. "And it looks as if Germain has already fled."

"Did you know of this man . . . Luzancy?" Elizabeth asked Castlemaine.

"Nay, I had never heard of him until today. But, from what I've picked up, he's a rogue and the son of some French actress."

Elizabeth frowned. "Today's events have distressed Mary Beatrice, and I have concerns for her safety. Without a doubt, this will cause anti-

Catholic feelings to resurface."

So Luzancy was a known rogue. Elizabeth doubted whether Father Saint Germain had accosted anyone and suspected Luzancy had been hired to stir trouble. But who had hired him? She grew concerned. The night priest hunters had invaded her home, as a child, still haunted her. The sound of the mob throwing bricks and then lit torches through the windows invaded her dreams. She lived in fear of the mob setting fire to her home.

"Do you think there's any truth in what Luzancy says?" she asked.

Powis let out a loud breath. "Luzancy did convert recently. And he did preach at the French Chapel, at the Savoy. So that part of his story is true –"

"Though the dagger is likely an invention," Castlemaine added.

"Hmmm," Elizabeth muttered and sat back in the chair. "There does seem to be some substance to his story." She looked at Castlemaine. "What did Luzancy say at the enquiry?"

"He claimed that before Father Saint Germain forced him to retract his words, he had tried to persuade him to return to the Roman Catholic Church, by telling him York was a confessed Catholic and the King one at heart. He also said all England would acknowledge the Pope within two years."

"Dear God," Powis said and rubbed his hands together. "Several other people have now come forward testifying to similar threats."

"Where will all this lead?" Elizabeth looked at Powis. "I don't believe a word of it."

"Regardless of whether this is true or no, the anti-Catholic faction will use this to their advantage," Castlemaine said with disdain.

Elizabeth didn't like what she was hearing and leant forward. "Do either of you see Shaftesbury's hand in this?"

"I'm unsure . . . tempers are frayed," Powis said. "The dispute Shaftesbury set in motion between the Commons and the Lord continues and all parliamentary business has ground to a halt. Charles had no choice but to prorogue Parliament."

"It does all seem very convenient," Castlemaine added.

Elizabeth raised her eyebrows, urging him to explain.

"Though published anonymously, the 'Letter' . . . denouncing Danby's Test Bill has Shaftesbury's name written all over it —"

Powis interrupted. "Any uncertainty I had about this disappeared when the second pamphlet, 'Two Seasonable Discourses', appeared, arguing for Charles to call for a new Parliament."

"And all of this so soon after Mary Beatrice still-birthing a boy," Elizabeth said. "Yes, it is all too convenient. But Mary Beatrice is only seventeen and has plenty of time to produce a male heir. Shaftesbury is playing a dangerous game."

CHAPTER EIGHTEEN

The Storm Breaks

A week later, the distant pounding on the front door startled Elizabeth awake. "Powis!" she called. Reaching out in the darkness she found an empty space beside her. Despite the late hour, Powis had not yet returned from Whitehall Palace. Her heart raced. Had something happened to him? She crossed herself. *Dear God, keep my husband safe.*

She pulled back the velvet drape, and a dull light filtered in. Scrambling out of bed, she barely felt the cold beneath her feet.

"Beth! Beth!" she called out for her lady's maid. Without waiting for her to arrive, Elizabeth hastened into her slippers and pulled on her robe.

The pounding on the door grew louder. God's truth, where were the servants? Why was no one answering the door? Surely they weren't still sleeping. The infernal noise would wake the children.

With trembling hands, she lit a candle from a burning ember in the grate and pushed it into a latticed metal casing. The candle flickered as she raced down the staircase, casting a wavering shadow in her wake. Reaching the hallway she saw the house servants, who on hearing the commotion had huddled together there. They stopped chattering on her approach.

"What's happening? Why has no one answered the door?" she asked in a shaken voice. Her heart still raced, and by now she could barely think clearly.

"It could be Priest hunters, my Lady," Evans, her butler said over the loud noise and took the lantern from her. "The King's men searched some houses earlier."

The banging on the door had nothing to do with Powis. Elizabeth gave a deep sigh of relief. She turned towards Evans and tried to disguise her confusion. "You should have informed me."

She was duty bound to allow the King's men in to search her home, but Powis was still at the Palace, where he had been ensconced all day in discussion with the other Lords. It was only a short coach ride away. She could send someone out the rear door to fetch him, but he could not return back in time to help her. Why had this happened tonight?

"A servant from one of the neighbouring houses informed me earlier," Evans said. "They were searching the other side of the Fields." He took a deep breath. "I didn't think they would come here. I . . . I saw no reason to disturb you then."

Elizabeth swung around, at the sound of glass shattering. The noise echoed throughout the hallway. It came from the cloakroom behind her. She gasped and looked wildly about.

The servants exploded into wild chatter and some threw themselves onto the floor. She continued to look around, bewildered. Beth came and stood beside her. "Dear God, 'Ma'am."

The scullery maid screamed and rushed towards Elizabeth. "In God's name, please don't let them in, 'Ma'am." Cook pulled the girl back and shielded her in her arms.

Evans opened the cloakroom door. A mob had gathered outside and their roars grew louder. "Papists! Papists!"

Evans bent down and shuffled into the cloakroom. He returned a few moments later. "If you don't let the searchers in the mob will escalate." He held out a brick. "This is a warning."

"Mama," a voice called.

Elizabeth turned. The children's nurse stood on the stairs with five-year old, Lucy. Her daughter sobbed and reached her arms out to Elizabeth.

The light from torches flickered outside the window. She had to protect her children. She had to quieten the mob. They might burn her home down if she did not heed their warning. "Gather the children together and take them into to the nursery. Make haste," she called out to the nurse. "Beth, go and assist her," she added and turned to refocus her attention on Evans.

She raised a hand to silence him. "Tell me, is anyone hidden in this house?" Evans had no need to consult her if someone needed their help, he would know what to do. He knew the location of the priest-hole.

"Nay 'Marm, no one. As God is my witness," Evans replied.

What should she do? Even if they were common priest hunters, she couldn't refuse them entry. If she did, the mob might think she was hiding who they were searching for. She would have to face this alone. She had no other option. Going by past searches, it could last a day or even a week. Pulling her robe tight around her, Elizabeth nodded for Evans to open the front door.

Three men pushed past Evans and rushed into her home. An icy, December blast followed them through the open door.

"Find the Papist dog," the leading man called out to the others.

On seeing the wooden stick in this man's hand, Elizabeth shivered and gestured behind her to one of the kitchen maids to go for help. Her fear turned to indignation. This was *her* home. *Her* children were upstairs. By their worn clothes and rough appearance, she reckoned these men were commoners looking for a reward. Concluding that they were most certainly not Court officials, she stepped forward. "Why have you come here?"

A short, stocky man made to move past her carrying a sharp metal bar. Elizabeth stepped into his path. "Explain yourself, or I'll have the King's men on you." His pockmarked face formed into a grimace.

The man who appeared to be in charge opened his mouth, revealing a row of stained teeth. "A Jesuit priest was seen preaching outside, in Lincoln's Inn Fields. We need to root out the Papist dog."

The last of the three men shifted towards the staircase as if heading upstairs to begin his search. Elizabeth swung around. "Desist. There are no Jesuits here. I can assure you of that." She turned back to glare at the leader. "Where's your warrant to search my home?" Only the Privy Council had the authority to issue such orders. This ragged bunch would have no such warrant in their possession. She remained wary of them, but would have to stand firm if she wanted them to leave.

The ringleader shuffled from one foot to the other. "We're searching all Papist houses in Lincoln's Inn Fields. The dog's hiding in one of them, and we will bring him in."

Keeping her gaze fixed upon him, Elizabeth considered what to do. "Evans, fetch the Parish Constable." Though she knew they wouldn't find the Jesuit priest and would leave of their own accord when they had finished searching, she would not have them storming through her home or distressing her children.

Giving out a mocking laugh, the man in charge waved for his men to start searching.

A rug was thrown back by the stocky man. Using the metal bar, he began to lever up the floorboards in the hall.

The man in charge raised a wooden stick and tapped along the walls. He pulled down paintings as he passed and threw them at his feet.

Starting at the bottom, the third man prodded a metal pole onto each wooden step. Tip-tap, tip-tap, he made his way up the staircase.

A loud thump caused Elizabeth's shoulders to sag, and she sank back onto a chair. Her eyes remained riveted on the portrait of her dead mother, now lying atop those of Powis' ancestors on the floor.

The servants stood around as if rooted to the spot.

When a fourth ruffian hurried through the door and entered the hallway, Elizabeth startled.

"There's been a sighting. Make haste," the man called to the others. "The Papist dog is hiding in a house further down the Fields."

As the four men hurried from her home, Elizabeth let out a sigh of relief. *Praise be to God, they've gone.* Filled with guilt at such a selfish thought, she crossed herself. *"Dear God, keep that poor Jesuit safe."*

The master from the neighbouring house entered through the front door, with the kitchen maid who had gone to fetch him. His eyes scanned the desecrated hall and then fixed on her. "Are you harmed?"

Elizabeth rose to greet him. "No, and you?" Now the immediate danger was over, she trembled. She gestured for the maid to leave them.

"My home hasn't been searched. No doubt I would have been next," the neighbour said.

Elizabeth's hands shook, and she clasped them together. "There's good money to be had from handing over a Jesuit. How soon before this applies to all Catholics?" She bit back tears of frustration. She had lived her life under a dark cloud of fear and hatred towards Catholics. A bad storm was gathering again, threatening to rain down on her and her family, she could sense it.

The neighbour nodded. "I blame York's marriage for stirring things up again."

Elizabeth agreed but felt torn in her loyalties. She already regarded Mary Beatrice as a dear friend and didn't want to get into a debate with her neighbour. She said, "That . . . and other matters." Last year, she'd attended the funeral of a fellow Catholic noble, Thomas Clifford. He'd resigned from his position as Royal Treasurer and then hung himself rather than renounce his faith. She shuddered at the image of his wife finding him hanging from the rafters of their bedroom.

"Where will it end?" Elizabeth paused. "Have you heard yet? Who they're looking for? Which Jesuit?"

"I don't know who it was, but an elderly priest was seen preaching in Lincoln's Inn Fields."

After her neighbour left, Elizabeth sank back into a chair. She'd seen little of Powis over the last few days. What new business was afoot, to keep him all hours at the palace? Her childhood years had been spent yearning for her absent father. She didn't want such a life for her children.

Rising from the chair, she called out for Evans. After he had replaced the portraits back onto the wall, Elizabeth made her way into the withdrawing room, to await Powis' return. Even the warm glow of the fire in the grate could not dispel her dark mood. What of the Jesuit? Was it possible the elderly priest had evaded capture? Though she tried to remain hopeful that he was still safe, visions of him lying fettered and filthy beside many other Jesuits in Newgate prison filled her thoughts.

She shook her head.

Perhaps Powis would know if the Jesuit had been caught? He would surely have heard news of the priest. Once again, she was filled with a longing to leave London. Her eyes fixed on the embroidery of their family home, Powis Castle, which she had worked on earlier. She would speak to Powis tomorrow about returning home to Wales. With Charles leaving for Newmarket and Parliament prorogued, perhaps they could have an extended stay in Wales, with her eldest daughters. The thought brought her some comfort.

But, what was keeping Powis? Trouble was surely afoot, and there was nothing she could do to stop it.

Part Three: The King's Prerogative

1676

'I always admired virtue, but I could never imitate it.'

King Charles II

CHAPTER NINETEEN

The Return

In the late morning of the third of January, Titus Oates cowered as the doors of the hold on the Adventure opened. Squinting against the daylight, he was blinded and stumbled back against a stack of crates.

"Oates, get 'yer sorry arse out here. Move it now! 'Yer wanted," bellowed one of the seamen, who had come to collect him.

Titus grabbed onto the rope ladder the seaman dropped down and, with great difficulty, climbed up. He didn't care what fate lay above. It couldn't be any worse than incarceration in this stinking hole.

Though the rope, tied around his neck and onto his ankles, chaffed his skin and prevented him moving with any great speed, he managed to pull himself up. On reaching the top, two seamen dragged him out and marched him across the deck, down the main gangplank and onto the dock below.

Struggling to keep his balance, Titus roared, "Stop blaady pulling. Let me be!"

Once on shore, they untied the rope around his neck and unfastened it from his ankles. Then, the men turned and re-boarded the Adventure.

Left on his own, Titus rubbed his aching neck and looked around. His heart raced. The ship had docked at Billingsgate. He was in London, and lucky to be alive. When he'd been reported for lewd behaviour on board ship and charged with sodomy, he'd begged the Captain to spare him. He had been thrown into the fetid hold unsure of his fate. But, the Adventure had docked back here. It was a miracle, and he thanked the Lord.

Unable to return to Hastings, he jingled the groats in his pocket and decided to remain in London. An icy wind howled along the quayside, and he stamped his feet to keep warm. Droplets of icy water blew onto his face, and he rubbed them off with his hands.

Amidst the existing bustle and noise, passengers started to alight and seek porters to carry their baggage. Titus walked up the quayside, out of their way.

Beside the Adventure, a barge was being unloaded, and crates of figs and dates and spices were piled up beside containers of coal. The smell of spices replaced the rank stench of tar and waste from the hold, and he welcomed the pleasant aroma.

Upriver, a boat carrying crates of wine was also being unloaded. The workers wore coarse-woven cloths tied to their heads, to keep out the biting wind. Titus salivated at the sight of the food and his stomach rumbled.

Using London Bridge as a marker, he headed for Thames Street and made towards the area of the fish market. Remembering the fishwives of Hastings, he kept his head down as he walked. These women were coarse both in language and nature. He knew this to his cost and had no desire to repeat the experience.

On reaching the market, his belly protested the smell of raw fish, brought from the coasts around London and piled up in crates. It also

143

protested the stench of the rotting fish waste littering the ground. Cold and unable to eat anything, he crawled into an empty cellar to sleep for a few hours before embarking on the final stage of the journey into the centre of London.

Dirt-encrusted, and now near frozen, he needed a plan. Lying in the dank cellar, Titus remembered his father's patron, Sir Richard Barker, asking him to call the next time he was in London. The strange looking man, Israel Tonge, lodged with him. He would seek them both out.

CHAPTER TWENTY

The Mode

Elizabeth looked over at Powis and smiled. They were heading to the Dorset Garden Playhouse, on the south side of Fleet Street, to see George Etherege's new play, 'The Man of Mode'. Elizabeth adored the theatre and had looked forward to today's production. York's secretary Stafford and his wife Mary travelled with them in their carriage. Two guards on horseback followed behind.

With Parliament prorogued, the family had stayed in Wales two months, and had returned last week. Her eldest daughters stayed behind again, but Elizabeth had made the most of her time with them. On her return, she'd been surprised to find London still in an uproar following the Luzancy affair. The elderly priest who'd been preaching outside Lincoln's Inn Fields, had been caught and taken to Newgate. Mrs Cellier had taken alms into him, but he hadn't survived the harsh conditions and died soon after arriving. Though there had been no more searches of her home, Powis had employed two armed guards, as protection against the anti-Catholic mobs which now milled about outside public venues.

The carriage clattered to a halt outside the playhouse, and an overwhelming vista of row upon row of boats, either arriving or already docked on the waterfront, caught Elizabeth's attention. Their lights glittered in the water and, against the dull March afternoon, created a magical aura.

"Oh, do look. It's beautiful," she said and stepped out the carriage.

The two guards stepped in front of her and Powis and cleared a path for them through the crowd. Powis' arm encircled Elizabeth, guiding her steps. She kept her head down and pushed forward. Stafford and Mary followed close behind them.

An angry mob milled around the playhouse, shouting, "No Papists. No Papists."

As Elizabeth neared the entrance the shouts grew louder, and her thoughts returned to another time and another place. "Father! Leave father be!" she had screamed at the soldiers who had battered down the door of their lodgings, to haul him off to the Tower of London. Elizabeth had been nine-years-old, and the Civil War had started. Her mother had been long dead, and her father had since remarried and spent large periods of time with his new family in Ireland. Apart from her brother, sister and the servants, Elizabeth had had no one to turn to for help. Unable to comprehend why her father had been arrested, Elizabeth had sobbed for days, unsure what fate awaited her.

The yells of the mob merged with Elizabeth's memories. "No Papists! Go, and take your Papist heir with you!"

"Are you all right?" Powis asked once they were safely inside the foyer.

His gentle voice drew Elizabeth back to the moment, and she nodded. As they hurried up the great staircase, making for one of the boxes on the first level, Elizabeth's legs felt unsteady, and she kept a tight grip on Powis' arm.

She gasped as she entered and looked around the auditorium. The interior proved every bit as lavish as the exterior facade. The ornate carvings of eagles and wild animals adorning the lower and upper galleries took her by surprise. The elegant statues of the great poets placed throughout the auditorium and forestage served as a stark contrast to the baying mob milling outside.

Tears stung her eyes, and she looked away. She had to shake off the despondent mood that had enveloped her since her return from Wales. It had taken days for the children to settle after the search of her home. But, she would not let the mob keep her from going about London. By all accounts, all they were doing was letting their anti-Catholic sentiments be known. Other than taunts, they had not harmed any Catholics.

"I missed the theatre during Cromwell's time," Stafford announced and took the seat beside Powis.

"Mmm. And, it's not only the buildings that have changed. I was no lover of Shakespeare. I prefer the modern plays," Mary replied. "I do like the challenge of working out who they're about."

Elizabeth removed her cloak and sat down beside Mary. "The decoration is magnificent."

"I've heard it said it's finer than any in France, and I have to agree," Stafford said.

Elizabeth turned her attention back to the playhouse. Along with Powis, she supported the Theatre Royal in Drury Lane. She hadn't visited here before but had been drawn today by the promise of a new production. The pit formed a semi-circle in front of the forestage. Between this and the main stage, was seated a musical band with over twenty violins, harpsichords and other instruments. The stage itself filled the width of the theatre. Elizabeth found the whole effect dramatic, but something unsettled her, and she couldn't identify what it was.

Mary leant over and pointed to one of the boxes. "Who's that woman sitting at Pepys' side? Not Sarah Jennings, the other one."

Elizabeth peered over to where Mary pointed. One of Mary Beatrice's ladies, Sarah Jennings, sat on Samuel Pepys' left. Nineteen-year-old Catherine Sedley sat on his right. Renowned for her extravagant clothes, which she wore in an attempt to compensate for her plain looks, Sedley had on an elaborate bronze and yellow gown. Looking up at the Royal Box, Elizabeth noticed it was empty; Charles and York were in Newmarket. The gilded box was decorated with the Royal coat of arms, and towering above it was the figure of Apollo.

Elizabeth turned to Mary. "That's Catherine Sedley, one of Mary Beatrice's ladies. I think the King's box looks splendid."

"Catherine Sedley? I did wonder if that's who it might be." Mary leant over and whispered, "Why, there's much gossip about her. Her father's a rake and a libertine. Humph! Notorious for showing his prick to all and sundry from the balcony of an alehouse. By all accounts, his behaviour pushed Sedley's mother to insanity."

Elizabeth frowned. Sedley had notoriety of her own – for saying out loud what others only thought. A known wit, she could curse as course as any man.

"Look, there's Buckingham with his wife, sitting behind them." Mary pointed over to the box again.

Shifting her gaze, Elizabeth scanned the faces. Then it struck her – what had unsettled her before – a definite divide existed. She glanced around, and her thoughts were confirmed. Catholics and Protestants were clearly divided in where they sat. She'd never seen this before at any theatre. A chill enveloped her, and she tried to shrug it off.

Continuing to scan the boxes, looking for Buckingham, Elizabeth noticed Rochester. "Look, there's Rochester with his mistress. She has one daughter by him and another by today's playwright. I do not envy his wife."

Looking over at Rochester, Mary scowled. "I agree, Elizabeth. He's also a drunk and a libertine. His behaviour's a disgrace. He claims not to have spent one sober day in the past five years. He's always in trouble for brawling. But he's only following the mode set at Court."

Elizabeth nodded. "Yes, but to be landed with such a rake. He spends his days languishing at court, drinking, and engaging with common whores. They say he's always seeking treatment for the pox."

"And yet, for all that his wife is still beautiful," Mary replied.

"They say today's play, is based on Rochester," Elizabeth said. "It's about the life of a wit, who seduces women."

"Hmm!" Mary uttered. "It does indeed sound like Rochester. But it could apply to any rake at Court."

"Yes, Indeed. Ah! I can see Buckingham and his wife now."

Mary looked over. "I'm glad he came to his senses and stopped his scandalous affair with Talbot. I got the full details from Pepys, who was a good friend of her husband. Buckingham's behaviour shocked me."

Elizabeth turned her attention back to Mary. "Pepys told you. What did he say?"

"To have killed his mistresses' husband in a duel was scandalous enough, but Buckingham then installed Talbot, the widow of his making, into his matrimonial home."

Elizabeth held her hands to her mouth. "Can you believe such wantonness?"

"Scandalous!" Mary raised her eyebrows. "Then they had the

audacity to have their bastard baptised in Westminster Abbey."

"Nothing stays secret for long in London," Powis said, interrupting the conversation. "The affair was debated in the Lords. They were ordered to apologise and forbidden from living together."

Elizabeth leant forward and lowered her voice. "Talking of bastards, I hear Monmouth has aligned himself with Shaftesbury." She glanced around. Reassured no one could hear her over the music playing in the auditorium, she continued. "Shaftesbury's turning Monmouth's head with tales of his legitimacy. They are refuelling the rumours about a black box."

"Charles marriage to Monmouth's mother is the talk of the taverns," Stafford said. "People talk as if the box exists. It doesn't bode well for York."

"Or us. Mary Beatrice is with child again. This one could prove to be the boy we yearn for," Elizabeth added. "But, do you think the box exists?" She shivered. If it did Monmouth would replace James of York as heir.

Powis glared at them. "Pish! It's a ploy to draw Monmouth towards the Country Party. They want a Protestant king who'll do their bidding. By talking about the box as if it exists you also are doing their bidding. I assure you there is no such box."

While they had talked, a small production had been enacted on the front stage. The burners at the front of the pit were now lit to form the footlights. A red curtain rolled up in the middle of the stage, and the audience responded with thunderous applause. The candelabras hanging above the stage illuminated a frenzy of artefacts and scenery.

Elizabeth finished clapping and settled back to enjoy the play. But, try as she might, she couldn't push aside the thought of Shaftesbury collaborating with Monmouth to bring about his succession. She wondered what Charles made of this alliance.

CHAPTER TWENTY-ONE

The Writ

Late on a dull afternoon, Shaftesbury sat opposite his wife, Margaret, in the withdrawing room of their home, engaged in a fiercely-fought game of cribbage. Flames from the fire flickered onto the dark oak wainscoting, casting a warm glow around the room.

Margaret's dark brown hair was pulled back from her forehead, and loose tendrils fell onto her delicate face. She adjusted the embroidered shawl around her shoulders and, with an air of triumph, moved her peg three places up the cribbage board.

A butler entered, bowed, and informed Shaftesbury that Sir Joseph Williamson, Secretary of State for the Southern Department, had arrived and required to speak with him.

Excusing himself, Shaftesbury left the comfort of the room and walked down the dark oak staircase to the hall below. He felt unsettled by Williamson's visit.

On reaching the hallway, he bowed his head to acknowledge the visitor and raised his eyebrows. "Williamson, I've not had the pleasure of your company in my home before."

Bowing back, Williamson coughed. "I've come with an urgent

message from the King. You're to vacate Exeter House immediately and leave London."

Shaftesbury stared at him and let out a mocking laugh. "Please thank the King for his kind concern, and tell him I'm most comfortable where I am. My butler will show you out."

As he climbed back up the stairs, Shaftesbury's legs sagged, as if they might give out beneath him. Pushing himself forward, he willed them to keep moving. So, this is my punishment. No doubt Danby would be behind this. He shook his head, dismissing the order to leave his home. Charles would never enforce it. He wouldn't tell Margaret. It would only distress her.

A few days later, on hearing the clatter of hoofs in the courtyard below, Shaftesbury hurried to the window and observed Sir Joseph Williamson, accompanied by four of the King's guards, riding in from the Strand. Williamson dismounted and beckoned to two guards to follow him.

Shaftesbury picked up his walking sticks, and hurried down to answer the door. A flash of anger flooded through him at the sight of Williamson and the two guards standing there. Looking into the courtyard, he noted the presence of the other guards. What now? Would Danby never give up? Williamson stepped forward and handed him a parchment. After reading the open writ ordering him to depart London immediately, Shaftesbury crunched it in his hands and thrust it back. Turning on his heels, he slammed the door of Exeter House behind him.

Returning to the withdrawing room, Shaftesbury sat down beside Margaret and told her about Williamson's visits.

He looked around the room, a room which held many memories. "This is one of my favourite places." Family portraits adorned the walls.

Today was Anthony's fifth birthday, and earlier they had entertained family, friends and some Members of Parliament. "I won't be forced to leave."

Margaret rubbed her hands together. "What can you do? If the King orders you gone –"

A surge of anger flared through Shaftesbury. "This is Danby's doing. Charles would never order me from my London home."

Margaret nodded. "I have many happy memories of here. Today we celebrated Anthony's birthday, but it seems only yesterday he was born."

"That child means everything to me. I have such hopes of him having a distinguished political career. I will do everything in my power to help him in this." Shaftesbury still believed Charles was trying to limit Parliament's function. He had to ensure he did not achieve this.

"Of course, you will help him." Margaret frowned. "Though pain blights you, do not underestimate the strength of your character. I've never known you to fail at anything you set your mind to." She let out a throaty laugh. "I'm married to a very stubborn man."

The tension of the day drained from Shaftesbury, and he smiled. Margaret was right. Though weak in body, his intellect was strong, and the dissolution of the Cavalier Parliament had now become his number one goal. "I want a new parliamentary body. One representing the interests of the people, not the King and his Court."

Everything seemed clearer. In agreeing to have him removed from London, Charles had only succeeded in strengthening Shaftesbury's resolve to stay and fight. Any doubts he had had about opposing Charles vanished like shadows brought into bright sunlight. Yes, he *would* lead the opposition against the Crown, and he'd do his damndest to succeed.

Charles could order his removal from his home, and even London, but it would *not* stop him fighting for a new Parliament to be formed. Charles would know this. Danby, however, was another matter altogether. A matter he intended to deal with.

Shaftesbury walked along Gresham Street with Buckingham. "In the end, Williamson refused to sign the warrant for my arrest," Shaftesbury said, concluding his story about Danby's failed attempts to have him removed from London.

"Poor Danby," Buckingham replied, between fits of laughter. "He seems to have the great misfortune of always losing out to you."

"Ha, ha! Indeed. To bring matters to a conclusion, I'm moving to Aldersgate Street." Shaftesbury's new house was smaller than his current mansion, but it was a compromise he had willingly made. If he'd been forced from London, he would have been finished as leader of the opposition. Without doubt, this had been Danby's intention.

Reaching the corner of Basinghall Street, Shaftesbury stopped and urinated in the gutter before entering the Guildhall building. Why had he been dragged here? "Come, Buckingham, what's afoot?"

"A surprise awaits you. But you'll have to be patient. All will become clear."

"You have me intrigued," Shaftesbury raised his voice, in order to be heard over the thrum in the packed vestibule. Though all the Lords were invited, few attended the Livery Companies elections to appoint the Sheriffs for the City of London.

Entering the Great Hall, Buckingham looked around. "Thanks be to God, it's busy." He pointed towards some empty places near the front. Around the hall people jostled for seats, and Shaftesbury stayed close behind Buckingham as they pushed their way through the throng.

They found seats together and watched as Aldermen from the Worshipful Companies were escorted in by their deputations. When they were all seated, a livery gown was placed on a Freeman from the Goldsmiths Company. Loud applause followed – The man could now trade gold or silver within London.

Shaftesbury felt even more confused. Nothing out of the ordinary had taken place. He tapped a hand against his mouth. The proceedings finished, with the election of two Sheriffs, as assistants to the Lord Mayor. He joined in the applause and rose to leave.

Buckingham grasped his arm, to stop him. Frances Jenks, a linen draper of the Worshipful Company of Drapers, stood up and asked for the attention of the hall. Shaftesbury looked at Buckingham and raised his eyebrows.

Smirking, Buckingham whispered, "Here comes your moment. Listen well."

Shaftesbury sat forward and afforded Jenks his full attention.

Jenks cleared his throat. "Thank you for your time. My speech will be short. My purpose is to furnish you with information of which you may not be aware. Two statutes dating from the reign of Edward III require Parliament to sit every year. Because of the long prorogation, the Cavalier Parliament is now dissolved. No Parliament is now legally in existence. Ipso Facto dissolved."

Shaftesbury shook his head in amazement. His ears buzzed with the loud discussions erupting throughout the hall. He turned to Buckingham. "Parliament is dissolved? The Restoration Parliament no longer exists? Am I dreaming?"

Buckingham roared with laughter. "I said you would like it. Nay, you are very much awake, but Danby and the King's worst nightmare has just begun."

Three weeks later, Shaftesbury engaged in a heated debate with Buckingham and the King's bastard son, Monmouth, in Wills coffee house. At separate benches beside the fire sat the poets, Otway and Dryden, surrounded by their followers; who drank up their witty repartee along with their coffee. At a table behind them sat some playwrights including Matthew Medbourne, their heads bent close, debating some issue.

"And how did your Royal visit go?" Monmouth asked Shaftesbury and Buckingham.

Although it had been Buckingham who'd guided Jenks in his speech, many thought Shaftesbury responsible. Shaftesbury had, however, been involved in writing a number of pamphlets arguing that Parliament could restrict the royal prerogative and had the right to legislate on the inheritance of the Crown.

"York was enraged," Buckingham said. "He slapped one of our pamphlets onto the table and pointed and stabbed at it with a finger. 'Bind, limit, restrain and govern the descent and inheritance of the Crown,' he roared at me. 'What do you mean by this?' I informed him Shaftesbury had drafted the passage in question."

Shaftesbury looked at Monmouth. "And I told him this passage was inserted without my knowledge. I thought that would be it. A short time in the Tower perhaps, as has happened many times before. But I didn't expect . . . this!" Shaftesbury said, holding up an anonymously written pamphlet, 'Pacquet of Advices to the Men of Shaftesbury'. "I am done for. My character is blackened. This tract presents me as a traitor. No one will respect me now." Copies of the pamphlet littered the tables, chairs and even the floor of the coffee house, and he winced.

Dryden sat down beside them and picked up one of the pamphlets. As a loyal supporter of the King, Shaftesbury couldn't fathom why he would join their table, especially while Buckingham was present. The antagonism between these two was well known.

Dryden pointed to the pamphlet. "Shaftesbury, you are in difficulty, Needham wrote this. I knew him as a scurrilous pamphleteer during the forties." Dryden looked over at Monmouth. "He played a significant role in the blackening of your grandfather's character, Monmouth. The Lords stepped in, and they sent Needham to the Fleet. On his release he retired from pamphleteering, to work as a doctor. He looked more ghost than man then, and it seems he's now haunting you Shaftesbury."

Monmouth roared with laughter.

Shaftesbury glared at him. "This is no time for gaiety. I'm being turned into a laughing stock. My dear friend, John Locke, who helps draft my pamphlets, has fled abroad in fear for his life."

Monmouth flushed. "Forgive me. I am of course laughing at Needham."

"I made some enquiries," Dryden said with a hint of a sneer.

"And?" Shaftesbury asked in a tremulous voice.

"From what I could determine all Needham's recent publications are on medicine," Dryden said. "Finding this strange, I asked around and found his motive to be financial. After your pamphlet appeared, Danby sought him out and gave him five hundred pounds to write this pamphlet discrediting you, and a further fifty pounds to distribute it."

Shaftesbury reeled. Five hundred pounds. Damn Danby. After delaying discrediting *Danby*, he now cursed his stupidity. He should have acted sooner. He should have known Danby wouldn't stop at evicting him from his home. But why was Dryden telling him this?

Dryden let out a mock sigh. "I'm afraid this isn't the only pamphlet."

"What . . . there are more?" Monmouth asked.

Shaftesbury's belly tightened. How did Dryden know this? He glared at him.

"Yes, two more." Dryden gave a mocking laugh. "Two more accounts of a small Goblin leading the noblemen of London into the Pit of Destruction."

Shaftesbury leant back in the chair and seethed. He would have his revenge. He didn't care how long it took. Danby would suffer for this. And, he would keep a watchful eye on Dryden.

CHAPTER TWENTY-TWO

Ripples

St Bartholomew-Tide was warm and sunny, and the crowds headed in droves to the ale houses to celebrate. Around mid-day, Titus crawled out of a cellar in Whitehall and donned his clerical robes and faded white hat. Picking up his cane, he set out towards the lower end of the Mall, to beg for alms. The tree-lined Mall offered a promenade for people of means, and by presenting himself as a poor churchman returned from studying abroad, he managed to procure a few small coins.

By two o'clock, his belly bemoaned its lack of food. The smell of roasting meat, sweet cakes and ale surrounded and tormented him. "I'm blaady starving," he murmured. Why should he have to beg for food?

"Dogs the lot of you," he muttered, as he watched throngs of well-dressed people hurrying to and from the taverns. While the occasional person threw down a small coin, most walked past. Titus raised a hand and considered his dirt-encrusted nails. Glancing down, he frowned at the shabby state of his clothes.

"Alms, please. Help a poor churchman," he called to three long-coated and lace-frilled gentlemen who passed without glancing his way. The clip-clop, clip-clop, of their high heeled shoes striking the cobbles grated in his head.

Arm in arm, a young couple, strolled along the walkway. An elderly female chaperone followed behind.

"I've just returned from abroad. I am but a poor churchman," he called to them.

He winced and flushed a deep red, when the young woman, dressed in a lilac gown and wearing a small feathered cap, looked back at him, gripped the man's arm and hurried him away.

Titus glared at the throngs passing by. So caught up was he in the injustice of his situation he failed to stop two ragged and filthy children descending on some coins tossed to him. His stomach rumbled with hunger and his resentment grew.

"Sinners all. Repent or you shall be damned in Hell. The Divinity is false. There is only one God and one spirit," he shouted, and an angry crowd gathered around. "The Holy Trinity is a falsehood. 'Tis a lie!"

Three well-dressed and able-bodied young men sprang from the crowd and manhandled Titus to the ground. They pummelled, kicked and slapped him until he swore to stop preaching and move on.

Rising to his feet, he grunted and dusted himself down. The alms he had received lay scattered on the ground, and he cursed as he picked them up. He kicked out at a small arm, snaking its way towards a stray coin that had rolled away. He lifted his cane, placed his hat back on, and set off in search of shelter.

Bruised and sore, he arrived back in Whitehall. Casting his eyes around, he spotted an open cellar in one of the grander houses near to the Admiralty Buildings. Stooping, he limped inside, and lay down and wrapped his arms around his painful ribs. Although it stank of mildew and coal, the cellar was cool and dark, and he welcomed its security.

Moments later, he found himself being dragged out by his legs. Moaning with pain and frustration, he looked up to see a handsome and clean dressed young man frowning down at him.

"Please," Titus sobbed. "Dear Gaad, don't hurt me."

"What are you doing in the Earl of Suffolk's cellar? I saw you enter a few moments ago and followed you here. Explain yourself."

"I am a poor churchman. Ahem. . . Set upon for my religious dress. A gang of ruffians beat me, and –" he heaved a sigh. The stranger was listening to his account. "And forced me to denounce God. But I couldn't. Now here I am battered and bruised and seeking sanctuary where I can find it. I don't blame my attackers. 'Tis the work of the Devil himself. They were sent to test my faith."

The stranger looked at him with suspicion, and Titus realised he was taking in the dishevelled state of his clerical robes. The man hesitated a moment longer, then helped him up. He held out a long-fingered hand. "I'm Matthew Medbourne, of the Duke's Theatre Company. You may, or not, have heard of me."

Titus had heard of the playwright and actor and moreover knew he was of the Roman Catholic faith. "Titus Oates," he replied, shaking his hand.

"I'm meeting a friend to sup, why don't you join us?"

Titus looked at him and then nodded. "Thank you. Thank you. I would like that very much."

They arrived at the Sun Tavern in Aldersgate Street, and Titus limped behind Matthew Medbourne as he climbed the stairs to the first floor. Following him across the tavern, Titus hesitated. At the table, they were heading towards, sat William Smith, his former master from Merchant Taylors' School.

Pish. He'd been caught out, and would have to make an escape. But, he needed this meal. Damn Smith to Hell, for being here. Titus bowed his head and waited for William Smith to deride him. But, wait. He was a good friend of mother's and held her in high regard. Perhaps it would be alright.

Matthew Medbourne gestured for Titus to sit at the table, and turned towards his friend. "William, I apologise if I've kept you waiting."

"No, not at all, Matthew. Titus Oates, is that you?" William Smith said. "I didn't recognise you. What are you doing here?"

"So, you know each other already?" Matthew Medbourne said and glanced around for someone to serve him.

"Yes, a long time ago. Titus was one of my boys at Merchants Taylor's." William Smith frowned. "I don't think you stayed with us long Titus? Taking in your clerical robes, I suppose you've made good."

Before Titus could answer, William Smith asked. "Why, Titus. Are you injured?" In fussing over him, he seemed to forget his concerns.

After placing an order for three servings of potage of mutton, small ale and bread, Matthew Medbourne turned his attention back to the conversation.

"I was making my way to meet you, William, when I spied this minister taking refuge in Suffolk's cellar. The poor man had been set upon by a gang of ruffians. Something I dread happening. It is intolerable one can no longer walk the streets in safety. Now, let us eat. I'm famished, and you must be as well, Titus."

By the time they'd taken their last sups, they were all on friendly terms. Titus thanked them for their hospitality and regaled them with accounts of his life as a churchman.

"I apologise for my poor state of dress and lack of money, but I've just returned from abroad, as part of my work for the church."

Before they left the Sun Tavern, on Matthew Medbourne's

introduction, Titus had been accepted as a member of a club, which met at the Pheasants Inn, in Fullers Rents.

Two months later, Titus turned off St. Clement Danes, on the Strand, and walked up a tree-lined driveway to the courtyard of Arundel House. A chill wind penetrated his lightweight clothing, and he shivered. Cold, bedraggled and hungry, he gazed over at the large townhouse, surrounded by numerous out-buildings. A smile widened on his face. A series of strange events had brought him here.

On hearing that the Parkers had dropped all charges against him, and remembering Matthew Medbourne's generosity, and his introduction to the club in Fullers Rents, Titus had made his way there. In the packed room, he'd been surprised to see priests milling around. He'd never mixed with priests before and had shivered at the thought of doing so.

On learning Titus remained destitute Matthew Medbourne had offered to speak on his behalf to his Catholic friend, Henry Howard, the Duke of Norfolk, who required a Chaplain for the Protestants living in his home.

The Bells from St Clemens Danes church, peeling out the morning hour of eight, broke Titus from his thoughts. Tapping the cane against his leg, he pushed his head down and limped over to start his new position as Chaplain to the Protestants of Arundel House.

Elizabeth entered the withdrawing room of Arundel House with Powis. Stafford and his wife, Mary, accompanied them.

Elizabeth scanned the room, where a number of other guests had already gathered, looking for their host. She spotted Norfolk standing by the fire. His back was stooped, and his jowls hung in their usual melancholic manner. A fire glowed in the grate, casting a warm aura around the room. Jane Bickerton, his mistress of many years, sat by Norfolk's side. Her long, grey-streaked auburn curls hung in ringlets and soft tendrils framed her face, making her appear younger than her fifty-eight years.

Elizabeth slipped her arm into Powis' arm, and they made their way over to them. Norfolk, a Catholic nobleman, lived a semi-reclusive life in Arundel House. Though good-natured, he took little interest in Parliament, or the running of his great home, which was sadly neglected. Following the death of his wife, Elizabeth's sister, Anne Somerset, some years before, he'd fallen into deep despair. Tonight gave Elizabeth a rare chance to spend time with Norfolk. Like most Catholics, they delivered their foreign correspondence to Arundel House. Norfolk's letter carriers then took them abroad. Other than handing in and collecting their letters, they rarely called.

"Ah, Powis, Elizabeth, welcome. Come, sit down. We will get started soon. Hmm?" Norfolk said.

Elizabeth smiled at Jane Bickerton and sat beside her, leaving Powis in a deep discussion with Norfolk about the birth of Mary Beatrice and York's daughter, Isabella.

Stafford's wife, Mary, joined the women, while Stafford himself, a relative of Norfolk's, remained talking to someone at the rear of the room.

Servants busied themselves offering red wine to the guests. Elizabeth accepted a glass, took a sip and rested it on her knee. Why had they been gathered here this evening? It was out of character for Norfolk to socialise on such a scale. No doubt she would learn of his reason in good time.

Looking around, she felt saddened by the state of disrepair Arundel House has fallen into. A few years earlier Norfolk had sold off a section of his land, where it joined the Strand. Mrs Cellier's townhouse had been built on this stretch of ground. Thinking of the midwife, Elizabeth decided to call on her. If the weather remained clement, she would do so tomorrow.

When Norfolk dismissed his servants, Elizabeth looked on in surprise. After the door had closed behind them, Norfolk bowed and offered his hand to Jane Bickerton. Jane took it and stood up by his side. Norfolk called for order, and a hush settled over the room. Elizabeth caught Powis' eyes, and he moved over to stand beside her.

Norfolk cleared his throat. "I've asked you here to share with you that Jane and I are to be married."

A number of guests clapped. Elizabeth glanced around and joined in.

Norfolk held up a hand to halt them. "No, we do not want your applause. Our intention is simply to inform you that in a few weeks time we shall go abroad and will return as husband and wife."

When the other guests started to depart, Elizabeth made to leave. Stafford asked her and Powis to remain behind, telling them he needed to talk to Norfolk. No sooner had the last guest departed than Stafford launched into an angry tirade. Elizabeth held her hand to her mouth and looked up at Powis in bewildered surprise. Stafford and Norfolk frequently argued together, but she'd never seen Stafford so enraged.

"In God's name, you're sixty-two. What the damn are you doing getting married again? Have you lost your senses?" Stafford pointed to Jane Bickerton. "And to *her* of all people."

Norfolk glared and stepped towards him. "You've gone too far this time. Leave my home and do not return. I've had enough of this family and their jealousies and squabbles. Even if I did *not* marry Jane, you wouldn't see a penny of *my* inheritance."

Stafford's face flushed a deep red. "This isn't to do with money. But, so be it. We will part on ill terms . . . once again," he said and turned on his heels and stormed out the room.

Elizabeth followed behind with Powis and Mary. Glancing back at Norfolk, she shrugged her shoulders. Making her way out the door, she almost bumped into an Anglican minister lurking outside. Something about this unusual looking man in a clerical cloak unnerved her. Where had she seen him before? As she passed, the man dropped his large chin onto his chest and averted his eyes. A shiver ran through Elizabeth. The minister had been listening outside the door.

.

Part Four: The Pawns

1677

'Ill habits gather unseen degrees,
as brooks make rivers, rivers run to seas.'

John Dryden

CHAPTER TWENTY-THREE

A New Order

After its long prorogation, Charles opened Parliament in February. He informed both houses he intended to rejoin the war effort and asked them to finance this.

"Your Majesty, we should align with the Dutch," Danby said.

"France has always been loyal to us and will continue to be so. We must remain with France. To side with the Dutch is unthinkable," James of York stammered.

"It's imperative the King has a place at the peace table, but we should not support France," Danby said.

The debate raged on. Ten minutes . . . forty minutes, and then the decision was announced: "Your Majesty, Parliament agrees to fund England's re-entry into the war . . . On the proviso England joins with the Dutch."

Charles remained quiet, his brows furrowed. Then, he nodded.

As he stood to leave, Buckingham leapt up, "Your Majesty, Lords and gentlemen, this was not a legitimate session. What we agreed cannot be. Because Parliament did not meet in '76 the current Parliament has ceased to exist."

Charles hesitated. His gaze turning towards Shaftesbury, who, along with Salisbury and Wharton, stood in support of the motion.

Charles sat down in shocked bewilderment.

Buckingham and Shaftesbury tried to persuade the other Lords to support their motion. When none would, their shouts grew louder. Chaos ensued.

Cries of, "Order! Order!" mingled with raised voices; unheard or ignored by protagonists and protesters alike.

Finally, Charles let out a loud exhalation. Parliament rejected the motion and concluded that while the long prorogation was unconstitutional, the session itself was not.

Buckingham, Shaftesbury, Salisbury and Wharton heckled and ridiculed the now quiet House. "Pish, what nonsense is this? Support the motion. It's your duty. Are you blind? Parliament is dissolved."

Charles asked them to apologise to the House. Twice he offered, and twice they refused. When they refused for a third time, he ordered their immediate arrest and removal to the Tower.

The fools, Charles thought, and stood up and marched out of chambers.

Titus lazed on his bed within the servant's quarters of Arundel House. Compared to the cellars he'd slept in since arriving in London, the room was more than comfortable. Furnished with a wooden three-drawer chest, a washstand with a bowl and jug, and a sturdy oak table and chair, it had everything he needed. To his disappointment, the position of Chaplain didn't pay well and was considered on a level with the upper servants. Despite this, he found the post agreeable, and he could come and go as he pleased.

When the bells of St Clement Danes pealed out the hour of six, he rose and stretched. Picking up his coat, he made his way to the main hall for his evening meal. He sat down at a long table, alongside the upper servants, and bowed his head. "Bless, O Father, thy gifts for our use; For Christ's sake, Amen."

Helping himself to a generous portion of fish pie, Titus salivated in anticipation. It smelled delicious. He savoured the first mouthful, and nodded his approval to the cook.

"He's to marry Bickerton. Norfolk's marrying his mistress," Titus repeated, on seeing their stunned faces.

"Where did you hear that?" the housekeeper asked. "Are you sure? I've heard nothing about this," she added and frowned.

"If this is true, then the man's as mad as his brother," the estate manager said.

The housekeeper laughed.

Titus joined in their laughter. He'd soon discovered the rightful Duke of Norfolk was, in fact, Norfolk's older brother Thomas, who resided in an institution abroad.

"Soon they'll all be abroad," the housekeeper said and turned the conversation to Norfolk's other brother, the Jesuit Priest, Cardinal Howard, who had fled abroad three years before.

Titus had never lived amongst the nobility and was shocked to see the wealth and status such Papists had. He envied their privileged lifestyle. He'd also seen Norfolk's relative, Viscount Stafford, at Arundel House. In recalling him, he realised Stafford hadn't been back since his argument with Norfolk. Stafford had been accompanied that night by the Earl and Countess of Powis.

Hmm, he mused, he was learning a great deal living here. What he didn't see for himself, he gleaned from eavesdropping on the household gossip. He'd learned the names and positions of many of the leading English Catholic nobles and clerics. He'd also met some of the runners, who carried their letters abroad. One of these letter carriers intrigued Titus, and he beamed to see him enter the hall and make his way towards the lower servant's tables.

Titus wiped his mouth with the back of his hand and rose to join him.

"You off out again, Titus?" the housekeeper asked.

"I wish I were so lucky," the head butler said and snorted. "What exactly are you employed to do here? I've yet to see you provide chaplaincy services to any Protestants."

Titus picked up his coat and glared at him. "You blaady heathen. Make sure you lock your door tonight," he said and limped off after Bedloe. He didn't care if the butler reported him. He'd soon learned Norfolk disliked confrontation.

Catching up with Bedloe, Titus sat on a bench beside him. The other servants were already departing. Bedloe accepted a bowl of fish pie from a young kitchen maid. Titus waved the blushing girl away, and poured a cup of small ale and placed it in front of Bedloe.

Twenty-six-year-old William Bedloe was tall, dark and handsome, and employed as letter carrier by many Catholics and Jesuits. His main employer was Baron Belasyse.

"Belasyse is so incapacitated by gout he can barely stand. He has no clue as to what goes on around him," Bedloe said.

Titus sniggered.

"It's becoming easier to cheat the old man," Bedloe continued.

Though he suspected Bedloe was bragging, Titus was impressed. "Cheat him, how?" In his capacity as letter carrier, Bedloe travelled throughout Europe. The last time they'd met, Bedloe had regaled Titus with wondrous tales of high living and adventure.

"Ah, by many means. Belasyse pays me to deliver these letters abroad." Bedloe tapped the leather bag slung across his shoulder "Do you want to read one?"

Titus flushed with excitement. He'd never met anyone like Bedloe. The sense of adventure and danger emanating from him intoxicated Titus. "You'll let me read one?"

Bedloe roared with laughter. "Nay, but one day I'll tell you how I really make my money. Until then, *au revoir*." He strode from the hall, the young servant girl following close behind him.

With little in the way of amusement at Arundel House, Titus spent his evenings at the club at the Pheasant Inn. Pulling on his coat, he set off towards Fullers Rents. He made first for Islington, to meet up with William Smith, his former schoolmaster. When he arrived Matthew Medbourne was with William Smith, and they all walked together to the club. A light drizzle fell, and they hurried along.

On their arrival, Medbourne bought Titus a tankard of ale and introduced him to his acquaintances. Later, they dissected the current gossip doing the rounds in London.

"Do you think it right Shaftesbury was sent to the Tower?" Medbourne said.

"No. Not for the sentiment behind his actions. But, for his behaviour, yes," Smith replied.

Titus raised his chin and looked at them. He had no idea what they were talking about. He felt on safer ground when the talk turned to simpler topics, such as the new monument to the Great Fire of London, designed by Christopher Wren.

"Have you seen the monument?" Smith asked. "The copper-gilded ball with flames sprouting out of it is magnificent."

"Yes, and I'll never forget the experience," Medbourne said and snorted. "As I attempted to climb it, I became giddy and near collapsed. I had to venture back down without reaching the top."

Titus roared with laughter.

On leaving, Titus waited outside for Matthew Medbourne and his friends. The rain had stopped, and they walked together towards the Strand. As the club comprised both Catholic and Protestant members, religious discussions were prohibited. Outside, however, members freely discussed religion. For the first time, Titus conversed with Jesuit Priests. Whenever their conversation included reference to Popery, Titus turned his full attention to it.

"Where do you think Germain is?" someone asked.

"Why, France of course, where else?" someone replied.

The Luzancy incident was being kept alive by pamphleteers intriguing about the whereabouts of Father Saint Germain. Titus had read many of their pamphlets.

"The incident has caused greater hostility towards Catholics. I was accosted as I left the theatre last night," Medbourne said.

William Smith halted and touched Medbourne's arm. "Were you harmed Matthew? Why didn't you mention this before?"

Medbourne shrugged, and they continued on their way. "I'm unharmed. The blaggard merely shouted at me about the 'Sacred Heart.' But, what has this got to do with me?"

Intrigued, Titus moved beside him. "The Sacred Heart? I've not heard of this."

"Mmm." Medbourne uttered. "Since the arrival of Colombière, as

Mary Beatrice's chaplain, there's been growing hostility towards Jesuits."

William Smith nodded. "There's also growing concern about the number of conversions to the 'Sacred Heart'."

Titus hadn't realised so many different factions existed. For the first time, he grasped the distinction between contemporary Catholics and the extreme faction of the Society of Jesus; the Jesuits.

Later that week, the Earl of Norfolk summoned Titus to his large book-lined study. Norfolk paced the room with his hands clasped behind his back. Candles flickered in his wake. Titus intended going to the club at Fuller's Rent and hoped the meeting would be brief.

Norfolk came to an abrupt halt and turned around. "Well Oates, what do you have to say for yourself?"

"Aah, Your Lordship. 'Tis all lies. The devil himself must be in them." Titus didn't know what Norfolk had heard, but from his demeanour, it was clearly serious.

"I count myself a fair man, and as such, I asked my staff to tell me how you were progressing. Not one person in my household had anything good to say about you. They tell me you are lazy, ill-tempered, rude, blasphemous and lewd. Are they *all* lying?"

"Blaady heathens the lot of them."

"Refrain from swearing in my house. You can gather your belongings and leave."

Titus dropped to his knees. "Please, I'm but a poor churchman with nowhere else to go. I promise to try harder. I'll do all you ask. I am weak." Titus could tell from Norfolk's grim demeanour that he was serious about dismissing him and collapsed onto the floor in tears.

"I expect you to be gone within the hour." Norfolk waved a frail hand, dismissing him.

Rising from the floor, Titus glared at him. "So be it! I never liked the blaady position anyway." He stormed from the study and banged the door behind him.

Twenty minutes later, he limped out of the grounds of Arundel House, onto the Strand. He hoisted a small bag, containing a few items of clothing and his bible, onto his shoulder. With no destination in mind, he walked along St Clement Danes. As he walked, he came to the cold realisation that his life as an Anglican minister was over.

He recalled the gossip he'd heard outside the club at Fullers Rent, about the glorious future for Catholics. Tonge had told him converts were being lured towards Catholicism through promises of money and great futures. Titus envied the merry and licentious life Jesuit emissaries led abroad. He had read Tonge's pamphlets, and the more he had read, the more he had wondered if Catholics might just succeed.

On Ash Wednesday, he met in secret with Father Richard Strange, an elderly Provincial of the Society of Jesus.

Father Strange remained solemn. "I've been informed you wish to convert."

"I do indeed, Father. My heart lies with the Catholic Church."

"This is not a simple matter. By making this conversion, you will place yourself in danger. Do you understand this?"

Titus licked his lips. "Yes. Yes, I do Father."

With a large liver-spotted hand, Father Strange picked up a sheet of paper. "I must stress that if you are accepted into the Jesuit order, you will have to assume an alias and live a secretive life."

"I can do that."

Father Strange held the paper as if to hand it to him, but laid it down.

"I have to be certain you understand what this will mean. It's a felony to attend Mass, and a serious offence to be in possession of religious artefacts, including rosaries."

"Yes, I understand." Titus would do whatever it took. Nothing so far caused him concern.

"You must keep secret everything about our order. As it's treason to convert anyone, you must never approach me directly."

Titus skimmed the sworn deposition Father Strange handed him – denouncing and disowning allegiance to any heretical king, state or Protestant, and to keep secret and private all counsels entrusted, and not divulge these either by word, writing, or circumstances.

A smile played on Titus's lips, as he read, signed and dated the oath.

CHAPTER TWENTY-FOUR

Suspicions and Spanish Shoes

In a stone cell, in the Tower, Shaftesbury bent over his desk. He stabbed a quill pen into a silver inkstand and splashed the black liquid across the words on the page. Never before had he experienced such a sense of impotent rage. Charles had incensed him many times through his words and actions, but this . . .

He threw the quill down. He'd sent a letter to Charles, explaining that the poor air in his cell had affected his health and he feared he wouldn't recover. Today, he'd received Charles' curt reply, written by one of his aides. Shaftesbury lifted the ink-stained page, on which Charles informed him he would 'seek a prison for him with better air'.

"Damn him!" Scrunching the letter into a ball, Shaftesbury threw it across the cell. After five months, he craved release, but Charles' response made him more determined than ever not to apologise. He scraped back the wooden chair and stood. "Nay, I'll not apologise for speaking the truth," he called out. Pouring a cup of ale, he downed it in one swallow.

He picked up his walking sticks and winced. The pain in his side had become intolerable. His wife visited him every morning with food and fresh clothes and remained a few hours to help draft letters and pamphlets. He didn't know how he would have got through this without her.

He could only sit for short spells. The build up of pressure in his side then became unbearable, and he had to stand up to relieve the pain. Outside, a hot summer sun shone, and the air in the cell had grown thick and humid. Sweat coursed down his back, and his legs felt stiff from inaction.

Shuffling around, Shaftesbury contemplated what to do. He remained suspicious of Charles, who was now raising an army in readiness to rejoin the war. He didn't believe the army would be used to fight the French. Instead, he thought Charles was preparing to rule the country through a standing army, and remove Parliament completely.

Believing Parliament's future to be in great jeopardy, he couldn't even contemplate apologising. If this meant dying in the **Tower, so be it. He stretched out on the small bed and closed his** eyes.

The following day proved hot, even for July. Buckingham, Salisbury and Wharton clustered together in his cell, drinking ale and discussing their recent incarceration in the Tower. After apologising, Buckingham, Salisbury and Wharton had been released two weeks earlier.

Buckingham removed his cravat. "Apologise, Shaftesbury, and have done with it."

"Never." Shaftesbury wiped perspiration from his brow, with the cloth he kept clutched in his hand.

"You've no option," Wharton said. "What good are you to the cause, locked in the Tower? We're all better placed to work outside. The writ proved a stroke of genius." The habeas corpus writ had been presented to the King's Bench and required Parliament to determine if they had cause to continue to detain them.

They all nodded their agreement.

"Charles will use any money granted by Parliament for the war to raise a standing army," Shaftesbury said.

"Many others are beginning to fear the same," Wharton said. "Parliament must delay funding the war for this very reason."

"You must also bring Danby down," Shaftesbury said. "As long as he leads Parliament by his purse-strings we're all doomed. France is offering high bribes to anyone willing to contribute to his fall. Let us pray there are sufficient takers."

Buckingham leaned back and laughed. "And where do you think all these new coaches are coming from, my own included?"

"Ha, ha! And much more besides," Wharton exclaimed through his laughter. "The gowns of the ladies at Court are very grand this year, more so than usual."

"Now that you come to mention it, even the whores on the street are wearing diamonds," Buckingham said, raising more laughs from around the table. "But this brings us no nearer to releasing you from the Tower, Shaftesbury. But there is some good news of sorts. People are elated at the announcement of a marriage between York's daughter and Orange. It aligns us with the Dutch and should ensure a Protestant succession."

"For now, we have little to fear," Shaftesbury said. "But, Mary Beatrice is with child again. If she births a boy, it will take precedence over York's daughters. People fear it would mean another Catholic rule over England."

"Do you suppose Papists still pose a threat?" Salisbury asked.

"To rich and poor alike," Buckingham replied. "Many of the nobility live in estates taken from Catholics. Rest assured under Catholic rule these would be restored to their families or the Church. The poor fear the tyranny of a Catholic rule. Yes, many live in fear of Popery. Listen to the panic raised after the Great Fire. Rumours still abound about Catholic plots to kill Protestants as they lie sleeping in their beds. The slightest thing restarts the gossip. People haven't forgotten the tales of the Catholic rule of Queen Mary."

"Then we need to bring about York's downfall," Shaftesbury said. "For, without doubt, he's a Papist. The evidence is clear."

"I'm planning a visit to France," Buckingham said. "I'll do my utmost while there to hinder any supply of money to Charles or York. I hope I don't find you still languishing here on my return, Shaftesbury."

Six weeks had passed since Titus had been received into the Roman Catholic Church, yet here he remained with Tonge, writing pamphlets that rarely sold. Having cast aside his clerical robes, he had dressed in a dated and shabby campaign coat, black hat and black Spanish-leather-heeled shoes. He took the scrap of paper Tonge handed to him.

"Can you solve it, Titus?" Tonge asked. "I made it just for you."

To please him, Titus puzzled over the anagram "They see." He deliberated for a few minutes. "The eyes."

"Ah, well done. Well done." Tonge handed him the draft for a new pamphlet. "Read this. I heard it again yesterday. There's a plot afoot to kill the King and replace him with his Papist brother. The Jesuits are behind it. There's to be a massacre of leading Protestants."

As Tonge ranted, Titus nodded. He could no longer distinguish between fact and fiction in the tales Tonge told. Hour after hour he'd sat with this little grey-haired and bearded man writing about Catholic conspiracies, planned massacres and threats from Popery.

Titus had sworn himself over to the Jesuits but needed money – now.

Yesterday, with his belly rumbling from hunger, he'd gone to Queen Catherine's residence, Somerset House. Presenting at the Chapel as a Catholic convert, he'd begged the priests for their charity. After feeding him a meal of meat and bread, Father Fenwick had given him three shillings, telling him he could return the money when good fortune shone on him again. Titus cursed Father Fenwick for looking down on *him*. Alms indeed.

Tonge continued. "I had my dream again last night, of Papists roaming London, murdering Protestants as they slept. It was most vivid. Are you listening to what I'm telling you?"

"Your dream," Titus said.

"My visions have returned." Tonge leant closer. "I see Jesuits huddled together . . . plotting against Protestants for the slaughter of the King, as they gloat over London burning. It's coming. The signs are all there. First, there was pestilence, in the form of the plague. Then the Great Fire. Then the sky blackened over. People fear the meaning of these signs."

The following day, Titus met again with Father Berry. "I do, Father. I profess a sincere desire to study for the priesthood."

Father Berry nodded. "I had to be sure. As a convert in need of help, Father Strange has agreed to give you a trial at our College at Valladolid, in Spain. It's a Jesuit seminary for the higher study of philosophy and theology."

Titus let out a loud exhalation. "Thank you. Thank you. I won't disappoint you. I'll work diligently at my studies." His dark mood lifted, his future suddenly looked brighter.

Four days later, he donned the summer suit Father Berry had given him. Feeling happy, and unusually prosperous, he attached ribbons to his jacket and a large bow on his shoulder. Under the alias of Titus Ambrose, he embarked on the Merchant of Biscay, bound for Bilbao, on the Northern coast of Spain.

Standing on deck, Titus imagined himself dressed in a grand Catholic robe, carrying secret dispatches for the Society of Jesus. When the ship set sail, he had no regrets as he watched both England and his Protestant faith disappear into the horizon.

CHAPTER TWENTY-FIVE

The Bells Ring Out

On the seventh of November, bells rang throughout London. Mary Beatrice had birthed a boy. A strange phenomenon occurred that day, causing murmurs something bad was afoot – A black dot moved across the face of the sun. Adding this to the plague, the Great Fire and two eclipses of the moon, many viewed this as a sign of impending doom.

Elizabeth sat beside Mary Beatrice in an anti-chamber at St James's Palace, embroidering baby linen. Catherine Sedley and Sarah Jennings, Mary Beatrice's ladies, sat on a window seat cooing over her fourteen-month-old daughter, Isabella.

Lying on a daybed, Mary Beatrice rocked her four-week-old son, Charles, in her arms. "Look, *amica cara*, isn't he healthy and strong."

The child did look robust, and Elizabeth nodded. "As healthy as any I've seen, and a good set of lungs too." At last, they had a Catholic heir.

Mary Beatrice smiled. "Tell me the news *amica cara*? I hear Shaftesbury's still not apologised."

"No. Ten months in the Tower, and still no apology," Elizabeth said and selected a pale blue thread from the basket. "Have you read the latest pamphlet? It portrays him as a traitor."

"Oh yes, how clever. But, unless more follow, some other scandal will come, and all will be forgotten."

Elizabeth added the final stitch to complete a blue flower. "I've heard he may well die in the Tower, and to think Buckingham has not only been released but is back on friendly terms with Charles."

"It's not the first falling out between Buckingham and Charles, or likely the last. Shaftesbury will be enraged."

"Charles has taken to referring to Shaftesbury as 'Little Sincerity'. And, it seems the name will stick. Soon everyone will be addressing him as –" Elizabeth looked up as the Lady Anne, Mary Beatrice's twelve-year-old stepdaughter, entered, accompanied by her ladies. Elizabeth pulled a silk thread through her work and laid it aside.

Anne rubbed her rheumy eyes and hurried over to the window seat. She beamed at Sarah Jennings, her truest friend. Gripping into Sarah's arm, Anne gave a quick curtsy to Mary Beatrice and walked Sarah over to the low table. Lifting a sweetmeat from a dish, Anne popped it into Sarah's mouth and said, "If it wasn't enough to miss my own sister's marriage, I was then denied the chance to say my goodbyes to her."

Elizabeth raised her eyes. "Now, now, Lady Anne. It's not your stepmother's fault. You were ill with smallpox. It couldn't be helped."

"And the Lady Mary was shocked to be told she must leave straight away," Mary Beatrice said. "She sobbed to say her goodbyes to you and to remain to see you recovered, but her husband, he must return to Holland."

Anne snorted. "Hmph! Well, I'm recovered now. Am I scarred?" She leant over Elizabeth so she could check her face for scars, and winced as she did so. Her illness had left her wracked with joint pains.

"The spots are disappearing, with few marks left behind. I cannot see even one deep scar. You are lucky," Elizabeth said and laughed.

Still linked into Sarah's arm, Anne stood over Mary Beatrice, "Can you arrange for my bedroom to be painted? Doctor Wakeman had it painted red to stop me scarring. It seems to have worked, but I can't abide to look at it any longer." Anne bent down and peered at Baby Charles through her rheumy eyes. "A brother, at last. Isn't he handsome? Can I hold him?"

♛

Four weeks later, Elizabeth sat beside Mary Beatrice in her apartments. Mary Beatrice's ladies were conversing with the Lady Anne, leaving Elizabeth free to talk to her.

Mary Beatrice's eyes were red-rimmed and her face pale. "I had a healthy son and heir. To witness the death of another bambino, this time from smallpox, it's more than I can bear. Why my son?"

Elizabeth struggled to find words to comfort her friend. There was none to be had. All she could do was be there for Mary Beatrice, as she had been throughout her darkest moments. Her own children had survived, but she would continue to keep a watchful eye on them.

The Lady Anne joined them beside the fire. She winced, as she held a hand mirror up to her face. "Dear God. How bloated I've become."

"You have been very unwell my Lady, and are lucky to have fully recovered," Elizabeth said. It was unfortunate smallpox had left Anne with stiff and painful joints, but she'd kept her life and for that, she should be thankful.

Laying down the mirror, Anne looked towards the window. Elizabeth followed her gaze. The snow, which had started the day before, fell in soft flurries. Sensing her own joints reacting to the cold, Elizabeth experienced a sudden longing for spring when she could walk in the park again with Mary Beatrice, her dearest friend.

Anne looked over at Mary Beatrice. "I hear I am to visit my sister in Holland. Are you planning on taking me soon?"

Mary Beatrice appeared startled by the question. "I am not sure, my Lady Anne."

"Please say you'll not force me to go just yet," Anne said and wrinkled her nose.

"But you know your stepmother has no say in this matter," Elizabeth said.

Anne glared at Elizabeth and withdrew into herself.

Unconcerned by Anne's dark mood, Elizabeth turned her attention back to Mary Beatrice.

CHAPTER TWENTY-SIX

St Omer

Five months after leaving London for Valladolid, the Jesuit seminary in Spain, Titus returned. Once again destitute and without prospects, he turned to Israel Tonge.

"Tell no one else," Titus whispered, as they huddled together in a booth in the White Horse Tavern in the Strand. "To infiltrate the Jesuits, I undertook a *mock* conversion to Catholicism." He watched in delight as Tonge paled as he absorbed his words.

"You infiltrated the Jesuits? But how?"

Titus glanced around the busy tavern and leant forward. "By pretending to be a Jesuit convert."

Tonge's eyes gleamed. "I could never have taken such a risk. You placed your life in danger."

"It was worth it. At Valladolid, I heard the Fathers talking about all manner of things. You would be appalled by what I uncovered. I could have learned more, but they weren't exactly forthcoming about their secrets. But I did overhear them talking about removing Protestants from positions of power and replacing them with Catholics. God's wounds, I think you are right. Papists are plotting again."

"We need to find out how they aim to achieve this." Tonge fidgeted with excitement. "We have to know what they're planning. Our lives depend on it."

"How? How can we find out more?" Titus regretted saying so much. He shook his head. "No, we just need to take care. You should stop writing your pamphlets against the Jesuits. If you don't draw attention to yourself, you should remain safe. Did I tell you William Bedloe, the letter carrier, visited me at Valladolid?"

"But, if there's a Papal plot afoot to replace Protestants, then we need to stop it. We need to find out more."

"God's truth," Titus said and sighed. "The Jesuits are hardly likely to inform us about their plots."

"I have an idea. Rumour is rife the Catholic boy's school, St Omer, is, in fact, a seminary for Jesuits. You could apply for a place there. You could uncover more of their secrets."

Titus sipped his ale and considered this. If he went to St Omer, he wouldn't be destitute. What had he to lose? "Yes. Yes, I think I will."

Reaching Calais in early December, Titus stepped into a coach bound for St Omer and settled back into a seat. Ignoring the other passengers, he pulled his hat over his eyes. Regardless of what he'd told Tonge, he intended to make a success of his time, and he fell asleep to visions of the glorious life he would lead as a Jesuit priest.

Arriving at the entrance of St Omer, he stopped at the porter's room. "I'm a student. A new recruit." He retrieved a paper from his coat pocket and handed over his letter of introduction from Father Strange.

The porter took the letter and disappeared. Ten minutes later, Titus went through the door the porter had gone through and arrived in a vestibule. A group of Fathers were gathered around the porter. Walking towards them, Titus could see their surprise that a grown man was starting as a pupil at their boy's school. He ignored it.

"I am Samson Lucy," he announced. "I've suffered greatly in the cause of the faith. But I do it because I'm dedicated. I'm well travelled and speak many languages, as well as having studied Latin, theology and philosophy." He was relieved it was an English college, and he didn't have to speak French.

The Fathers stared at one another, as if unsure what to do. A Father read his recommendation and passed it to another Father, who stepped forward. "Samson Lucy, I'll show you to the student quarters. We erm . . . There's no need for you to use your alias here, but you should use it wherever else you go. Your name?"

He beamed at him. "Titus Oates, Father."

"We have thirty Fathers and over a hundred boys. You can go in with the senior boys," the Father said and set off at a brisk pace.

Titus picked up his bag and followed him. "Thank you, Father. You'll find me a willing student. The setting here is magnificent, as is your school."

That evening, Titus was shown to a single table and chair, which had been erected for him at the side of the dining room. Sitting alone at his table, he devoured a meal of fresh fish with herbs and washed it down with a tankard of ale. As he ate, he watched those around him, trying to gauge which boys were leaders and which were of no account.

Part Five Game Start

1678

'The dread of evil is a much more forcible principle
of human actions than the prospect of good.'

John Locke

CHAPTER TWENTY-SEVEN

Champagne and Secrets

On the evening of the fourteenth of March, a storm built, whipping trees and causing havoc for carriages and those on foot alike. The accompanying rain fell in torrents. Elizabeth relaxed with Powis on a settee by the fire, in their temporary room, at Whitehall Palace.

"The storm shows no sign of abating. I think we'll be here all night," Powis said.

Elizabeth snuggled into him. "The children will be fine, they were safely tucked abed before we left, and with God's blessing, we can return home in the morning. As long as the storm doesn't wake them, we won't even be missed."

"Ah!" Powis sighed and pulled her closer. "You are right, but what a week this has been. Shaftesbury's apology and release from the Tower infuriated Charles. It stoked his temper, which was already raised by missing out on the peace negotiations. He hasn't settled since." Powis snorted. "By the time Parliament released the funds for us to re-enter the war, peace had already been declared and the spoils divided. And, all of this will please Shaftesbury."

"On the war ending I agree with Shaftesbury, though not for the same reason. The last thing we need is another war."

A knock came on the door, and one of Louise de Kérouaille's maids entered, curtsied and handed Elizabeth a note.

Elizabeth scanned it and said to Powis, "Louise returned from France this morning. Hearing we're detained here, she's invited us to her apartments to share news of her sister, Henrietta." She looked at Powis and shrugged her shoulders. "We need to inform Louise about Pembroke, and this could provide us with the ideal opportunity."

"Yes, of course. I wonder how Henrietta's faring in France."

They found Louise relaxing in front of a fire of roaring coals, in the withdrawing room of her luxurious apartments.

"Ah Elizabeth, Powis, come sit beside me," Louise said and beckoned them over to the settee. "I have such news of Henrietta and my darling niece, Charlotte."

As they warmed themselves in front of the fire, Louise furnished them with tales of Henrietta's new life in France, after fleeing from her husband, Pembroke.

"Pembroke's a monster," Elizabeth said. "He's lost all sanity. Dear Henrietta had no choice but to leave. As a Catholic, she couldn't divorce him."

Powis nodded. "None of us had any doubt he would have killed her had she remained. While you were in France Pembroke was charged with murdering a man. As a peer of the realm, he intends claiming privilege of statute and will no doubt be released."

"I am unsurprised to hear this, and have no desire to know the details," Louise said. "No doubt he was in one of his drunken rages at the time."

"Yes," Elizabeth said. "But with no one willing to prosecute him, he almost walked free."

"All good faith to Edmund Berry Godfrey for stepping forward to do it," Powis said. "Though likely, Godfrey now lives in fear for his own life. I've heard Pembroke rages and threatens to murder him too."

"We tried to help," Elizabeth said. "But there was nothing we could do. Pembroke wouldn't listen to reason."

Louise smiled. "I know you tried to help Henrietta, and I appreciate your efforts. Even Charles spoke to Pembroke, but he was beyond talking to. God knows who he will kill next."

"Powis and I have had no dealings with him since Henrietta fled. We will not condone such behaviour."

Catherine Sedley tapped on the door and entered. Louise's closest friend, she too had received a note.

Powis stood and bowed. "I've some business to attend to, and will leave you ladies to your talk. I'll return soon, Elizabeth, to see you safely back to our room."

Elizabeth nodded.

Dressed in a bright yellow gown, Sedley wore an equally bright smile.

"What is amusing you, Sedley?" Louise asked after Powis left. "That smile tells a million tales. Come sit here where it is warm."

Sedley nodded to acknowledge Elizabeth and, throwing her skinny frame down beside Louise, she laughed. "Mmm. Move over and I will tell all. I'm pleased you've returned. I'm anxious to confide in you."

"And I am anxious to hear what you have to say," Louise replied.

Sedley gripped her nose. "Louise, we all smell bad but you more than most. There's a stench of stale sweat coming from you. Do you not have some rosewater to hand?"

Elizabeth scowled – Sedley said out loud what others only thought. "Sedley, tut tut. Louise has been travelling."

"Nell is with Charles, so I have no need to care," Louise said. "He is dining with her at her dwelling, so I am free to do as I wish. Leave my toilette be. I will attend to it when I am ready. Now come, tell us your news. You have me intrigued."

Sedley glanced at Elizabeth. "Louise am I not the plainest of your friends? Are my breasts not the size of the toadstools we tread on in the park? Do my ribs not stick out like the washing boards used by the scullery maids? Do my eyes not squint, and are my legs not so thin my knees rattle together when I walk?"

Elizabeth pulled her hands over her mouth, to stifle the giggle starting in her belly.

"Why then would any man find such a wretched body so desirable he cannot have enough of it?" Sedley asked.

Louise's eyes widened in surprise. "Who is this man?"

Sedley became serious. "It's not just any man. It's James, Duke of York."

Elizabeth glared at Sedley. She felt confused. Although York was considered a greater rake than his brother, it had been some time since he'd taken a new mistress. "Dear God, York is another woman's husband. Have you lost your wits?"

Sedley snorted. "I said this intentionally in your hearing Elizabeth. Who better to inform Mary Beatrice than you? I'm not as hard-hearted as you think. I want her to be one of the first, not the last, to know. If it wasn't me, it would be someone else."

"This will devastate Mary Beatrice," Elizabeth said.

"Mary Beatrice will quite rightly be enraged," Sedley said. "She has long informed York she will not tolerate his infidelity. I'm concerned for her, as she is once again with child. But her body is worn out with childbearing. I can provide him what she *should not*."

Elizabeth shook her head but remained quiet. Mary Beatrice *was* worn out with childbearing. No sooner had she birthed or lost a child than she was with child again. But . . . York and Sedley. She couldn't take it in. She didn't know how she would tell Mary Beatrice?

"When? How?" Louise asked.

"I'm to become his mistress," Sedley replied. "It's no casual affair he seeks. I'm more surprised than anyone. He claims to have fallen passionately in love with me and cannot abide us being apart."

Elizabeth could scarcely believe what she was hearing.

"But . . . I thought you already had a true love," Louise said.

"Why yes, I do and he always will be my true love," Sedley replied. "We're madly in love. But why should it only be men who behave as rakes? But stay hush on that one dearest, we don't want a fuss when York's new bastards arrive do we?" Smiling, she added, "I jest. York's handsome, but if he has wit, he has yet to discover it. Without doubt, he's dimmer than his brother."

Louise roared with laughter. "Sedley, you give me more wit than anyone else I know. We are now related . . . as royal mistresses. I have a confession for you as well."

"Pray tell. I'm all a flutter to hear. Are you with child?" Sedley asked.

Rising from the seat, Louise poured three glasses of Champagne. "I brought some luxurious bottles back for Charles. I do hope he likes them," she said and handed a glass each to Elizabeth and Sedley.

"To think the French despise the bubbles. I adore them," Sedley sipped from the glass. "Mmm. This Champagne's delicious. Now, do tell. Are you big-bellied?"

Louise shook her head and sat back down. "No. No. Nothing like that. It is strange. I never thought I would say this, but . . ." She looked at Elizabeth.

"Say what? Come. Come. What ails you? Why so serious?" Elizabeth asked. Surely it couldn't be anything more shocking than what Sedley had told her.

"France. . . It was not the same. The French Court is . . . I took no enjoyment from being there. I barely knew anyone. And worse, I missed Charles dreadfully. I was no sooner there than I wanted to return here to be with him. But, he is with Nell tonight," Louise bristled. "It is my first night home, and he chose to be with that whore. Did he not miss me at all?"

"But of course you would miss him." Sedley frowned. "I'm surprised you thought otherwise."

"I mean, I *really* missed Charles," Louise said. "While I was in France I came to realise that I *loved* him." She looked at Elizabeth again. "I also came to the realisation that I would not divulge any more of his secrets to France, even if it did help the Catholic cause here. Instead, I will feed France whatever false intelligence I am instructed to. Elizabeth, if ever you have need of information, ask me and I will find out for you. No longer will I be King Louis' marionette, but for now he does not need to know that."

Elizabeth's mouth opened in surprise. Louise de Kérouaille had offered to act as her spy.

CHAPTER TWENTY-EIGHT

Judas

Titus sat in St Omer, brooding. Life at the Jesuit College proved comfortable. Despite this, he felt resentful. Along with the other senior boys, he'd been instructed to remain in the common room and wait to see the provincial, Father Whitbread, who was conducting his annual visit to the seminary.

Titus had just listened to yet another boy announcing he'd been approved by Father Whitbread for the Society of Jesus. He glared at the boy and seethed – he held no hope of being recommended. Lying back in his chair, he clasped his hands behind his head and chanted the boy's name over and over. "Smith. . . Smith. . . SMITH!"

Receiving no response, Titus called out, "The Stuarts are stained with bastards and tyranny." He tried again to force a response. "The death of York's son, Charles, caused me no more concern than if it had been one of his dogs."

When this also failed, Titus ruminated over being refused admission into the Society of Jesus. Soon after arriving, he'd pestered the Fathers for entry into the Society. To demonstrate the strict nature of the training, they arranged for him to visit the Jesuit novitiate at Watten. The Rector of Watten took an instant dislike to him and told him so.

There had also been a meeting of Jesuits, on the twenty-fourth of April in London. This rankled with Titus. He'd hounded the Fathers for more information, and the more they refused to give it, the more intrigued he became. Hmm, what had they discussed?

When his turn came to see the provincial, Titus stood in front of Father Whitbread and felt an instant dislike for him, which he thought to be mutual. He bowed his chin onto his chest.

After listening to the damning report Father Whitbread presented, Titus held his hands together, as if in prayer. "I beg your forgiveness. I had a poor upbringing. They're poor religious men who would cast out a sinner who's trying to repent and change."

Father Whitbread scraped back his chair and stood. "I was educated at St Omer and have worked in the priesthood for more than thirty years since. In all these years, I never met anyone who held so little religion in their heart or soul as you do. I don't know why you asked to come here. It's evident it wasn't for academic or religious study. Neither do I know why you persist in seeking admission to the Society of Jesus. You've had six months to prove your worth, and failed to do so." Father Whitbread shook his head. "You must leave first thing tomorrow."

The next morning, dressed in the lay clothes he'd arrived in, Titus prepared for his return to London. Before leaving, he approached Father Whitbread and roared, "You'll suffer for expelling me. I'll be revenged for this insult."

Boys and Fathers rushed over to find out the cause of the commotion.

"If I cannot be a Jesuit, I'll be a blaady Judas! You should think twice before offending *me*!" Titus screamed at Father Whitbread and stormed out.

At St Omer, he'd received regular meals and been given comfortable living quarters. He'd also enjoyed a certain status as a scholar. Now, he would return to his former existence of near starvation and paltry handouts. He couldn't allow this. From now on, everyone would call him Doctor Titus Oates. After all, he'd studied in Spain and received a Doctor of Divinity from the University of Salamanca.

Titus travelled by coach to Calais, from where he sailed to Dover. For the duration of the crossing, he kept to himself, seething with anger and resentment. Almost all his money had been spent on the boat fare, and he would have to walk part of the way from Dover.

He arrived back in London, tired, hungry and bedraggled. Though his time at St Omer had come to nothing, he'd gained a better understanding of Jesuit activities. He remained curious about the meeting that had taken place in London in April.

Tonge seemed pleased to see him and secured a cheap room for him in Cockpit Alley, close to his own lodgings in Sir Richard Barker's home. Throughout July, Titus met Tonge every day in The Flying Horse, in Westminster. In this tavern, Titus whispered to him the information he'd gleaned at St Omer and the Jesuit College, at Watten. He also told him about the Doctor of Divinity he'd received from the University of Salamanca.

While Titus talked, Tonge supplied him with food and ale and urged him for more details.

With an air of secrecy, Titus leant closer and whispered, "I've learned many of the inner secrets of the Jesuits. I heard about a secret gathering of them here in London in April."

Tonge flushed with excitement. "These are the details missing from my own theories. Now I have evidence to support my claim a plot is afoot to establish a Catholic supremacy. I was right all along."

Titus recalled his dismissal from St Omer. "You were indeed. The Provincial of St Omer, Father Thomas Whitbread, is a key figure in this

Catholic plot to return England to Rome." Titus also recalled the priest he'd met at Queen Catherine's residence, who had looked down on him as he handed him three shillings in alms. "Father Fenwick, from Somerset House, is involved in this plot with Father Whitbread, as are many others." Titus named the priests and Jesuits he'd met at Matthew Medbourne's club in Fullers Rent. He also named Father Berry, who'd recommended him for the Jesuit seminaries.

"Part of their plot was to kill you," Titus whispered. Watching Tonge grow delirious with a mixture of fear and excitement, he fed him more details. "I heard Father Whitbread say you had to be murdered, as you knew too much."

Tonge's eyes filled with fear. "Accusations have already been sent to Parliament naming Colombière, of the Sacred Heart, one of Mary Beatrice's priests."

Titus hadn't heard about this, and his heart quickened. He was onto something huge, and turned his full attention to what Tonge said.

"While you were at St. Omer, two Protestants accused Colombière in Parliament, of spreading the Catholic religion and of having a close connection with Edward Coleman. He had told Protestants that York openly, and the King secretly, were Catholics, and soon all England would be Catholic again. Colombière was arrested and banished to France."

"Edward Coleman you say? Mary Beatrice's secretary?"

Tonge glanced around and lowered his voice. "Yes. Before that, he was York's secretary. They're all Papists. Do you see how they're plotting together? What should we do? We must make this known. But how? It's so big. I fear retaliation. I don't trust the papist dogs not to kill us if we divulge their plotting. They're the Devil's spawn. There will be more of them, and we need to establish who they are before we act. We cannot risk speaking out only for them to silence us by murdering us as we sleep. We must remain cautious, and disclose this valuable intelligence to no one until we know who we can trust."

"We need a plan," Titus said.

After much discussion, Titus agreed to write everything down. A string of accusations soon emerged, around a Papal Plot to kill and overthrow the King and replace him with his Catholic successor, James of York. Names, dates and places formed together into a narrative account of how this would be achieved.

More names were added, as Titus formed the parts into a whole that proved shocking in its disclosures. The plot centred around a meeting of Jesuits, held in April at the White Horse Tavern in the Strand, to decide how to kill the King. At this meeting, the King was referred to as a bastard and an excommunicated heretic, whose death was necessary to the Catholic cause. On the order of Pope Innocent XI, the King was to be shot in St. James's Park. Irish ruffians had been hired for this purpose. If they failed, a Jesuit would stab him. If this also failed, Queen Catherine's physician, Doctor Wakeman, would poison him. A large cash reward would be paid by French and Spanish Jesuits, to whoever killed the King. Thereafter, Protestants would be massacred, and York placed on the throne, under Jesuit control.

After many rewrites a great plot emerged, containing the names of ninety-nine people. It included all those who would hold office under the new Jesuit Government. Titus named Edward Coleman. He also named five Catholic Lords he'd met or heard about at Arundel House; Arundell, Stafford, Belasyse, Petrie and Powis.

The range of the allegations became enormous, and Titus' excitement grew in proportion. He titled his manuscript – 'True and Exact Narrative of the Horrid Plot and Conspiracy of the Popish Party against the life of His Sacred Majesty the Government and the Protestant Religion'. It filled all of sixty eight pages.

When he had finished, Titus organised his narrative into forty-three clauses. After copying everything out, he concluded it was time for his 'Popish Plot' to be presented to the King.

CHAPTER TWENTY-NINE

Informing the King

Remembering the humiliating outcome of his allegations against young William Parker, the schoolmaster in Hastings, Titus feared pushing his narrative forward. He thought it best to remain in the background until he'd gauged the King's response.

"You must be the one to bring the plot to the King's attention," he said to Tonge.

"I could do that, but my pamphlets aren't very popular. Few, if any, sell. Our narrative might even be dismissed as another of my tracts against Catholics. It would be better if my name's not connected with the writing of it."

This suited Titus. Having written the narrative, he didn't want anyone else taking the credit for it. "I could be its secret author."

"Yes, that would work, but we need someone to bring it to the King's attention." After considering a few unsuitable candidates, Tonge suggested an acquaintance of his, Christopher Kirkby. "The King knows Kirkby by sight. He sometimes works for the Lord Treasurer, Danby, and holds a position in the Royal Laboratory."

Titus beamed. He thought Kirkby an ideal person to take the news to the King of a plot against his life and agreed Tonge should call on him.

Early the next morning, Titus called on Tonge at Richard Barker's house. Bathed in sweat, from fear and the oppressive heat enveloping him, Titus had a copy of the narrative tucked under his coat. While Tonge kept watch, Titus pulled back a loose piece of wainscoting and dropped the copy behind it, making sure a section remained visible.

Later, Tonge would pretend to find it, in Richard Barker's presence.

As he made his way out of Whitehall Palace, to take his usual morning promenade around St James's Park, Charles strode ahead of his courtiers. He was setting off early in the morning for Windsor, and would let Danby sort out the funding mess. Parliament had withheld his funds again. Unable to persuade them to release his revenues, he'd prorogued Parliament. So incensed had he been, he'd walked out without making his closing speech.

Storming past Shaftesbury, he'd heard him mutter, "Popery and slavery go hand in hand." Shaftesbury was causing him no end of trouble. The distance between them had grown so great it was like looking at a stranger.

Pushing all thoughts of Shaftesbury and Parliament aside, Charles anticipated the pleasures of hunting and fishing at Windsor. He might even play some pall-mall. He looked forward to seeing the improvements he'd commissioned at Windsor; the fresco paintings by Verrio and the wood carvings by Gibbons.

Coming out the outer gallery, a man stepped in front of Charles, and he startled. He recognised the man's face but couldn't recall how he knew him.

"Your Majesty, it's most urgent I speak with you," the man whispered. "Your life is in the greatest danger, and you must take care."

Charles experienced more surprise from the man's sudden appearance than from any sense of pending danger from his words. He gave the man a puzzled look, and as he did so, he recognised him. "Kirkby. God Bless you. But how is my life in danger?"

"Well . . ." Kirkby licked his lips and glanced around. "It might be by being shot, but I need privacy to tell you more."

Anxious to continue his walk, Charles ordered Kirkby to walk with him and indicated to his courtiers to remain behind them. "Pray explain the reasons for your concern."

As they walked, Kirkby told Charles about the plot to shoot him in the Park, and how Doctor Israel Tonge had stumbled upon the plans for this. "I have all the details. Two men, Pickering and Grove, are watching for an opportunity to shoot you. If they fail, you're to be poisoned."

"How do you know all this?" Charles asked. He'd heard so many false plots against his life he'd already dismissed this as yet another.

"Your Majesty, I received the intelligence from a friend, Doctor Tonge, who will appear with papers whenever the King commands."

"Bring Doctor Tonge, to see me this evening," Charles ordered. He didn't have time for this nonsense but supposed he could give fifteen minutes over to it.

Later that evening, Charles had Kirkby and Tonge brought to the Red room. He regretted agreeing to meet them. What a strange story Kirkby had told. God's truth, he had more pressing concerns.

When Tonge and Kirkby entered and bowed, Charles thought them an odd pair. Tonge carried a document and presented it to him.

Charles scanned the pages. "Where did you get this?"

Tonge bowed again. "Your Majesty, It was behind some wainscoting at my lodgings. I don't know who wrote it, but suspect it's someone living amongst Jesuits."

Charles stared at the strange figure of Tonge, and then at the papers in his hand. "Jesuits take vows of poverty and live to help others. They aim to educate. Their tools are books and quills, not . . . guns. I find it very strange Jesuits should wish *me* dead, or start any kind of battle to return England to a Catholic state."

None of the articles made sense to Charles, and he didn't want to waste any more time on it. "I'm bound for Windsor in the morning and need to retire. Make an appointment with my Lord Treasurer, Danby. I will keep this manuscript," Charles said and made ready to leave.

"Your Majesty," Tonge said. "I implore you to keep these papers safe, or the lives of those who discovered this plot will be placed in danger. Only your trusted cabinet should see its contents."

"That won't be necessary," Charles replied. He had no intention of attending to this. He would leave for Windsor as planned, and aimed to enjoy himself. "Call on Danby tomorrow," he said and turned and left the room.

♛

Two days later, Danby yawned and rubbed his eyes. After questioning Tonge once again about the details of the plot against the King's life, he'd set off at once for Windsor. He had barely slept – Shaftesbury was trying to oust him from his position as Royal Treasurer. The minute Danby read the manuscript, he'd realised it provided him with the ideal means to distract Parliament's attention from himself.

On entering Charles' privy chamber, Danby bowed. "Your Majesty, I urge you to order a warrant to apprehend Pickering and Grove, and have this whole affair brought before the Privy Council."

"Odd's fish, I can't have the Privy Council's time taken up by this nonsense," Charles replied. "You forget my brother sits on the Privy Council. I'll *not* have him concerned by this. On the contrary, I *forbid* you to mention anything about it."

"But, Your Majesty... your life's in danger... and perhaps that of your brother." Danby felt confused.

Charles waved away his concern. "I'll take care of myself until more is known. You can let me know of any developments." Charles laughed. "This whole business is absurd. Let us keep these events to ourselves."

Danby coughed and cleared his throat. Dear God, he needed this distraction. "But, Your Majesty, a plot has been made against your life."

"I have reason to doubt these stories," Charles said and frowned. "This morning I had a private meeting with the author. I thought him a strange and... yes, an odious man who asked not to be named. I found it hard to believe one word he said. Well, perhaps one, but certainly no more than that."

"Your Majesty. Your safety is paramount."

"Yes, but some of my most loyal and trusted servants have been accused . . . Powis, Arundell, Petrie, Stafford, and even Belasyse who is so incapacitated by gout he can barely stand. Odd's fish, these are people who serve me faithfully. Nay, none of these accusations make sense. Don't disclose anything about this to anyone. *And*, let this nonsense die a natural death."

Elizabeth walked arm in arm with Mary Beatrice through St James's Park. Though the air was filled with the sweet perfume of the last of the roses, she felt too distracted to appreciate it. Her nine-year-old daughter, Lucy, and Mary Beatrice's two-year-old daughter, Isabella, walked in front of them, holding hands. As they strolled along the gravel path, their satin gowns billowed in the breeze.

Isabella's nurse walked behind them with one of Mary Beatrice's ladies, Sarah Jennings.

"Milk! A can of cow's milk, sir? A can of milk, ladies?" called out a young girl standing alongside a tethered milking cow.

"Cow," Isabella called out and made to race over to it. Lucy pulled her back.

The thought of the refreshing milk made Elizabeth salivate, and she looked at Mary Beatrice. "Shall we?"

Mary Beatrice nodded. "Children, do you want milk?"

Isabella rushed towards her mother, and Mary Beatrice scooped her up in her arms and said, "Milk it is then,"

Laughing, Lucy hurried over to them. "Do you have money, Mama?"

Elizabeth dug into her skirt pocket and produced a small purse. Raising it up to Lucy, she smiled. "Warm milk the Lady Isabella wants and warm milk she shall have."

After buying a small can for everyone, Elizabeth ushered them over to some benches so they could sit and savour it.

"It tastes so much sweeter drawn fresh from the cow," Mary Beatrice said, as she sipped from the small metal cup.

Elizabeth nodded. "It's fashionable to drink fresh milk in the park. Does this mean we are now of the mode?"

Lucy giggled and pointed to a group of pelicans which had come into view.

After finishing the milk, they resumed their walk. Lucy continued to hold Isabella's hand and pointed some ducks out to her.

Elizabeth linked into Mary Beatrice's arm, and they strolled along in silence. Mary Beatrice had refused to acknowledge that Catherine Sedley, one of her ladies, had become her husband's mistress, and this suited Elizabeth. The alternative would be for Mary Beatrice to distress herself over it. Elizabeth linked tighter into her friend's arm.

Surprised to see Louise de Kérouaille rushing towards them, Elizabeth stopped. Louise's pale green cloak, billowed behind her, and she held her skirt as she hurried along the gravel path.

"Dear God in heaven." Louise gasped for breath. "I have to speak with you both. It's most urgent."

Seeing the concern on Louise's face, Elizabeth called to Isabella's nurse, "Take the children back to the nursery."

"Go with them," Mary Beatrice said to Sarah Jennings. "Elizabeth will escort me back."

When they'd left, Louise looked around and continued, keeping her voice low, "Please keep walking. I do not want to be overheard. It's why I waited until you were outside. I have come from Windsor, on the pretext of an appointment with my dressmaker. I would have come sooner, but couldn't get away."

"What is it? Has something happened?" Elizabeth felt alarmed by Louise's distressed state.

"Something and perhaps nothing, but it concerns you both," Louise said. "Charles has been told of a new plot against his life,"

Elizabeth's hand shot to her mouth and she felt Mary Beatrice' grip tighten on her arm. "When? What has happened?"

"Please listen, I don't have much time," Louise continued. "I do not know all the details, and Charles is regarding it as another false plot."

"And is it?" Elizabeth asked as they walked along.

"Like Charles, I think it is but . . . It is a Catholic plot intended to replace Charles with his Catholic heir, York," Louise said.

"Why now?" Mary Beatrice worried at her pearl necklace. "Why can we not be left in peace?"

Louise stopped walking and looked at them both. "Charles wants this contained, but Danby's nurturing this plot to distract Parliament's attention away from himself. I will find out what I can and tell you more when I return. For now, don't utter a word of this to anyone. As only Charles and Danby are party to this knowledge, you mustn't tell anyone or you will throw suspicion onto me. Do not betray me as your source, or I may be unable to help you further. Keep watchful."

Titus continued to loiter in the precincts of Queen Catherine's Residence, Somerset House, begging alms from Jesuits. Aware of his dismissal from St Omer, they refused to help him.

Titus exploded with rage. "You'll curse the day you turned me away."

When he returned to his lodgings, Titus added the Jesuit's names to the manuscript of the plot. The forty-five articles had grown to sixty-eight.

CHAPTER THIRTY

The Magistrate

Shaftesbury had pushed the members of the Country Party to seek out new recruits and had admitted anyone arriving with an introduction. Along with Monmouth and Buckingham, he used drinking to draw them in. To accommodate their growing number, they moved their meetings to the Swan Tavern in King Street.

The Swan Tavern belonged to Sir Edmund Berry Godfrey, the magistrate who'd prosecuted Henrietta de Kérouaille's husband, the Earl of Pembroke, for murdering a man in a drunken attack. Godfrey's brother, Michael, sat on the bench beside Shaftesbury.

Despite the large number in attendance, Shaftesbury felt unsettled. He still couldn't shake his conviction that Charles intended to rule the country through a standing army. As long as the Restoration Parliament remained, this was likely – few if any of the members spoke out against Charles, particularly the Catholic Lords.

Shaftesbury's frustration mounted. "The war is no more, so why hasn't Charles disbanded the army?" he asked the large table of members.

"Parliament voted a sum to disband the expeditionary force, but Charles used the money to maintain it instead," Buckingham said.

"And when I raised for the Commons to support us, Charles closed Parliament, and the army remained in place *and* intact," Shaftesbury said.

"Has anyone heard rumour of a new Catholic plot?" Buckingham asked. "It has a very tight lid on it, but I've heard a whisper. It's nigh impossible to get any details about it."

"Tell us more," a member said and shifted forward in his seat.

"I've heard no word of this," Shaftesbury said. "What have you been told?"

Buckingham frowned. "Nothing, but Danby was forever going back and forth to Windsor to see Charles. Curious as to his purpose, I slipped one of Danby's servants a few shillings to find out what he could about his business there."

"And?" Shaftesbury urged. He'd heard nothing about this. Was Danby drawing closer to Charles?

"The servant found some papers lying on the desk in Danby's study. He managed to read the top sheet –"

"And," Shaftesbury said again, a lack of patience showing in his voice.

"God's truth, Buckingham, what did it say?" a member said.

"Pish! If you would stop interrupting me, I will tell you." Buckingham sat back and laced his fingers behind his head. "The man couldn't remember much. But, from what he could recall, it said, 'A plot afoot by Papists to kill the King and all Protestants'."

Shaftesbury gasped. "Why has the Privy Council not been informed?"

"Did the man read it correctly? Can he read at all?" Godfrey's brother, Michael, asked.

Buckingham laughed. "Of course he can. Though a servant, the man can read as well as any of us. I assure you of that."

"We need to find out more, and bring this to the attention of the Privy Council," Shaftesbury said. Damn Danby for keeping this from them. Was this another indication of Charles's intention to rule without interference? Well, he for one wouldn't allow it. "Does anyone have friends who socialise with Danby?" He frowned at their silence. "Come on, think!"

"My wife calls on Danby's wife, but I can't involve her in this," one of the new recruits said.

Shaftesbury stood and banged a hand on the table. "Dear God, man, sort out your priorities. Get your wife to find out what she can. We need all the information we can gather. Anyone else?"

Sir Edmund Berry Godfrey stared into the mirror in the small changing room attached to his office beside the Parliamentary offices at Whitehall. He looked and felt better than he had in a long time.

After seven years as a magistrate, he'd earned a reputation for pursuing justice. Colleagues hailed him for his courage in prosecuting the Earl of Pembroke; when no one else would. His knighthood had been awarded for bravery during the Great Fire, yet he didn't feel worthy of such recognition and reward. He didn't feel at all brave.

At fifty-six he remained unmarried and burdened by melancholia and deafness. A few months earlier his spirits had been so badly shaken he'd not even wanted to rise from bed. His physician dispatched him to the South of France, where he'd remained four months.

Two weeks ago, he'd returned to London. Though he felt better, his face remained set in a sad expression. The broad forehead, hooked nose and jutting chin looked carved from cold, hard stone. A dark periwig did these features no favours. He wiped his mouth with a handkerchief, and the overly tall, stooped figure did the same. He continued to stare at his image and was saddened to see how old he'd become.

Turning away, he removed his new gold-rimmed hat and hung it on a hook on the wall. Taking off a fashionable French coat, he shook it and placed it on the hook beside his hat. He straightened his lace cravat and pulled on his robe. As he walked into the office, his eyes, as usual, remained fixed on the ground.

At exactly nine am, he unlocked and opened the door. Three men entered and started talking all at once. They introduced themselves as Doctor Titus Oates, Doctor Israel Tonge and Mr Christopher Kirkby.

After much hard effort, partly from his poor hearing but mainly from their incessant chatter, Godfrey ascertained that they wanted him to act as a witness to the veracity, sworn under oath, of various pieces of information Doctor Oates had written.

Stunned by their secretive manner and brash way of talking, Godfrey decided to refuse. "I apologise, but I cannot do this unless I read the content of what I am swearing to."

The three men shook their heads, then huddled together whispering. After a few minutes, they turned their attention back to him.

"No Sir," Tonge replied. "His Majesty has a copy, and the contents are not to be disclosed to anyone. It contains intelligence of treason."

Realising the King had already seen the content of the paper, Godfrey hesitated. If the King was involved, he had no choice. "Very well I'll take your deposition, but you have to give me the details of what I am swearing to."

When the three men huddled together again, Godfrey thought them an odd bunch. After a few minutes, Titus Oates nodded and handed him a document. "This is a summary of the narrative. We cannot let you have the original."

After the men had left, Godfrey wiped his mouth. The insufferable drooling never stopped, and seemed to be getting worse. After a slight hesitation, he untied the ribbon from the document and sat down.

It didn't take him long to realise he was reading a fabrication. He didn't doubt there were some truths within these pages, but his trained eye picked up a lack of detail such as he would never countenance in his own proceedings. He found some of the content preposterous and recognised the whole thing as an extended and elaborate version of the anti-Catholic pamphlets littering the streets. But, his friend, Edward Coleman, was implicated in planning to assassinate the King, and he grew alarmed. He asked his secretary to go post haste to Whitehall and tell Edward Coleman he must speak with him.

That evening, Godfrey ushered Coleman through to his parlour. Anxious for his friend's safety, Godfrey related to him the details of the narrative of the plot to kill the King. He refrained from mentioning anyone else who'd been named.

As they warmed themselves before the fire, Coleman admitted he *had* written to La Chaise, the French King's Confessor, but assured Godfrey his intention had been innocent. "There's also a major flaw within the narrative," Coleman continued. "A pivotal point of this plot is a Jesuit congregation held on April the twenty-fourth, at the White Horse Tavern in the Strand. This is a lie."

"What do you mean? How can you be so certain? Speak up."

Coleman hesitated, and Godfrey urged him to continue. "Because no Jesuits met there. They did, however, meet on that very same day at St.

James's Palace."

Godfrey startled. "Did you say the residence of the Duke of York? Jesuits met there?"

"Yes." Coleman nodded. "To choose who would take their annual report abroad."

Godfrey rose from the chair and walked over and looked out the window. Dear God, what mess had he got himself into? Turning around, he walked back and sat down. "Oates is sworn and is perjured, but we can never expose him."

Coleman sighed and leant closer. "No, we cannot. Unfortunately, the truth of the matter is far worse than the lies written and sworn by Titus Oates. If the truth leaked out the discredit it will bring to Oates, would be nothing compared to the gains for the Country Party who aim to discredit York, and have him removed from the succession."

"York received Jesuits in his home? It's against the law for Jesuits to gather in London. In enabling Jesuits to meet, York has committed an act of treason."

"Exactly, and this would be used by Shaftesbury to bring about his downfall... if not his death. It could also bring down the King. In the outcry that followed, many would say he had been aware of it. Apart from York, and the Jesuits who attended the meeting, we're the only ones who know of this, and God help us we need to keep it this way."

Godfrey nodded and wiped his mouth. "Meantime you *must* remove *all* communication you have had with Jesuits, Catholic priests, and all letters to and from France. I urge you, as a friend and magistrate with knowledge of these matters, do this as soon as you return home."

CHAPTER THIRTY-ONE

The Privy Council

Titus sat with Tonge in the Flying Horse Inn, in Westminster, extending and copying out the manuscript of their Popish Plot. Kirkby rushed in and made straight to their table.

"Make haste, the Privy Council has called for you to appear before them," he informed Tonge, between ragged breaths.

Titus bundled his papers into his bag, grabbed his hat and hurried out of the Inn behind Tonge, making towards Westminster Halls. Holding down his ill-fitting wig, Kirkby raced along behind them. By the time they arrived, however, the Privy Council had already finished, and they were asked to return in the morning.

Out of breath and panting, a strange sense of relief flooded through Titus. He'd been unsure of the Council's intentions. What if they took his document as their own and dismissed him? "I think we should safeguard the plot manuscript," he said to Tonge and Kirkby. "We should hand the original over to the magistrate."

Tonge and Kirkby agreed, and they made their way back to Godfrey's office. Handing over the original of the 'narrative' to Godfrey, for safe keeping, Titus said, "We're appearing before the Privy Council tomorrow."

The following day Titus and Tonge made their first appearance before the Privy Council. Titus had dressed in the light campaign coat with the ribbons on it, which he'd been given before he left for Valladolid, and his Spanish high-heeled shoes.

Titus trembled as he knelt before the Council. On being told to stand, he handed over an abstract of the plot, which included a list of the plotters' names and places of residence.

"Who is this person Doctor Titus Oates, to you?" a member of the Council asked Tonge.

"He's an acquaintance of short standing," Tonge said.

"What do you know of this plot to kill the King?" another member asked Titus.

"I beg you my lords, don't make me recite the long details again. I've placed before you an abstract," Titus replied.

Along with Tonge, he was asked to leave while they read through the document. As he headed out, Titus bristled. A member had tittered. Titus stopped and looked back into the room. Danby shook his head, picked up the document and began reading it aloud for the benefit of the others.

The next morning Titus was called on his own before the Privy Council, and examined again on the details of the plot. The members listened to his long account and made little comment as he spoke.

After two hours, Danby spoke to Titus on behalf of the exhausted and concerned Council members. "You will be provided with a bodyguard, a band of soldiers and the authorisation to arrest and seize the papers of Edward Coleman and all the Jesuits mentioned here."

Dressed in a new Parsons gown, with white bands that glowed in the light of the lanterns carried by his men, Titus tramped the streets late that night with his cane held aloft. He wore a new light coloured periwig and felt full of his own self-importance. He'd set out with a bodyguard, warrants for arrests and armed men to do his bidding.

Puffed up to his full height, and with his chin pressed against his chest, he limped along shouting orders. "This way I said! Move 'yaar selves! When I say move I mean now!"

At one am, they entered Wilde Street, the Residence of the Spanish Ambassador. By the light of the lanterns, the soldiers battered on the door until a servant opened it. Dressed only in his night attire, and with a blanket wrapped around his shoulders, the servant stared at them.

"Stand aside. I have warrants from the King!" Titus roared. Barging past the servant, he entered the Spanish Embassy. Hurrying up a large staircase, he bellowed at his men to follow.

The armed men banged open every door as they passed and searched each room. Coming to the one in which Father Edward Mico lay, Titus snorted with delight. Rushing over, he attempted to drag the fevered man from his bed.

"Far Gaads sake, help me!" he roared to the soldiers, and they rushed over to assist him.

Father Mico struggled pitifully against them, and one of the soldiers struck him in the stomach with the butt of his gun. They hauled the moaning, delirious man from his bed and dragged him along as they continued their search.

Titus soon found the main person he'd been looking for. Although the man looked paler and older than when he'd last seen him, Titus recognised the body lying in the bed surrounded by foreigners, as that of the Provincial of St Omer, Father Whitbread. Titus smiled as he shook the warrant in his hand and ordered the men to remove him.

As he tried to resist their attempt to drag him from his bed, Father

Whitbread whimpered and waved his thin bruised arms. A soldier stepped forward and struck him. Father Whitbread moaned in agony and collapsed back onto the bed.

The Spanish Ambassador rushed forward. "Show some mercy. I beg you. These Fathers are ill and have received the last sacraments. They have foreign immunity. Dear God, leave them be."

"I have warrants for their arrest," Titus said and turned his back on the Ambassador.

Despite their best efforts to remove him, however, Father Whitbread proved too ill to be moved, and Titus placed him under house arrest until he could have him taken to the Tower.

"Father Whitbread cannot leave the Embassy. Under pain of death to him and anyone who assists him," he said.

Elated by the success of the raid on the Embassy, Titus continued his search. Now a man of importance and power, he had the means to bring in Jesuits of his choosing and intended to use this to his advantage. From the Spanish Embassy, he and his buoyed up band of men, headed towards 66 Lincoln's Inn Fields.

♛

The banging at the door startled Elizabeth from her bed. It was after two am, and although the noise had woken her from a deep sleep, she'd been instantly awake and heading towards the source of the disturbance. Pulling a robe around her, she raced down the stairs.

Powis hurried behind. "Go back upstairs Elizabeth. I'll see to this."

Recalling the priest hunters searching her home, she shook her head. "Please Powis, let us deal with this together. If it's priest hunters again, I need to learn how to handle such matters."

When Powis opened the door, a band of men pushed past him. A large figure stopped in front of him, brandishing a warrant for the arrest of their friend, Father William Morgan. Despite protestations by Powis that Father Morgan wasn't in London, the men searched the house looking for him.

Whiles the men rampaged through their home, the children huddled together with her and Powis. Elizabeth hushed Winifred and Lucy, who pushed their faces into her and sobbed. William and Anne stood beside their father, their faces filled with fear.

Elizabeth recognised the large man in the Parson's gown, but couldn't remember where she had seen him before. She watched in stupefied silence, as the men pulled up rugs, tore tapestries and paintings from the walls, scattered books to the floor, broke down the walls behind cupboards and lifted random floorboards. As she looked on in stunned silence, Powis shielded her with his arms.

Once they were satisfied Father Morgan wasn't there the band left, announcing their intention to arrest Father Harcourt instead.

While the raiders had carried out their search, two faithful servants had slipped out the house and raised the alarm that would spread through the Catholic community.

♛

Titus grew impatient. Despite a vigorous search of his known abode, he'd been unable to find Father Harcourt. He suspected the priest had gone into hiding. It was now four o'clock in the morning, and rain bounced off the cobbles. Frustrated at not finding the key people on his list, Titus sought out and arrested those he could find.

Before dawn broke, Father Ireland of the Society of Jesus, Father

Fenwick from Queen Catherine's residence, and many other Jesuits made their way to Newgate prison. Titus watched from his carriage, as his armed soldiers marched the shackled men along in the downpour.

While Titus carried out his search, Danby, accompanied by the King's men, set out to arrest Edward Coleman. Danby had pushed for Coleman's papers to be brought before the Privy Council and decided to supervise the search himself. He'd heard gossip York had warned Edward Coleman about his correspondence. Of all the accusations Titus Oates made, this seemed the most promising line of enquiry. If there was evidence of plotting against the King to be had, then Danby suspected it could be found amongst Coleman's papers.

"I have a warrant for the arrest of Mr Edward Coleman, and for the search and seizure of his papers," Danby informed Mrs Coleman when she opened the door to him.

"My husband's abroad. I don't expect him back anytime soon," she replied and made to close the door.

Danby pushed it open. "Step aside. I have a warrant to search this house."

Wiping rain from his face, Danby set the search in motion. He ordered his men to start in Coleman's study. A large volume of letters found stuffed into drawers and left lying around were placed beside those lying on top of the desk. Danby scanned the room, making sure they had left nowhere unchecked.

When a soldier put his arm up the chimney and pulled out a nailed down deal box from a hidden recess, Danby shuddered. "Bring that over here."

The soldier laid the box in front of Danby, and at his urging, levered it open. Danby raked through the contents, pulling out letters and scanning them. It contained Coleman's private correspondence and some letters to and from Queen Catherine. Danby reeled at the content in a letter written by Coleman to la Chaise, the French King's confessor, suggesting King Louis should send him money to use in the French and Catholic interest to bribe members of Parliament. This letter alone would persuade the Privy Council of the truth of Titus Oates' claim that a Catholic plot was afoot.

Danby handed the letter to Mrs Coleman. "Read this, and be clear about the nature of the letters found by us."

Mrs Coleman sobbed as another letter found in the deal box was read out. She looked on aghast, as the soldiers ransacked her home.

Finally satisfied all Coleman's correspondence had been recovered, Danby had the papers bundled together and carted off to be read by the Privy Council. Wanting to leave Mrs Coleman in no doubt that the Council would spend as long as it took to search through these papers, he said, "Each letter, each document, each scrap of paper will be scrutinised for evidence of high treason."

The next morning, Titus wandered along the Strand and listened in on the talk in the coffee houses and taverns. As word of the arrests spread, public concern grew. Everywhere Titus went, conversations were entirely taken up with news of his Popish Plot, and he grew delirious with excitement.

CHAPTER THIRTY-TWO

Questions

Elizabeth sat in the withdrawing room at 66 Lincoln's Inn Fields, with Powis and Castlemaine. She was concerned that the accusations against Powis still hadn't been thrown out by the Privy Council. Along with four other Catholic Lords, he'd been named as complicit in a plot to kill the King. When Danby had first informed Powis of this, Elizabeth's fury had known no bounds. Now, it was as if it was happening to someone else. She couldn't comprehend it.

Earlier today, she'd spent over an hour trying to reassure her son, William, that the charges against his father and the other Lords were an invention made up to stir trouble against Catholics. Rumours about a new Papal plot were rife around London, and it was inevitable he would hear about this. William had also heard talk of the Duke of York's conversion to Rome. Elizabeth had struggled to answer his questions.

She trusted Castlemaine with her life, and he now tried to answer her questions about the King's response to the supposed plot.

"Charles remains doubtful about Titus Oates's claims, but can't be seen to stifle this," Castlemaine said.

"No," Powis agreed. "Of course, Charles has to be seen to examine the matter. Only then can he make the truth known."

Elizabeth frowned. "Meanwhile, for the fourth night, Titus Oates has been sent on his rounds, armed with warrants for the arrest of those he has falsely accused." She drew in a deep breath. "I don't like it. That he invaded our home . . ." She sobbed and wiped her tears away with her hand. "Why's this happening to us?"

Powis rubbed his hands over his face. "I don't know. I wonder the same myself."

"It all seems too convenient." Anger coursed through Elizabeth. "Who is Titus Oates? Why has he appeared now? Why is he telling these lies?"

"No one knows much about him," Castlemaine replied. "We need to think this through. Though I'm not suggesting you have any involvement in this Powis, do you believe there could be any truth to the matter? The letters found in Coleman's house do establish some credibility to Oates' account of a Catholic plot."

Guilt flooded through Elizabeth. She wondered the same. Had Coleman become involved in a French plot to re-establish the Catholic faith in England? Powis had warned him on more than one occasion to leave matters be. She recalled the letters Mary Beatrice had found amongst her correspondence. Had Coleman inadvertently become involved with French plotters? She pushed the thought from her mind.

"Edward Coleman is loyal to the Stuarts," Powis replied. "His intention was to raise funds for the King and York. He sought only to ensure their independence from Parliament –"

"It is too much of a coincidence that this has arisen now," Elizabeth said, interrupting him. "First, York converts and marries a Catholic. Then Buckingham leaks the King's secret treaty with Catholic France. This is followed by the Luzancy allegation, which reignited the old fear and distrust of Catholics. And now . . . a Catholic plot against the King's life.

228

No, this is a deliberate attack against Catholics, and we need to determine who's behind it."

"It is not Titus Oates," Castlemaine said. "He's someone's agent, for sure, but whose?"

Powis nodded. "Do you think the Bishops have fabricated this plot to stir hatred against Catholics? They would have to respond to the rumours of York's conversion. They'll not take the risk of surviving under a Catholic King. Coleman had been Secretary to both York and Mary Beatrice. He's an obvious target."

"As all the Catholic Lords are," Castlemaine added. "Perhaps the Bishops are attempting to remove all Catholics from Parliament. Or . . . dear God, from any position of power."

"Aided by Shaftesbury?" Elizabeth said. "He's behind Buckingham leaking the King's treaty with France. He's behind all of this. Of that, I now have no doubt."

Powis startled at the strength of her conviction. "What you say makes sense. But how can we fight the Bishops *and* the Country Party?"

"We can't," Castlemaine said and sighed. "Charles said he wanted the whole matter speedily resolved, but, Danby delayed."

"Anything which distracts Parliament's attention from him," Powis said.

Elizabeth didn't know what to do. Castlemaine looked her in the eye. "Instead, Danby's nurturing Titus Oates' accusations."

Elizabeth felt as if her breath had left her body and she gasped. For the first time, she realised the enormity of the accusations. "Powis, you have to leave London. We should return to Wales," Elizabeth said and went over and, kneeling in front of him, grasped his hands.

"No Elizabeth," Powis said. "I won't be driven out of London by lies.

If I leave now it may be taken as proof of my guilt. I would be thought a coward. I can't run from this."

"Powis' word should be enough against that lying knave," Castlemaine added.

Elizabeth gripped her husband's hands tighter. That these allegations were false was not an issue. Powis had become a pawn in a much bigger game.

♛

Edward Coleman was thrust into a cell in Newgate Prison. The dark, stone room held nothing of comfort – a pallet bed, a thin blanket and a single candle. He paced the small space. Having been away from home, he'd returned to the news that his papers had been seized and a warrant issued for his arrest. As there was only Titus Oates' word against his own, it was insufficient for the charges to stand. Seeing no point in delaying the inevitable, he offered himself up to the Secretary of State.

Two hours earlier, he'd stood before the Privy Council, informing them of his innocence and that Titus Oates had failed to point him out as the person he'd witnessed plotting with Jesuits. This came as no surprise to Coleman – he'd never met Titus Oates. But his relief had been short lived. When his letters were read out, the Council members had been so shocked at their content they signed a warrant for his immediate removal to Newgate.

So sure had he been of his innocence, he'd failed to protect himself. He'd also failed to listen to advice to destroy all his papers. But he'd only done what York had asked him to do. Though it might be difficult, York would find a way to make this known.

For now, his papers were being examined in detail by the Privy

Council. He sat down on the bed and held his hands against his face. Dear God, what had he written?

CHAPTER THIRTY-THREE

In Too Deep

Edmund Berry Godfrey hadn't slept. He hadn't even made an effort to go to bed. When his maid, Eliza, and then his manservant, Moor, padded downstairs the next morning he called out to them, "I need your help, now! God's truth I'm going to be the first martyr made in this Hellish Plot."

First, he addressed Eliza, "Gather all my papers. Bring them all. Hurry, there's no time to waste."

When the maid rushed off to do his bidding, he turned to Moor. "Get that fire blazing, and then leave me be."

Waiting in his parlor for Eliza to return, Godfrey paced the room. His brother, Michael, had turned traitor, and could no longer be trusted. Yesterday, Michael had informed Godfrey that Shaftesbury had offered a large sum of money for the original manuscript of the Plot. The brazen cur had then approached Danby asking him to up Shaftesbury's price. Now here he was, stuck in the middle, sure each one of them would see him dead over the matter.

Eliza hurried in, holding her apron out with both hands. It overflowed with his personal papers.

As she headed off to get more, Godfrey sat close to the fire and threw each sheet into the flames. He then burned his pocketbook, containing the names and addresses of all his friends and business associates.

When Moor knocked and entered, Godfrey startled.

Moor handed him a note. "A messenger called and left you this."

Godfrey read the note and threw it in the fire. "Wait," he called out, to Moor's retreating back. "Bring me my coat. I have to go out."

When Moor returned and put his new French coat on him, Godfrey shrugged it off. "No. Not this one. Get me another. It's best I am not too well dressed today. And . . . bring my sword."

Fifteen minutes later, Godfrey wiped his mouth with his handkerchief and looked along the length of the Strand. Once he was certain no one had followed him, he lifted his cane, put his head down and turned out of Green Street.

The sky was overcast. As it was October, and early on a Sunday morning, the Strand remained free of its usual street vendors, shoppers and promenaders.

Thoughts swirled around in Godfrey's head, making it difficult to concentrate. He should have spoken to the King straight away. Why hadn't he checked then that Charles knew about the plot on his life? What if he hadn't known about it?

Godfrey faced a huge dilemma. He'd been told about a plot on the King's life and hadn't informed him of it. That was treason. If he passed on the narrative of the Popish Plot to him now would he be charged with trying to conceal it? Would he be accused of being one of the plotters, if it came to light he'd known about this all along and hadn't informed anyone?

Last night, he'd sent the original narrative of the Popish Plot to Chief Justice Scroggs to pass to the Privy Council. But was this enough to protect him? York had told him the Popish Plot would have died a death if he hadn't fanned the flames. He cursed himself for taking Oates' deposition.

Godfrey willed himself to focus. He was in this much deeper than he wanted to be. He also held information that could destroy the Duke of York and possibly the King. He was one of only a small number of people who knew York had secretly allowed Jesuits to meet in his home. By law, Godfrey should also pass this information on, but to do so would be catastrophic for both the King and James of York.

What day was it now? Yes, Sunday. He had to remain focused.

Thursday remained cold and overcast. At two o'clock, a young working man made his way to the Whitehouse Inn, with his friend. They were both tired and anticipating the ale and food they would order. Like many others, they'd set rabbit traps around the area, and they kept a look out for any trapped ones they could sell. The rain fell in a steady drizzle, and the men quickened their pace, their eyes scanning for rabbits.

As they walked across the fields at the foot of Primrose Hill, the young man stopped and looked at his friend, puzzled. At the edge of a ditch lay a walking stick, a scabbard, a belt and a pair of gloves. Bending down, he pushed aside the brambles and staggered back horrified. Lying head down in the ditch was the body of a dead man, a periwig and hat beside him.

When his friend made to touch the corpse, the man grasped his arm. "Leave it be. Let the Constable see to it."

"But look at the gold rings on his fingers," his friend said. "I thought he 'ad been killed 'an robbed, but nothing seems to 'ave been taken. Any thief would 'ave took these rings."

"Any lowlife murderer would 'ave as well. This is very strange," the young man agreed.

On Saturday morning, Elizabeth awoke to headlines in the London Gazette that struck terror into her heart; '*Sir Edmund Berry Godfrey's Murder Revealed*'.

Sitting with Powis at the breakfast table, she spread the Gazette out between them. Powis moved his chair beside her, so they could read it together. Godfrey had been missing for four days and rumour had been rife as to his whereabouts. When his body had been discovered in a field at the foot of Primrose Hill, like many others they had believed he'd committed suicide. Godfrey's melancholy nature had been well known.

"What? Godfrey has been murdered? No, I cannot believe this." Scanning the page, the content sent Elizabeth further into panic. "Tell me what it means Powis, for I cannot take it in."

Powis lifted the Gazette and finished reading the report. "They traced Godfrey's movements to five days before his body was found, the day he went missing. He was seen in the Strand that day. There's also evidence the ditch where he was found had been empty two days before. Godfrey's neck had purple creases, suggesting a cloth had been tied tightly around it. Most striking of all was the absence of blood where the sword had been plunged into his body."

This puzzled Elizabeth. If Godfrey had been stabbed his clothes would have been saturated with blood.

Powis continued. "It seems Godfrey was strangled, and a sword thrust into his body sometime after his death."

Elizabeth stood up and wrung her hands together. Godfrey had been murdered and his body taken to Primrose Hill. "If Godfrey had been strangled, why was a sword plunged into his body?"

"None of it makes sense," Powis agreed. "Had Godfrey committed suicide, and been stabbed to make it look like murder?"

"Perhaps, it was widely known he was melancholic. But it doesn't explain where his body lay for four days, or why?"

♛

With Mary Beatrice in Holland, visiting her step-daughter, Mary, Elizabeth called on Mrs Cellier. She desperately wanted to talk to the midwife about Godfrey's murder.

Sitting before a roaring fire, they took turns reading out snippets from the latest broadsheets.

"Ha! Israel Tonge has formed Edmund Berry Godfrey's name into an anagram." Mrs Cellier snorted. "Dy'd by Rome's reveng'd fury."

Elizabeth gasped. "And look here," she said and stabbed her finger onto the page. "Titus Oates claims Catholics murdered Godfrey to steal the original of the narrative he'd lodged with the magistrate. Oh, Mrs Cellier, what shall we do? Powis has been named in this plot." Along with many others, Elizabeth had ridiculed Titus Oates' claims as nonsense. And, believing Edward Coleman had been caught and thwarted in his plans, people's interest had started to wane.

Mrs Cellier stopped reading. "Godfrey's murder is being taken as proof a Papal Plot exists, and Titus Oates is being hailed for bringing this to light. They're calling him 'The Saviour of the Nation'."

"Dear God!" Elizabeth exclaimed and gripped Mrs Cellier's arm. "Powis. What about Powis? His life's in danger."

Over the coming days, Elizabeth watched in a daze as events unfolded. She couldn't turn around, but a new piece of information was brought to her. It was as if nothing else mattered. Titus Oates' Popish Plot had become the focus of everyone's conversation.

"Titus Oates has been moved into Whitehall Palace and given an allowance and a bodyguard," Castlemaine informed her.

Mrs Cellier retold the gossip she heard in Newgate and on the streets. "A servant named Dugdale, who was being dismissed for embezzlement, claimed his employer was involved in the Popish Plot. His employer was arrested."

It was as if a fever had gripped the country. Freedom of speech had all but disappeared. To question the truth of the Popish Plot became dangerous, and speaking out on behalf of the accused was tantamount to admitting involvement. Anyone who did was brought in for questioning. Elizabeth no longer knew who to trust and, apart from family and close friends, kept her own council on the matter.

She spent hours on her knees praying for Powis' safety. Each night before retiring, she thanked God Powis had not been arrested.

Whether she remained at home or ventured out, she was reminded of the Popish Plot. Protestants carried Godfrey daggers, with the words, 'Remember the murder of Edmund Berry Godfrey' on one side and 'Remember religion' on the other. These daggers were sold by street vendors, to help Protestants protect themselves from Papist attack. Fashionable ladies carried them hidden in specially added pockets and slept with them under their pillows. Shaftesbury's wife had a miniature pistol made for her muff and set a trend amongst the ladies of the Protestant nobility.

Under Shaftesbury's lead, the Country Party promoted the idea that Godfrey had been killed by Papists, and he took Titus Oates into his personal care.

Brooches with Godfrey's Portrait were sold, ballads composed, sermons preached, commemorative medals struck, and pamphlets printed. But there was still no details forthcoming about the accusations made against Powis, or the other Catholic Lords. For Elizabeth, the wait was insufferable, and she constantly took to her bed with headaches, feeling as if her head was gripped in a vice.

As the public fever reached its peak, Godfrey's body was carried through London in State, and the open coffin placed in the street. Elizabeth and Powis joined the long procession queuing to gaze at the body of the dead magistrate. Elizabeth walked away from the corpse feeling cold terror in her heart and burning fear in her bones.

Posters, offering a reward of five hundred pounds, to anyone whose evidence led to the apprehension and conviction of Godfrey's murderers lined Elizabeth's route home to Lincoln's Inn Fields.

Parliament opened the next day. Filled with uncertainty about how the other Lords now viewed him, Powis took his place beside them.

The King didn't mention the plot against his life in his opening speech, and Powis relaxed.

As Danby argued for funding for a standing army, Shaftesbury stood and asked leave to speak. "Not one person has mentioned a word about the plot on His Majesty's life," he said and glanced around. "Neither army nor money, will protect the King from the knife of a murderer. Could Edward Coleman, so inconsiderable a person, be the chief agent in such a great plan? It's now days since the Magistrate was found dead. Were a spaniel lost, an inquiry would be made in the Gazette. Yet a worthy gentleman has been murdered, and no search is underway for his murderer. The Privy Council is overwhelmed with work. Dozens of witnesses have been examined, without getting any closer to finding out who murdered Godfrey, or why. Let Parliament proceed with greater vigour."

Powis looked on bemused as Parliament took on the task. He winced but remained silent when Shaftesbury proposed a Bill to disable Catholics from sitting in Parliament, and again when an address was made to remove all active Catholics from within ten miles of London. A Committee of Secrecy was appointed by the House of Commons, and a similar one set up by the Lords – to investigate the Popish Plot and Godfrey's murder.

All other Parliamentary business ground to a halt, and the Catholic Lords were excluded from sitting on any committee.

Powis didn't know what to do.

On the last day of October, bells rang throughout London, as Godfrey's body was brought for burial at St. Martin's in the Fields. Seventy clergymen walked before the black-draped coffin, and over a thousand dignitaries followed behind. When the procession reached the church, Elizabeth and Powis joined the other members of the Catholic nobility.

Godfrey's friend, Dr Lloyd, preached the sermon, based on a verse from the Bible –'Did Abner as a Fool Dieth?'

"Did Abner die like an inexperienced fool, who did not know how to defend himself? No, he fell victim to a wicked, deceitful plot. He was slain in a city of refuge, and the residence of the King. And the King lamented over him and said, did Abner as a fool dieth?

"And they buried him, and the King wept at his grave, and all the people wept with him. As a man falls before wicked men, *so* you have fallen. And all the people wept again. And the King said unto his servants, 'there is a prince and a great man fallen this day. The Lord shall reward the doer of evil according to his wickedness.'"

After extolling Godfrey's achievements, Dr Lloyd launched into a damning tirade against Catholics. To protect Dr Lloyd from any attempt by Catholics to kill him, a strong divine stood on either side of the pulpit.

Elizabeth and Powis sought out and gripped each other's hand.

There was no respite for Elizabeth. The hysteria continued. Anyone suspected of being a practising Catholic had their house searched and driven out of London.

When Louise de Kérouaille informed Elizabeth that Titus Oates had been praised in Parliament and been granted an annual income, she had listened in shock. It had become increasingly clear to her that the majority of members feared Titus Oates. Rumours even circulated that he was to marry a member of Shaftsbury's family.

Over the following days, Elizabeth watched in silent fury as the gentry, judges and jurors, who were fearful that Titus Oates would cite their names, fawned over him. And, she looked on bemused as large crowds turned out to greet him wherever he went.

CHAPTER THIRTY-FOUR

What Will I Tell the Children?

Danby pushed for a full enquiry into the Papal Plot against the King's life. The sheer volume of names to be investigated overwhelmed him, and he was anxious to get started. He'd delayed long enough. If Charles hadn't stopped him making this business known when he first heard about it, he could have had this seen to already. Now the work stretching out before him seemed like a monumental task. At least it had turned Parliament's attention away from him, and for that he was thankful.

The Council proceeded by approving the arrest of the five Catholic Lords, on a charge of treason. They were to be removed to the Tower, to await trial.

Danby accompanied the Officers of the King's Guard, as they made their way to make the arrests.

The first Catholic Lord to be removed to the Tower was fifty-two-year-old Baron Petre. He begged Danby, "Leave me be. I'm not guilty of conspiring with anyone." Baron Petre would remain in the Tower until his trial. Danby would let the jury decide if he was guilty, or not.

Sixty-four-year-old, Baron Belasyse was blighted by ill-health, riddled with gout and unable to walk any distance. Danby arranged for a coach to take him to the Tower.

Stafford was removed to the gatehouse of the Tower. As a Viscount, he would have rooms there.

The oldest Catholic Lord, seventy-year-old Baron Arundell, was arrested for conspiring with the other impeached Lords. It was common knowledge he hadn't spoken to Stafford in years. It was not up to Danby to judge whether or not they had been in secret communication. That's what the Old Bailey was for. He would not let emotion or reason get in the way of the task at hand.

There was still one Lord, who'd been named by Titus Oates, and Danby called for his immediate removal to the Tower. He would supervise the arrest himself.

Powis stood in the corridor of the House of Lords with his cousin, Castlemaine, listening to the heated conversations around the impeachment of the four Catholic Lords. Tears came to his eyes when he heard that his good friend, Stafford, who'd raised the toast for his own Earldom, had been arrested. "I cannot believe this is happening," Powis said to Castlemaine.

"Stafford's home is being searched, and all his papers are to be brought in for examination," Castlemaine said.

Danby, accompanied by four Officers of the Guards, entered the corridor and walked towards them. A deep sense of foreboding flooded through Powis. This feeling was confirmed when two guards moved alongside him, and each grasped one of his arms. The third guard positioned himself behind Powis. All conversation in the corridor stopped.

The fourth guard stood in front of him. "William Herbert, Earl of Powis, you are to be removed to the Tower to await trial for treason for involvement in a Papal plot against the King."

What about Elizabeth and the children? Were they safe? Powis turned and called out to Castlemaine. "Tell Elizabeth what has happened. Pray, do not let her come to any harm. I beg you."

An hour later, Powis bent forward and wiped tears from Elizabeth's eyes. They'd been given a few moments, outside the Tower, in which to say goodbye. Powis had no idea when he would see Elizabeth again. He was to be held in the gatehouse. He wondered where the other Lords were being held. No one would tell him.

"What will I tell the children?" Elizabeth asked between sobs.

Powis was overcome with a need to reassure her. She needed to focus on looking after herself and the children. He was certain Charles would sort things out as soon as he learned of their impeachment. "Tell them this nonsense will soon be sorted," he replied, stroking her hair. "Charles doesn't believe in this plot, but must be seen to investigate it, or *he* will be accused of Papism."

"But why you, Powis? Charles trusts you with his life. He must know you're innocent."

Powis tilted her face towards his own and looked deep into her eyes. "The public are baying for blood. Charles cannot risk another civil war. He's merely riding the storm, as we must."

"Yes, a storm in which his subjects may die," Elizabeth whispered as she held her husband close.

Two days after the arrest of the five Catholic Lords, Titus ambled along beside Shaftesbury, on his way to a meeting of the Country Party in the

Swan Tavern in King Street. As Titus passed through the tavern, men tipped their hats to him. He saw people pointing, and heard them referring to him as, 'The Saviour of the Nation'. He shook in ecstatic delight.

Shaftesbury ushered Titus over to a crowded table and introduced him to the King's son, Monmouth. On sitting down, Titus lifted a jug and poured himself a glass of cider. This should have been his life all along. Accustomed to drinking watered-down ale, he savoured the fruity flavour of the drink. Why had he been forced to beg for his living? Tonge had deliberately placed him in dingy lodgings. He, who people referred to as 'The Saviour of the Nation', had been made to feel like a common street beggar.

A comment from Shaftesbury caught his attention. "Let Danby shout all he likes about this Papal Plot. I'll shout louder and put myself at the head of it. Wouldn't it be a fine stroke of luck if we could implicate York? Perhaps we could start by implicating him in Godfrey's murder. Samuel Atkins, Pepys clerk, was arrested last night, for being concerned in the murder. If Atkins were to implicate Pepys, then the Duke of York, under whom he works at the Admiralty Office, would prove an easy target. But, for the law to stand, we need another witness to validate Titus' accusations against Atkins."

Titus leant forward and smacked his lips together. "I know of another witness."

The next day, Captain William Bedloe, Titus' handsome letter-carrying acquaintance from Arundel House, who'd visited him at Valladolid in Spain, came forward as a second witness to Godfrey's murder. Bedloe had been released from Newgate prison, so he could testify all he knew. He submitted a written deposition.

Testimony submitted by William Bedloe; 6th of November.

Two Jesuits, Walsh and Le Fevre, offered me money to help them kill a man. When I arrived at Queen Catherine's residence, Somerset House, Le Fevre told me the man was already dead. I was shown the body. I saw four men there; Walsh, Samuel Pepys' clerk, Atkins, a man of Lord Belasyse's employ, and an attendant from the Queen's Chapel. By the light from a lantern, I recognised the dead man as Sir Edmund Berry Godfrey. His corpse was to be left at Primrose Hill. I promised to assist but left.

The next day Le Fevre told me how the murder had been committed. They threatened Godfrey with death unless he handed over the deposition of the Popish Plot. Le Fevre wanted to make a new one, contradicting the original, in order to exonerate the plotters and make the informers out to be liars.

Titus sat in the House of Commons, seething with anger. He was the author of the 'Narrative', not blaady Tonge. Tonge was addressing the House as if he had discovered this Papal conspiracy. Titus lifted his cane, tapped it against his nose and stood.

Thumping a fist against his chest, he asked leave to speak. "I, Doctor Titus Oates, accuse Queen Catherine of plotting with her physician, Doctor Wakeman, to poison the King."

Faces turned and stared at him in stunned silence. No one uttered a sound as they waited for the King's response. The deathly silence continued. Shaftesbury had discussed Wakeman's involvement in the conspiracy with Titus and had urged him to hold back on suggesting Queen Catherine knew about this. Why had he spoken out now? Worse, why had he accused her of high treason? Shaftesbury would surely disown him.

Eyes latched onto the King. Titus shuffled in his seat. Perhaps all was not lost. This was the King's chance to be rid of a barren Queen.

Titus watched in horror as a livid flush spread up Charles' face, and his dark eyes blazed. Titus gazed around then dropped his chin to his chest. Beads of perspiration formed on his forehead. Dear God, what had he done? Unable to resist looking, his eyes strayed towards the King.

Charles fixed him with a cold stare. "And how do you know this? Pray, tell me."

Titus froze. Rooted to the spot, he avoided the King's gaze. He'd spoken too soon and needed time to think. His intention had been to draw attention away from Tonge. Titus replied with the only thing that came to mind. "Your Majesty . . . your life is in danger."

Charles stood. "So you keep saying. Now! Tell me *how* my life is in danger from my own Queen?"

Sweat coursed down Titus' face, and he wiped it away with his sleeve. He had to think before replying. Wakeman was the Queen's physician. Titus had written in his Narrative that if Pickering and Grove failed to shoot Charles, the physician would poison him. He had his answer. "Your Majesty, yesterday afternoon, someone overheard Wakeman, plotting with the Queen to poison you . . . Your Majesty."

"Ah! And where did this conversation take place?" Charles asked. "And . . . when?"

Titus hesitated. Queen Catherine resided at Somerset House. He licked his dry lips. "Your Majesty, it was at Somerset House . . . in the grounds there. Yes, it was in the garden. At just after two o'clock. They were both heard plotting together." He visualised it.

Charles spun on his heels and pointed to a guard. "Have this lying knave arrested. Queen Catherine spent the afternoon at Whitehall. God's truth, I saw her there myself."

Titus paled, and his body shook, he slumped against the seat. What had he said wrong? "I may have been given the wrong day."

All hell broke loose, as members argued for Titus' release. The guards hesitated. Titus let his breath out. The Lords believed him.

Charles waved a hand for the guards to continue. Titus was dragged from his seat and brought before the King. A guard gripped each of his arms, and another stood behind him. Looking around for a means of escape, Titus sagged forward. There was no way out.

Charles held up his hand. Silence ensued, and all eyes again fixed on the King.

Titus' breath came in short bursts, and he gasped for air. It was as if he were choking.

"Very well," Charles said, breaking the silence. "This goes against my better judgement. I won't have you arrested. I will, however, have you watched night and day. Apart from attending as a witness, you are confined to your apartments at Whitehall."

Charles addressed the guards. "Have all Oates' papers seized and given to the Privy Council. Dismiss all his servants and restrict access to his rooms. Don't afford this liar any means of collaborating further about this fanciful allegation against *my* Queen."

Titus let out a loud gasp. Charles ignored him and stormed out.

After a heated debate, the members of the Commons voted for the Queen and her retinue's removal from Court. The Lords rejected this, and Shaftesbury entered a formal protest at their decision.

Two guards marched Titus to his apartments. He couldn't fathom what had happened.

The following morning, two guards collected him and brought him before the King's Bench. The Lord Chief Justice, Sir William Scroggs, members of the Privy Council and a number of other Judges were in attendance. Titus baulked when he saw them. Were they going to charge him? Would he be thrown into Newgate? He wasn't certain. For the moment he seemed safe, Scroggs was asking Tonge questions about the plotters.

Tonge testified, "Catholics caused the Great Fire, and I have evidence of plans for another such fire."

Titus scoffed at his words. Tonge was ranting, again. All his old conspiracies were tumbling out of him. He wasn't saying anything new. "Protestants are to be massacred as they sleep," Titus mimicked under his breath. He'd heard it all before. Realisation dawned on him. They were preparing for the trials of the accused.

When Tonge finished, Titus stood and asked leave to speak. When this was granted, he beamed over at Scroggs. To outdo Tonge, he said. "My Lord Chief Justice, it's my opinion that in attempting to remove the Protestant religion through French assistance, William Herbert, the Earl of Powis, committed high treason." He waited to see how Scroggs reacted.

Turning to the other Judges, Scroggs asked, "Does it, or does it not, constitute high treason if attempts are made to remove our established religion through the assistance of foreign powers?"

After debating the issue for a few minutes, the Judges agreed that it was indeed an act of high treason.

"I would have reached the same conclusion myself," Chief Justice Scroggs said and nodded. "Have the Earl of Powis moved from the gatehouse to the Tower. Once there, place him in solitary confinement and allow him no visitors."

Reluctant to leave matters there, Titus raked his memory for something else to say. He recalled that the actor, Matthew Medbourne, was a Catholic. Medbourne had introduced Titus to a club, frequented by Jesuits. He dismissed Medbourne's kindness as a ploy to entrap him. Why, Matthew Medbourne had even secured a position for him as Chaplin to Arundel House, a Catholic home. He flushed as he recalled Matthew Medbourne correcting *him* on aspects of the Bible. "My Lord Chief Justice, may I have leave to speak again?"

Titus shook with pleasure when permission was granted. "On a number of occasions I overheard Matthew Medbourne, the playwright and actor, conspiring with Jesuits to turn people towards Rome through membership of a club held in Fuller's Rent. Why, he even tried to persuade me. He's involved in this Papal conspiracy."

Scroggs nodded. "No matter how famous Matthew Medbourne is, we cannot condone such behaviour." Scroggs addressed the court. "Have Matthew Medbourne arrested and committed to Newgate. Place him in solitary confinement and have him clad in irons.

CHAPTER THIRTY-FIVE

Hell Hath No Fury

Elizabeth couldn't rouse herself sufficiently to get out of bed. The mere thought had her burying back under the covers. Why was this happening to her again? It was as if she had been thrust back into childhood, her father in the Tower. All her lonely years came tumbling back in a wave of self-pity. With no mother to turn to, she'd experienced her father's absence as a sense of acute loss, sending her into a spiral of despair and anxiety. Now Powis had been taken in the same way . . . on a charge of high treason. Dear God, the penalty if he was found guilty was execution. As a Lord, he wouldn't be hung and quartered but, at this moment, this provided little consolation to her.

"Dear God in Heaven help me, for I cannot bear the pain." Why was God refusing to hear her call? Powis had been moved from the gatehouse into the Tower. Now, he was allowed no visitors. How would she know how he was faring? How would he prepare for his trial? No, it was all wrong. A feeling of helplessness overwhelmed her. There was nothing she could do to help him.

Castlemaine had been the one to bring her the news of Powis' removal to the Tower. "On the word of that liar, Titus Oates," she reminded herself. Her feeling of fury towards this man held no bounds. "And Shaftesbury?" she uttered out loud. Why was he encouraging such lies against his fellow Lords? She couldn't fathom such disloyalty.

Then, as she'd stood by unable to stop them, guards had searched her home and removed Powis' letters and papers. With all her heart she believed Powis innocent. Goodness did not always bring just rewards. She'd learned that as a child. Over the years she'd lost sight of this, cocooned in the world of her family. . . The family she loved beyond all reason. She would do anything to secure Powis' release. She too could move from goodness. The thought gladdened her heart. It brought no guilt. If she could free Powis through foul means, then so be it. She would do it.

Once more she tried to rouse herself from her bed, without success. Four days she'd lain here. Her children needed her. She had to get up. She had to help Powis. With that thought, she laid her head back onto the pillow and drifted off to sleep.

Later that afternoon her maid knocked and entered. Beth informed her Mary Beatrice had called and was waiting for Elizabeth in the withdrawing room.

Rousing herself from slumber, Elizabeth opened her eyes and sat up. When had Mary Beatrice returned from abroad? This placed her in a dilemma. She'd instructed her staff that apart from Castlemaine and Mrs Cellier, she didn't want to see anyone. Mary Beatrice never called on her. It was always the other way round. She couldn't refuse to see Mary Beatrice.

Stepping out of bed, she winced as she caught her reflection in the mirror. She hardly recognised the pale and bedraggled figure who glanced back at her. "Pass me my robe and show the Duchess of York into my small sitting room. Dear God, I cannot see her like this for I need to bathe and change. What am I to do?" Covering her face with both hands, she burst into tears.

An arm slipped around Elizabeth and pulled her close, the scent of bergamot and lavender filled her senses. Startled, she looked up into Mary Beatrice's face. Elizabeth made to speak, but instead, let out a series of racking sobs. It was as if the heavens had opened releasing a long overdue gale of lashing rain. Clinging on to Mary Beatrice, Elizabeth's suppressed fury tumbled from her.

When Elizabeth stopped crying, Mary Beatrice said, "I am sorry to come to your room unannounced, but I was concerned for you. I returned to news of Powis' arrest and removal to the Tower and did not know what to do. When you did not come to see me, I –"

"God's truth, Mary Beatrice, my own dear children couldn't rouse me from that bed." Elizabeth gave a snort of laughter. "I've prayed for three days for God to help me. Now I'm out of it, and it's all thanks to you."

Elizabeth looked at her bed and had no desire to retreat back into it. "Thank you, Mary Beatrice. Thank you, my dear friend."

CHAPTER THIRTY-SIX

The Bell Tolls

The first Plot trial started three days later. Inside the Old Bailey, Elizabeth took a seat beside Castlemaine and Mrs Cellier. Castlemaine would take notes and set a notebook, quill and inkpot onto a small knee desk. When the courtroom had filled to capacity, the doors were shut.

To protect the occupants from gaol fever, the Old Bailey had recently been rebuilt as a three-sided structure, with huge columns holding up the roof. The open wall led onto a courtyard, and today this was packed with people looking into the courtroom.

Gazing around, Elizabeth noted that Shaftesbury and many other members of the Country Party were present. At the sight of Titus Oates sitting in the witness section, Elizabeth's heart lurched. Bile rose to her throat, as she watched the man who'd falsely accused her husband and invaded her home. She shuddered and closed her eyes. *Lord in heaven, show mercy to the innocent people accused by this man.*

After the jury had taken their seats, Elizabeth's attention turned to the front. Three bewigged judges entered. Once they were seated, Chief Justice Scroggs asked for the prisoner to be brought in.

When Edward Coleman entered a loud roar erupted from the crowd, "Papist plotter!"

Coleman looked pale and unshaven. Without his periwig, his shaven head revealed dark tufts of thin hair. Elizabeth stifled a moan. Coleman's meddling to bring about religious freedom for Catholics had brought him here, but she could not believe he'd been plotting to kill the King. His innocence would surely be revealed.

The Clerk of the Court opened proceedings and read out the charges. "The prisoner stands indicted for no less than an intention and endeavour to murder the King, change the government of the nation, alter the Protestant religion and introduce Popery instead. How does the prisoner plead?"

Edward Coleman was appalled that a charge of high treason had been brought against him. He'd dedicated his life to the Stuarts and remained confident no evidence would be produced showing otherwise. He addressed his reply directly to Chief Justice Scroggs. "Not guilty. I deny all these charges, my Lord."

Titus Oates stood and licked his lips. "I overheard Edward Coleman expressing his agreement when told Jesuits were to kill the King. He attended the Jesuit consult held at the White Horse Tavern in the Strand on April twenty-fourth, '78, to plan the King's death, and distributed letters carrying instructions for the assassination."

When Titus Oates finished, Coleman asked leave to reply. "What nonsense you speak. Pray tell me how you observed me at this time in the Whitehouse Tavern when I wasn't even in London on that date?" Edmund Berry Godfrey had informed him no Jesuit conference had taken place in any tavern, so he felt on safe ground denying his presence there. Oates, however, persisted in stating he was, but provided no evidence to support this.

William Bedloe stood and presented his testimony. "I swear I carried treasonable letters between Edward Coleman and Jesuits in London and Paris. I also overheard him discussing treasonable consults he attended in Paris."

Coleman was called to answer Bedloe's accusations. "My Lord, I insist the court acknowledge that all these letters were written before'75. I ceased all correspondence after that time. I –"

Titus Oates stood. "That's a lie! I carried a treasonable letter from you to the Rector of St Omer, containing a sealed answer to Father La Chaise, giving thanks for the ten thousand pounds given to him for the propagation of the Catholic religion, and . . . to kill the King."

When letters, selected from Coleman's correspondence with Catholics, dated '75 or later, were read out by the court clerk, Coleman's belly lurched and he trembled. Dear God, these letters proved beyond doubt that his communication had continued after he had finished as York's secretary. But, how did Bedloe know this? The main evidence against him centred round letters to and from Throckmorton, Cardinal Howard and la Chaise in France. He couldn't fathom how Bedloe knew about them. He suspected Bedloe had known nothing before the search of his home and removal of his letters.

Coleman looked at Oates, and realisation dawned. He had informed Bedloe of their content. He gripped the edge of the dock. How could he prove this? He needed to explain his reasons for writing these letters. "I only ever tried to gain liberty for Catholics . . . Legally, through Parliament. I sought money for this reason. God's wounds, I'm not involved in *any* plot. Oates' testimony is false. How did he not . . . He failed to identify *me* as the person he saw carrying out these acts."

"When this man was brought before me," Titus Oates said, pointing to Edward Coleman, "The candles in the room were dim I couldn't swear positively to his identity. I couldn't see properly. But I can now, and I say it was him I saw."

"Then why didn't you charge me then, with all you're charging me with now?" Coleman asked.

Scroggs leant forward, "Doctor Oates, why is this? Why was Edward Coleman not charged at that time with attending the Jesuit consult and plotting to kill the King?"

Titus Oates looked away. "I was tired. I'd been up all night carrying out raids gathering in Catholic dogs. My eyes were tired. I –"

"Keep to the point! Answer the question," Scroggs demanded.

Coleman foresaw the Popish Plot crumbling around Titus Oates. "Why couldn't you identify me?"

Titus Oates tilted his chin. "The candles in the room were dim."

"Enough! We've already addressed the issue of the candles. I've no intention of going through all that again," Scroggs announced and started summarising the evidence for the jury. "It's my opinion the explanation given by Edward Coleman for his letters is feeble and cannot be entertained."

Coleman was aghast at these words. "But I'm innocent, my Lord."

"Your letters alone are sufficient to condemn you." Scroggs banged his gavel to end further discussion.

The jury huddled together for less than five minutes before returning their verdict – "Guilty of high treason."

Fearing he might collapse, Coleman gripped onto the dock. Never had he imagined this outcome. There had been no evidence presented to warrant convicting him of high treason. His letters had been his undoing.

He listened in shocked silence as sentence of death and confiscation of his property was pronounced. A silent scream started in his head. He would be drawn to Tyburn, hanged to unconsciousness, castrated, disembowelled, quartered, and beheaded.

On Monday the second of December, the eve of his execution, the prison chaplain attended Edward Coleman in Newgate. Supposedly concerned with bringing him spiritual comfort, Coleman knew the chaplain's main purpose was to get his last words to sell as a broadsheet after his execution. He remained silent.

As the church bells struck midnight, the bellman of the Holy Sepulchre emerged from the tunnel, connecting the church with the prison. Reaching Coleman's cell he stood outside, rang a hand bell and called out:

"All you that in the condemned hold do lie
Prepare for tomorrow you shall die

Coleman tried without success to block out the words.

And when St Sepulchre's bell tomorrow tolls
The Lord have mercy on your souls."

The bellman's words pierced Coleman's conscience. He wished he had spent more time with his wife. So engrossed had he been in working for York he'd neglected her. Even at this late stage he still believed York would obtain a pardon for him.

He could have shown Titus Oates as a liar and a perjurer, but his loyalty to York wouldn't allow him to utter one word of the information that would save his own life. The Jesuit gathering Oates claimed to have attended had been held at the Duke of York's residence, and *not* at the White Horse Tavern. York would know he had shielded him, and would seek a means of gaining his freedom. He clung to that belief and prayed.

Later that morning St. Sepulchre's bell rung out – announcing that an execution was to take place. Before the sun was up, and in the bitter cold, Edward Coleman was taken to the condemned room where his manacles were removed. He was escorted from the prison, placed in a cart and strapped onto his own coffin.

The prison chaplain blew into his hands and climbed onto the cart. When it drew away, Coleman murmured, "There's no faith in man." The pardon he'd expected from York hadn't arrived.

As he rolled along to certain death, Coleman cursed the man he'd faithfully served. When the procession reached the steps of St. Sepulchre, friends and family threw small posies onto the cart. Against the darkening sky, their faces appeared as a blur to Coleman.

The church bell sounded, and the clerk chanted:

"You that are condemned to die repent with lamentable tears,

and ask mercy of the Lord for the salvation of your soul."

When the cart passed, the clerk called out:

"All good people pray heartily unto God for this poor sinner

who is now going to his death, for whom the great bell tolls."

The long journey to Tyburn took over two hours. Crowds lined the route. As he rolled past on the cart, most cheered and shouted, others stared, and some threw stones.

The taverns overflowed. As it was a hanging day, people had been granted a *Tyburn Fair holiday*. As they passed a tavern, the guards were offered drinks to see them on their way. At least a thousand people now followed Coleman on his last journey to Tyburn.

As he clattered along on his way to the gallows, Edward Coleman recalled the day he'd attended the hanging of the young woman, Anne Jurejon. She'd stood there in her green dress, red cloak and the black hat with a red feather on it, declaring her innocence and hoping for a reprieve. He'd dismissed her as a common thief, and guilt overwhelmed him.

When he arrived at the gallows, the King's Commission was read out, and the crowd were asked to move back from the scaffold.

Titus watched from a prime position as Ketch, the hangman, stripped Coleman of his shirt, bound his arms in front of him, drew a cap over his eyes and fixed the knot from the rope.

At five to nine the signal was given, and the cart shifted.

The crowd surged forward.

Coleman hung for a few minutes, with his feet still touching the cart. On the sheriff's orders, the cart was removed, leaving him suspended in mid-air.

The crowd roared and surged forward again, to check if he was still conscious. Coleman's entrails were removed and burnt, and his heart removed. The smell overpowered Titus, and he gagged.

At nine thirty, the body was cut down and laid on sawdust. The head was severed, and the body chopped into four pieces. The quarters were removed from the gallows in a basket and parboiled. They would be put on display, as a reminder to others of the penalty for high treason.

The crowd fought to buy pieces of the hangman's rope and clambered for the broadsheets containing Coleman's crimes. Titus basked in the scene of his own creation and whetted his lips in anticipation of those who would follow.

CHAPTER THIRTY-SEVEN

The Pit

London remained in a state of frenzy, and the mob roared for Godfrey's murderers to be hanged. Queen Catherine's residence, Somerset House, became the main focus of attention. The three Catholics, Titus had accused of killing Godfrey, worked at the Chapel there. Robert Green was a cushion-man. Lawrence Hill was a servant, and Henry Berry, a porter.

Almost three months after Godfrey's death, Miles Prance, a Catholic silversmith occasionally employed by Queen Catherine, was also accused of his murder. Prance's lodger, who owed him arrears of rent informed the Privy Council he had been away from home for the four nights Godfrey had been missing.

Under examination, Prance denied murdering Godfrey or helping to remove his body. "I haven't been to the Queen's Chapel for over a month."

Despite protesting his innocence, Prance was lowered into the condemned hole in Newgate. He lay in the pitch dark, airless hole, manacled, freezing and dreading execution. As he shivered in the hole, a man called down to him, "Say you were involved in Godfrey's murder, and your life will be saved."

Prance wasn't sure if he'd imagined the voice. He was so cold he could barely focus and had been drifting in and out of consciousness. Had someone spoken? Had he dreamt it? A feeble scream sounded in his ears and grew in intensity. When the scream reached a crescendo, he couldn't bear it any longer. He clasped his hands over his ears and rocked his body back and forth. On each forward move the manacles on his ankles dug into his flesh, he welcomed the distraction.

On his second day in the freezing pit, he sent a message to the Lords, offering information in return for a pardon. Buckingham arrived to take his statement.

Prance looked up at Buckingham, who stared down at him. Shivering and hungry Prance pleaded, "Please, I beg of you have mercy. I'm frozen and near death. I've not eaten in two days. Help me!"

Buckingham's reply echoed around the pit. "You wish to confess?"

Prance pulled his hands over his head. He had no knowledge to impart about Godfrey's murder. He'd barely even followed the gossip surrounding it. He shouted up to Buckingham, "I'm involved in Godfrey's murder."

"Did you see Green, Hill and Berry, the servants from Somerset House murder Godfrey?" Buckingham called down.

"Yes. These men told me Godfrey was to be killed."

"And Lord Belasyse paid you all a reward to do this?"

"Yes! I agreed because of a grudge I held against Godfrey. We followed him . . . and held him until we could murder him."

When a rope ladder dropped into the pit, along with the key to his leg manacle, tears sprung to Prance's eyes. His hands were so cold he could barely feel the key, and struggled to turn it in the lock. When it finally opened, he limped over to the ladder and dragged himself up. On reaching the top, Buckingham placed a blanket around his shoulders and he relished its warmth. His stomach rumbled with fear and hunger. Buckingham walked from the room and indicated he should follow.

That evening lying in a cell, and covered with a blanket, guilt overwhelmed Prance. He'd eaten a bowl of warming broth and had swilled it down with ale. Though he remained cold, he was no longer freezing, and he gave thanks to God for that. Why had he accused three innocent men? Would God forgive him? Wracked by doubt and guilt, Prance slept fitfully and woke to his own screams.

A few days later he withdrew his confession and was placed back in the condemned hole. At various times throughout the day he became aware of someone up above.

A voice asked him, "Were the five Catholic Lords . . . Powis, Petre, Belasyse, Stafford and Arundell to command the new Papist army?"

Prance refused to answer. He heard the tapping of walking sticks as the man moved about but couldn't see anyone. He'd been loaded with irons and couldn't adjust his position to get a better look. It wasn't Buckingham's voice.

"Perhaps the rack will help you see the error of your ways? No? Then mayhap your wretched body could be stuffed inside a barrel of nails and rolled into the Thames?"

Tears coursed down Prance's face. "Please, I have a wife . . . children."

After a few days, his resolve broke. When Buckingham appeared at the top of the pit again, Prance reluctantly called up to him, "My original confession is true. I am one of the murderers. Please let me out. Throw down a ladder. Dear God help me. For God's sake, get me a pardon."

When he was removed from the condemned hole, Prance fell to his knees. "Everything I confessed is untrue. I'm innocent. I knew nothing of

Godfrey's murder."

In her apartment, Louise de Kérouaille sat on Charles' knee stroking his wrinkled face. "I would say not to fret Your Majesty, but these are dangerous times, and this is very worrying."

"I know darling Fubbs. I have to protect myself. Midnight will bring in a new year, but I am in no mood to celebrate. I'm inflamed Parliament dared pass their Act excluding Catholics from Parliament. Thanks be to God my brother is exempt."

"We can sit here until before twelve o'clock and join the revelries then. *Oui*? The tables are full tonight. Think how much I'm saving you by sitting here instead of losing my purse to the banker."

"Fubbs, you do my heart good, but since Danby's arrest, I cannot trust him to remain silent. What are your thoughts?"

"I suspect they're the same as yours, for I don't trust Danby not to save his own head." Since losing his position as a diplomat in France, Montagu had turned against her and Danby. "Montagu's vindictive. I fear his attack on my character will be believed. That he dares say I am a Catholic whore, converting *you* to Papist ways. It makes me fear for my life."

"Darling Fubbs you know I won't let anyone harm you. Montagu's words are just that – words."

Louise sneered. "That he should also turn on Danby. Why? Danby's done nothing."

"Ah Fubbs, it's not Danby Montagu is after, it is me. It's clear to everyone Danby's letters seeking funds from France were penned by him, but were dictated by *me*. No one's accusing me directly of receiving money from France, but... if Danby implicates me –"

"But . . . he's been accused of trying to conceal this plot on your life. If he speaks out now, it will be taken as proof of his intention to cause you harm."

"Perhaps, but I cannot risk him talking. I will prorogue Parliament to delay his trial and those of the Catholic Lords. I'll also call the Country Party leaders together and see if I can negotiate a way out of this damned mess."

Fubbs yawned and stretched out her arms. "Let us pray '79 is a better year for the King and for England."

Part Six: Counterplay

1679

'*True and false are attributes of speech, not of things.*'

Thomas Hobbes

CHAPTER THIRTY-EIGHT

A City of Madness

Sitting around a burning fire of logs, in Mary Beatrice's apartments at St James's Palace, Elizabeth chatted with Mary Beatrice and Mrs Cellier about the growing number of imprisoned Catholics.

They'd gathered together to sort clothes and blankets to distribute and struggled to cope with the overwhelming amount who were in desperate need of their help. The weather remained bitter and showed no sign of relenting. Frost lay so thick it remained day and night without thawing. Occasional flurries of snow alternated with falls of sleet-filled rain. Thin layers of ice coated the insides of the windows.

Elizabeth huddled closer to the fire. "I wish we could do more to help these poor souls." The mere thought of them triggered her concern for Powis' safety. She hadn't seen him for almost three months, and had heard no news of him or any of the other imprisoned Catholic Lords. Father Mico, arrested on the night of the raid on the Spanish Embassy, had died soon after being placed in Newgate. Like many others, he hadn't survived the harsh conditions. Elizabeth shivered and tried to blot out the image of Powis in a cold cell in the Tower.

"I know. *Che so*, hundreds imprisoned and many more turned out of their homes and barred from London." Mary Beatrice said and placed an old shirt she'd finished folding onto a pile of clothes at her side.

Elizabeth nodded her agreement. Every day brought news of further arrests or deaths of Jesuits and Catholic priests. "They're being hunted down like animals. It's too much to bear." Adding to her distress, Mary Beatrice had birthed a daughter in November. Elizabeth's namesake had died within a few hours of her birth.

"What more can we do?" Mrs Cellier said. "There must be some way of stopping this madness."

"Shaftesbury's using the nonsense spouted by the accusers of a Papal Plot to further the interests of the Country Party," Elizabeth said. "They now refer to themselves as the Green Ribbon Club. Pah! Have you seen the ribbons they wear in their hats?"

"There are so many. They're hard to miss. It is to provoke," Mary Beatrice replied.

Elizabeth picked up a loose bundle of socks and started folding them into pairs. "Shaftesbury won't stop until he gets what he wants. He aims to destroy Danby."

"Humph! And my husband," Mary Beatrice replied. "Shaftesbury wants him removed from the succession, and will do anything to achieve this. It is folly . . . A city filled with madness. No one knows where the finger will point next. Protestants live in fear of Catholic assassins. There's no real threat at all. Yet patrols march the streets and cannons have been placed outside my home. Why? On the word of liars, that is why. Not a day passes but new accusations are made against our friends and holy Fathers. Dear God . . . How these good men suffer while their false accusers live in luxury and are fawned over. *Si*, Mrs Cellier, I agree. There must be something we can do."

Tears welled in Elizabeth's eyes, and she brushed them away. "Anyone speaking out risks being charged with involvement, no one dare move against the accusers. Powis is still not allowed visitors. I cannot get news of him. My only small comfort is that if anything had happened to him, I would have been informed. Still, every day remains a torture."

Mrs Cellier patted Elizabeth's arm. "My dear, you are strong and a credit to us all. Tell me how the children are. It must be hard for them also."

Elizabeth paused before answering. At thirteen, her son was growing into a young man. "William tries to act as my protector, but… he's so young. When the mob attacked my home, I thought we would all surely die. When they gathered outside . . . and I saw their torches, I thought . . . I thought they would surely burn my house down."

Elizabeth recalled the horror she'd experienced that night, knowing her children were in the house. "Instead, they threw stones, breaking the front windows and yelling, "Papists! Papists!", until I granted admission to search my home. Lincoln's Inns Field is home to more Catholics than anywhere else. It's the main target now for the mob. I've been lucky, many of my neighbours have had their houses desecrated . . . Walls pulled down, and floors lifted, looking for priest holes. Unfortunately, they sometimes find them.

"On Powis' arrest, I did consider returning my eldest daughters to London, so they could be with me. But they're old enough to be held to account. I kept my youngest children close by me, but won't hesitate removing them to Wales if the need arises."

"Dear God, there is something we can do," Mrs Cellier said. "Do you remember my reading from Bridgefield, Elizabeth?"

Elizabeth looked blankly at her. "Bridgefield? You have had so many readings, I –"

"The one where he said someone would infiltrate the Catholic Church. I looked at it again yesterday. Not to say there's any truth in his prediction, but it set me thinking. What if someone did infiltrate our Church? What do we know of this man, Titus Oates?"

Dawning flooded Elizabeth. "Do you think it referred to him?"

Mary Beatrice looked flummoxed, and Mrs Cellier explained to her about Bridgefield's reading. "But my point isn't to look at the truth or no of this," Mrs Cellier continued, "But perhaps we should find out more about Titus Oates. Do you think Castlemaine would help?"

"I'm sure he would consider it. I'll ask him," Elizabeth said. "But what are you proposing?"

Mrs Cellier laid down the bundle of shirts she was sorting. "We need to find out everything we can about Titus Oates. Where is he from? Where did he study? Let's start there."

"Oates' Doctor of Divinity was from the University of Salamanca," Mary Beatrice said. "We could find out about his time there. Dear God, it is a Jesuit College."

Elizabeth thought of Powis. She needed to do this for him. "How should we go about this? We need a plan."

As snow swirled outside, Prance lay in Newgate, dirt-encrusted and hungry and near death. The day before, he'd been removed from the freezing pit, where he'd lain on a board, and placed into a bed in a cell and covered with blankets.

Prance groaned and opened his eyes. At the bottom of the bed sat his old friend, Mr Cooper.

". . . and so having sought me out, Shaftesbury asked me to spend the day with you," Cooper said, finishing his explanation of the reason for his visit.

Prance shivered. He was freezing. Cooper's face seemed out of focus. He desperately needed Cooper to help him. "I fear for my life. I've been wrongly accused. I'll never see my wife and children again . . . I'll hang. Shaftesbury has me terrified with his threats. Will I hang? I hear no news of events here. Did Green, Berry and Hill hang? I didn't mean to accuse them. I am also the Queen's servant."

Unable to stop himself, Prance ranted on. He wanted Cooper's help, but couldn't make him understand this. Finally, exhaustion overcame him, and he fell into a fitful sleep. Now and again he woke and cried out. "Guilty, guilty! Not guilty, not guilty! Murder! No murder!" Even in sleep he couldn't escape the horror of his situation.

That evening, after hearing Cooper's concerned report, Shaftesbury asked Dr Lloyd to accompany him to Newgate to examine Prance. When they arrived in the cell, Dr Lloyd made his way over to the bed and lifted one of Prance's closed eyelids. "This man is barely conscious. Unless he's provided with heat and nourishment, he will die. His health is failing."

Shaftesbury shivered and pulled his cloak tight around him. The cell was indeed icy cold, and the blankets covering Prance were both threadbare and inadequate for their purpose. To remove York from the succession, he needed this man's evidence to back up Titus' accusations.

Prance moaned and opened his eyes. He looked startled to see Shaftesbury standing over him. "I'm innocent. Please help me, I'm innocent."

As Shaftesbury turned to leave, Prance reached out a cold hand to stop him. "I beg you, don't leave me here. For the love of God, get me out. If you grant me a pardon, I'll tell you everything I know."

Shaftesbury nodded to Dr Lloyd. This was all he needed to hear. Shaftesbury helped Prance from the bed and wrapped a thin blanket around his shoulders. Prance shivered so violently his whole body shook. Shaftesbury gripped onto one of his arms and guided him through a stone passage, heading towards the main hall. Once there, he sat Prance down beside the warmth of a coal fire. Still shivering, Prance pulled his legs up and curled onto the bench.

Scraping a small bench over, Shaftesbury sat beside him. If Prance followed through on his statement, that he'd seen Green, Hill, and Berry murder Godfrey, then there would be sufficient witnesses to enable the trial to commence.

After a while, curled up in front of the warm fire with the blanket pulled tightly around him, Prance stopped shivering.

"Here, drink this. It will warm you further." Dr Lloyd placed a tankard of heated ale into Prance's hands.

As he sipped on the warm drink, Prance became more alert and started talking. "My original confession . . . that I was involved in Godfrey's murder along with Green, Hill, and Berry, the servants at Somerset House . . . this was true."

"And you'll swear to this in court?" Shaftesbury asked. The man had changed his mind so often. He wondered if he'd do it again. The best way to ensure Prance stuck with his story was to keep him close.

Prance looked at him. "Could you arrange for me to be moved to a warmer cell and have these leg irons removed?"

"Nay, but I can secure your immediate release from here,"

Shaftesbury replied.

Prance turned his eyes from the fire and stared at him.

"I'll arrange for your immediate release, provide you with food, clothes, money and an apartment at Whitehall Palace, beside Titus Oates and William Bedloe."

Prance nodded.

That evening, after dining with his growing band of accusers, Shaftesbury allowed himself a smile as he limped away from Whitehall Palace.

Charles' face flushed and his brow furrowed in a deep frown. Parliament had refused his request to grant a Royal pardon for Danby. He harboured mistrust of many members of Parliament, seeing them as Country Party sympathisers, and now determined to distance himself from their sphere of influence. He resented their attitude and would no longer confide in them. Instead, he would draw closer to those he *could* trust, and who respected his Royal position. From now on, he'd make it abundantly clear who *was* and who *was not*, in Royal favour.

Looking at Shaftesbury, whom he had invited along with other parliamentary leaders to negotiate a way forward, Charles' long fingers flipped the pages outlining their proposal for him to dissolve Parliament and call for new elections. "God's nails, I can't agree to this. I've told you this before, and nothing's changed." In truth, he was taken aback by the stark clarity of the argument contained in this document.

Shaftesbury glared at him. "This *will* happen. It's a question merely of when . . . and how. If this document is not presented to Parliament, many will suffer as a consequence."

"God's truth, even a coin has two sides. I granted a Royal pardon to Danby, yet you refused to acknowledge this." Charles sighed. "Why then should I do your bidding?" He tried to calm his rising temper. Shaftesbury was attacking everyone close to him. He saw it clearly now. They were trying to remove his supporters. They'd even attacked his Queen and his mistress, Louise.

Shaftesbury consulted with the other Lords around the table and then said, "If you call for new elections, we'll not proceed against Danby."

Charles blew out his cheeks and let out a loud exhalation. Damn them. He needed Parliament to sit to obtain the funds due to him. "And you'll pay the funds due to me, along with those already withheld?"

The Lords whispered together again, then Shaftesbury nodded and said, "If you announce the dissolution of the present Parliament, then yes, we'll pay all you are due."

After Shaftesbury and the others had left, Charles sent a summons for the French Ambassador, to speak with him in private. He would ask him to approach Louis to ask for his support again, this time against the Country Party. The Exchequer lay empty, and the royal accounts had plunged into a loss. It incensed Charles that vast amounts of money were being ploughed into feeding, clothing, entertaining and housing the accusers of the fabricated plot against his life. He wondered where it would all end.

Charles had agreed to Shaftesbury's demands. He would announce the dissolution of the Cavalier Parliament, which had sat for eighteen years. A great feeling of sadness coursed through him. But, for the time being at least, he himself, his Queen, Louise, York, Danby, Powis and the other Lords were safe from Parliament's interference. He wondered how much longer he would be in a position to sustain this.

CHAPTER THIRTY-NINE

A Dilemma

The mob milled outside the Old Bailey, baying for blood. Inside, Chief Justice Scroggs adjusted his robe and reached a decision that he would give them what they wanted. He now knew a not guilty verdict in the Plot trials was not an option. Not only did he know it, the common people knew it, and the jurors knew it. Truth be told, everyone was trying to save their own necks.

Scroggs was well aware of Titus Oates' flexible memory – he'd witnessed it often enough. But, any attempt by him to dispute Oates' testimonies led to uproar – Hissing, jeering and chants of 'Coleman's letters' invariably followed any of his interjections against the accusers and resulted in further protests, directed at him. No, he would not become their next target.

Swallowing a large mouthful of ale, Scroggs reached a decision. He would stop being impartial. He now wanted the guilty verdicts passed as speedily as possible. Every day the prisons took in more of the accused. No one was immune.

Three Catholic priests, Father Whitbread, Father Fenwick and Father Ireland, stood before him in the dock, along with Thomas Pickering and John Grove – the two men Oates claimed were to shoot the King. Apart from Father Whitbread, who'd been brought directly from the Spanish

Embassy, they were dirt-encrusted and dishevelled.

All five stood accused of involvement in a plot to kill the King and return England to a Catholic state. These were indeed grave charges, and Scroggs was aware the eyes of both Parliament and the public were fixed firmly on him.

Father Whitbread, from St Omer, had not recovered his full strength following an illness and stood shaking in the dock. Titus Oates had just stated that Father Whitbread had attended a Jesuit consult at the White Horse Tavern in April. Titus licked his lips and concluded, "Father Whitbread conveyed sealed commissions for a new Popish army."

Scroggs frowned. Titus had laboured over his accusations against Father Whitbread. Thanks be to God he'd finished at last.

Father John Fenwick, the London agent for St Omer, had been carried into the dock. So tightly had he been manacled, his foot needed to be amputated, and he grimaced from the pain.

Again, Titus Oates stood and presented his evidence. "I swear Father Fenwick witnessed Edward Coleman paying a guinea to the person who delivered the message stating the King would be killed. He also instigated a plan to raise rebellions in Scotland and Ireland."

Father Fenwick requested leave to speak. Annoyed at the interruption, Scroggs only nodded.

"I beg you to allow me to have a document sent over from St Omer," Father Fenwick said. "I can prove Titus Oates was there during the time he says he attended this consult in London."

Scroggs hadn't anticipated this turn of events and needed time to think. "Bring refreshments for Doctor Oates," he called out to a court clerk. "Doctor Oates, pray sit down and rest." He considered the best way to refuse Fenwick's request. When Oates had presented his evidence his statements had drawn 'oohs' and 'ahhs' from the crowd. 'Fenwick called the King a black bastard.' 'Whitbread said the King spent his days drinking and whoring,' Titus Oates had announced to murmurs of shocked protest. No, the crowd wouldn't tolerate him agreeing to such a request.

"I've considered your request, and cannot agree to it," Scroggs announced. "It's not admissible evidence to have such a letter sent from abroad."

While Titus devoured his refreshments, Scroggs called William Bedloe. Scroggs regarded Bedloe's fine dress and admired his lace cravat.

"All I know of the plot against His Majesty, I've already stated," Bedloe said, as he puffed on his pipe. "I stand firmly by it. I discovered all of this from carrying letters abroad between Jesuits and Lord Belasyse . . . and other Catholic nobles. Of the priests in the dock, I can speak about Father Ireland, but I only know the other two by sight."

The last statement left Scroggs in a dilemma. Although he had Oates' evidence against Whitbread and Fenwick, he needed two witnesses to secure a conviction for high treason. He should release the prisoners, but hesitated. "Have Whitbread and Fenwick retained in Newgate." He would address the issue another day.

He recalled Titus Oates to the bench to give his evidence against Pickering and Grove – the 'would be assassins', who had stalked the King in St. James's Park.

Thomas Pickering, a Benedictine, and John Grove, a Jesuit lay-brother, both proclaimed their innocence. John Grove spoke first. "I have met Doctor Oates once before . . . but not as he describes. He was destitute and begging alms. I felt sorry for him and gave him a few coins and said he could pay me back when he could."

Slapping his hands onto the bench, Scroggs snorted with laughter. "Are we expected to believe *you* lent money to a . . . a destitute stranger, begging alms? Do you expect us to believe such an unlikely tale? Mmm!"

Thomas Pickering spoke next. "I swear I never met Titus Oates . . . or William Bedloe, before seeing them here today."

Scroggs shook his head in despair and waved his hand for Father Ireland to speak.

"Your Honour, I wasn't in London at all between April and September last year and hence could *not* have attended any meetings during this time. I have witnesses to prove it."

Witnesses? Scroggs was taken aback by this but nodded for the witnesses to present their evidence.

Father Ireland's sister, Anne, rose. "I can verify my brother wasn't in London during the times stated."

Father Ireland's coachman then swore he'd been with him in Staffordshire throughout August, and another witness said he'd talked to him in Wolverhampton in September."

Alarm coursed through Scroggs. So many witnesses had come forward in Father Ireland's defence, and he wondered at their motive.

The prosecution called a respected local woman, who swore she had seen Father Ireland in London in August, in Fetter's Lane.

"I also swear to that," Titus added. "I also saw Father Ireland in London at that time."

Anne Ireland then spoke of the perjury charges brought against Titus Oates, by a schoolmaster in Hastings, William Parker. She submitted written evidence to Scroggs about this, from the Attorney General.

Scroggs read the statement and passed it to one of the other Judges. He looked over at Titus Oates, who was wiping the back of his neck with his hand.

"This material is unfit to be read," he said to Anne Ireland. "You cannot introduce evidence from another judiciary at this stage in the proceedings. The jury should ignore this as a malicious attempt to discredit a Crown witness. Do not let this prevent you from bringing a guilty verdict."

Scroggs summed up the evidence for the jury. "Much has been said here today by the defence, and in truth, I've forgotten most of it. But that is neither here nor there. The main issue is whether Father Ireland attended the treasonable meetings in which the King's death was planned. Who are we to believe? The word of lying Catholics, who eat the body of their own God and martyr their murderers or the witnesses who brought their foul plans against all good living Protestants to our attention? Had they not been stopped they would have brought their Popery to us all in a cruel and bloody way. Two witnesses have proved this.

"That a witness attempted to trick us by trying to discredit the good name of Doctor Titus Oates, so the accused could escape justice, in itself beggars belief. A woman of good standing testified to seeing Father Ireland in Fetters Lane at the time in question. It's my opinion evidence was presented that Thomas Pickering and John Grove attempted to shoot the King in St James's Park. You, the jury, must decide if all three men are guilty as accused. But be quick about it for we've already lost much time today!" He nodded to Judge Jeffreys to take over.

Five minutes later, Judge Jeffreys pronounced the jury's verdict. "You the jury are all good Protestants. Father Ireland you have been found guilty of heinous crimes against our King and country. You would do well to pray to that God of yours. Let it be known we will not tolerate such an abomination to occur. Many more lying Jesuits will follow you before long. I hope God Almighty shows compassion to you in the next world, for you'll receive none here. You think the Pope invincible? Well, we shall see."

Turning to the two men who had been accused of attempting to shoot the King, Jeffreys said, "Thomas Pickering and John Grove, you have both been found guilty of attempting to kill our King. What good have your forty thousand masses done you, I ask?"

Jack Ketch, the hangman, stepped forward. He placed each of the prisoner's hands behind their backs and tied their thumbs together.

When the hangman had finished, Judge Jeffreys announced, "Father William Ireland, John Grove and Thomas Pickering, you will be drawn to Tyburn, where you will be hung by your necks. You will have your privy members cut off. Your bowels will be removed and burnt in front of you. After you are dead, you will be cut down. Your heads will be removed and your bodies cut into quarters. Others will be reminded of the penalty for daring high treason. May God be merciful on your souls."

The packed court burst into thunderous applause. On hearing the applause, cheers of delight erupted from the mob outside. Chief Justice Scroggs smiled his approval.

Elizabeth hurried out of the courtroom with Mrs Cellier and the Earl of Castlemaine. They climbed into Castlemaine's carriage, and it clattered away from the Old Bailey.

"Did you get all that?" Elizabeth asked. "St Omer . . . Titus Oates was at St Omer and could not have been in London at the time of the Jesuit meeting he speaks about in April." Tears formed in her eyes and she wiped them away with her hand. "I must go to St Omer. I have to get evidence to help Powis."

Sitting opposite her, Castlemaine held up his papers. He'd taken detailed notes of the trial. "No Elizabeth, I cannot allow you to travel to France. The children need you. You cannot be the one to go."

"Then you go. You're the ideal person." Mrs Cellier said to Castlemaine. "If you can get anyone from St Omer to come here and speak out against Titus Oates, Scroggs will have to listen. They can stay in my townhouse. All you need do is get them here. Many of their Fathers have been named, including Father Whitbread."

Castlemaine nodded. "Yes, Yes. I'll do that. But there was another important detail raised." He picked up his notes. "Yes, here it is. Ann Ireland said Titus Oates had been charged with perjury in Hastings over. . . ." He scanned his notes. "Yes, here it is. Parker, the schoolmaster. We have to make contact with Parker and find out what transpired."

"I'll find out what I can through my contacts in Newgate," Mrs Cellier said. "Someone there may have heard about this. I'll also make a trip to Hastings."

♛

On finishing his meal, Charles excused himself from the evening's entertainment. Noticing him leave, Louise de Kérouaille rose and joined him, and they made their way to his apartments.

Charles was not in the mood for the repartee of the wits. Reaching his ante-chamber he threw himself down on a settee and pulled Louise onto his knees. "I'll not be much company, my dearest Fubbs. Think twice before staying with me. I know you adore the tables. Feel free to join the others."

"But not as much as I adore you, *mon chéri*," Louise said and snuggled into him. "More and more I treasure our time alone."

"Mmm, I know what you mean. I'm getting old, for although I need my raucous Court, its constancy bores me."

"You are not âgé. You speak the truth. Court is better for time away. The skaters were magnifique today. York is one of the best sliders at Court . . . Yourself excepted, *mon chéri*."

Charles smiled and relaxed. "Yes. I enjoyed today, but let us sit quietly. I need to concentrate my mind. There is much I have to think over."

He'd received word of the guilty charges brought against Ireland, Pickering and Grove. He couldn't believe Father Ireland had been involved in any plot to kill him. Was he sending an innocent Father to his death? Yet, a jury had declared him guilty. Neither did he know if Pickering and Grove had attempted to shoot him – but there had never been any ring of truth to it.

He saw Shaftesbury's hand in this. How much he'd been involved in the early stages, Charles wasn't certain, but he was involved now. Shaftesbury gave lavish handouts to his roguish band of accusers - his marionettes. But, Charles couldn't declare them liars. To do so could point the finger at him. York was already in danger, and Charles was sure his brother's conversion lay at the heart of all his current problems. What better way to ensure the Exclusion Bill, preventing Catholics from succeeding to the throne, was passed, than to stir up an anti-Catholic frenzy and prey on the fears of the common people?

What should he do? How should he act to ensure the best outcome?

The problem lay with Titus Oates. People lived in fear of him pointing a finger at them. In conversation, Oates always implied that what he still had to say was bigger than anything he'd already disclosed. Charles acknowledged the implicit threat to himself and his brother and shuddered at the false accusations that could be laid before them.

All Catholic peers had been removed from their seats in the Lords, and the Popish Plot consumed all parliamentary business. Five Catholic Lords lay in the Tower. Edward Coleman and numerous Jesuits and priests had been executed. Charles had no doubt many more would follow, and he decided to move York and Mary Beatrice overseas out of harm's way.

To protect his brother's right to succeed him, Charles would prorogue Parliament indefinitely if he had to. He would also delay the Catholic Lords' trials, and protect Danby from further accusation. The problem was his income would also stop. He would contact Louis again, and ask for French funds to see him through the Exclusion Crisis facing him. He would remove his son from Shaftesbury's control, and delay Father Ireland's execution.

Satisfied with this plan, Charles relaxed and snuggled into Louise, who giggled as he tugged at her gown.

Father William Ireland closed his journal for the last time. As he stared at the journal, he thought back over his life. He'd been educated at St Omer and admitted to the Society of Jesus at Watten. Religion had been his life. It was all he'd known.

On the day he was brought to Newgate, he began the journal, in which he accounted for every day of his time between April and

September '78; when it was claimed he'd attended treasonable conferences in London. He wasn't writing the journal out of any hope of being saved, but from a belief that one day those accused would be found innocent. The journal was his record of the truth of the matter.

Placing the journal beside all his worldly possessions – his bible, robes and a few silver coins – Father Ireland resigned himself to the fact that his life on this earth was over. He would miss the summer sun, the sea breeze, the call of the birds and seeing his family home one last time. He moved his thoughts forward to leaving this earth as he had arrived in it, with nothing.

Taking off his ring, Father Ireland placed it on top of the bundle and knelt down in prayer. "God forgive those who falsely accused me. I pray for the safe deliverance of John Grove and Thomas Pickering. Tomorrow John Grove will travel with me to Tyburn. Grant us strength to see us through this journey with dignity. Forgive me for any sins I committed throughout my life."

The following morning, along with John Grove, Father Ireland was removed from Newgate, tied to a sledge and pulled behind a cart. Despite the bitter, cold weather, over a thousand people followed him to Tyburn. As he was dragged along, Father Ireland felt dazed by the motion of the cart and the stones pelting down on him.

Standing on the gallows, he maintained his innocence. As the rope slipped around his neck and the cap fell over his head, he repeated over and over, "We are innocent and have been wrongfully condemned to die. God forgive those who caused it."

As the cart rolled away, the crowd remained silent. Their silence filled Father Ireland with hope, and he smiled.

CHAPTER FORTY

Discoveries

Elizabeth received a note inviting her to join Queen Catherine, Mary Beatrice and a guest for low tea. Intrigued, she set out for Somerset House. Her lady's maid, Beth, accompanied her. Arriving at the withdrawing room door, in Queen Catherine's apartments, Beth remained in the ante-chamber while Elizabeth went inside.

Queen Catherine ushered her over. "*Meu amigo*, Elizabeth, come join us by the fire."

Mary Beatrice stood and hugged Elizabeth, and she returned the embrace. The room was different from any Elizabeth had seen before, and her eyes scanned the vast array of lacquered tables, cane chairs and porcelain artefacts Catherine had brought with her from Portugal. Calico prints adorned the backs of chairs and settees, and more hung on the walls – vibrant orange and green hues competed with subtle blue and yellow tones. Baskets of sweet herbs, placed throughout the room, filled the air with their smells.

Drawing her eyes away, Elizabeth turned to Mary Beatrice. "I've brought a gift for Isabella." She handed Mary Beatrice a silk pouch containing an exquisite silver bracelet, engraved with tiny entwined flowers.

After Queen Catherine and Mary Beatrice had admired the bracelet, Elizabeth joined them beside the fire.

"Our guest should be here soon," Queen Catherine said, and her voice broke. Tears rolled down her face, and she held up a hand, indicating that Elizabeth and Mary Beatrice should remain where they were. After a few moments, she took a deep breath and said, "All of these deaths, Father Ireland, John Grove, and many more. I blame myself."

Elizabeth startled at Queen Catherine's words. "But you are not to blame. Whatever makes you say that?"

Catherine looked over at her with tears in her eyes. "When I arrived in England in the summer of '62, and married Charles, I came to realise that his first mistress, Lady Castlemaine, had more influence than I did as Queen. She chose to birth their second bastard at Hampton Court Palace . . . while we were *honeymooning* there.

"She then *demanded* to be appointed as one of my Ladies-of-the-Bedchamber, despite me raging, imploring and pleading for this not to happen. I even threatened to go back to Portugal, and I meant it. To force me to conform, Charles returned my retinue to Portugal. I was grief stricken.

"But, I held on to the belief that when I produced my children, I would become the most important person in my husband's life. I consoled myself with the knowledge that Lady Castlemaine could provide him with bastards, but when I birthed Charles' heirs, Castlemaine would lose her hold over my husband."

Mary Beatrice made to speak, but Catherine held up a hand to stop her and said, "I had three miscarriages. In '63, '64 and '65, while I grieved for my dead children, Castlemaine was large bellied with child and flaunted this in front of me. It was humiliating. It was humiliating for me also that she could enter my bedchamber, touch my belongings and blemish my day with her presence. I was frustrated beyond all measure.

"When Lady Castlemaine ceased as one of my Ladies, I vowed never to be humiliated like that again. To prevent it happening, I reduced the number of my Ladies, had a Mother of the Maids appointed - to shield them from my husband - and reduced their status."

Catherine touched her pearl necklace. "Louise de Kérouaille was Maid of Honour to the King's sister, Henrietta. When Henrietta died, Louise was appointed my Maid of Honour. Although she held out, in the hope Charles would divorce me and marry her, she finally relented and became his mistress.

"Once again my husband's mistress was attending me. The following year she gave birth to a son, Charles Lennox. That was humiliating for me also.

"But my humiliation then is nothing to what I now feel at causing the deaths of so many of our dear friends and Fathers. I am barren. I am a barren Queen. Had I produced an heir, none of this would have happened."

Mary Beatrice spoke with a quiver in her voice. "And my arrival in London, as York's new wife, provoked fear of a Catholic heir and return to Catholicism in England. But . . . none of my sons survived."

Elizabeth said, "The burden for us all is great, but as our Lord did, we need to accept our burdens. I pray every day for the faith to carry on."

The door swung open, and Elizabeth stood up. "Mrs Cellier . . . What are you doing here? You are the mystery guest?" Three days before, Mrs Cellier had departed for Hastings to see what she could find out about Titus Oates. Elizabeth shivered and sat down.

"Yes, Mrs Cellier is here to relate her findings, but it must wait until our tea has been served." Catherine inclined her head towards the maids who had entered behind Mrs Cellier.

The maids placed two low tables between their chairs. Tea, in a silver pot, was set down on one, along with fine porcelain china cups. China plates of crumpets, and wafer thin crust-less sandwiches - of shrimp and fish pastes - were placed on the other.

Catherine excused the maids and poured tea for them all. "I do prefer to pour myself. I regret that it is winter, and we cannot walk outside. The winters are so long and hard here, and I yearn for sunshine. But it is to hear Mrs Cellier's findings that I called you here."

Mrs Cellier swept back a stray wisp of hair with her fingers. "What I found out about Doctor Titus Oates was very strange, very strange indeed."

Eager to hear what Mrs Cellier had discovered, Elizabeth tapped her foot. Her hands shook, and she laid her cup down.

"No one in Hastings had anything good to say about Titus Oates," Mrs Cellier said. "I was told all sorts of tales about him. During his last stay in Hastings, he worked as his father's curate."

Mrs Cellier rubbed at her temples. "There is so much. I don't know where to start. The tales about him seemed never ending. Blaspheming during sermons . . . Arguing with the parishioners while drunk. These tales . . . were mere hearsay and I grew despondent of finding out anything of value.

"But I was fortunate. Turns out Oates' mother, Lucy, is a midwife like myself. We had a long talk together and what she told me was most interesting. Not that she would speak ill of her son. Very protective she was. But, as she didn't know my reasons for asking, she was happy enough to talk about him. I learned a lot about Titus Oates.

"His mother felt sorry for him when he was a child because he suffered from convulsions and he'd been ridiculed for his strange way of talking. His father was an Anabaptist minister who changed to the

Anglican Church during Cromwell's time. And . . . well, Reverend Oates and Oates' mother now live apart. Reverend Oates left Hastings and joined Mr Lamb's Anabaptist church here in London . . . as an ordinary member. Lucy Oates remained behind in Hastings."

The door opened, and a maid came in with a fresh teapot and removed the old one.

"Did you find out anything about the Parker incident?" Elizabeth asked Mrs Cellier as soon as the maid left.

"In truth, not very much that can help us." Mrs Cellier frowned. "In Titus Oates' absence, the Parkers dropped all charges against him."

"Dear God, no. Then all is lost?" Elizabeth felt as if the bottom had fallen out of her box of hope.

"I don't think the Parkers would appear as witnesses against him," Mrs Cellier said. "They were sickened by the whole affair and wanted no more to do with Titus Oates. I think they would fear being charged by him again."

Mary Beatrice gasped. "How can this be? How can we fight back if everyone fears Titus Oates?"

"While taking alms to Newgate I managed to glean some information from one of the warders," Mrs Cellier said. "The keeper of the Inn, where they took Godfrey's body after it was found. . . I don't know the truth of the matter, but the warder told me the innkeeper was tortured until he admitted running a Catholic club and that Miles Prance had been a member. It's all so confusing.

"I also heard some interesting details about that other accuser, William Bedloe," Mrs Cellier continued. "He's well known in Newgate. By all accounts, he received a reward of five hundred pounds for revealing the names of the Magistrate's murderers. Hmph! Bedloe swears Godfrey was murdered here, and his body removed to Primrose Hill in a sedan chair."

Catherine touched her pearl necklace. "Bedloe has named three servants from my chapel. Robert Green, Henry Berry and Lawrence Hill have been arrested for Godfrey's murder. They've been removed to Newgate, shackled and incarcerated in freezing cells." Catherine looked at Mary Beatrice with tears in her eyes. "Charles is arranging for you and your husband to be moved abroad out of harm's way."

Mary Beatrice startled. "How can this be? Why should *we* leave England? Do you know where we are to go?"

"No. Not yet." Catherine shook her head. "Holland, Brussels perhaps?"

Elizabeth considered this. "Shaftesbury's stirring great trouble for your husband, by pushing to exclude him from the succession. Yes . . . I can see the sense in sending you both abroad."

"Charles will have York moved from harm's reach before Parliament reopens," Catherine added.

"Dear God." Elizabeth tapped her forehead. "I've just recalled where I've seen Titus Oates before. It always bothered me that I thought I recognised him but couldn't remember where from. It was at Arundel House. On the day Norfolk announced he was marrying Jane Bickerton. Yes. I almost bumped into him as I was leaving. I can ask Norfolk about Titus Oates. Perhaps he knows something."

"And William Bedloe was a letter carrier at Arundel House," Mrs Cellier added.

CHAPTER FORTY-ONE

Unexpected Visitors

Titus turned to view himself in the full-length mirror and admired his new red hat. If he hadn't known otherwise, he would swear it was one of the Bishop's own. He smiled as he studied his reflection. This new light-coloured periwig also suited him.

Turning away from the mirror, he strode across the floor of his large apartment at Whitehall Palace. Made from the purest silk his gown swayed and whirled as he walked, and he delighted in the swish of silk accompanying his movements.

As he paced back and forth towards the mirror admiring himself a servant entered and informed him that Doctor Israel Tonge had called and wished to speak with him.

Titus hurried to the door and, on opening it, stared at Tonge. "What do you want?" he said, then turned and walked into his apartment and sat down beside the fire.

Tonge followed and sat opposite him. "Titus, I'm leaving my apartments and won't be returning. I will stay with my son, Simpson. He's completed his studies at University and has his own rooms now. The idea pleases me. I'll not be missed here. I've no evidence to present against anyone. In truth, I never did."

As Tonge spoke, Titus grew alarmed. Tonge was distancing himself from the Plot. Over the last few months they'd started to argue, and hadn't talked to each other since quarrelling at a supper given last week in Titus' honour.

♛

Tonge recalled the meal in Titus' honour. During it, he'd grown increasingly resentful of the attention showered upon Titus, while *he* remained ignored. Unable to contain himself, he had announced to the assembled company that Titus had no knowledge of the Plot, other than what he had told him. Shocked silence had followed his outburst, and he left soon after.

Hurt and angry, he'd returned home and thought long and hard about Titus Oates. Although Tonge believed with all his heart in the truth of the Popish Plot, he came to the cold realisation that Titus was using this for his own means. More and more of the accused were people Titus wanted to avenge for some action or slight against him. To begin with, Tonge hadn't seen this, but the more he thought about it, the clearer it had become. He was intelligent, and once he began analysing the events, he had started to see things in a different light.

To begin with, he'd been flattered that the Country Party had championed their cause, and felt privileged by the flattery Shaftesbury heaped upon him. Then, as if a shutter had been opened in front of his eyes, he saw that Shaftesbury was also manipulating the Plot for his own means. Tonge's anger flared again as he considered, not for the first time, whether Shaftesbury believed any of his accusations to be true. His main concern, and this sorely troubled him, was that Shaftesbury seemed intent on removing York from the succession and replacing him with the King's Protestant bastard, Monmouth.

Shaftesbury also seemed intent on bringing about Danby's downfall, and had set up the Country Party, by and large, Green Ribbon Club members, in opposition to the Crown. Increasingly, to Tonge's disquiet, Shaftesbury was drawing in all sorts of shady characters as accusers in the Plot. As far as Tonge was concerned, these new accusers were either low-life scoundrels or hardened criminals. He didn't trust William Bedloe and thought him an opportunist. Prance seemed different. Tonge believed Prance had been tortured at Newgate, and now tried to please those who had clearly schooled him in the events of Godfrey's death. He was certain Bedloe and Prance knew no more of the murder than he did.

Tonge also harboured suspicions about Titus' claim he had gained a Doctor of Divinity at the University of Salamanca but feared asking him about this. Tonge had checked and double checked his memory about the time Titus had spent in Spain, and always concluded that it was no longer than six months. In his opinion, it wasn't possible for Titus to have studied for a Doctorate in this short time.

Tonge looked over at Titus, who appeared lost in his own thoughts, and took in his fine gown and puffed up demeanour. Who could blame him, for he was the champion of the Country Party? He kept an excellent table, and was dressed every morning by servants who vied with each other to attend to his every whim. Despite his insolent manner, Titus frequently dined at Shaftesbury's home, where he was a welcome guest. His sermons, when he could be bothered delivering them, were treated as great public events.

Wherever Titus went, great crowds followed him and parted to let him pass. He had had odes written, declaring him a saviour and worthy opponent of the Pope, and grand formal dinners held in his honour. Tonge had even seen Titus' health toasted along with the King's. Everywhere Titus went, he was courted, feted and acknowledged, and was conveyed around the city in a grand carriage, with bodyguards riding aside it. Members of the Country Party defended him to the Privy Council and advised and supported him during the Plot trials.

Tonge had decided to remove himself from it all, and the sooner the better as far as he was concerned.

♛

Titus grew increasingly concerned by this new stance Tonge was adopting. He frowned and looked over at him. Would Tonge speak out against him? How much did he know? "I am sorry we argued," he said to him. "The Plot is still yours if you want it."

When Tonge merely stared at him, Titus begged, "Please stay and help me."

Tonge rose from the chair and without a word walked from the room, leaving Titus staring after him in disbelief. The effect was momentary, and Titus shrugged it off, comforted in the knowledge that Tonge couldn't speak out without incriminating himself.

Later, as he finished off some refreshments at his table, a servant informed him a lady had called wishing to speak with him. Rising to his feet, Titus pushed the man roughly on his shoulders. "Well, blaady show her in then. What are you paid for?"

With all thoughts of Tonge forgotten, Titus peered at his reflection in the mirror and adjusted his periwig, in anticipation of the female visitor. He'd grown accustomed to ladies calling – most were of the Protestant nobility. William Bedloe, the letter carrier, was now engaged to be married to such a woman of notable wealth.

When the woman entered, Titus startled. "Maather! What brings you here?"

"I've come to see you. What's this I hear of conspiracies and plots you've uncovered? I found it all hard to believe, but when I learned you were living in the Palace, I wondered if there might be some truth to your claims. So I ventured from Hastings to speak with you."

Titus puffed himself up and showed his mother around his apartments. With great pride, he told her of his pension from Parliament. After showing her the plates he'd had made, with his crest, he sat beside her and recounted his finding of his Popish Plot.

When he started to implicate William Smith, the schoolmaster, Lucy shook her head. "You forget I know you, Titus. This accusation is surely an exaggeration of the truth. I remember well the false allegations you laid against William Parker, the schoolteacher. Now, if you will excuse me, I have the beginnings of a headache."

"Maather, I'll call my carriage. It has my crest emblazoned on its side." Titus smiled. "You will never have seen such a carriage. It's among the finest in London."

Lucy walked to the door. "No thank you, I've seen enough grand things already. The walk will clear my head. Personal carriage, indeed. A crest? Holy God, what next? I'll bid you goodnight."

Shaking his head at his mother's hasty departure, Titus sat down at his desk. Pulling a sheaf of paper towards him, he beamed. He didn't need Tonge. In front of him lay evidence of this. Besides his 'Narrative of the Horrid Plot and Conspiracy of the Popish Party', he had other publications in progress, and what was more, unlike the works he published with Tonge, people would clamour to buy them. That much of the material had been borrowed from the pamphlets he'd laboured over with Tonge was forgotten, as he gloated over his recent successes.

By nine o'clock he felt restless. The visit of first Tonge, and then his mother, had left him unsettled. Calling his servants and bodyguard into the room, he informed them he had a headache and would retire for the night *without* their assistance. He ordered them to leave his apartments and told them on no account were they to return until morning.

When he was certain they'd gone, he removed his hat and periwig and placed them on wig stands. He put on a long grey coat and a large-brimmed hat and wound a long black scarf around the lower part of his face. Slipping out of the Palace, he headed for Lincoln's Inn Fields. Tonight he needed company, and there were plenty of vagrant boys out there who would provide this for a few coppers. Though he disliked himself for doing it, and his stomach churned at the thought of being caught, Titus wandered the Fields on the lookout for just such a person.

CHAPTER FORTY-TWO

Transforming Traitors Into Martyrs

Chief Justice Scroggs peered round the door of the ante-chamber and watched the commotion erupting in his court. Damn it. He'd overindulged on wine the previous evening, and his head ached. What had he been thinking? He should have known people would turn up in droves for the trial of Godfrey's murderers.

Hoping events would proceed swiftly he pulled on his periwig and walked in. The other judges followed behind. Once he had taken his seat silence ensued.

Robert Green, Henry Berry and Lawrence Hill, servants from Queen Catherine's chapel at Somerset House, were appearing at the Bar of the King's Bench, accused of the wilful murder of Sir Edmund Berry Godfrey.

After the jurors had taken their seats and the three bedraggled men brought to the Bar, Chief Justice Scroggs ordered the public to be silent and addressed the jury. "How far will Catholics go to further their own cause, I ask you? What we have before us today is the horrid death of a learned man who found himself in the way of Papists."

He now believed Catholics would stop at nothing to achieve their aims, and felt enraged at the death of one of his colleagues. "It is chilly today, but better cold here than burning at Smithfield," he said and glared at the accused. When he had finished decrying the Roman Catholic Church, he called the first witness for the Crown.

William Bedloe retold the account he'd given to the Privy Council, but Scroggs noticed the details differed. Points had changed about how he'd met Green, Berry and Hill, the way Godfrey had been murdered and where the murder had been carried out. Bedloe also seemed vague about what he'd been told about the murder. As Bedloe's previous statement wasn't available, Scroggs didn't challenge these variations. He hadn't brought all the relevant documentation with him and, while he could send someone to retrieve the papers, he had no desire to delay proceedings any further. His head throbbed, and he poured himself a glass of ale.

Prance stood and gave a confident, if different, account from Bedloe. He presented each point as he'd previously stated it to the Privy Council, and gave consistent answers to all the questions. Scroggs smiled in his direction. At last a credible witness. He jotted down points from Prance's statement, to use in his summing up.

Scroggs called each witness for the accused and openly sneered as they presented their evidence. He doubted the truth of their words and wanted them to know it.

Lawrence Hill's wife stood. "Prance is lying. He said that –"

"What!" he shouted at her. "You cannot think he would swear three men to their deaths over nothing. Call the next witness."

Two guards, who were working at Queen Catherine's residence, Somerset House, the night Godfrey's body was said to have been removed in a sedan chair, stood and swore no sedan chair had passed them.

Scroggs bristled and leant forward. "That you did not see a sedan chair is neither here nor there. It could easily have slipped past without you noticing."

When Lawrence Hill's wife stood and said that the evidence presented by Bedloe and Prance differed from each other, Scroggs leant back and raised his eyes. He was in no mood for debate. His head ached, and he felt tired. He'd awoken in the early hours of the morning in a strange bed and had no memory of how he'd arrived there.

He decided to bring the business of the court to a speedy conclusion and commenced his summing up. He skimmed over the evidence provided by Bedloe and concentrated on Prance's evidence. He concluded by declaring that Edmund Berry Godfrey's murder was in itself undeniable proof of the truth of Prance's evidence.

After a few minutes deliberation, the jury returned a verdict of guilty against Robert Green, Henry Berry and Lawrence Hill.

"I would have reached the same conclusion," Scroggs said and rose to his feet.

Loud shouts of approval erupted around the crowded courtroom.

Elizabeth sat in her withdrawing room, working a stitch on her embroidery of Powis Castle. She'd instructed her staff not to disturb her. The day after their trial, Chief Justice Scroggs announced Green, Berry, and Hill's sentence. Despite them maintaining their innocence, Green and Hill were sentenced to be hanged at Tyburn. Berry, a Protestant, had been granted a respite.

This morning, Castlemaine brought her the news that Berry had now followed Green and Hill to Tyburn. Berry's respite had lasted one week.

Despite inducements that his life would be spared if he confessed, Berry resolutely refused to admit to any knowledge of his or any other persons' involvement in Godfrey's murder.

Elizabeth pushed the needle through the fabric, again and again. Working on the embroidery was the only thing that soothed her righteous anger. She lived in fear for Powis' life. He remained in isolation, and she'd not had news of him in months. No one would tell her how he fared, or whether he was well. He could be hanged, just as quickly as Berry. Pushing the thought aside, she jabbed the needle into the fabric.

As these men had been hanged for Godfrey's murder, Samuel Pepys' clerk, Atkins, was released. Elizabeth sighed. This ensured, at least for now, that York's name wouldn't be mentioned during any of the trials, through his involvement with Pepys and the Naval Board.

Rumour had spread around the coffee houses that Green, Berry and Hill were innocent of any involvement in Godfrey's murder, and as a result, questions were surfacing about who *had* killed him. Elizabeth allowed herself a small smile. People were now openly debating whether Green, Hill and Berry had been wrongfully executed. Elizabeth prayed they would now question Titus Oates' word.

Thanks be to God, Castlemaine was leaving soon for St Omer.

A week later, Elizabeth stood outside St James's Palace saying goodbye to Mary Beatrice. Elizabeth hugged her dear friend and fussed around her making sure she had everything for the long journey to Brussels. Elizabeth stroked her finger along the strand of pearls showing around Mary Beatrice's neck and wished her good luck for a safe journey.

Three carriages were readying to leave, and two bodyguards climbed onto the back of each one. Mary Beatrice was travelling in the first one, with her husband, York, their daughter Isabella, and Isabella's nurse. Their small retinue of aides would follow in the others. Their departure had been arranged in haste; before the newly elected members of Parliament assumed their seats in two days' time.

"When Shaftesbury found out York was leaving he ranted and raged to anyone who would listen," Elizabeth said. "Take care. Shaftesbury will push the Exclusion Bill in York's absence."

"Pah! Shaftesbury," Mary Beatrice spat out. "He encourages my husband's exclusion for his own means. Only a few months ago, Danby shouted loudest of all about this Plot and supported Titus Oates. You do see, without Oates' claims the Country Party would not have such support. Hah! Now Danby has been defeated by Shaftesbury. Oh, how the mighty one has fallen, and many more with him. Now, the Country Party is ensuring Parliament prevents my husband or any other Catholic succeeding to the throne." She shook her head in amazement.

"Then Charles was right to prorogue Parliament and have you both removed abroad. But why he appointed Shaftesbury as Lord President of his new Privy Council is beyond my reasoning. Perhaps he aims to keep him sweet. God speed your journey away from this nightmare." Elizabeth hugged Mary Beatrice one final time before ushering her to climb aboard.

She watched with tears in her eyes as the carriage carrying Mary Beatrice and her family clattered out of the palace grounds – the carriages carrying their retinue and luggage trundling along behind it.

Fresh elections had taken place, and these were hard fought. When the results were announced Shaftesbury was elated – the Country Party members dominated over the King's supporters. To add to his delight, on hearing this, the imprisoned Danby resigned.

On the first day of the new Parliament, Shaftesbury addressed the Lords. As president of the new Privy Council, he had pushed for the Exclusion Bill to be heard – To remove York from the succession and have Monmouth acknowledged as the legitimate heir.

"My Lords," Shaftesbury began. "We've heard much about a plot to murder our King and return England to a Catholic state. But it is wrong to take such a short-sighted and narrow view of the crisis facing us. You allow yourselves to forget the Crown is larger than England. The threat of Popery is rife throughout Ireland, and now, we hear, it's creeping its way like a disease into Scotland. The threat of Popery abounds everywhere. But what do we hear of such threats? Nothing, I would say.

"Ask yourself why this is? I would suggest that just as Danby has done in England, Ormonde in Ireland and Lauderdale in Scotland have been governing independently of the Crown. What do we hear of their policies? Are Ormonde and Lauderdale free to administer as they wish? Are they free to allow this Papal Plot to grow and fester, while we in England toil to remove it at its roots? It would appear so, and I move that this stops herewith.

"Do not be misled. There *is* a most horrible plot afoot to murder our King and replace him with his Catholic successor, James of York. Oh yes! There's a definite plan afoot to return us to a Catholic state. We have seen how easily this could be achieved? And yet, Ormonde and Lauderdale do nothing to stop it. I denounce their policies, and I put it to you that there is an urgent need to review the administrative policies, not only Danby's within England but also Ormonde's in Ireland and

Lauderdale's in Scotland."

Shaftesbury smiled when his speech was greeted with loud shouts of approval. Both houses agreed a plot existed, as did the impending threat of a Catholic supremacy throughout all three territories. They agreed that the administrative policies of England, Ireland and Scotland should be urgently reviewed.

Matthew Medbourne, the young, intelligent, talented playwright and actor, who had helped Titus without thought or hesitation and had invited him as a member of his club at Fullers Rent, lay shackled to a wall in Newgate prison.

Delirious from fever, Medbourne's mind moved back and forth through his life, and he smiled as his memories settled on his finest hour; playing the part of Trico in the play, Ignoramus. The Gazette had gone as far as reporting he had 'owned the part'. He allowed himself another smile, at the sheer irony of this – for the play was a farce.

As his thoughts flitted between past and present, Matthew Medbourne recited his lines. "Approach not near *him* sir, take my advice - ," he uttered and gave a last feeble gasp.

CHAPTER FORTY-THREE

Dangerfield

Elizabeth laid down her quill pen and moved aside the letter she had written. Standing up from the desk, she welcomed Mrs Cellier into Powis' study. A smartly dressed and handsome young man accompanied the midwife.

The man stepped forward and bowed to Elizabeth. "Thomas Dangerfield, Ma'am. I hope I can be of assistance to you."

She smiled at him. "Mrs Cellier's told me all about you, and your help will be most welcome. The situation here in London is far from good. We need all the able hands we can muster if we're to stop this absurd situation from continuing. Welcome to our fold."

After a year in the debtor's side of Newgate prison, Dangerfield had been planning a way out. He'd drawn up a list of complaints against the keeper and persuaded a visitor to deliver it to a Justice of the Peace. When Mrs Cellier learned about his clever plan, she realised she could do with the aid of such a resourceful fellow and had visited him in his cell.

Impressed to find he was a clerk and the son of an attorney, she employed him as her assistant. She paid off the twenty-nine-year-olds' debts and discharge fee, gave him lodgings in her home and arranged for him to be fitted with two suits, two shirts and a pair of shoes. She then summoned a barber to attend to Dangerfield's appearance. With his long handsome locks, he had no need of a periwig.

Elizabeth was charmed by Dangerfield's eagerness and good manners and handed him £30 to help secure Powis' release. "My husband remains in isolation in the Tower," she informed Dangerfield. "I've had no communication with him since the day he was moved there. His trial date was fixed for the middle of May, a few weeks from now. Fortunately, it has been delayed."

Mrs Cellier nodded. "And we need to make the best use of this time to secure Powis' release. The Earl of Shaftesbury's using this Papal Plot to incite fear and hatred towards Catholics and will use any means to achieve this, even if it leads to the death of every Catholic Lord."

"Shaftesbury's playing a dangerous game, and I'm determined to fight him back," Elizabeth said to Dangerfield. "I thank you for your help in this. We must work to force the release of my husband and the other Lords. This won't be an easy task. My husband's cousin, Castlemaine, will help us. We've already formulated a plan, and I can go over the details of this the next time we meet. I think you are the perfect person to help make it work. Well done for finding him, Mrs Cellier."

"Everything's in place for Powis to receive information today," Mrs Cellier informed Dangerfield. "The gaoler's been bribed to admit you to Powis' cell, under the guise of a doctor visiting him for severe belly-ache. Once there, you will slip Powis a letter and relay his responses back to us. You will deliver the first letter this very evening."

When she retrieved the letter from the desk and handed it to Dangerfield, Elizabeth's eyes filled with tears. "God be with you. The letter is unsigned and has no revealing details in it so it cannot be traced back to me. It breaks my heart not to be able to send my husband words of love or news of the children. Please . . . let this be known to him."

Dangerfield scanned the letter.

The third day of April 1679

Shaftesbury and his supporters are becoming more extreme in the lengths they are prepared to go to exclude York from the succession. They are pushing for an 'Exclusion Bill' to be passed, which will remove York from the succession on the grounds of his Catholicism and relationship with France. For his protection, he has gone abroad.

Country Party members mill around the lobbies of the Commons, pressing their pamphlets and arguments upon the members. To stop the Bill from being passed, and to prevent you and the other Lords from trial, the King has prorogued Parliament.

Danby has also been removed to the Tower.

Do not despair. A means for securing your release will be found.

William Smith trudged towards Whitehall Palace. He remained deep in thought and kept his head bowed low. Titus had summoned him to his apartments, a summons he couldn't ignore.

As he walked along, he felt as if a great weight pushed down onto his shoulders. The scuff of his worn shoes against the ground served as his constant companion. By the time he arrived at Whitehall his stomach growled, from both hunger and fear.

Last year, on the day of Godfrey's funeral, Titus had ordered William Smith's arrest. When William Smith appeared before the Lords, he'd been stunned into shocked silence by the charges laid against him. Titus had informed the Privy Council someone had overheard him swearing to 'harm the King'. The Privy Council agreed, however, that the evidence was hearsay, and on that basis, he would not be charged with high treason. Before William Smith had exhaled a sigh of relief, Shaftesbury announced that as he had brought disgrace upon himself through this accusation, his licence to teach would be revoked.

Tears had coursed down William Smith's face as he had walked from the hearing. Unable to teach, he had lost his position as schoolmaster. With no income, he'd been driven to beg for money to pay for his food and lodgings. Good fortune had been with him, in that people had shown him kindness. So far, he'd always managed to scrape together the three pence each week for his rent.

William Smith tried not to think about what further humiliation Titus intended for him today. For humiliate him he surely would. As he walked along his thoughts drifted to his good friend, Matthew Medbourne. He cursed himself for a fool for ignoring his instinct to warn Matthew to stay away from Titus Oates, when he'd first brought him to their club in Fullers Rent. Now a great actor and wonderful man had died. The charges against Matthew had never been brought to trial – there had been no other witness to support Titus' accusations.

Determined William Smith would be that witness, Titus had first threatened and harassed him and then physically beaten him to make him testify. Exasperated by his continual refusal to act as a witness against Medbourne, Titus brought the charges against him. Still he'd refused and, through not doing Titus's bidding, had lost his teaching licence, his employment, his income and his status in the world.

Now, he'd been summoned by Titus again. "Oh, dear God, what

now?" he softly intoned, as he found himself standing outside the door of Titus' apartments.

"Ah! Schoolteacher Smith, you've arrived at last," Titus called out. "Come sit beside us."

With reluctance, William Smith walked over and sat at the table.

Titus laughed, and Bedloe and Dugdale joined in. Prance sat between them looking dazed and unhappy.

"What do we know of the murder of Edmund Berry Godfrey?" Titus said and sneered at William Smith. "Nothing. Blaady nothing, that is what."

Bellows of mirthful laughter erupted from Dugdale and Bedloe.

Titus stood up. "Ooh, schoolmaster Smith, do not be shocked. 'Tis nothing compared to what's coming next. Godfrey's death –" He stooped and wiped bread crumbs from his breeches. "His death was merely an appetiser."

Dugdale and Bedloe roared with laughter. William Smith could only stare back at them.

"Ah! Do not look so shocked." Titus laughed and slumped back onto his seat. "The King's a Papist just like his brother. I know it, and you know it."

Bedloe pointed his glass at Smith. "And the whole of bloody London knows it," he slurred, and downed the wine in one swallow. Bedloe wiped his mouth with the back of his hands and reached out for a carafe of red wine. "The common people will believe anything the 'Saviour of the Nation' says. You fool, the King himself is in on the Popish Plot," he added and refilled his glass, splashing wine over the table in the process.

William Smith thought he might collapse. He felt light headed and couldn't make sense of the words he was hearing. His thoughts raced. As far as he was concerned, there was more treasonable talk in this room than there had been accused across the whole of the Plot trials. He wanted to get up and leave but felt rooted to the spot. Titus' next statement sent him reeling.

"Smith, I need you to swear you dined with me in London during the time of the Grand Consult. I need to shut up those who say I was at St Omer at that time. If you do this, I will get you your teaching licence back."

"Even if I got my licence back no one would employ me as a teacher again," Smith croaked.

"Then I'll give you fifty pounds for doing this," Titus said and beamed.

William Smith was so poor he didn't know if he could pay his rent for the coming week. He prided himself on being an honest person, but the thought of being thrust into the debtor's side of Newgate prison terrified him. He looked at Prance, who had sat quietly throughout the exchange, and realised they were in a similar position.

"I'll say I dined with you around that time . . . in London, Titus, but –" Smith straightened up in the chair. "But I refuse to be specific about the date."

As Titus reached over and handed him a glass of wine, William Smith's stomach heaved.

King Charles played a vigorous game of tennis with a courtier. He seethed with anger and thrashed the ball back and forward, growing impatient when the courtier missed a return.

Despite his attempts to delay it, the Commons had voted for the

Exclusion Bill to be heard, to remove his brother from the succession. That York had converted was now widely acknowledged, and it was also rumoured that Charles was allying himself with France again. For the first time, he realised how organised the opposition had become. He had underestimated their power, but no more.

Sweat coursed over him, as he smacked the tennis ball back. He acknowledged the game the Country Party played. He was nothing if not a good sportsman and decided to adopt their strategy.

Moving to retrieve a missed ball, he cursed, "Damn them for arrogant beings." The Country Party was playing on Protestant fears of the country returning to a Catholic regime. Well, he could play that game too. There were far more dangerous things to fear than mere Papists, and he would show the Country Party for the self-serving tyrants they were.

As he returned the ball with a resounding whack, the thought came to Charles that the opposition was growing and spreading like a disease that had to be stopped. He resolved to be the one to do it.

CHAPTER FORTY-FOUR

The Five Jesuits

In Mrs Cellier's townhouse, Elizabeth and Mrs Cellier fussed around the boys who had come over from St Omer to testify at the trial of the five Jesuits. Castlemaine had accompanied the sixteen boys - aged between twelve and fourteen - over from France. Four would lodge with Elizabeth at Lincoln's Inn Fields, and the other twelve would lodge with Mrs Cellier. The trial was in two days time, and Elizabeth prayed that the boy's presence would not become common knowledge.

Elizabeth smiled as she watched Mrs Cellier helping the cook serve up bowls of mutton broth and handing out bread to each of the boys in turn. Surely the word of sixteen students would convince people Titus Oates had been at St Omer in April when he claimed to have witnessed the Jesuit gathering in London.

Now June, she hadn't seen Powis since November. He remained in solitary confinement. She treasured the words Dangerfield had brought back from Powis after visiting him in the Tower. In two days' time, these boys would present the evidence which would hopefully secure his release.

Two days later, Elizabeth stepped down from her carriage and helped the four boys from St Omer out. She adjusted a summer shawl around her shoulders and glanced around. Noting that Mrs Cellier, Castlemaine and the other boys hadn't arrived yet, she looked for somewhere to wait on them.

The clear morning sky carried the promise of another hot day. She was weary of the heat and felt all of her forty-six years. Dear God, how her life had changed. To think she'd once considered herself fortunate – now her life was fragmented, broken by lies. Glancing around, she spotted a space on the other side of the road, where they could wait.

Pushing through the crowd gathering outside the Old Bailey, she called out, "Move aside. God's truth, let us pass."

Chants of "Coleman's letters," and "Papist plotters," rang from the assembling mob.

"God, grant me strength to see this through," she muttered and continued to move slowly through the mass of bodies.

As she ushered the children across the road and away from the crowd, a rank smell assaulted her. She held a hand to her nose and skirted around the layers of horse droppings littering their path. Reaching the other side, she gathered the four boys close around her.

Carriages clattered past, and anchored above her head and overhanging the cobbled road, painted boards swung and creaked as they announced the names of the establishments within. Open shutters displayed tallow candles, powders and periwigs. Turning her back on them, she looked over towards St Paul's Cathedral, which was still being rebuilt following the Great Fire.

Her respite was short lived. A young girl with a basket on each arm approached and called out in a shrill voice, "Pastries, sweet pastries, m'Lady." Elizabeth waved the girl away.

Eager to find out what news had been distributed about today's trial, she gestured over to a black-toothed man to bring over one of his broadsheets. Her hands shook as she pulled a penny from her purse and thrust it into the man's open palm. After reading the announcement that the boys from St Omer would be appearing as witnesses for the five Jesuits, Elizabeth scrunched the broadsheet and tossed it into the gutter. She chewed her bottom lip and prayed the boys' evidence would prove Powis and the others to be innocent.

As two carriages clattered to a halt and Mrs Cellier and Castlemaine alighted with the other boys, relief flooded through her. She adjusted her shawl and hurried over to greet them.

"Thanks be to God, you're here." Elizabeth gave a wavering smile to Castlemaine and hugged Mrs Cellier.

Mrs Cellier waved a hand for the sixteen boys to gather round. "God Bless these brave boys. I pray no harm comes to them."

Castlemaine took command of getting the boys safely inside the court. "When we start towards the Old Bailey, stay close together. The mob may try to stop you but keep going. Make haste towards the front door and go straight into the building. Do not wait for each other. Go . . . Now!"

No sooner had they started towards the Old Bailey when the mob gathered around the boys. The chants grew louder: "Papists! Papist Plotters! Coleman's letters!"

Moving forward, Elizabeth's stomach churned. The crowd thronged tighter around them and tried to bar their way. As the boys neared the courthouse, stones showered down around them. A large stone hit one of the boys on the back, sending him sprawling to the cobbles.

Elizabeth stopped and looked back. A group of men were gathered around the fallen boy, kicking and pummelling him while he lay helpless on the ground. The boy screamed out in terror, and dogs barked as they joined in the melee. Rooted to the spot, Elizabeth called out to the other boys to keep moving.

Noticing Elizabeth had stopped, Castlemaine shouted to her. "Keep going! Get into the courthouse! Make haste! I will bring the boy!"

On shaking legs, Elizabeth staggered forward. She glanced back to make sure the child was safe. Castlemaine gripped the screaming boy under the arms and dragged him away from the mob. He pulled the boy in through the doors of the courthouse and continued to pull him until he reached the rear of the entrance hall, where he laid him onto a wooden bench.

Elizabeth rushed over to help. At forty–five-years of age, and of only a modest and slight physique, Castlemaine had struggled to lift the large boy. Sweat coursed down his face and a rasping sound emitted from his chest. He bent down and placed his hands on his knees, and gulped in a few deep breaths. When he straightened up, his gentle face broke into a smile. "Heavens above, lad, we did it. We outran them. Like great foot soldiers. Now rest yourself, while I inquire after the others."

Mrs Cellier gathered the other boys together and brought them over. Most of them had received kicks and been hit by small stones but professed to be well enough to continue. Mrs Cellier checked their cuts and bruises and dusted them down.

The injured boy's whimpers tugged at Elizabeth's heart, and she knelt beside him. He was no older than her son, William. "Shush child, we won't let them harm you again. You're safe now," she said and checked his injuries. The boy's lip had started to swell, and blood seeped from his nose. Tears streamed from his eyes and streaked his face. Elizabeth's chest constricted with her own unshed tears. Taking off a glove, she wiped the blood away. She glanced up at Mrs Cellier and saw her own concern mirrored in the midwife's face.

When Castlemaine had finished checking that no one else had been seriously injured, he drew Elizabeth aside. "You must go into court as planned," he said in his soft-timbered voice. "I'll remain with the injured boy. We can't let the mob stop these boys from giving their evidence. Do not let their injuries be for nothing."

Elizabeth nodded and ushered Mrs Cellier and the other boys into the packed courtroom. As they walked towards the witness section - at the front of the court - baying and hissing erupted from the crowd. Once the shaken boys were seated, Elizabeth made her way to the back of the room and secured seats for herself and Mrs Cellier. The smell of stale periwigs and body odour followed her steps.

People continued to file in and find places to sit or stand, and loud conversation and the sound of scraping benches resounded through the courtroom. The gallery had already filled to bursting point. As Elizabeth gazed around, she noted the presence of Shaftesbury and other members of the Country Party. She shuddered and closed her eyes. *Lord in heaven, show mercy and grant the safe keeping of these dear children.*

After the jurors had taken their seats, Chief Justice Scroggs asked for the prisoners to be brought in. Entering the dock - surrounded by sprigs of rosemary, to guard against gaol fever - were Father Thomas Whitbread and Father Fenwick. Their health had declined since their last appearance, and Father Fenwick had to be carried in because of the weeping, suppurating sores on his leg - from where he had been manacled too tightly. The foul stench from the wound invaded the courtroom. Three other Jesuits appeared for the first time.

Around the courtroom, heads turned as Doctor Titus Oates swaggered in, to be greeted by thunderous applause. Elizabeth's heart lurched. She wanted to swallow, but her throat was too dry, and she gave a feeble cough instead. Clamping a hand over her mouth, she stared at the man who had invaded her home and removed her husband to the Tower.

As he limped past her towards the front of the courtroom, she heard the swish of silk and the sound of the crowd hailing him as 'The Saviour of the Nation'. Elizabeth looked at Titus Oates sunken eyes and large face and believed him to be the devil himself. Fighting the urge to cross herself, she sat rigid in her seat.

Titus Oates dipped his chin, and fixed his beady eyes on Father Thomas Whitbread, from St Omer. As he made his way, officers of the court jumped up and fussed around him, clearing a path.

"Get out of my blaady way," Titus Oates bellowed and shoved one of the officers aside. "When I say move I mean move, for Gaads sake," he added, elbowing past the others.

Praise for him thundered from the gallery, and he puffed himself up and sneered in Father Whitbread's direction. On reaching the boys from St Omer, he stopped, glared at them and then smiled. He was still smiling when he seated himself in his reserved place at the front.

"Fetch some refreshments for Doctor Oates, it is a warm day," Chief Justice Scroggs instructed one of the attendants. "I hope this doesn't take too long."

The clerk of the court opened proceedings. The five Jesuits stood trial for high treason, in consorting to kill the King and change the established religion.

Father Whitbread stood at Father Fenwick's side, holding him upright. Elizabeth hoped they took some small comfort from seeing their students, who had come to speak in their defence. Father William Harcourt stood beside them in the dock, deep in prayer. To Father Harcourt's right stood Father Anthony Turner. Next to him stood the

317

youngest of the accused, John Gavan, who had not yet taken his final vows. Like everyone else charged with complicity in the Popish Plot, they each held up their hand and answered not guilty to the indictments against them.

Ketch, the hangman, stood by, awaiting the verdict. As Elizabeth took in Ketch's impassive face, he removed a long-stemmed pipe from a bag, filled it with tobacco and lit it. Then he turned and looked out through the open wall of the courthouse.

Titus Oates rose as the first witness for the Crown. He swaggered, sneered and stared at the five Jesuits as he presented his evidence. "I swear that in April last year, these . . ." He turned and pointed to the men in the dock. "Those Jesuits attended a Grand Consult in London, where 'twas agreed to kill the King. I travelled from St Omer and attended the Consult myself. I also saw letters sent and received by these Papist dogs, planning to set up an army as part of a Popish Plot to make England Catholic again."

Filled with his own self-importance, Titus Oates snubbed Chief Justice Scroggs, when he interrupted him. As he outlined the Jesuits' involvement in the Plot, Titus Oates retorted back to Scroggs, "I haven't finished speaking. That is irrelevant. I didn't say that. If I say I can't remember a date or time, then that means I've forgotten. Don't interrupt me again."

The main defence of the five Jesuits was that Titus Oates was a perjurer and had not travelled to London at this time. The boys from St Omer were called as witnesses to this.

The first boy to stand kept his eyes fixed on Father Whitbread; as if reminding himself of the purpose of his evidence. His right eye had started to swell, and a livid bruise had formed on his cheek. As he stood up, a loud hissing erupted from the crowd.

"I… I swear Titus –" The boy swayed and righted himself. "Titus Oates never left St Omer during the time he said he attended the Jesuit Consult in London."

Chief Justice Scroggs giggled. "What? How can you say that with certainty? Are you employed as a watchman at St Omer?"

"No, Your Honour, I am a student."

The crowd chanted, "Papist plotters".

Undaunted, the boy continued. "Titus is a man . . . of some thirty years. He was the only adult studying at our school. I would have noticed if he was missing. He –"

"Yes! Yes! It's all very well to say that, but *how* would *you* have noticed?" Scroggs raised his eyes to the ceiling, setting off a roar of laughter amongst the crowd.

The boy ignored them. "As the only adult student, Titus took his meals at a table on his own, Your Honour. *Everyone* would have noticed his absence at meal times."

Elizabeth's heart quickened, and she reached out and gripped Mrs Cellier's hand. The boy had answered well, and his statement raised questions about the truth of Titus Oates' evidence.

As the other boys stood and presented their testimonies, Scroggs sneered and giggled, and the crowd heckled and hissed, making it difficult to hear what the boys said. Undaunted, they all swore that Titus had never left St Omer during the time of the proposed Jesuit meeting.

Elizabeth looked on with a growing sense of fear and bewilderment. What was happening? She struggled to make sense of events unfolding before her and shook her head in despair as the Chief Justice commenced his closing summary.

Scroggs yawned and sat forward. "I apologise to the Jury for having to sit through such a lengthy trial. It is my opinion that much of the evidence presented by the defence is irrelevant. Is it not suspicious each boy said the same thing? I ask you, were they coached? Does anyone believe their evidence is anything other than a part of a plot, and an indication of how far Papists will go? No Catholic witness can be believed."

Fear surged through Elizabeth. Titus Oates was the liar. Their efforts, in bringing the boys to prove this now seemed in vain. Scroggs had made it clear, no Catholic would be believed. Tears welled up, and she bit them back.

Realising there could be no justice in any of the Plot trials, she feared for her husband's life. Her hands clenched into fists. By God, she *would* fight back. She *would* see justice done.

Ten minutes later, when the Jury presented their guilty verdict, roars of approval erupted throughout the courthouse.

Anger rose within Elizabeth, and she jumped up. How in God's name had all this come about? Anger turned to suspicion. As she glanced around the full room, her eyes settled on Shaftesbury.

CHAPTER FORTY-FIVE

The Triple Tree

Jack Ketch, the hangman, sat astride the Triple Tree at Tyburn, smoking his pipe. Fog, drifting in from Wapping, marred what would otherwise have been a perfect June morning. As he sat in quiet contemplation, pipe smoke furled into the air and mingled with the fog.

As usual, he'd arrived as dusk broke, to ensure everything was in place and in working order. It never failed to amaze him to find people already present, having spent the night so they could secure a good vantage point.

Lounging back, Ketch ran over in his mind the arrangements for today's hangings. He believed in using good quality rope and had secured sufficient rope for today's purpose. It was no loss to him. A long queue always gathered, eager to buy a piece of the hanging rope and turning him a good profit.

Hearing a merry tune, he raised his head and looked in the direction of the sound. After stretching his arms, he slid down from his perch and made his way over to the scaffold. He watched as a procession of carts slowly approached, followed by drummers and a fife band. A group of soldiers marched behind, and a great host of people followed behind them.

Removing the stem of his pipe from between his blackened teeth, he moved forward to claim the condemned men. First, he removed Fathers

Whitbread and Harcourt, who were strapped prone onto one hurdle. Next were John Gavan and Father Turner, who were tied onto another. Lastly, Father Fenwick, who was strapped to a hurdle on his own, was removed. Father Fenwick could barely stand, and Ketch shouted to his assistant to carry him up to the scaffold.

Ketch led the others up and made his final preparations.

Despite its vast size, a hush fell over the crowd as the Jesuits uttered their last words. All five Jesuits proclaimed themselves innocent of any involvement in a plot to harm the King, or of attempting to return England to a Catholic regime. Each one finished by proclaiming, "God bless the King."

"The Grand Consult . . ." Father Whitbread informed the crowd, "was nothing more than a medium to select who should take the Province's annual report to Rome, as did Provinces the world over. We were forced to meet in secret because the laws in England forbid Jesuits to meet openly together."

Ketch felt moved by the dying men's speeches, and the crowd remained silent as he started to carry out their sentence. As he adjusted the ropes around their necks and pulled the caps over their faces, a horseman approached, speeding through the crowd and waving a piece of paper above his head and shouting, "A pardon! A pardon! Let me through!"

When the horseman reached the scaffold, the bewildered Sheriff, who was in attendance to oversee the proceedings, hurried over and snatched the paper from his hand. "It's a pardon from the King," he shouted.

The huge crowd gasped and surged forward, to hear his words.

"A pardon will be granted to any, or all, of the condemned men who admit their part in a Papal conspiracy and will provide more details of what they know," the Sheriff announced.

In turn, each Jesuit thanked the King for his offer of a pardon but declared they could not admit to something of which they had no knowledge. Each finished with the words, "God save the King, and grant forgiveness and mercy to all those who lied against us."

Ketch, who stood to the side, listened as each man again declared his innocence, and in doing so refused the Royal pardon to spare his life. He now had no doubt in his mind that these men were innocent of the charges brought against them, and felt moved to a level of compassion he'd never before felt as a hangman. Not one person charged so far in this Papal plot had admitted any involvement in it. Now, here were five men who refused to save their own lives, by admitting any knowledge of it. The significance of this struck home to Ketch.

Once the horseman departed, with the reply that none of the accused accepted the pardon, Ketch, despite a heavy reluctance, set about the task of carrying out their sentence. Contrary to instructions, he ensured they died quickly. To make sure they were indeed dead, he grabbed each man around the waist as they hung, and pulled downwards with all his weight. When he had finished, there were no roars of approval.

Most of the crowd drifted away with a piece of the dead men's clothing or bit of the hanging rope clutched in their hands and, Ketch had no doubt, questions on their minds. Even the broadsides distributed the following day, confirming that the five Jesuits were guilty of treason, did little to quieten Ketch's growing uncertainty.

The dying Jesuits had all prayed: "Blessed Jesus into thy hands receive my soul and my spirit. I am ready." When given the opportunity of a pardon, not one of them had sold their soul to save their earthly body. Ketch scratched his head, in bemused contemplation.

Doubts about the reality of a Papal plot seemed to be growing around him. In the tavern that evening, he listened in to talk that the Plot wasn't believed abroad. Indeed the accusers were laughed about in France. Everywhere he went, the roots of doubt were shooting buds, as questions were openly raised as to why not one single person accused had admitted their guilt, and why devout Catholics were prepared to face their God with lies on their lips and sins in their souls.

Attired in his new clothes, Dangerfield spent his days in the coffee houses, gathering whatever information he could about members of the Country Party. He took a seat near anyone he considered worthy of note and listened in on their conversations. When they grew accustomed to his presence, he joined their tables and their discussions. He even considered becoming a member of the Country Party but baulked at paying the hefty admission fee.

At the end of each day, he returned to Mrs Cellier's house, where together they wrote down the names, roles and discussions of each member he had met or heard about.

Parliament, prorogued in April, had re-opened and wherever Dangerfield went, Shaftesbury's speeches being hotly debated amidst the coffee and pipe smoke. Once again he was pushing to exclude York from the succession.

Dangerfield carefully noted the habits of Shaftesbury and his followers and, with Mrs Cellier's assistance, committed these to paper. When they were finished, they had before them a document containing evidence that Shaftesbury and his supporters were involved in a Protestant plot to replace James of York with the King's bastard son,

Monmouth. Satisfied they held intelligence that would cast doubt upon the integrity of the Catholic Plot accusers, they passed the document to Elizabeth, who in turn ensured its passage, person to person – amongst the Catholic Nobility, until it reached the hand of the King.

Charles passed the document to the Secretary of State, William Coventry.

Coventry informed Dangerfield that he needed to provide evidence to support his claims.

Undaunted, Dangerfield secured letters addressed to Shaftesbury, and with the aid of Mrs Cellier, published pamphlets highly critical of the accusers of the Catholic Lords.

CHAPTER Y FORTY-SIX

The Strategy

"To our continued success," Titus said and raised his glass in a toast.

Shaftesbury and the other accusers, Dugdale, Bedloe and Prance, raised their glasses in reply. They'd finished a meal of partridge followed by plum pudding, all served up in Titus' apartments. During the meal they'd worked out to their satisfaction a strategy on how their evidence against Doctor Wakeman, the Queen's physician, might best be presented at his trial tomorrow.

With Shaftesbury's help, Titus rehearsed each of his fellow accusers on their evidence. He wasn't concerned about his own statement. Chief Justice Scroggs was presiding, and would provide him with assistance if he needed it. The Bench had defended him up until now and would continue to do so. Proving Wakeman's guilt would be a significant step forward for the Country Party, and would cast doubt on Queen Catherine. Their next attack would be on York.

The following morning, Chief Justice Scroggs walked towards the Bench in the Old Bailey. As he passed the other judges, he nodded in acknowledgement to the Mayor.

The King and his loyal supporters sat on one side of the full courtroom, Shaftesbury and his followers sat on the other.

Scroggs' belly churned. This had to be the most important case he had presided over. *Lord God, do not let me get it wrong.* For the first time in the Plot trials, he faced a great dilemma. If Titus Oates' accusations against the Queen's physician were upheld, it could implicate Queen Catherine. He thought the accusers were now taking things too far, and had grown weary of hearing the same stories. The Papal Plot seemed to be falling out of favour, and Shaftesbury's influence over the King had waned.

Scroggs sat down, rubbed the stubble on his face and turned his full attention towards the proceedings. When Sir George Wakeman entered the dock, Scroggs was taken aback by his confident manner. When he considered this, he realised he shouldn't have been surprised. After all, the King had taken a personal interest in his trial and had ensured the attendance of good Protestant witnesses for his defence. Scroggs had no desire to fall foul of these people. The implications of a guilty verdict on Queen Catherine, and hence the King himself, were too obvious to ignore. He determined to exercise caution during these proceedings.

Titus Oates stood first and presented his account. "Doctor Wakeman was Physician to the Society of Jesuits. I saw his Patent. He held out for more money before agreeing to poison the King. I recognised his signature on letters about this because I'd seen it before . . . on a letter of prescription for the Rector of St Omer. I've submitted this letter as evidence. I also saw him at the Jesuit consult in April '78 where he agreed to poison the King if need be. 'Twas *not* his conscience preventing Doctor Wakeman accepting the money offered for doing this but his *greed* for more," he said and pointed over at Doctor Wakeman.

Scroggs groaned. Titus Oates was playing to the crowded courthouse and adding new details to his documented statement.

When Titus Oates finished, Doctor Wakeman challenged him. "You speak as if we've met before, yet you couldn't identify me as the person you speak about. Why is that?"

Titus scowled at Doctor Wakeman. "I *don't* have to answer that question."

"I insist that you do answer, Doctor Oates," Scroggs said and leaned forward. "I am also interested to hear your answer. If, as you say, you had previously met Doctor Wakeman, pray tell me why you were unable to identify him as that person? Mmm!"

Titus stared at Scroggs. "I beg to be excused. I'm not well."

The recorder jumped up. "Bring refreshments for Doctor Oates. Make haste! I want them now. You heard. He is not well. Move yourself!"

Scroggs remained focussed on obtaining an answer. "Doctor Oates, you must answer the question. Why were you not able to identify Doctor Wakeman as the person you witnessed plotting to poison the King?"

Sweat broke out on Titus' forehead, and he rubbed it off with his hand. "Because the light of the candle was in my eyes and I wasn't sure it *was* him. I have weak eyes. And the candle was held too close . . . blinding me. I'd been up all night bringing in Papists!"

Scroggs bristled and stared at him.

Titus returned the stare and sneered: "Anything else?"

Scroggs leant forward. How dare Titus Oates adopt this manner with him. "Yes, there is more. I've heard the excuse of the candle too many times. Surely if you met Doctor Wakeman, then you know him? Either you know him, or you don't. Pray, tell me, which is it?"

Titus sat in sullen silence until Scroggs asked him to present his evidence about Doctor Wakeman's signature on the commission.

"I recognised Doctor Wakeman's writing *and* signature because I'd seen it before, on a letter for medicine for the Rector of St Omer. It was the same signature as I saw on a letter agreeing to poison the King in exchange for £10,000."

"On any other occasion, you would be correct to assume I wrote the letter of prescription for the Rector of St Omer, for that is indeed part of my position," Doctor Wakeman replied in a steady voice. "But . . . as to the letter you refer to, I was too ill to write it myself and asked someone to write it for me. This physician will appear today to confirm it was he, and not I, who penned and signed that particular letter of prescription. A doctor who witnessed the writing of this letter will also be appearing to swear to this. So . . . how can *you* identify the writing and signature on this letter as mine? Hmm!"

Titus Oates turned ashen. Scroggs realised he was looking to him for support, but he was damned if he would help him out of this one without a satisfactory explanation. "The men who are appearing later are both good Protestant witnesses and should be believed. Now, answer the question!"

"These witnesses are mistaken," Titus replied. "It must be a different letter of prescription from the one I am referring to."

"The details you provided are the ones contained in this letter." Scroggs held up the letter. "Are you suggesting there is a second one?"

"Nay! The letter . . . The letter I saw. Yes, I did see it, but not that one. 'Twas . . . Yes. 'Twas written by Doctor Wakeman. I recognised his writing." Titus pointed to the prescription held in Scroggs' hand. "That is a forgery and not the letter I saw."

Scroggs felt anger rising within him. "What! Are you saying you were mistaken?"

"Nay. It was the Privy Council who got it wrong . . . not me!" Titus snapped back.

Scroggs shook his head at Titus' arrogance and observed the stunned silence of the court as they watched to see how he responded to this impertinence. "Pray do not address me in that manner, or tell *me* what to do. Remember, you are sworn on oath in front of God. You will mind your conscience before you speak, and not bear false witness. This is your last warning. SIT DOWN!"

The following day, Bedloe appeared as the chief witness for the Crown. As he puffed on his pipe, he struggled to answer even the most basic questions put to him. He swore he'd seen a paper appointing Wakeman to the post of physician-general in the new Popish regime, but couldn't remember where or when.

Scroggs harboured doubts about Bedloe's character. He felt concerned that this man delivered letters for many prominent people, including those to the Pope, yet showed no scruples in opening their private papers and reading them. Yet, the Commons had never questioned his integrity, in opening the mail he was commissioned to carry.

On the final day, Scroggs summed up. "This has been a long trial, seven days in total, and I thank the jurors for their patience. I would ask them to mind their conscience when determining if Doctor Wakeman is guilty or no of planning to poison the King. And to mind, that if they are not convinced by the evidence presented against him, to let their conscience prevent them from finding an innocent man guilty.

"I doubt the trustworthiness of some of Doctor Wakeman's accusers and warn you to be careful in accepting their evidence. You must all look to your conscience and determine if what has been sworn is true. You must be satisfied it is, before returning a guilty verdict. If you doubt the truth of the evidence presented against the accused, then you are required to acquit him."

The jurors huddled together, engaged in furious debate. After forty-five minutes, the spokesman asked if they might find the prisoner guilty of Misprision of Treason. For the benefit of those in attendance, Scroggs explained this was treason committed by someone who knows it has been or is about to be, committed, but does not report it. He turned to the jurors. "No you cannot."

Scroggs grew unsettled by how long the Jury was taking to reach a decision. He was now in a foul mood. In the course of the week, he'd received proof Father Ireland hadn't been in London during the time Titus Oates had sworn he was at a Jesuit consult there. Scroggs' conscience was now sorely troubled, and he wondered how many more innocent men would die on the false words of Titus Oates? From what he'd heard today, there was no evidence to suggest Wakeman had contrived to poison the King. He would leave it up to the jurors to look to their own conscience. He would see if they reached the same conclusion he had.

After an hour, the jurors announced they were ready to deliver their verdict, and Scroggs made his way back into the courthouse. When he sat down, the Clerk of the Court stood up and asked the jury, "Is Sir George Wakeman guilty of the charge of treason that he stands indicted for, or not guilty?"

"Not guilty," their spokesman replied.

"God bless the King and the Bench," Wakeman called out and slumped forward.

A stunned silence fell over the courtroom. It was the *first* not guilty verdict to be delivered against anyone accused in the Popish Plot.

Castlemaine looked blankly ahead. Elizabeth Herbert sat by his side, tears streaming down her face. King Charles looked stunned and stared around him taking in the scene as if he could not quite fathom what had happened.

When Scroggs stood up, William Bedloe, the letter carrier, pointed his pipe at him. "You haven't summed up the evidence properly. What about all that the accusers said?"

Stopping in his tracks, Scroggs turned and stared at Bedloe. "By what authority does this man speak?" he jeered and made his way out of the courtroom.

The court erupted into a frenzy of chatter and scraping of chairs. Shaftesbury jumped up from his seat and hurried from the court; followed by Titus and Bedloe. On reaching the door, Shaftesbury turned, pointed a finger towards Scroggs and shouted, "You let us down!"

Though he remained incarcerated in the Tower, it was a joyful day for Powis. For weeks now, he'd expected to hear that his own trial was imminent. He'd grown weary of watching the same stone walls, broken only by two windows set in deep arches and the width of the fireplace. Dangerfield had taken notes at Doctor Wakeman's trial and had brought these to Powis' cell to share with him.

Powis took the notes. "Have you knowledge of the other Lords here in the Tower?"

"There's no news, my lord, but I will find out what I can before my next visit."

"And our King?" Powis ran his hands over the stubble on his face.

"His Majesty seems . . . tired, my lord." Dangerfield replied. "The present situation has taken its toll on him. He's so active in habit any change is easily noted by his people."

Powis sat down at a small table and laid the trial notes out in front of him. "I've not set eyes on His Majesty these past two years. Like me, he is no longer young, but is strong nonetheless. He will come through this unscathed."

"Talking of illness, my lord, Bedloe looks as if drink is destroying him. His nose is red and swollen, and his skin is a pasty grey. At Wakeman's trial his memory was poor, and he staggered when he walked. He is not at all well. It also affects his temperament. He's never been jovial, but he's now foul-mouthed and ill-tempered."

Powis smiled. "God forbid, but Bedloe's death will mean one less liar in this world."

CHAPTER FORTY-SEVEN

Counter Plot

July gave way to August, and Titus ambled around Newgate in a foul temper. He had demanded admission to see if he could identify any of the priests incarcerated there, as having involvement in the Popish Plot. As he moved around the cells inspecting the inmates, he seethed at the painful memory of Scroggs' treatment of him during Wakeman's trial. He couldn't shake Scroggs behaviour from his thoughts.

"You! . . . Over there," he roared, pointing to a dirt-encrusted, fettered priest, who from his constant moans, appeared close to death. "What's your name?"

The priest's groans grew louder.

Without waiting for an answer, Titus turned to the warden who accompanied him. "Yes. This dog attended the Consult in April. Have him appear for trial. I'll leave now. I'm dining with Lord Shaftesbury in an hour. I'm starved with hunger. Mmm, we will be dining on roasted pork, my favourite."

Later that evening, Titus raised a glass of sherris sack towards Shaftesbury. They'd finished their meal and remained sitting at a small table in Shaftesbury's garden. "T'was not just Scroggs allowing Wakeman's release, but the way he talked to *me*. 'Tis my mind Scroggs was drunk during the trial. What do you say, my lord?"

Shaftesbury raised his brows. "I think it's likely, Titus. The more I think upon it, the more I recall he was. Scroggs is known to overindulge. Add it to our list."

"Scroggs was so drunk, I recollect that at a few points during the trial he closed his eyes and fell asleep. 'Tis my reckoning he was also... bribed."

After a few moments, Shaftesbury replied. "Wakeman's acquittal is our first failure. I want it to be our last. This has caused immeasurable damage to our plans. Had we succeeded York would have been next. Scroggs has fled abroad, but we can still wreak our revenge on him. Before leaving, he called on the King at Windsor. I wonder what they spoke about. I am incensed by his turn around, but it's only a slight setback. I have reservations about conducting further Plot trials if he is to preside over them."

"Then I . . ." Titus laughed. "No, *all* the accusers will refuse to testify, on the grounds that Scroggs doesn't believe a Papal Plot exists. Scroggs has been bribed by Catholics –"

"Slow down Titus. I think you might have something there. If Scroggs doesn't believe a Papal Plot exists, I can have him arrested. Both Parliament and the Privy Council voted it does. Mmm. Yes. Write treason down as well."

Shaftesbury refilled their glasses and laid the decanter on the table. "We must also move forward with our plans to have York impeached for high treason, but . . . we need witnesses. The Lady Anne travelled to Brussels, to see her father and Mary Beatrice. I've heard she'll remain there three months. This means York won't be back this year and perhaps not until the winter months have passed. Yet another one who has moved out of our reach. And, Charles is doing his damnedest to prevent us excluding York in his absence."

"I don't understand how he is managing to do that?"

"With his usual means," Shaftesbury replied, with contempt in is voice. "He's prorogued the October Parliamentary session until January."

"Is there no other way we can move forward?"

Shaftesbury sipped the sherris sack and laid his glass down. "Monmouth's our only hope. I'm working on my next tract, *An Appeal from the Country to the City*. This tract is an open incitement for Monmouth to strike out for the Crown. The tales of Popery within it will strike fear into the hearts of all Protestants in London. After reading this, they will call for York to be removed from the succession."

Mrs Cellier and Dangerfield arrived without warning at Elizabeth's home and informed her they had startling new information to impart. Elizabeth ushered them through to the withdrawing room, and asked a maid to bring tea and ensure they were not disturbed.

"I'll let Dangerfield explain," Mrs Cellier said, after their tea had been served and the door securely closed behind the maid as she left.

Dangerfield sat forward and rubbed his chin. "This could prove to be a most unexpected step forward in your quest to secure your husband's release, my lady. During my observations of Shaftesbury, it came to my attention that he is consorting with known Republicans."

Elizabeth's hand froze in mid-air. Recovering herself, she replaced her teacup on the low table. "What did you say? Are you sure? But... how?" Shaftesbury was mixing with Republicans again. God's wounds, if the King hears of this. Elizabeth chewed her bottom lip. "These are dangerous men, who were responsible for the Civil War and the execution of the King's father."

"There's more, my lady," Dangerfield said. "Once I became aware of this, I paid particular attention to Shaftesbury's actions. In the course of my investigation, I uncovered some startling information. From what I could gather, he's using the return of their property as a lever to pull the old Republicans back in. I entered his home in secret - don't ask me how- and retrieved correspondence confirming this.

"Those Republicans, whose lives were spared by the King, had their properties confiscated. They'll view this alignment with Shaftesbury as a means of restoring their finances . . . And their positions. After all, if York's removed from the succession, the Monarchy will be headed by the King's bastard son, Monmouth. As the Country Party's marionette, he will not object. Indeed he's agreed to all of this in return for their support."

Elizabeth's hand shot to her mouth, and she let out a gasp. "Charles will be enraged. You say these dangerous men are now in the employ of Shaftesbury?"

"I have letters to prove it, my lady."

Mrs Cellier nodded. "This constitutes a Protestant plot to change the succession. Monmouth, Shaftesbury and Buckingham are involved. Well done, Dangerfield, on gathering this intelligence."

Stunned by these revelations Elizabeth shook her head. *Shaftesbury and Buckingham . . . intriguing with old Commonwealth officers.*

Dangerfield's voice interrupted her thoughts. "My lady, we need to expose this Plot. I obtained information concerning Colonel Mansell. He has met in secret with Shaftesbury and Buckingham and has involved himself in exposing the Popish Plot. Mansell's a known Republican. Very soon, those who brought about the execution of the King's father will be controlling London. I would say this is indeed a Protestant Plot against the King, and the proposed Papal Plot a mere ruse to hide it. Are we agreed?"

Elizabeth and Mrs Cellier looked at each other and nodded.

"Do you think the other Country Party members are aware Shaftesbury is consorting with known Republicans?" Elizabeth asked.

"Nay, I am certain they're not. But, they soon will be," Dangerfield said.

"How should we proceed?" Elizabeth said. "This is dangerous, and we need to act with caution. Though tempting, we shouldn't rush things. For the moment, York and Mary Beatrice are safe abroad, and Charles is keeping Parliament prorogued. I think we should seek Castlemaine's council."

"The Civil War is still fresh in people's minds. Shaftesbury's pushing us towards another conflict," Mrs Cellier said and sighed. "This discovery will strike terror into the hearts of the ordinary people, and Protestant nobles will fear the loss of their homes. I think we have the weapon we need to fight back."

"While the accusations about a Papist Plot rests on lies, this Protestant Plot is founded on truths," Elizabeth said and stood up. "But we need to gather more evidence before we present this."

"I know where Colonel Mansell resides," Dangerfield said. "I could engage rooms in the same lodgings. It would enable me to find out more. If you trust me to do this, I will proceed."

Elizabeth pulled five pounds from her purse and pressed the money into Dangerfield's hand. "God be with you."

CHAPTER FORTY-EIGHT

Jesuit Powder

Under cover of darkness, three cloaked and hooded figures made their way into Windsor. Soft moonlight illuminated the Castle, and they remained in the shadows as they walked. The only sound was the soft clip of their shoes, against the cobbles. They remained silent and kept close together.

As they rounded the final corner, towards the rear of Windsor Castle, William Chiffinch – Keeper of the Backstairs – stepped out to meet them. He held a finger to his lips and ushered them through candlelit passageways, up the back stairs and into the King's bedchamber.

Once inside, James of York and two of the King's trusted aides removed their hooded cloaks.

"By God's good name, we made it. I only hope we were not followed," York stammered as he passed his hooded cloak to Chiffinch and made his way over to Charles' bed.

Charles' aides laid their own cloaks over a chair and stood beside the door.

Reaching the large ornately carved four-poster bed, York gasped as he gazed down on the pale, sleeping form of his brother. Crossing himself, he prayed for Charles' speedy recovery.

Three days ago he received an urgent message from Charles, asking him to return post-haste from Brussels, and to make the journey to London in secret. As heir apparent, he was to make ready to take the Crown, if Charles did not survive the wretched fever enveloping him.

Anxious for his brother's well-being, York set off that same evening, leaving Mary Beatrice and Lady Anne to follow when they could. He had not stopped until now.

Charles opened his eyes and smiled at York. "Dear Jamie, you are here," he said, between laboured breaths. "I had to urge for your discretion. If word leaked out you had returned because of my ill-health, there would be an uprising. The Country Party has already decided that I lie on my death bed." The effort of talking brought on a fit of coughing and Charles spat phlegm into a white cloth.

Bending forward, York helped his brother sit upright, and placed two pillows behind his back

"Fear not. I'm not dying," Charles said and smiled. "Though tell that to the Country Party. Even now they celebrate my impending demise, over their ale. If word reaches their ears that I summoned your return, they will view it as proof that I am indeed at death's door, and present Monmouth as the rightful heir."

York nodded his understanding.

"Odds Fish, I have a lot more life in me before you take the Crown, brother. Nay, I dined on partridge today and devoured it." Charles pushed himself upright. "Granted, two days ago the sweats were upon me, and I couldn't rise from this bed without stumbling."

"But . . . what happened?" York frowned. "You are so rarely ill."

"Truth be told. It was folly on my part. I built up a sweat playing tennis and then went for a walk by the river to cool down. I caught a chill," Charles said and coughed. "Of course, panic ensued amongst my

340

people, and a cry went out that I'd been poisoned . . . by Louise. My darling Fubbs! It struck terror into her heart to be accused. But darn them, I will soon be out of this bed."

"Your recovery seems . . . sudden."

"Along with my physician, Talbot, I had been working on a fever remedy, Jesuit Powder." Charles cleared his throat. "Damned good taste and it works too. I mixed Talbot's 'special bark' with two pints of claret, and take nine spoonfuls at a time. Now, pray let me sleep. Call on me tomorrow, as if returning to London unaware of my illness and I will feign surprise at seeing you. And Jamie . . . God bless you, for returning."

Having received news of the King's illness, Shaftesbury started preparing for an uprising, by pulling together a band of armed supporters. If the King were to die at Windsor, plans had been set in place to march on London, seize the Tower, Dover Castle, and Portsmouth, and then to place the members of the Privy Council under arrest.

Shaftesbury would then push to have Monmouth, acknowledged as the rightful heir.

"Pray be silent!" Charles held up a hand. "I need to think. I cannot reach any decision amidst all this jabbering."

Though it had been over a week since he'd risen from his sick bed, Charles remained fatigued. He walked over to the other side of Queen Catherine's bed and faced the wall. With the threat of a war against France rapidly becoming a reality, he had decided to use this to his advantage. King Louis continually urged Charles to maintain his Royal

Prerogative and establish the Catholic faith in England. The opportunity had now been placed before Charles to turn the French King's ambition to his own benefit.

During Charles' previous negotiations with the French Ambassador, Paul Barillon, Charles had turned down an offer of £200,000 to be paid over three years. To make his position clear to King Louis, Charles aligned himself with Spain, against France. The French Ambassador asked to meet with Charles again, in private, to reach a settlement. To ensure secrecy, they met in the Queen's bedchamber. York was present as a witness.

Charles was pleased with the timing. He'd delayed this meeting so he could dissolve Parliament immediately after it concluded. He was determined to achieve what he desired. Despite his long exile, he'd grown accustomed to having whatever he pleased. Indeed, people fell over themselves to ensure he did, with one exception; Parliament. The reason for this was clear to him. Parliament had developed its own power and what is more *it* held the purse strings, not him.

As he thought through his response, he stared over at the French Ambassador. He was dressed in a black jacket and breeches. The addition of a white frilled collar and cuffs gave him the perfect look of a nobleman. The fashion of Charles' own Court was for colourful, quilted silk coats, coloured breeches and high-heeled shoes with bows on them. Regardless of whether he was indeed a nobleman, Paul Barillon was Louis' spokesman, and Charles wondered how far his cousin could be pushed.

Turning around, Charles nodded to York and addressed Paul Barillon. "I'm willing to withdraw my alliance from Spain and align myself with France –"

"Your Majesty, King Louis, will not forget your loyalty. He –" Paul Barillon replied.

"Pray let me finish," Charles said. "You will understand that there are conditions attached to these actions. They will have to be agreed first. My *offer* does not stand alone. Nay, I'm willing not only to prorogue Parliament but to dissolve it altogether. Members, therefore, will not be able to interfere in any action we agree upon. You must realise that without a Parliament sitting, I will have no revenues paid to me. Your offer of £200,000, paid over three years, is insufficient for me to consider this."

York walked over and stood against the wall beside his brother.

"I'm aware that my cousin, Louis, will be well disposed to this," Charles continued. "Make me a decent offer, and you can return to him secure in the knowledge that you have acted as he would have wanted."

Paul Barillon walked over beside them and smiled. "Your Majesty, if you agree to disengage from Spain and dissolve Parliament, I can verbally offer you a settlement of £250,000, to be paid over the next three years."

Your verbal agreement for… £300,000, paid over the next four years will enable me to dissolve Parliament," Charles replied.

Paul Barillon bowed. "On behalf of King Louis XIV of France, I verbally agree for this amount to be paid in return for your withdrawal from Spain, and the dissolution of your Parliament."

Charles nodded. "Then let us dine. We will leave separately and restrain ourselves in company, for this meeting never took place."

As he left Catherine's apartments, Charles smiled. He now had the funds to be free of Parliament. He could move on to the next stage of his plan. To do this, he needed his brother out of the way. Though he had asked James to leave, following his return during Charles' recent illness, James showed no signs of leaving London again. Charles asked to speak with him in private.

Charles and James of York walked together in the Privy Gardens. It was a warm afternoon, and the gardens were bright with the last of the summer blooms. The leaves were starting to turn on the trees and a few lay on the ground.

Although his health had recovered, Charles remained fatigued, and he settled to James' slower pace. Two spaniels accompanied them, and they trotted on ahead.

"Jamie, you must leave England again, for I cannot carry through with my plans while you are here. I fear for your safety. My actions will result in the Country Party retaliating against you. We both know they will do this. A rising was planned on your return from abroad. You know I set guards to protect you, and had barges made ready to carry you to the Tower. You did not have need of them, but…"

"I understand your concern but feel slighted that I have to leave England while Monmouth remains to win the hearts of the people in my absence. He intends to take *my* place as the rightful heir. How can I leave knowing he will use this to his advantage?"

"I agree," Charles said and nodded "Monmouth has grown arrogant since my illness. He has also changed towards me. I sense his displeasure that I did not die and leave him to claim your Crown. God's wounds, that my son, whom I love beyond reason, would wish me dead."

"Nay! His head has been turned by Shaftesbury, to think he is entitled to more than he merits. Monmouth loves you but has grown to expect your forgiveness for his actions. Indeed I believe he seeks your approval for *his* 'brave' fight for the Crown."

"Then he will be most surprised to learn of my *disapproval*. But you are right about Shaftesbury's influence on him. Monmouth sulks when we meet, and argues for your removal from Court. Since your return, he has grown more arrogant and pushes my patience."

York stopped walking and touched Charles' arm. "Then send Monmouth abroad. Remove *him* from Shaftesbury's influence. Monmouth has changed since your illness. It is not that he desires your death, but he now realises the extent of support for *him* within England. It has increased his desire, for what he thinks is his rightful place as your heir."

"By God, you are right." Charles looked at York. "I don't know whether to be more surprised by what you said, or... that *you* said it. I did not credit you with such awareness of matters. Mmm, you surprise me, brother. Or are these Sedley's words?"

"Well... Well. Mmm. Y-y-yes. I suppose they are. B-b-but they are true," York said, and they continued walking.

Charles laughed. "Regardless, it has made things clearer and I appreciate that. What do you say to Monmouth going for an extended stay with your daughter Mary, in Holland?"

"I would say it is an excellent idea, and add that although the Palace in Edinburgh is not to Mary Beatrice's liking, I will make ready to sail for Scotland."

They walked on in silence.

"Your daughters, the Ladies Anne and Isabella *must* remain in London. It will remind my people that your heirs are Protestants," Charles announced.

"I will push for the trials of the five Catholic Lords held in the Tower,"

Shaftesbury said.

He had been called to Whitehall Palace to speak with Charles in secret, to find a mutually agreed way out of the current exclusion crisis. Shaftesbury wanted Parliament re-opened, but Charles refused to consider this while the Exclusion Bill was under debate.

"It's been almost two years, but I remain determined to see justice served on all those involved in this Papal Plot against your life, Your Majesty," Shaftesbury continued. "I wanted to give you fair warning of this."

Charles turned to face him. "How do you think that would sit on my conscience? To see five of my loyal Lords executed at your whim? It is not an option. I need you to drop the Exclusion Bill."

"Nay, that is impossible, Your Majesty. Not while a Catholic is heir to the throne. Divorce Catherine, marry a Protestant. You are virile. You have many lusty bastards to prove it. Face it! Your Queen is barren. I will make it easy for you to –"

"Never!" Charles said and stepped towards him.

"But, Your Majesty, if you produce a Protestant heir then James is removed from the succession. It is the solution we seek."

Charles walked away. Turning back around, he pointed a finger at Shaftesbury. "Nay, it is the solution *you* seek. Why has the Country Party turned against me?"

Shaftesbury hesitated before replying. "Some say you are too close to Catholic France."

"God's truth, Louis is my cousin," Charles said and glared at him. "He helped me during my long exile. Do these people expect me to turn away from him now? Well! Do they?"

Shaftesbury stared back. "Both King Louis and France are Catholic.

Protestants in London fear a return to a Catholic state, Your Majesty. There is even a rumour that Papists intend to poison the water supplies of every Protestant. Your subjects are now watching to see where your loyalties lie. It is not my doing. This is what your people fear. And you . . . You asked me to tell you."

"Yes! Yes, I did. I was nineteen when my father was executed. I never understood why people would turn against their King. But I understand the consequences well enough, for I have had to live with them."

Shaftesbury held up a hand. "We'll drop the Exclusion Bill and assure you have vast revenues if you consent to divorce Queen Catherine and marry a Protestant. That is all we ask."

"I have already told you that it is not an option. I will, however, re-open Parliament so that we can engage in *fair* debate. That is all *I* ask. I'm well aware my Queen and her physician were implicated by you in order to force our divorce. Stop playing with the lives of my family. And that includes my son, Monmouth. You are using his youth and ambition to your own ends. I love my son *and* my Queen, and will not stand by and watch you destroy them.

"As we do not seem to have reached any solution to our current differences, consider the October session of Parliament prorogued until January. If by then no solution is reached, well . . . . Consider it prorogued until we do."

Realising he had been dismissed, Shaftesbury bowed and, barely managing to control his seething anger, backed out the room.

CHAPTER FORTY-NINE

The Meal Box

While Colonel Mansell was away on business, Dangerfield reported to the authorities his suspicion that a parcel of Flanders lace had been smuggled into England by an individual, who, it turned out shared his lodgings. As no Justice of the Peace would investigate his allegations, Dangerfield continued to push the point, and eventually a warrant was obtained through customs to search Mansell's rooms.

Having managed to secure rooms in the same dwelling, Dangerfield met the customs officers at the entrance to the building and escorted them to Mansell's lodgings. After forcing the door, the officers went through the rooms, pulling out drawers, lifting rugs, opening cupboards, searching under the bed and mattress, before declaring they could find no trace of any Flanders lace.

Dangerfield paced the room. "I beg you, keep searching. I know the lace is here, for I saw him bring it in."

"These rooms have already been thoroughly searched and enough of our time has been wasted," the senior officer replied.

"No!" Dangerfield stood in front of him. "No, you have not looked everywhere." He moved across the small room. "You've not looked here." He reached behind the bed and pulled out a stack of papers. He flicked through the papers and shouted, "Treason! It is treason!"

The senior officer gaped at Dangerfield and retrieved the papers from his hand. "How did you know these were there?" he asked, while scanning through them.

"I … I did not know, but… I realised you hadn't searched behind the bed. It's the kind of place I would conceal something, and this put the thought into my head."

The customs officers moved towards the door.

Dangerfield paled. "Where are you taking these papers?"

The senior officer paused. "To a Justice of the Peace, and *you* are accompanying us."

As Dangerfield followed the men outside, a great sense of foreboding flooded through him. When they reached the offices of the Justice of the Peace, Dangerfield was told to wait in the corridor, while the officers went inside. Ten minutes later he was called into the room.

Looking over a pair of half-moon spectacles, the Justice of the Peace peered at him. "Thomas Dangerfield, I do not believe your account of how these papers came to be found behind the bed in Colonel Mansell's lodgings. It's my view this whole business is suspicious. How these damning papers came to be found at all, I'm not sure. I will have the Privy Council carry out an investigation into the matter."

Feeling as if the lifeblood was flowing from him, Dangerfield swayed.

Early the next morning, he sat on a bench in a corridor at Westminster, waiting to be called for examination by the Privy Council. A guard stood on either side of him. Running his fingers through his hair, Dangerfield pondered a way out of his present predicament. *There's no proof I placed the papers behind the bed. Pish, they contain the intelligence I gathered and documented for Mrs Cellier. She will surely stand by me? She will vouch for the truth of what I say. No, I'll deny it all. Damn, but how do I account for –"*

"Thomas Willoughby? I've 'bin looking for 'yer for quite some time," someone said, pulling him from his thoughts.

Glancing in the direction of the voice, Dangerfield found himself staring straight into the face of the Officer who had arrested him for forgery. He thought he had left that part of his life behind. Now it seemed his past had finally caught up with him. Thomas Willoughby, alias Dangerfield, glanced around for an escape route and made to stand up.

Hooking his finger, the Officer beckoned to the guards. "Arrest this man. He has twice stood in the pillory for theft, and dodged a sentence for forgery by escaping from prison."

Dangerfield slumped back onto the bench, laid his elbows on his knees and let out a moan.

Mrs Cellier was at breakfast when her maid brought a folded note into her. Opening it, she gasped as she took in its contents.

Mrs C, this morning I was committed to Newgate and

urge you to provide assistance to secure my release.

Dangerfield

Mrs Cellier dabbed her mouth with a napkin and rose from the table. "Fetch my cloak and gloves and... call for a coach. Make haste! I have to go out," she called to the maid, as she made her way through to her workroom. She was fearful of what Dangerfield could disclose.

In the workroom, she unlocked a cupboard in the oak bureau and retrieved a small metal cash box. Opening the lid, she counted out ten pounds. She prayed it would be sufficient to cover Dangerfield's bail. After locking the box away again, she stood up and pulled a sheet of paper from a drawer. Picking up her writing implements, she sat down and scrawled:

D, I never change.

Mrs Cx

Mrs Cellier pushed the money into her purse and hurried to Newgate to arrange for Dangerfield's bail and ensure he received her message.

Arriving at the gatehouse, she gave a sigh of relief to see the warder on duty was someone she recognised. She'd been visiting Newgate for years, distributing alms to the poor, and knew many of the warders and their wives.

Half an hour later, she climbed back into the coach and made her way to 66 Lincoln's Inn Fields, to share her news with Elizabeth. As soon as they were seated in Powis' study, Mrs Cellier handed Dangerfield's letter over.

Elizabeth read it and held her hand to her mouth. "I know you're *fond* of Dangerfield, but... I no longer trust him."

"And you have good reason, my lady," Mrs Cellier said and raised her brows. "I've just had a lengthy talk with an acquaintance of mine at Newgate. It seems *our* Dangerfield, who I put up in my own home, turns out to be nothing more than a common thief and scoundrel. He's been arrested as an escaped criminal, for having forged coins. Dangerfield's nothing but an alias. His real name is Thomas Willoughby."

"Dear God in heaven, what are we to do?" Elizabeth said and crossed herself.

"There is more, my lady. He's a friend of Bedloe's –"

"But... how? I don't understand."

"Ah! Dangerfield and Bedloe were in prison together. They know each other ...very well."

"Does this mean all his deeds and words to help us were nothing but lies? Surely not," Elizabeth said and wrung her hands down her linen gown.

Mrs Cellier shrugged. "The documents found at Colonel Mansell's lodgings didn't only contain the evidence we gathered. From what I could glean from the warder at Newgate, there are many additions." Mrs Cellier let out a loud snort. "He's extended our information into a Protestant Plot, implicating Shaftesbury, Buckingham, Monmouth, and Sir William Waller, amongst others. I don't know what Dangerfield, rather Willoughby, plans to do next? I managed to secure bail, so he'll be released until his trial."

"Waller, by God! Waller?" Elizabeth jumped up. "The Justice of the Peace who relishes catching priests and burning Roman Catholic books and vestments?" She slumped back onto her seat. "We need to inform Castlemaine. And . . . we need to distance ourselves from Dangerfield."

"He'll receive no further assistance from me, my lady."

The following afternoon, Mrs Cellier startled when her maid announced that Dangerfield had called. Rushing through to the hall, she ushered him into her workroom and pushed the door closed behind them.

"Dear God, what is happening?" she asked, as a flush spread across her cheeks.

Dangerfield bowed. "Ma'am, I apologise for having placed you in danger. I've brought you the original papers outlining the information we gathered. Many are written in your hand. I urge you to hide them."

"Thank you... Thank you for bringing these to me." She took the documents. "They contain dangerous information against Shaftesbury. God be with you," she said and tightened the red ribbon, tying the rolled up papers together.

"If you'll excuse me, ma'am, I've been called to attend an interview with James of York."

Mrs Cellier escorted Dangerfield out. Closing the door behind him, she leant against it deep in thought.

Minutes later, she entered the kitchen and called to her maid. She handed the roll of papers to the girl. "Hide these. You know this kitchen better than I do. Place them somewhere no one, not even I can find them. I should burn them, but they contain valuable information." She wasn't concerned the maid would look at the papers, for the girl could neither read nor write. "Please make sure you hide them well," she added and walked out the kitchen.

In the late morning, five days after Dangerfield's visit, Mrs Cellier was startled by pounding at her front door. Looking out of the workroom, she shuddered when she saw Sir William Waller waving a warrant in her maid's face. She walked over to meet him.

"Mrs Elizabeth Cellier," Waller said and stepped forward. "I have a warrant to search these premises."

She turned to her maid, who was now in tears. "Hush you. Go into the kitchen and leave this to me."

"Oh ma'am!" the maid wailed and set off along the hall.

"Carry out your search of my home, if you must. My husband is abroad. Apart from the servants, I'm quite alone. Am I permitted to ask whom or what you are searching for?"

"Nay," Waller replied and swept past her with his search party.

As they pulled her house apart, Mrs Cellier followed behind. She shrieked when a man picked up and discarded her precious midwifery notes. When pages from her manuscripts floated to the floor, she yelled at him to take care. She objected when another man examined her undergarments and pulled her dresses off their hangers and dropped them to the floor. She looked on as the men searched the servant's rooms, and ground her teeth as they searched her dining room, grabbing at her fragile glasses with their clumsy hands.

She dropped onto a chair and watched as they searched her kitchen. Sighing with relief, she followed them as they walked out the back door to search the outhouses. She froze when one of Waller's men pulled his hand out of a meal-tub and held up the papers she had asked the maid to hide.

These same papers, Mrs Cellier now knew, contained allegations of high treason. They named certain Protestants, including Sir William Waller, who now stood in front of her and said, "Mrs Cellier I am arresting you on suspicion of high treason, for attempting to fabricate a Protestant Plot against the Duke of York."

Mrs Cellier nodded and raised her brows to the sobbing maid.

Dangerfield soon realised no one wanted to hear about any Protestant Plot and his life would be in danger, were he to continue to claim such a plot existed. Elizabeth, Mrs Cellier and Castlemaine had withdrawn their support of him. Realising he was now on his own, he asked to speak to Robert Clayton, the Lord Mayor, to make a confession.

"The Meal-tub Plot is a sham," he told Clayton. "It was invented to cover the intentions of Papists. It was an attempt to discredit Shaftesbury and the Popish Plot."

"The papers found in the meal tub and the treasonable letters I placed behind Colonel Mansell's bed, were dictated to me by Elizabeth Herbert, Countess of Powis. I was employed by the Earl of Powis to assassinate Shaftesbury and was to be paid a sum of five hundred pounds for doing so. I went to Shaftesbury's home, with the full intention of murdering him, but couldn't bring myself to do it. I invented the Meal-tub Plot, to incriminate leading Protestants and conceal the Papist plan to murder the King.

"Lord Arundell, who is already in the Tower charged with treason, offered me £2,000 to kill the King. All of this was with the knowledge, and at the direction of Roman Catholic priests. Castlemaine coached the sixteen boys who came over from St Omer to attend the trial of the five Jesuits implicated in the Popish Plot. He told the boys what to say, and was also involved in setting up the Meal-Tub Plot, to discredit the Country Party."

Stepping down from her carriage, outside 66 Lincoln's Inn Fields, Elizabeth paused as a cold surge of fear flowed through her.

Castlemaine, who had stepped out the carriage just before her, held his hand out to help her down. "Dear God what is Waller doing here? And surrounded by the King's men."

With a sense of foreboding, Elizabeth linked into Castlemaine's arms and walked with him towards her London home. Evans, the butler, stood outside on the steps, beside the housekeeper and Elizabeth's maid, Beth.

The click-clack of Castlemaine's high-heeled shoes echoed off the cobbles.

Elizabeth stared at Waller's approaching figure and waited to find out what was happening. She did not have to wait long.

"Elizabeth Herbert, Countess of Powis, I am arresting you on an allegation of treason, for conspiring to forge a false Protestant Plot. You will be removed to the gatehouse of the Tower, and may ask a maid to bring your personal items and remain with you, but be quick about it."

Elizabeth felt a scream rising in her throat and made to run towards her house, she had to get to her children. "No! No! My children." Her legs buckled beneath her, and two guards placed an arm each under her arms and marched her towards a waiting coach.

Waller and two guards approached the Earl of Castlemaine and, placing him under arrest, marched him to a separate coach.

"Beth!" Elizabeth screamed out, "Beth! Arrange for the children to go home to Wales. Come to me when you can."

Before she was forced into the carriage, Elizabeth heard Evans, the Butler, shout back to her affirming that he would do as she asked.

CHAPTER FIFTY

Carnival of Lies

Shaftesbury stood on the double balcony of the Kings Head Tavern. Situated on the corner of Chancery Lane, the torch-lit balcony afforded him a superb view of the crowds below who for hours now had been gathering to view the spectacle of the Country Party's Anti-Popery pageant. Further up the street, at the next junction, a bonfire was being prepared in readiness for the celebrations.

Everywhere Shaftesbury cast his eyes, neighbouring balconies and windows were filling to capacity and from the streets below, loud cries of 'No Popery' rang clear and distinct in evidence of a vehement and almost tangible anti-Catholic sentiment pulsating through the crowd.

Since early morning, church bells had rung out in the capital's centre, announcing the Gaudy Pageant and heralding its citizens to the spectacle. People were turning out in their thousands to witness the event, and with a broad smile Shaftesbury removed his green-ribboned hat and whirled it above his head. As a blatant and open challenge to the accepted fashion of the Royal Court, none of the club members wore their periwigs. Raucous laughter broke out among the company, and Shaftesbury joined in.

The Country Party had spent months organising this event, with Buckingham orchestrating the theatricals. To achieve maximum impact, they had staged it on the seventeenth of November, to coincide with the anniversary of the Protestant Queen Elizabeth's accession to the throne; and the triumph of a Protestant rule in England.

Desperate to ensure the people of the capital came out in huge numbers, word had been sent out days beforehand that free alcohol and entertainment would be provided. Shaftesbury's aim was simple – to stir up anti-Catholic feeling. For the Country Party to succeed in removing York from the succession, the people had to be convinced of the veracity of the Popish Plot. Wakeman's acquittal had given rise to doubts as to the credibility of Titus and Bedloe, as Crown witnesses. The Pageant has raised the stakes again, he thought, as loud cheering broke out from the crowds below.

"Ah look. Look it's started," Bedloe shouted, as he removed his pipe and pointed the stem down Fleet Street.

Adding to the glow of thousands of torches, carried by the crowd, lanterns flared into life along the length of the route. At the front, six men, all dressed in distinctive red-coated livery, cleared the street to make way for the solemn procession that, having set out from Moorgate, now approached. As the red-coated men pushed onlookers aside, the noise from the crowd grew louder.

First to come into view was a bellman, carrying a lantern and staff. He rang the bell and in a loud sombre voice repeatedly called out, "Remember Justice Berry Godfrey." The awe of the crowd became almost tangible, as a second man appeared, dressed in the attire of a Jesuit priest.

Despite the rising excitement in the crowd, silence ensued as a horse appeared with an effigy of the murdered magistrate, Edmund Berry Godfrey, sitting astride it. A man on horseback, dressed as a Jesuit priest, followed behind carrying a second effigy of Godfrey's dead body – a very clear reference to the way his murderers might have conveyed him to Primrose Hill.

The crowd screamed out, "No Popery!" "Remember Godfrey!" "No justice!"

Drinking in the scene, Shaftesbury couldn't contain his delight and swirled his green-ribboned hat over the side of the balcony. Beside him, Titus twirled in a green coloured cloak and shouted. "Blaady Papists! Leave London now! You murdered Godfrey!"

The excitement of the crowd grew to the point of hysteria, as yet another man dressed in a priest's habit advanced with the parade – offering pardons to anyone who would murder Protestants. A further group of men, all dressed as priests, accompanied by six more dressed as Jesuits and holding up bloody daggers, followed behind.

The tumult of emotion in the crowd was spirited even higher by the emotive music sent out by a group of players, who moved alongside the procession.

Tears streamed down Shaftesbury's face. The display was everything and more than he had expected. The relief of seeing the total enthrallment of those watching this gaudy pageant was like a weight lifted from his shoulders. He had no doubt now that the interest of the Protestant public in the Popish Plot had been regained. *And be damned, he would repeat this pageant every year to maintain it.*

Shaftesbury's attention returned to the parade which, following a brief halt had now restarted. A series of effigies of famous Catholics of the day rode by on horseback. Two mounted men led the way. Firstly came a caricature of the King's Catholic cousin, King Louis of France, followed by a second likeness representing the Duke of York.

The crowd looked on in awe at the spectacle appearing before them and was once again whipped up into a frenzy of emotion when a long array of Catholic dignitaries appeared followed by . . . a glorious, golden tasselled, red velvet chair-of-state covered in golden balls and crosses. An effigy of the Pope sat on the chair. At the Popes' feet, two reclining boys swung the silver vessels Catholics used at Mass for burning incense. Sitting at his back, a man dressed as the Devil, caressed and hugged the effigy of the Pope and loudly urged him to forge a plot to kill the King. Finally, the Devil passed the Pope a burning torch and asked him to set London ablaze again.

The procession halted below the balcony of the Green Ribbon Club. Shaftesbury stood spellbound as fireworks exploded above it, illuminating the night sky, and the prepared bonfire was set alight. When the fire blazed, the actors jumped off the chair and tipped the effigy of the Pope into the burning flames. As carcases of dead cats and dogs were hurled into the fire, the roars from the crowd grew deafening.

A cheer went up from those on the balcony, followed soon after by a host of green-ribboned hats. Amidst the flickering flames, and the stench of seared flesh, Shaftesbury roared, "No Papists!"

The following morning, Titus still brimmed with excitement. He chattered nonstop to anyone who leant half an ear to his ramblings. At 10 am, when a servant showed Shaftesbury into his apartment, Titus whirled around with a smile on his face.

When Shaftesbury did not reciprocate, Titus baulked. "What naaw?"

Shaftesbury laid his sticks down, took off his coat and placed it on the back of a chair. Sitting down, he stretched his legs out in front of him, crossed his arms and stared up at Titus.

Determined not to be intimidated, Titus took a seat beside him.

"What a show, the Gaudy Pageant -," Titus blustered on. "I've never seen anything like it. It made them -" He licked his lips. "The Pope thrown into the burning flames. No Papery," Titus mimicked the cries of the Crowd.

When he stopped talking, Shaftesbury came straight to the heart of the matter. "Do you remember John Lane, a former servant of yours? He has brought charges against you for sodomy. The Country Party spent thousands of pounds on the Anti-Popery Pageant to revive interest in the Popish Plot. I will NOT have you compromise it now."

Incensed, Titus jumped up from the seat. "Charge him with... complicity. Have him indicted now for . . . Straight away. He's involved in the Plot. He's trying to discredit me. I'll see him HANG."

Shaftesbury looked up at Titus and said nothing.

CHAPTER FIFTY-ONE

River of Tears

As the year of '79 wore away, Powis languished in the Tower and listened to the bells of All Hallows. Over a year had passed since he first entered the Tower. It seemed like a lifetime since he had last seen Elizabeth and their children. From today, he was allowed visitors. He should have felt elated, and derided himself for wishing the privilege had not been granted. He longed to see his wife but feared her reaction on seeing him - this shell of his former self.

Powis struggled to remember how he had been then. But even here, he gave up. All he saw was a bitter, old and useless man, who was no good to anyone. All his fight had left him, and he had long ago resigned himself to his fate.

When the door of the cell squealed open, Powis stiffened.

When Elizabeth entered, tears erupted and trickled down his face.

When she smiled, his heart broke and his tears flowed.

When she held him, it was as if they had never been apart.

Elizabeth was the source of his strength, and it surged from her straight into his soul.

All his bitterness swept away in an instant.

Elizabeth looked into his eyes. "Powis, my darling, I thought I would never see you again. I have been but half of myself without you."

Powis nodded and drank in her presence.

Stepping back, Elizabeth kissed Powis' lips and linked into his arm. "Come, there is much we need to discuss, and we have such a short time. They refer to you all as the five Popish Lords. The King has been delaying your trials, but things have changed in recent days. It is not good. Not good at all. The Bill –" She saw the pain etched on Powis' face and held him close. "So much has happened, and it's vital you are kept informed. Mary has been visiting Stafford and has told him. Excepting York... a Bill has been passed by the Lords preventing Catholics from sitting in Parliament."

Powis trembled. "I cannot believe this. Never –" He shook his head. "Never, could this happen. Leave London, Elizabeth. Take the children and return to Wales. Castlemaine will help you do this. Please do it today."

Elizabeth winced at this new suffering she had caused her husband, but Powis had to be aware of everything if he were to succeed at his trial. She would not tell him she was also incarcerated in the Tower. He need not know of it . . . yet. She was being held in the gatehouse and had been permitted to retain her maid, Beth, and other privileges. For a fee, a prison warden had arranged for her to visit Powis' cell.

"I heard that those supporting York were shouted down with cries of, Coleman's letters!"

Powis closed his eyes. "By how many votes?"

"Two," Elizabeth replied and bit on her bottom lip. She held Powis close and informed him that his trial along with the other four Lords, which had previously been delayed by the King, was now imminent. The Privy Council had decided to proceed with the eldest member of the group, Lord Stafford.

"Dear God in heaven. Not our dear, dear friend," Powis said. "I can see him now, announcing the news of my Earldom."

"A lover of justice," Elizabeth added, with a snort. "And what justice is he rewarded with?"

Powis rubbed a hand over the back of his neck. "And the King, York? How do they fare?"

"People fear the Country Party's opposition to the Crown will incite another Civil War. When the King was indisposed with a fever, fear of a rising started when York returned from abroad. Guards lined the city, including outside our home in Lincoln's Inn Fields. Barges were readied to carry the Royal family here to the Tower. But so far –"

"Good God. I feel so helpless, trussed up in here. I have heard nothing about any of this. But, how are you . . . the children? You look tired Elizabeth."

"I have many people lending their support, as you know. We are doing everything we can to bring about your release."

"And Castlemaine, is he well?"

Elizabeth dipped her eyes. "Castlemaine is well. He is a great support."

The cell door swung open, and a head appeared round it. "Time! Gather yer things. C'mon."

As Elizabeth embraced Powis, she slipped him two pamphlets. One was 'London's Defiance to Rome', describing the Pope burning procession. The other was an account of a farce written by Etherege and currently playing, entitled, 'She Would if She Could'.

Powis smiled as he glanced at the second pamphlet, and as its full meaning dawned on him, he looked up at Elizabeth and roared with uncontrolled laughter.

Part Seven: The King's Move

1680

*'Wickedness may prosper for a while, but at the long run
he that sets all knaves at work will pay them.'*

Roger L'Estrange

CHAPTER FIFTY-TWO

Penny Lies

Titus' carriage clattered to a halt outside the Country Party Club in Chancery Lane. As he stepped out, a woman hurried towards him, dragging a younger woman by the arm. They were both dressed in fashionable satin gowns.

"Doctor Oates," the older woman called out and gasped for breath. "I am pleased to have caught up with you at last. I would like you to meet my daughter," she said and pushed the young woman in front of him.

Titus removed his hat and bowed to the girl. "A pleasure to make your acquaintance."

The girl blushed and glanced round at her mother, who raised her brows as if urging her to say something.

Though Titus thought the young woman attractive, he couldn't keep up with the sheer number of mothers who wanted him to marry their daughters. Assuming this was another such one, he smiled and excused himself.

He was still smiling when he entered the club. After calling out to the proprietor to bring him some ale, he joined the other members, gathered around a large table. Each man wore silk armour and held Protestant flails in their hands.

Shaftesbury patted his silk vest and laughed. "To think the public believe these are bulletproof. How gullible can people be?"

"And they carry their Protestant flails in their pockets." Bedloe bellowed with laughter. "What good would it do in an attack on their life? God's truth, Protestants are so afraid they believe anything possible."

Reaching out, Titus accepted the tankard, which had been brought over to him, and took a large swallow. Already in a jolly mood, the nature of the conversation made him laugh. "I hear Protestants are sleeping with pistols under their pillows. Should Papists swoop under darkness, then they will have met their match."

Around the table, the members erupted into roars of laughter, and Titus grinned.

Shaftesbury guffawed, wiped his mouth with a handkerchief and blew his nose. "I haven't laughed so much or so loud in a long time. It does us all good, I think. But... let us move on to the purpose of this meeting and the real cause of our good cheer. Chief Justice Scroggs."

On hearing Scroggs name, Titus straightened. "The man's an ass. He dared to –"

"Yes, Titus, but we must move on," Shaftesbury said. "We've much work to get through to ensure Scroggs' conviction . . . and removal from office. Placing an indictment before the Privy Council for his role in Wakeman's acquittal is but a first step. We need a plan to see this through. We also need a strategy for the upcoming general election. We have to remain focused. We need a scandal. Something to put out to the Protestant public. Something to justify the cost of their silk armour, perhaps?"

Titus roared with laughter. "Bogtrotters the lot of them. All Royalists are blaady Tories. They think us no better than . . . than the rebels of

Scotland. They think themselves cream and us as sour milk. They think of us as . . . Whigs!" He recalled names he'd heard bandied about and used them now in the hope it would cause further laughter.

"I like it," Shaftesbury said and snorted. "Bogtrotters indeed, Titus. Ha, ha! Tories. They should watch out for us . . . Whigs. Ha ha! I do like it."

Titus swelled with pride.

The press censor, Sir Rodger L' Estrange, read through the pamphlet 'Papists Plotting to Kill the King' and saw it as another poor attempt to turn the public against James of York and a Catholic succession. L' Estrange had tried to refrain from commenting on this latest plot. Too many people who'd spoken in defence of the accused had been implicated themselves. Having been imprisoned in Newgate, charged with spying during the Civil War, L' Estrange had no desire to repeat the experience.

As press censor, he was aware of *all* newspapers, broadsheets and pamphlets circulating throughout London, and regularly published articles to cast doubt upon those he considered untruthful. He referred to them as 'Penny Lies' and was intolerant of even the mildest.

He knew the Earl of Castlemaine as a kind and learned man, and had been shocked by his arrest along with the Countess of Powis and Mrs Cellier, the midwife. He realised with a growing certainty that the Country Party were trying to prevent a Catholic succession. He inhaled and rubbed at his chin. He needed to put aside fears for his own safety. The more he had thought about it, the more he realised he had to say something.

He didn't have to do anything which would draw attention to himself.

He could respond with wit, attack Shaftesbury and his growing band of Popish Plot accusers indirectly, using innuendo . . . just enough to raise questions about their trustworthiness.

As an experienced news writer and critic, L' Estrange determined that the best means of calming the present hysteria was through pamphlets challenging the truthfulness of the allegations made about a Papal Plot.

Titus Oates' latest accusations against Chief Justice Scroggs infuriated L'Estrange. Oates was refusing to attend trials over which Scroggs presided, claiming Scroggs cursed to excess and was against the Plot accusers.

These accusations disturbed L'Estrange. Never before had such blatant lies gone unchallenged. But, anyone speaking out against Titus Oates was revenged. He wondered who would be next. Perhaps it would be him. But he would make damned sure before this happened that doubt was raised about the *word* of Titus Oates.

Writing by candlelight, L' Estrange knew his actions were dangerous, but someone had to speak out. If he did, then others might follow his example. He'd never believed in the truth of the Popish Plot and thought it nothing more than a conspiracy. Now, as he pushed forward with his first attack on the credulity of Shaftesbury and his followers, using hints where points couldn't be made directly, he was determined to raise doubts in people's minds.

He developed a code: Aldersgate, referred to Shaftesbury. Billingsgate, to the Country Party, and Wapping meant Mob Rule. With care, he selected each word.

Mmm, how best to portray Titus Oates and William Bedloe, he thought, as he dipped his pen into the ink.

Citt and Bumpkin in a Dialogue Over a Pot of Ale, Concerning

Matters of Religion and Government, by Sir Roger L' Estrange

There appeared in London two heavenly witnesses, as from the book of revelations, whose mission is to prophecy. Based on the evidence of these informers every subject in England will hang - if found guilty.

These witnesses from Aldersgate were trained at the Universities of Billingsgate and Wapping.

Reading over his words, L' Estrange felt satisfied he'd made a start on his first onslaught. He determined that it would not be his last.

CHAPTER FIFTY-THREE

A Case to Answer

Night after night Elizabeth woke in a sweat, a dream hovering on the edge of her awareness, of Powis' demise. Each dream took on a different form of death. In this one, Powis had fallen from a cantering horse, and she had stood by frozen, unable to help him. Pulling her hands through her hair, she shuddered and forced the memory away.

Although it was still night, she lay there awake and would not be able to go back to sleep. She threw the blanket back and stepped out of bed. Taking care not to wake her maid, Beth, lying on the floor on a pallet mat, Elizabeth slipped on an over-robe and paced her cell.

Pushing a stray strand of hair from her face, tears formed and she let them flow. It had been eight months since her arrest, and seven months since she'd last seen Powis. Though she'd tried to keep her incarceration from him, he was now aware she was being held in the Gatehouse of the Tower.

She stepped up onto a small bench and looked out of the narrow window, overlooking the Thames. A mist hung above the water, cloaking it in a fine gossamer shroud. She shivered as she recalled looking out over the same river on the day Mary Beatrice had arrived from Italy as York's new bride. Six years had passed since then, and her circumstances had changed beyond all recognition.

Imprisoned in the bleak cell, she had had plenty of time to reflect over all that had taken place since York's marriage to Mary Beatrice. She missed Mary Beatrice and wondered if her dear friend was safe. She thought of Edward Coleman and shivered. She was certain now he had been guilty of nothing more than meddling in matters that were none of his concern. So many of her good friends and Fathers had been hung at Tyburn or died fettered and filthy in Newgate. Was this to be her fate, and Powis'?

Beth had informed her that the children had been removed to Wales, as Elizabeth had instructed. Her eldest daughters, Mary, Frances and Anne, would care for the younger children. William was now fifteen, Lucy eleven, and Winifred almost eight-years-old.

Gazing out the window, her thoughts turned back to Powis. What was he doing? All she had wanted was to be a good wife and mother and keep her family safe. All she had desired was to keep them close by her. She had failed both as a wife and as a mother. Her heart ached with a desire to see them all again.

She recalled the last Christmas they'd spent together at Powis Castle, enacting out a traditional Christmas. They'd gathered bunches of holly, tied coloured ribbons into bows around their stems and strung them around the hall. They'd eaten hot mince pies straight from the oven and sung carols.

"Peace on earth and goodwill to all men," she sang out, and her voice broke into a sob.

A few hours later, after Beth had dressed Elizabeth, a gaoler arrived. He escorted Elizabeth from the cell and brought her to stand before the King's Bench. She shivered and wondered what fate awaited her. Why was she so weak? She tried to keep her thoughts away from how the children would manage if she were to join Powis in the Tower. Or worse

. . . if they were both executed. She had fought to keep her family safe, now it all seemed in vain.

As she stood at the bar, the opening statements passed in a fog of confusion. It was as if Chief Justice Scroggs was referring to someone else. Elizabeth couldn't contemplate leaving Powis or her children. She looked over at the window, set high up on the opposite wall. The large, dark and dismal room provided a stark contrast to the sun shining outside. She wondered if she would ever feel the sun again.

Elizabeth's eyes widened when Chief Justice Scroggs advised the jury: "It is my opinion there is no case to answer."

Had she heard him correctly? She held her breath and studied the dust motes floating in the shaft of sunlight flooding through the window.

The jury consulted for a few minutes and then declared they were ready to deliver their verdict. Unable to turn away, Elizabeth looked directly at them.

The spokesman stood. "No case to answer."

A smile spread over Elizabeth's face. She had been acquitted, of all charges.

The following day, Elizabeth attended the Earl of Castlemaine's trial, with her lady's maid, Beth. Castlemaine had been accused of intriguing with Jesuits to kill the King, and instructing the sixteen boys who attended from St Omer, as witnesses against Titus Oates at the trial of the five Jesuits.

Elizabeth worried at her pearl necklace and said a silent prayer for Castlemaine's release. It seemed too much to hope for. Samuel Pepys, of the Navy Board's, case had been heard following hers, and he had also been released. After all this time, Elizabeth wondered if justice could prevail.

When Chief Justice Scroggs entered the courtroom, Elizabeth trembled. She realised how close she had come to being convicted of treason.

Castlemaine was brought into the dock and, despite his time in the Tower, looked clean and well presented.

When Titus Oates stood to give his evidence against Castlemaine, Elizabeth chewed on her bottom lip.

Titus Oates stood directly in front of Castlemaine and glared at him. "My Lord, Castlemaine was in correspondence with Jesuits in Valladolid in Spain and St. Omer. From reading his letters, I discovered that after his divorce from Lady Castlemaine, he had become a priest. It was Castlemaine who arranged for the sixteen boys to be brought over from St Omer, and he schooled them in what to say to discredit the veracity of the Popish Plot against the King's life."

Elizabeth looked on with complete confusion. God's wounds, why does anyone believe a word of his lies? The press censor, L' Estrange had begun to raise questions, but would this be enough? Her heart raced when permission was granted for Castlemaine to speak.

"You claim I'm a priest. Perhaps you saw me while studying at the University of Salamanca where you obtained your Doctorate. Perhaps it was at Valladolid where you also say you studied in Spain. I have been to neither of these places . . . yet. As for the letters, where are these letters? You mention my correspondence but don't produce any of it."

Leaning forward, Scroggs addressed Titus Oates. "Yes, you mention many letters in your testimonies against Lord Castlemaine, but I have yet to see any of them. I suppose you have these letters?"

"Really, My Lord, no I do not," Titus Oates said and stared at Scroggs. "How could you expect me to have them? God's truth, I read them and then delivered them."

"Then I wish to hear no more about these letters," Scroggs replied. "Do you have anything further to say, Lord Castlemaine?"

Castlemaine produced a record of William Parker's trial at Hastings, which included the verdict that Titus had perjured himself.

The Bench read the trial record but refused to allow young Parker to appear as a witness.

Dangerfield stood as the next witness against Castlemaine. "I was released from prison, by Mrs Cellier, on the condition I assassinated the King, Lord Shaftesbury, and others. Under Castlemaine's instruction, I was to manufacture false plots upon anyone known to be unfavourable to the Catholic cause. Castlemaine told me that the crowd would 'cheer a good dying'."

Scroggs leant forward and summed up the evidence for the jurors. "We have heard today from men grown so insolent they speak against parties when they are guilty of numerous crimes themselves. Though I hold little store by the evidence presented about the Parker trial in Hastings, we have proof Dangerfield has a history of numerous convictions against him. Take care in deciding who to believe.

"If you believe Doctor Titus Oates' testimony but not Dangerfield's, then you must return a not guilty verdict against the accused, for it takes two witnesses to convict a man of treason."

After consulting with each other for a few minutes, the jury pronounced their verdict. "Not guilty."

Elizabeth jumped up and applauded.

A few days later, Elizabeth returned to the Old Bailey with Castlemaine, this time for Mrs Cellier's trial. Elizabeth prayed to Almighty God that her good friend would also be acquitted. It seemed too much to believe that they would all be found not guilty.

Mrs Cellier stood and confirmed that she had taken the details of a Protestant plot from Dangerfield. "I was deceived by him. He led the Crown step by step into finding the information against me."

The charge against Mrs Cellier was high treason. A guilty verdict would mean certain death. Elizabeth thought back to the day Mrs Cellier disclosed Bridgefield's reading to her. Bridgefield had forewarned that someone would infiltrate the Catholic Church, and become a threat to a senior member of State, and England. How right Bridgefield had been. He had also foreseen Mrs Cellier's involvement in these events. Her own and Castlemaine's release had already been achieved. Would Mrs Cellier be answerable for them all? Elizabeth sagged. Her head ached, and she rubbed at her temples.

At long last, Chief Justice Scroggs summed up. "Mrs Cellier has been charged with high treason. It requires two witnesses to bring about a guilty verdict. Only one witness has appeared against her. It is my belief that Thomas Willoughby, alias Dangerfield, is an unreliable witness. As no other witnesses have appeared to speak against her, Mrs Cellier is acquitted of all charges."

A squeal rose in Elizabeth's throat, and she tried to hold it back without success.

Scroggs banged his gavel. "Silence! Pray, be silent. Thomas Willoughby, alias Thomas Dangerfield, you will be removed from here and placed in Newgate prison where you will serve out the remainder of your sentence on the outstanding charge of making false coins."

Elizabeth stared in disbelief. Mrs Cellier had been released, and Dangerfield returned to prison. For the first time in years, Elizabeth allowed herself to truly believe that Powis could also be released.

CHAPTER FIFTY-FOUR

Little Sincerity

William Bedloe stared at Lucy Oates through a drunken haze. Pish, of all the distinguished guests in attendance, he'd been seated next to this woman of a thousand questions. He'd been surprised to receive the invitation to attend a meal in London for himself and Titus, in honour of their good work towards the Protestant religion.

Titus's mother, Lucy, had questioned him endlessly about his wife. "Yes, Anna remained in Bristol," he replied. "No, she's not English, she's Irish."

He found her questions annoying and wondered where she was going with them. Along with her sister, Anna was co-heir to hundreds of pounds per year. No doubt she'd heard rumour of this from Titus. Well, she could prattle on all she liked, he would not confirm this to her.

He could see the gleam in Lucy Oates' eye, reflecting a hope that Titus would also marry into a good family. Her questions were driven by self-interest, rather than any genuine concern for him, he concluded in his alcohol befuddled state.

When Lucy asked him about Titus, Bedloe's head swirled. She had come knocking on the wrong door if she expected him to satisfy her curiosity about the truth of Titus' accusations.

"Indeed I do not like it at all," Lucy said. "God bless Titus, for I'm concerned he might end up in trouble again," she confided, as they stood up from the table.

Bedloe remained silent. He had concerns of his own to contend with and made no effort to reassure her.

The following day, Bedloe rushed back to Bristol to see Anna. He had received a letter from her that morning, informing him that she was ill and needed him to return home. As he cantered along the rutted roads, his stomach heaved, and sweat poured from his brow. Slowing the horse to a gentle trot, he drank another swig of wine from a flagon attached to the saddle. Almost at once he leant over to the side and vomited up the contents of his stomach. His thoughts raced. Pish, how would he make it home? He dare not stop to rest. He knew without a doubt that if he stopped he would not have the means to resume his journey. Better to keep moving ...Moving. Not far now, he told himself.

Bedloe dug his heels into the horse's side, and it set off again at a canter, which sent fresh waves of nausea through him. Why had he returned to London? He should have bloody stayed away. While there, he had attended as a witness at another of the Plot trials. But . . . he had immediately sensed a change. The judges no longer had any reservations about challenging what he said. He'd been questioned beyond his endurance and asked to state and restate his accusations. He shuddered as he recalled how close he'd come to being thrown into Newgate for perjury. He decided that he had attended his last Popish Plot trial, ever. Never again would he attend as a witness to any bloody Plot trials.

On arriving home in Bristol, Bedloe slid from the horse and staggered into his new home. His last image before he passed out was of Anna trying to catch him in her arms as he collapsed onto the wooden floor.

For two days he slipped in and out of consciousness. His body shook, from both the fever which had claimed him on his way home from London and a lack of alcohol. Whenever he awoke Anna was sitting by his side, tears trickling down her face as she stitched her embroidery. He wanted her to fetch someone to take his dying deposition. "Inform them I will tell everything I know. Tell them I have new information I wish to disclose before I depart from this earth. And Anna . . . don't be denying a dying man. Bring me something to drink, for I know from experience that only alcohol will stop these violent tremors."

The following day, the Chief Justice arrived in Bedloe's bedroom to take his dying statement. Anna remained by Bedloe's side and held his hand.

"Everything I've said is true, my Lord," he told the Chief Justice. "If you secure some money for me from the Crown, I'll provide information I've not yet disclosed. I've no need of money myself, for I'm past cure, but I'll leave a wife of less than one year as a widow."

Two days later, Bedloe died. Despite his promise he disclosed nothing that he had not already revealed.

Titus sat alone at the dining table in his apartments at Whitehall Palace. Papers covered the gleaming oak table; elegies to Bedloe – he had either picked up or had been discretely slipped under his door.

He'd been shocked to learn of Bedloe's sudden death. He felt heartbroken by the loss of such a trusted friend. He'd always looked up to Bedloe, admired him even, and had envied his good looks and charming nature. Above all, he had considered Bedloe as the only real friend he had ever had; and now he was gone.

He scanned the many works scattered about the table and pulled sections out to read.

An elegy written upon the unfortunate death of Captain William Bedloe, who departed this life on Friday, 20th August. 1680.

"Could Bedloe fall so softly to his tomb. Without a comet to foretell his doom?

Titus smiled at the thought that he would receive even grander elegies on his own death. His smile turned to a deep frown, when he read:

> *'The Lord is pleased when man does cease to sin;*
>
> *The Devil is pleased when he a soul does win;*
>
> *The world is pleased when every rascal dies:*
>
> *So all are pleased, for here Will Bedloe lies.'*

As summer turned to autumn, Charles removed himself to Newmarket. On receiving word that Shaftesbury had called an extraordinary meeting of the Privy Council, to discuss Charles' decision to move York to Edinburgh, Charles returned post-haste to London.

He summoned Shaftesbury before him to account for his actions, in daring to call the Privy Council together in his absence. On seeing Shaftesbury entering the room, Charles's neck flushed red. *Little Sincerity, he bows before me but mocks me behind my back.* He stood up and said, "I've had enough of your insubordination. I will *not* tolerate it for one moment longer. You've made a wrong move this time against me and my brother. Explain yourself!"

Shaftesbury leant onto his walking sticks and paled. "Your Majesty . . . I was acting only in my capacity as Lord President of the Privy Council. A position you gave me."

Charles tilted his head and strode over to stand in front of him. "I will ask you once again. Explain yourself!"

Shaftesbury shrugged and looked up. "I apologise, Your Majesty. But you must understand that the Privy Council has a right to discuss your decision to remove York from London. It –"

"Nay! I do *not* understand," Charles said and shook his head. "Pray tell me. God's truth, do you think I don't know why you did it? Do you? Do you think I cannot see your ploy in trying to keep my brother here while you push through... *your* Exclusion Bill against him?"

As Shaftesbury slumped forward, Charles flicked a hand in the air. "You say you were acting only in your capacity as Lord President of the Privy Council . . . a position *I* gave to you. Well, just as I gave you the position, I am now removing it. You are also dismissed from my presence."

Charles returned to his seat and watched as Little Sincerity, as he now thought of Shaftesbury, ambled from the room. Having vented his rage, it now subsided. Surprised that his usual reluctance to confront Shaftesbury had gone, he realised this was because he no longer admired or respected him.

For some time now Charles had noticed Shaftesbury becoming frailer. Shaftesbury had also started to make wrong moves, and this could be to Charles' own advantage. While the other Country Party leaders focussed their efforts on maintaining the power and position of Parliament, Shaftesbury had become fixed upon the issue of a Catholic succession. It was Charles' view that Shaftesbury was disgruntled by the public acclaim of York when he had returned to London from Brussels.

Charles smiled. Little Sincerity would be the source of his own undoing. Meantime, Charles would ensure York's remained out of his reach. He would have York return to Edinburgh with Mary Beatrice, but their daughter Isabella would remain in London – to remind the public that York's daughter was Protestant.

In order to prove he was not enforcing arbitrary rule, and because he needed his revenues, Charles opened Parliament. The first reading of the Exclusion Bill was held in the Lords. Charles heart raced as the debate raged on . . . and on. When Shaftesbury or his followers spoke, Charles scowled, and he smiled and applauded when York's supporters spoke.

Lord Halifax led the cause for York. For ten long hours, the debate raged on. Halifax answered every point raised by Shaftesbury, and Charles' emotions soared.

"York is a Catholic. All Catholics should be excluded from the succession," Shaftesbury argued.

"York is well thought of. The people like him." Halifax replied.

"I object. The people do not want a Catholic heir," Shaftesbury said.

"York has prestige within the Navy and within England, Scotland and Ireland. He is regarded with esteem. The people will not tolerate his removal, nor do they want it." Halifax replied to his objection.

Shaftesbury stood again. "I call for members to support this first request for the Exclusion Bill."

"To pursue York's removal from the succession leads to the danger of a revolution," Halifax replied. "The people do not want or need another civil war. The Civil War is still fresh in their memories. I urge you to consider reducing York's power on his succession. Pursuing his removal spells disaster for the King, the public and for Parliament."

As the debate wore on, and it darkened outside and the room grew dim, Charles sensed Shaftesbury wearying. His supporters were also intervening and contributing less and less to the debate. Shaftesbury's support was faltering. His autocratic ways were alienating a number of his followers, who had at first argued with him to see reason and then to fall silent. Charles realised that the members were growing more and more fearful of a Civil War, but Shaftesbury talked on. Shaftesbury remained set on pursuing his original course of action — to exclude York from the succession. But, he started to sag, his speech grew slower, he yawned and he fidgeted. Charles' spirits lifted further.

Finally, votes were taken.

At nine o'clock that evening, the spokesman bowed and informed the packed house, "Your Majesty, Lords and Gentlemen, The Exclusion Bill has now been voted in the Lords. Sixty-three members voted against the Bill, and thirty voted for it. The Bill is now rejected."

Charles slumped back onto the throne and breathed a deep sigh of relief. He had done it. His perseverance had won out. By God, the Exclusion Bill had been defeated in the Lords. But, he would not let his guard down, yet. This result would infuriate Shaftesbury. He did not trust Little Sincerity to accept this outcome.

Charles would continue with his plan to keep York from Shaftesbury's reach.

CHAPTER FIFTY-FIVE

God Bless His Highness

James of York looked out the window of his carriage, as it clattered along towards Merchants Taylors' Hall. Although darkness fell, York could see the crowds lining the streets along his route. He smiled and waved out at the public, who had gathered to see him before he left for Edinburgh tomorrow.

To mark his departure, the Mayor and Aldermen of London were hosting a meal in his honour. As he arrived at the Hall and stepped down from the carriage, shouts of good wishes for his journey north erupted from the crowd.

"A York! A York!" people called out as he passed. He did not understand why he had to leave – the Exclusion Bill had been thrown out.

On his return home, the streets were once again lined with people cheering him as he passed. York relaxed into his seat. He'd enjoyed a splendid meal and good conversation. As he waved out at the people, his thoughts drifted. He did not want to move to Edinburgh, but Charles had insisted on it. He would leave behind Catherine Sedley, now big-bellied with their first child. Though he would miss her company, the impending break eased the conflict he felt about how the affair fitted with the doctrines of his Catholic faith.

Sedley was his love, and he found it hard to stay away from her.

Perhaps time apart would help him make a complete break. Besides, heavy with child, she was unavailable for sexual liaisons. Loud shouts roused him from his thoughts, and the carriage slowed almost to a stop. Startled, York glanced out the window and saw the source of the commotion. On a balcony above a bookshop, stood Shaftesbury, Titus and Prance.

Titus Oates leant over the balcony and shouted, "A Pope! A Pope!"

The others joined in. "A Pope! A Pope!"

A soldier cocked his gun in their direction, causing them to withdraw.

The crowd yelled back. "No Pope! No Pope! God bless, His Highness."

York sank back into the seat. Thank God he was leaving for Edinburgh in the morning.

On returning from the bookshop, Shaftesbury withdrew to his study. Tonight had not gone as planned. Support for him was falling. He'd alienated a lot of Country Party members, by his actions over the Exclusion Bill, and whenever the Country Party members now met, arguments arose. Pish! How should he proceed?

The latest argument had arisen because he'd been infuriated the Lords had voted out the Exclusion Bill. He believed the opinions of others were now listened to before his own. Younger leaders were emerging who held a different agenda from his own. No, he would not give up his goal of ensuring Parliament's continuation.

He'd been so close to succeeding in his quest to exclude York. Apart from Buckingham, none of the other Country Party members understood Charles as he did. Given enough pressure, Charles *would* have given in and passed the Exclusion Bill. For this to happen now, the public would have to be reminded of the harsh realities of a Catholic succession. The death of Bedloe in August served a hard blow to progress in this direction, but Shaftesbury would succeed.

The trials of the five Catholic Lords would refocus attention back onto the Popish Plot. William Howard, Viscount Stafford, a weak and gentle man, was the obvious Lord to target first – he was also old, infirm and distanced from his family.

Shaftesbury would also call for York to be tried as a Papist, Louise de Kérouaille to be tried as a whore, and both of them to be tried for being in league with Catholic France. No, he was not finished yet.

Incensed by the Country Party's latest antics in calling for his brother and his own mistress to be tried as traitors, Charles strode with an even brisker pace than usual through St James's Park. Three spaniels yelped and barked, as they ran at his side.

"Your Majesty," a commoner called out.

Charles turned and called back to him, "God Bless you!" and strode on. This latest attack against his family made Charles even more determined to play the Country Party at their own game. This time, he determined, there would be no half-measures, no negotiating and no compromises. He would let the Country Party members destroy themselves, and provide them with the means to do so.

Reaching the lake, Charles dodged out of the way of a flock of swans, which scattered at his approach. Buried in his thoughts he hadn't even seen them. The day after the exclusion Bill failed, Shaftesbury presented a motion for him to divorce Queen Catherine, marry a Protestant and produce a Protestant heir for the Realm. The Lords had not supported the motion. That evening Charles had dined in Public with Queen Catherine. In publicly demonstrating that his loyalty lay with his Queen, he hoped to pull support from Shaftesbury.

By now calling for the trial of the five Catholic Lords, Shaftesbury was testing his tolerance to the limit. Charles, however, was working on his own negotiations. His public did fear a return to a Papal State, but they also feared another Civil War. Shaftesbury had not reckoned this into his strategy. Through L'Estrange, Charles had the press on his side, and he would limit the ability of the Country Party to influence further *his* people; through lies printed in broadsheets and pamphlets. From now on, all unlicensed publications would be banned; as threatening to the public order.

He'd also built up a strong following, and they were publishing their own propaganda, designed to show the Country Party as anarchists' intent on dividing England and throwing the country into a Civil War. His counter strategy involved exposing the Country Party members as threatening the security of England and highlighting that a Civil War could result from their actions. By instilling fear into the nation, people would think twice before supporting the Country Party against the Crown. Charles had also got rid of trouble-seeking members from within the Privy Council and the Lords, and replaced them with his loyal followers; to neutralise the previous Country Party control.

His good friend Rochester had died in July. Charles thought of him often. Oh, how he missed Rochester's witty repartee. Charles prayed for his soul. At the age of thirty-three, Rochester had died riddled with pox. His wife and child died soon after, from the same condition. Charles was grateful for his own good health, and his doctor's success in treating the pox whenever he caught it.

Charles had spent time at Newmarket with Rochester and had noticed his decline. A shadow of his former self, Rochester had known he was dying, and had had a religious conversion. Charles found this intriguing; even Rochester had turned to God in the end, asking forgiveness for his bawdy days and even bawdier nights.

The following evening, Charles pulled back the curtain and looked out from Louise's apartments. His belly lurched. "Fubbs! Make haste!"

Louise rushed to his side. "*Mon chéri*, what is it?"

"Look! You must see this. By God, is it happening?" Charles pointed out the window at a mass of bright light with a very large tail trailing down from it in the sky.

"Come away from the window Your Majesty. Find the children. *Non.* I will gather them together."

Charles laughed. "Fubbs it is but a comet, and by the look of that tail, a very great one indeed," Charles said and turned and pointed to one of his attendants. "You sir, have my horse readied to leave. I have to view this from the observatory at Greenwich."

With her face full of concern, Louise touched his arm. "But. . . Your Majesty. It fills me with great fear."

"This is most exciting, Fubbs," Charles said and raised his arms. "It must be the largest comet yet. Excuse me, for I must leave. And... do not fret. It will cause you no harm. Gather together your ladies and go up to the rooftop, you can watch it from there."

Drawn to the spectacle occurring, Charles rode with haste through London. The comet was even larger than he had first imagined. It filled him with awe. He smiled to see crowds standing out on such a frosty night, staring at the sky in wonder. He frowned to see others, running towards churches, no doubt lamenting the great omen signalling bad things to come. For him, it was a thing of wonder and intrigue.

As Charles' retinue slowed to a trot, along the cobbled streets, he watched as women gathered children and rushed them indoors. Observing the fear in the eyes of a group of men, huddled outside an inn, a trickle of doubt flowed through him. Had the good Lord been angered? Was England to be avenged? Similar phenomenon had appeared before the thirty years war, the plague and the Great Fire of '66. There had even been sightings before the Civil War. Was the Great Comet a bad omen? Placing such dark thoughts aside, he pushed forward at greater speed towards Greenwich.

CHAPTER FIFTY-SIX

Double Death

Lord Viscount Stafford, a Catholic Lord accused along with Powis in the Popish Plot, sent a message to the Lords, informing them he would confess everything he knew. The following day, Stafford was marched from the Tower and brought before the Bar of the Lords. He looked frail and unkempt. His long, thin grey hair hung lank to his shoulders, and unshaved stubble covered his pale face. Shame swept through him as he watched his peer's expressions change to pity as he entered.

"You have decided to tell all," their spokesman said and peered over at him.

"Yes . . . Yes, I will tell you what you want to know," Stafford said and bowed his head. Standing in front of the Lords, he felt uncertain about how what he had to say would be received. "I had much time to think in the Tower, My Lord, and some things came to my mind. I remember a debate . . . Yes, one concerning the Catholic and Country Parties joining forces to dissolve Parliament and gain religious toleration. The Earl of Shaftesbury was present and –"

"Are you admitting involvement in trying to alter the established faith?" one of the members asked and cleared his throat.

Stafford looked up, and his eyes welled with tears. "To debating religious toleration, yes, My Lord. Yes, I do. I attended a meeting in which an 'Oath of Allegiance' was discussed. I disapproved. I thought the Oath too severe. Others were not of the same opinion. Shaftesbury thought it –"

"When was this meeting *you* attended?" the spokesman asked.

Realising the futility of his endeavour to inform the Lords what he knew, Stafford now regretted asking to appear before them. Whenever he had mentioned Shaftesbury's name, his explanation had been cut short. He determined to tell them no more and answer only no, or yes, My Lord, to their questions. When the Lords realised he had nothing to tell them, they dismissed Stafford.

On his way back to the Tower, Stafford worried over the fate of the four other Catholic Lords held there. Like him, Powis, Belasyse, Petre and Arundell had spent the last two years incarcerated without trial. Stafford knew his own life to be over, but prayed for the safekeeping of his friends.

A few weeks later, Stafford was brought before the Lords again, this time to stand trial for high treason. At nine o'clock on that bleak morning, he was removed from the Tower. As the Black Rod escorted him over to Westminster Hall, Stafford bowed his head in shame, his humiliation complete. A baying crowd shouted for his blood. Cries of "Papist!" and "Papist plotter" rang in his ears.

White frost covered the ground, and he was saddened to see the trees bare of their leaves. Having been enclosed in the Tower for so long, he had hoped to feel the heat of the sun on his face. He had not slept well. Try as he might, he could remember very little about the events he had been accused of. It was all very vague in his mind now. It all seemed such a long time ago. Distant memories surrounded in fog.

In Westminster Hall, Elizabeth sat beside Stafford's wife, Mary, and the Earl of Castlemaine. Elizabeth had her arm around Mary, who looked dazed and red-eyed.

At eleven am, the Lords dressed in their scarlet robes, four serjeants carrying maces in front of them, and another four following behind the Lord High Steward, the judges and their assistants, walked two by two from the House of Lords and filed into the courtroom. Stafford's two eldest sons, Henry and John, walked behind them. The Deputy Black Rod followed, bearing a white staff. After bowing to the King, they each took their places. The Serjeants with their maces walked over and knelt down, four on each side of the throne. Opposite the Bar sat the Lord High Steward. Beside him sat the prosecution lawyers; six members of the House of Commons.

"Serjeant at Arms make proclamations," the Clerk announced. "O, yes! O, yes! O, yes! The Lord High Steward of England commands all manner of persons here assembled to keep silent, upon pain of imprisonment. God save the King. O, yes! Constable of the Tower bring in the prisoner William Howard, Viscount Stafford."

Elizabeth glanced around. From her seat in a private box, Louise de Kérouaille distributed sweetmeats. Queen Catherine sat in another box with several of her ladies-in-waiting. Near the front, Shaftesbury huddled together with other Country Party members.

Stafford was brought to the Bar, and the Lord High Steward addressed him. "Your Lordship stands charged with the crime of high treason, for plotting to kill the King and return England to a Papal State. I urge his Lordship to use the utmost caution in stating his defence. As a Lord, you are judged by your peers. Such is the gravity of the charges laid against you that the Commons and the King are in attendance."

Titus Oates stood as the first witness for the Crown. "I swear I delivered a commission to Viscount Stafford from the Pope, referring to Stafford as the General of his new Papist army."

"And you saw the content of this commission?" the Attorney General asked.

"Yes, My Lord. I was suspicious of the letter and read it before handing it over."

"What aroused your suspicion?" the Attorney General asked.

"During the year of '76, I was employed by the Duke of Norfolk at Arundel House. During my time there I heard many things. I heard Stafford say he had worked with the Duke of York, to plot and arrange the Great fire of '66." Titus Oates replied and licked his lips.

Elizabeth gripped Mary tighter.

The Lord High Steward turned to Stafford. "Does Your Lordship want to reply to these charges?"

"I've nothing to say that would be believed, My Lord." Stafford realised no one was attending to what he said. The thought made his heart beat faster. Over sixty witnesses were called against him; Titus Oates and Stephen Dugdale presented most of the evidence.

Many spoke in Stafford's defence, and he was uplifted to hear them.

On the afternoon of the seventh day of the trial, the Lords adjourned. Two hours later they returned. One by one the eighty-six Lords were asked if Stafford was guilty, or not guilty, of high treason. As each Lord was asked, they stood up from their seat, placed their right hand onto their breast, replied and sat down.

Fifty-five found Stafford guilty, and thirty-one found him not guilty of high treason.

The Lord Steward called for silence, and turned the edge of the axe to face Stafford. "I pronounce sentence of death by drawing, hanging and quartering."

The Black Rod broke his white staff, dismissing the court.

Two days later, Elizabeth waited outside the Tower with her arm around Stafford's wife, Mary. Elizabeth watched events unfold through a haze, and her mind blotted them out as soon they had happened. She had no memory of their journey here.

"Peace and goodwill to all men." The voice of the carol singers sung out beside them. To Elizabeth, their words served as a lance to a festering wound. Charles had reduced Stafford's sentence to beheading, and Louise de Kérouaille had told Elizabeth he had signed the warrant with tears in his eyes. Louise had also informed her that the evidence against the other four Lords, Powis, Belasyse, Petre and Arundell had been ordered to be made ready. To prevent this, Charles would delay opening Parliament.

When Stafford was brought out, Elizabeth felt Mary stiffen and step forward. Elizabeth tightened her grip on Mary's shoulder and held her back. "No, Mary. You must remain strong. I know it's hard, but it will be worse for your husband if he sees you in distress. Remain dignified for his sake."

As Stafford passed, he cast a forlorn look at his wife.

Mary stared back at him and held her hand over her heart.

Elizabeth's legs shook, but she moved Mary forward, to watch as Stafford was placed in the open coach, taking him to his place of execution. Along with Stafford's family, Elizabeth threw a posy into it and walked over to the mourning coaches, which would follow him to Tower Hill. Elizabeth would watch the execution with Mary, from inside the coach.

Though her heart beat loudly and she feared she might collapse, Elizabeth willed herself to keep moving and tried to keep her thoughts from Powis' trial, which would surely soon follow.

The following month, Titus rested in his apartments at Whitehall. He picked up the Protestant Mercury, lounged back in a chair and scanned the paper. Doctor Israel Tonge's name caught his eye. After reading the content, he stood up, walked over to the fire and held his hands out to warm them.

Doctor Israel Tonge had died ten days earlier. Titus frowned – King Charles had paid for Tonge's funeral, for his services to the Realm. Titus had liked Israel Tonge, but his death came as a huge relief – he no longer needed to worry about Tonge spreading lies about him.

SHEENA MACLEOD

Part Eight: The Endgame

1681-1682

'When we have feared three years we know not what,

till witnesses begin to die o' the rot.'

Otway 1681

.CHAPTER FIFTY-SEVEN

The Petition

"Charles totally ignored this," Shaftesbury said, holding up a petition, containing over 20,000 signatures, asking for Parliament to be opened at Westminster and not Oxford. "Charles' response was to prorogue Parliament again. As usual, he chooses the same strategy. Well, I for one am bored with his game. Nay, do not give up. Push further."

"But . . . few refused to sign the petition," a voice from the other side of the table in the club in Chancery Lane said. "Those who did were hailed as Papists. How many more names can we gather?"

"I say we move to action rather than words." Shaftesbury replied. "Charles has made the wrong move in recalling York from Scotland. Perhaps we can use this to our advantage. I say we bring another indictment against York, this time before a grand Jury at the Old Bailey."

"And Charles' Catholic whore?" a voice shouted.

"Well, I'm all for exposing Louise de Kérouaille as a spy for France. Are we in agreement, York, *and* Charles' mistress?" Shaftesbury asked and smiled as his question was answered by a roar of "ayes" from around the room.

Later that evening, after dining with his wife, Shaftesbury retired to his study. Rain fell in torrents, and he looked out the window and watched it splash off the cobbles below. Though today's meeting had gone well, he couldn't settle, and a great anger towards Charles built within him.

Sitting down at his desk, he picked up a quill and dipped it into the ink.

> *Monmouth,*
>
> *Things here are ripe for your return from your enforced exile in Holland. We, your loyal supporters, will provide all you require on your return.*
>
> *Make haste, for our plans for you are worthy of your consideration.*

Shaftesbury pressed his seal onto the rolled parchment. He would use every advantage to further his cause, and felt no qualms at the timing of his actions – Mary Beatrice had birthed another stillborn son.

The following evening, Shaftesbury dined alone with Titus.

After taking a long drink of wine, Titus thumped the glass onto Shaftesbury's dining table. "What else would you have me do? I have to do it! It's been two years. Why else is Charles proroguing Parliament but to stop the trials of the Popish Lords? No, I'll not have it."

Shaftesbury also felt angry that Charles had prorogued Parliament, again. It served as a huge blow to his plans to remove York from the succession. "I share your frustration, but we must think this through."

Titus accepted a large helping of roast pork from the dish a servant held in front of him. Picking up his fork he stared at Shaftesbury. "Well I say we charge York as complicit in the plot to kill the King."

By God, Titus was right. This could work. Excitement coursed through Shaftesbury. "Yes. I think we should raise a charge of treason against York. The Privy Council and both Houses of Parliament will be made to vote on it. We will see York in the Tower."

Titus chewed his meat and grinned over at Shaftesbury.

"But, first things first," Shaftesbury said. "For the moment, I need to focus on the Opening of Parliament in Oxford."

The following Sunday, surrounded by a small army of armed guards, the Country Party, now referred to as Whigs, rode into Oxford. Crowds lined their route, and cheered as they passed. Every Whig wore blue satin ribbons in their hats – to indicate their support of Monmouth. Woven into the ribbon was their new motto. 'No Popery. No slavery.' The sun shone down upon them and their ribbons blew in the gentle breeze, as they walked their horses through the narrow streets.

"'With all my heart.' God damn him. That was Charles' reply," Shaftesbury said to a fellow Whig, riding beside him. "I told Charles all leading Whigs would resign if he brought York back, and he replied, "With all my heart. The man's a fool."

"And for him to insist upon opening Parliament in Oxford, how strange," the Whig replied.

"No doubt to keep us away from York. The welcome he received on his return enraged me."

The Whig shifted forward. "A banquet hosted by the Lord Mayor and shouts of welcome from the people . . . The English public have short memories."

Shaftesbury nodded. "I'll not give up. We've put a rumour out that the black box has been found, containing the marriage documents for Charles and Lucy Walters. This will confirm to the public that

Monmouth is the legitimate heir. But damn and blast, more than anything, the situation with Scroggs stoked my fury. I cannot fathom why the Privy Council released him . . . and why they accepted his reasons for his damnable conduct during Wakeman's trial."

"Scroggs has retired to Essex and can trouble us no more. But think on it. There is now talk of an armed rebellion, and I'm not at all surprised."

The next day, Charles arrived to address the Oxford Parliament. As the Royal standard was hoisted to announce his entrance, he walked through the chambers to take his place on the throne. His white puffed, and ribbon-bowed shirt sleeves billowed, and a blue velvet cloak blew out in waves behind him. The fall of his high-heeled and ribboned shoes, on the stone floor, created the only sound in the otherwise silent chamber.

As he made his opening speech, all eyes within the packed chamber remained fixed upon him as they waited to hear what he had to say.

"My Lords and gentlemen, pray be seated." Charles took a deep breath and informed both houses, "I will not be bullied, coerced or pushed. I, who never use Arbitrary Government, will not tolerate it in others. Make the laws of the land your own rule, as they are mine. The very idea of exclusion is at odds with natural succession and I dismiss it as an option. In order to ensure peace in my kingdom, I will, however, consider Regency. After my reign, this will enable Parliament to run the country and leave James of York as King in name only.

"My Lords and Members of the House of Commons, I pray that the blessing of Almighty God may rest upon your wise counsels."

Having concluded his opening speech, Charles strode around the hall, listening in as the Whigs debated the Exclusion Bill. As he had expected, they dismissed out of hand his idea of Regency, and continued to push for exclusion. So entrenched were they in a battle against him, the needs of the public were forgotten. By refusing to debate Regency, the Whigs showed themselves to be pursuing their own interests. He, on the other hand, had shown willing to compromise. *And, his people would hear about this.*

Satisfied, Charles settled on the throne, and waited. *Let the Whigs destroy themselves.* He'd given them enough rope, now he would wait for them to hang themselves with it.

On the last day of the Oxford Parliament, Charles entered the Hall of Christ Church - where the Lords had spent the full week debating nothing other than the Exclusion Bill. As he strode towards the throne, the Lords stood and stared at him in stunned silence.

Once seated, Charles summoned the Black Rod to also bring the Commons before him.

Surprised by the order to join the Lords in the Great Hall, members hurried down the winding stairs. Charles smiled at the uproar that followed and watched as the chattering members of Commons were stilled by the Serjeant-at-Arms. "Silence, I order you to be silent. Silence! I will not ask again for your silence!"

One by one, members of the Commons hurried to the front of the hall, and Charles watched their mouths drop open as they took in the sight of him; seated on his throne, dressed in his robes of state and … with the Crown upon his head.

There was no longer any need for orders of silence. As they bowed before him, taking in his sombre and stately mood, for once the members of Parliament stood in awe before him. Events were not as they had expected, and Charles smiled at their discomfort.

With a powerful voice, and in his position as King, Charles declared, "All the world may see what point we have come to. When the divisions at the beginning are such, we are not likely to have a good end." He stood, bowed, and walked out, leaving behind a stunned silence of uncertainty.

He made haste back to London. *Let them wonder what his intentions were, for he'd wondered long enough about theirs, but no more. He would never call another Parliament.*

After a light meal, he set out for Windsor – heavily guarded and with his trusted friends and servants in his wake. To prevent such a crisis occurring again, he would make some examples. Along with other Whig leaders, he would order Shaftesbury's removal to the Tower – charged with high treason – for attempting war on the King, using force to push the Exclusion Bill through, and uttering treasonable words against York.

He smiled at Queen Catherine, sitting opposite him. She had always given him her loyal support, and he determined to spend more time with her. For almost ten years, Shaftesbury had pushed for him to divorce his Queen, marry a Protestant and produce a Protestant heir. If Shaftesbury had only known the truth, he could have saved himself the trouble.

Since his youngest bastard with Louise, Charles Lennox', birth in '73, Charles had known he'd fathered his last child, illegitimate or otherwise.

CHAPTER FIFTY-EIGHT

Harsh Reality

During his morning meal, Shaftesbury engaged in deep discussion with his wife, Margaret "The bounds of the Popish Plot are larger than first realised," he informed her and pushed his empty plate aside. "The Plot is rife throughout the kingdom. I –"

Looking up, Shaftesbury scraped his chair back and stood up. *God's truth, what now?* Four soldiers stood before him, bearing arms. They'd marched, without invitation, into his dining room.

Behind the armed soldiers stood a shaking servant. "My lord, I couldn't stop 'em."

Shaftesbury dismissed the servant and walked around the table and placed his hands on Margaret's shoulders. She was shaking, and looked at him as if he could provide the answer to this intrusion.

The senior officer stepped forward. "Anthony Ashley Cooper, Earl of Shaftesbury, I'm arresting you on an accusation of high treason. You will be committed to the Tower to await trial."

Shaftesbury held up his hands in supplication. "Ah! I will come with you, but as to the reason for my apprehension I have no clue." He glanced down at his wife. "Do not fret dear Margaret, I have done nothing wrong."

As the soldiers marched him out, Shaftesbury said, "I trust you have my *usual* room prepared for me in the Tower."

Despite his show of bravado in front of the officers, Shaftesbury now lay in the Tower, unwell and dispirited. So many of his allies had spoken out against him, and their betrayal wounded his heart. His physical health had declined.

He'd been imprisoned in the Tower many times before, and had always been able to see it through. Was this the end for him? Concerned he would die in the Tower, he penned a note to Charles promising to withdraw from all politics and political intrigues, if he dropped the prosecution against him.

Shaftesbury called out for the warder and, slipping him a silver coin, asked him to have the note delivered post haste.

On receiving the communication from Shaftesbury, Charles shook his head. *Little Sincerity deserves no clemency.* Charles no longer trusted his word. Shaftesbury would see him for a fool if he released him, and would start his intrigues all over again.

Charles thought Shaftesbury too ambitious to retire from public life. The time had arrived to destroy Little Sincerity. If he did not see through Shaftesbury's destruction, then Shaftesbury would surely ensure his own.

He would *not* grant Shaftesbury a Royal Pardon.

At ten o'clock the following morning, Titus reclined in bed. He had overindulged on food and wine the evening before, and felt tired. He refused the hot chocolate brought to his bedside and informed his attendant he would eat and sup later. He yawned, stretched and turned back over and fell asleep.

As he dozed, the bedroom door burst open.

Titus startled and opened his eyes.

The Black Rod stepped forward. "Doctor Titus Oates, you must leave this apartment by midday today, the last day of August, and not return. Take all your possessions with you."

"Do you know who you are speaking to?" Titus said and sat up. "I *am* the Saviour of the Nation. 'Tis the wrong apartment you have. Now leave me to rest."

"Titus Oates, the King himself has instructed you leave. There is no mistake," the Black Rod replied. Laying the warrant on a small table, he ordered his men to remove Titus from the bed.

The men laid down their guns and pulled Titus onto the wooden floor.

"Move 'yerself, and don't take anything belonging the King," one of the soldiers said.

Staring up at them, Titus grimaced. "I'm staying where I am. If the King wants *me* out, he can blaady well tell me himself. Blaady King! He's involved in the Popish Plot. He's had me arrested to stop me disclosing this. God damn you! Both the King and York are Papists. CAN YOU HEAR ME?"

Receiving no reply, Titus stood up. "God's wounds, turn around until I dress. Have some decency."

Tears formed in his eyes as he collected the plates with his crest on them. As he left the apartment at Whitehall Palace, soldiers checked through his bags to ensure he hadn't taken anything belonging to the King.

Titus glared at them. *Rot 'em.*

Shaftesbury looked out the window of his carriage. He was heading home and couldn't arrive soon enough. In October he'd moved for a writ of habeas corpus and his case had finally come before the grand jury. The case against him was weak and the evidence inconclusive.

As the carriage clattered along, he reached his hand out the window and waved to the people lining his route. They called out to him, "No Popish Successor, No York, A Monmouth," or "God bless the Earl of Shaftesbury."

On returning home he retired to his study, where he sat alone nursing a glass of port between his hands. Staring at the deep red liquid, he realised his time in the Tower had shocked his senses. Adding to Shaftesbury's misery, he'd learned that one of the Plot accusers, Dugdale, had been willing to appear against him.

"Damned traitor!" he muttered. *Dugdale is nothing but a scoundrel. A rat making his nest from other people's misery. Piss on him and his kind. Were the accusers now turning against him?* As he thought about this he acknowledged that all the Popish Plot accusers were vermin amongst men. They had no code of honour, no backbone . . . no knowledge of events. They were liars.

Shaftesbury sipped the port, relishing the warmth of its slow descent into his belly. He needed to wash, shave and change his clothes. The damp fetid smell of the Tower clung to him and seeped from his pores, but he couldn't rouse himself into action.

My God, he had lost sight of his goal to serve the people, and been deceived into executing innocents . . . on the word of liars. *Dear God forgive me, for it suited my own needs to listen to these false accusers.*

Never before had he questioned why everyone executed for complicity in the Popish Plot had protested their innocence. Nor, why public feeling had moved away from the Plot itself towards the accused, particularly the Jesuit Priests, the majority of whom were part of communities, and horror had been aroused by their deaths. As he considered this now, shame swept over him.

God's wounds, he knew some of the families of the priests languishing in prison accused of complicity in the Plot. Standing up, he paced the room as specific individuals competed for a place in his thoughts. He would arrange for their release and . . . he would watch his own back.

CHAPTER FIFTY-NINE

Entwined Lives

As spring turned to summer, Elizabeth lay beside Mary Beatrice, on a blanket under a budding tree in St James's Park, outpouring to each other from their pained hearts. Around them, bees buzzed and birds chirruped, and a warm, gentle breeze blew over them. Mary Beatrice's ladies sat a short distance away, their heads bowed, deep in conversation. Elizabeth wore a flowing green dress. Mary Beatrice, who was big-bellied with child, wore a loose lilac one, and rested her head on Elizabeth's arm.

"My dear, how do you bear it?" Elizabeth soothed as she turned on her side and stroked Mary Beatrice's dark hair. "You are like one of my own dear daughters, and it pains me to see you so forlorn. Your situation is different from mine, but we both carry heavy burdens. Three years now Powis has been in the Tower. I may yet see him returned to me, and you my dearest may yet bear a healthy child who will live to old age. I pray every day that your burdens are lifted, and your heavy heart soothed."

Mary Beatrice winced. "I thought I was losing my mind. I could not bear to think of the loss of my darling *bambino*, Isabella. That she died when I was apart from her tore at my heart. Isabella had reached four years. I thought . . . I thought this is the *bambina* who will grow into womanhood. When the news was brought to me . . . Oh, Elizabeth I cannot express my grief in words. Four bambini I have borne and all of them taken. I believed I was being punished, and took to constant prayer for forgiveness for my sins. Indeed I still think I am to blame."

Elizabeth felt tears form in her eyes. "Why would God punish you? You have led a devout life."

"And where has it led me?" Mary Beatrice let out a mocking laugh. "I cannot bear to think that the *prostituta* Sedley's *bambino* thrives while my own die. York's mistress's bastard thrives, but not his wife's. Why Elizabeth? *Amica cara*, why? I feel wicked for thinking it should have been her bambino and not mine who died."

Sitting up, Elizabeth brought Mary Beatrice's head onto her lap. "I don't know. I honestly do not know. I've often wondered if the reason lay with the pox, for York has surely had this many times from his whores . . . but it cannot be. Why would the children of his whores thrive? I cannot understand it. I have wondered if children born to the pox suffer. Mrs Cellier agrees, and she reads widely on such subjects. Does York have signs of the Pox?"

Mary Beatrice closed her eyes against the bright sunlight. "Many times, but the mercury treatments have always worked. So this cannot be the cause."

"Then I cannot fathom it. You must remain strong. Let us pray the child in your belly is healthy."

"And Powis?" Mary Beatrice said. "The letters in this week's Observator should help his cause. How brave of L'Estrange to publish the letters between himself and Tonge's son. These letters have raised questions about the Popish Plot. I wonder if the truth will ever be revealed."

Elizabeth's heart quickened and she chewed her bottom lip. How many times had she let her hopes be raised for Powis' release, only to have them dashed? But, she would *not* give up hope. Titus Oates had been removed from his apartments, but it wasn't enough.

Mary Beatrice sat up, interrupting Elizabeth's thoughts. "I missed you while I was away, *amica cara*. I'm leaving again for Scotland. York and I will return to Edinburgh. I don't know when we'll be permitted to return, but I pray it will be soon." She reached into her pocket and pulled something out.

"I would like you to have this mio amica cara." Mary Beatrice handed her the Indian silver bracelet she'd given to Isabella, years earlier. "Keep this and think of me while I am gone. Pray for me as I do for you my dear friend."

A few weeks later, Mary Beatrice gave birth to a daughter, Charlotte Maria. The following day, Elizabeth called on Mrs Cellier.

I cannot wait to see my children again," Elizabeth said. She was leaving for Powis Castle in the morning, and would bring her youngest children back with her when she returned to London.

"You should remain in Wales, where it's safer," Mrs Cellier said. "The troubles here are far from over."

Elizabeth stiffened. Castlemaine had said the same. "I cannot leave London while Powis is in the Tower. No, I cannot do it."

"I understand, but you have to consider your own safety. Look how quickly we ended up in the Tower. God forbid, that you should end up there again. For myself, it's highly likely, but you have the children to think about."

"Do you really intend to publish your account of the Meal-tub incident?"

"Indeed I do. And don't raise your brows like that. Nothing will stop me from exposing the lengths Shaftesbury has gone to remove York from the succession. Do you think Dangerfield was also working for Shaftesbury?"

Elizabeth did not need to consider this. She'd thought long and hard about Dangerfield's role in uncovering Shaftesbury's plan to replace York with Monmouth. "I think Dangerfield would have remained with the winning side, regardless of who it was. I believe the information he brought us was true. I think there was a Protestant plot to replace York with Monmouth. And, yes. I do think Dangerfield was playing a double game. Had his true identity not been discovered I dread to think what might have become of us. You need to take care, Mrs Cellier. These are difficult times. Trust no one."

"With Shaftesbury's decline, Titus Oates has no one to guide him. A marionette without a master, he'll soon become entangled in his own strings," Mrs Cellier said. "But until he does, you also should also take care. Without doubt Titus Oates is a dangerous man."

"Castlemaine's trying to find out what he can about Titus Oates. He's convinced he never received a Doctor of Divinity at Salamanca, or anywhere else, and is also suspicious about his time at Valladolid. It will be interesting to hear what Castlemaine finds out in Spain."

"I pray he finds something soon. I can't bear to think of Powis spending any more time in the Tower. The children miss him, as do I." Tears came to Elizabeth's eyes and she wiped them away. "Winifred no longer remembers her father. She was too young when he left. Louise told me Charles will never call another Parliament in his lifetime. As long as no Parliament sits, Powis cannot be brought to trial. She assures me my husband is safe, for the time being."

CHAPTER SIXTY

Retreat

Under cover of darkness, Shaftesbury strapped his meagre belongings to the saddle, and pulled himself up on to his horse. As the horse skittered on the frost laden cobbles, he patted the breast of his topcoat, and was reassured when he felt the bundle there.

He'd taken enough money for his needs, and had left the rest for his wife, Margaret. He had left her sleeping, unaware of his intentions. The letter placed by her bedside would explain everything. What else could he do? He feared for his life. One day he *would* return, but in the meantime he would continue his work in exile. *God bless The Prince of Orange and his continued support of our cause.*

It was a particularly cold November night, and his warm breath clouded as it hit the frost bitten air. Kicking his horse into a gentle canter he made his way towards the port and a ship to Brielle, in the province of South Holland. From Brielle he would make his way North to Amsterdam, and safety.

By early morning, and despite regular rests, his horse began to tire. Shaftesbury booked a room at a coaching inn, and after breaking his fast, slept for five hours solid. He set off again after dining, and made good progress, arriving in Dover the following afternoon.

Amidst the noise and bustle of the busy port, he found a trader to buy his horse. He set sail the following morning, and arrived in Calais that afternoon. Using the money from the sale of his horse, he purchased food and lodgings for the evening. The following morning he took the coach to Rotterdam, and arrived there two days later.

Waiting in the inn, for the coach bound for Amsterdam, he vomited. Wary he'd eaten something that had disagreed with him he drank only water, and stayed in the coaching inn for another night. Tomorrow, he would continue on the final part of his journey.

As another wave of nausea hit him, Shaftesbury rushed to vomit in a pail. Weak from the effort he lay down beside the pail, pulled a rough blanket from the bed and closed his eyes.

By the following morning he'd developed a fever but, as he hadn't eaten or drank anything for the past day, the vomiting had stopped. Climbing aboard the coach, he was relieved to see only two other passengers sharing his journey. Throwing himself down on the full length of the seat opposite them, he closed his eyes. The long journey to Amsterdam passed in a haze of nausea and pain.

Another winter had arrived, and still Powis remained in the Tower. Elizabeth's gaze shifted towards the blazing withdrawing room fire. Would Powis have a fire to warm him today? She had paid a warder to light one every morning, but could she rely on him to do it? The frost already lay thick on the ground, promising another hard winter. She would visit Powis this very afternoon and check for herself.

She had tried to fight back by playing Shaftesbury at his own game, but it had all come to nothing. But she could not give up, she had to do something. She had a great need to get people to understand the lies they were being told, and expose the Popish Plot accusers for the tyrants they were. Dear Mrs Cellier had been pilloried for publishing her book, *'Malice Defeated'*. For three days she'd been subjected to jeers and pelted with rotten waste.

Elizabeth recalled, lying in the park in the summer with her dear friend. Mary Beatrice had been big-bellied with child, and Elizabeth had prayed it would live to old age. But, it was not to be. At eight weeks old, Charlotte Maria had died of convulsions. Deep in thought, Elizabeth laid her fingers on the keys of her harpsichord and played out the tune to Packington's Pound.

A few years ago, the words of the popular song had been changed to a 'Ballad of the Popish Plot'. How clever of them, she mused, to have their lies sung by the common people as they drank their ale. Even those who couldn't read learned the words of the latest ballads. Why, even children sang along to the popular tune.

She continued to play out the tune and formed her own ballad as she did so.

"Whether you will like my song or like it not, it is the downfall of the Popish Plot."

She pressed the keys and sang on, "With characters of plotters here I sing, who would destroy our good and gracious King."

Pushing the harpsichord stool back, Elizabeth stood and hurried through to Powis' study. Sitting down at her husband's desk, she picked up a quill and dipped it into the ink.

A Ballad Upon The Popish Plot. Written by a Lady of Quality.
Whether you will like my song or like it not,
It is the downfall of the Popish Plot

For a full hour Elizabeth wrote, shushing away the servants when they interrupted her asking if she wanted anything. All she wanted was peace to write. On and on she wrote. The words tumbled from her – releasing her pent up anger at the Popish Plot accusers – and she wrote verse after verse ridiculing them. Finally, and with a great flourish, she wrote her final word on the matter – *FINISH.*

Wiping her ink-stained fingers on a rag, she called out for her carriage to be brought to the front and for her winter cloak and outdoor wear to be made ready. She would call on Castlemaine. He would know how to have her ballad printed and then distributed throughout London. Though people may suspect she was the author, she would ask Castlemaine to leave no trail back to her.

Satisfied by her morning's work, Elizabeth hummed the tune to her new ballad and hurried off to change into her outdoor clothes.

SHEENA MACLEOD

Part Nine: Checkmate

1683

'A day shall come when in thy power,
the cruel Foes shall be.'

Dryden

CHAPTER SIXTY-ONE

Regrets

Almost two months after leaving London, Shaftesbury realised he would never return – unable to eat, his health declined by the hour. He had regrets, many of them and, confined to bed, had plenty of time to contemplate them. Indeed, he spent all his waking hours thinking about how things had turned out as they had.

Rubbing at his balding scalp with a frail hand, he recalled the time in London when he had been a favoured member of the King's retinue. He could hear the laughter as the restored King announced the ministers who would oversee foreign affairs. 'C-A-B-A-L is an acronym of the names of my five new Privy Councillors; Clifford, Arlington, Buckingham, Ashley-Cooper (Shaftesbury) and Lauderdale,' Charles had announced, amidst gasps of surprise and roars of approval.

As they swore their allegiance to the King, the Cabal members had laughed together. As a trusted servant, Shaftesbury's heart had filled with pride. His thoughts turned to the day he learned from Buckingham that Charles had deceived him, and he had become hell-bent on revenge. He'd never accepted it could finish there, and had continued to believe a secret treaty with France existed. When York married Mary Beatrice, a Catholic, his suspicion that York had converted to Rome had been confirmed. He had been damned if he would let Charles lead the life of a merry King and allow England to return to a Papal regime.

Shaftesbury thought of his grandson, Anthony, and his heart swelled with pride. He loved the boy beyond reason and would do anything for him. He still believed Charles intended to rule without a Parliament, and that Anthony's future in the Lords was at stake. Had Charles succeeded? Would others continue to fight to retain Parliament? The arrival of Titus Oates, with his Popish Plot, had provided Shaftesbury with the ideal means to put an end to the King's plans, and he'd become blind to anything else.

He lay back on the pillow and closed his eyes. He regretted that his fellow peers had had to be imprisoned and that Stafford had been executed. In thinking about Powis, he recalled walking into the palace with Elizabeth, on the day Mary Beatrice had arrived in London. He had told Elizabeth then that he had no particular dislike of Catholics, and it had been true. But, he had deliberately played on Protestant's fear of England returning to a Papal regime, in order to turn the public against York.

He also regretted that so many Jesuit Fathers had died by his words. He knew the Jesuits to be kind and honest men, whose aim was to teach and help those less fortunate than themselves. Before fleeing London, Shaftesbury had arranged for many of them to be released from prison. Was this enough to make amends with God for his wrongdoing?

♛

A week later, Charles received a message from one of his spies in Holland, informing him of Shaftesbury's death. The sixty-one-year old, had never recovered his health following his flight to Amsterdam.

Charles looked out a window at Whitehall Palace. It was proving to be the bitterest winter in living memory. Snow lay thick on the ground, and frost had turned the trees a permanent glistening white. For days at a time the roads and streets had been blocked.

He recalled looking out this same window during the harsh winter of '74; the day he acknowledged to Powis that his trusted advisor and friend, Shaftesbury, was gone from him. He had grieved for this loss and thought his heart had been wrenched from his body. Today, he had learned Little Sincerity had died, and felt nothing.

Titus' hands shook and a strange sensation enveloped him. He knew where he was, but . . . at the same time, it was as if he was not in the room with his mother. All feeling had left his body, and he stared at her, blank faced.

"Oh Titus, I'm sorry. I didn't think this would affect you so. Sit down, come on, sit here," Lucy said, guiding him onto a settee.

Titus heard his mother's voice as if it was coming from somewhere far away, and yet he could see her leaning over him. It was like when he had one of his convulsions, but different. He took a deep intake of breath and shuddered.

"Maather. What you say cannot be true. I saw Faather last month and he was . . . maather, he was well. I cannot believe it."

A few minutes before, Lucy had knocked on the door of his lodgings. She'd told him that his father, Reverend Oates, had been found dead in his lodgings above the pie shop, in King Street.

He couldn't comprehend it and shook his head as if to clear his thoughts. "Was father poisoned?"

"No Titus, he wasn't poisoned. What made you say that? Your father has been unwell for some time and . . . it was his time. God Bless him and look after him. Although I remained in Hastings when he moved to London, he was still my husband and, as you know, I visited you both when I could. It's a sad loss for us, Titus, but just as spring is our life start, so winter is our life end."

Though he knew his mother spoke the truth, Titus couldn't control the sudden surge of anger that raged through his body, and tears flowed down his face. "Blaady Papists!" he roared and stood up.

Turning his mother to face him, he gripped her arms. "Maather, I'll miss Faather." He drew her into him and held her close.

When Titus awoke it was dark. He didn't remember his mother leaving. He must have fallen asleep on the settee, and had slept for hours. Lying there, he thought about the news of his father's death. When he'd learned Shaftesbury had died, he'd believed himself to be grief-stricken, but it was nothing compared to the pain he now felt.

He shifted and adjusted a cushion beneath his head. He hadn't eaten since morning, but didn't feel hungry. Why was everyone leaving him? With Tonge, Bedloe, Shaftesbury and his father dead, who would help him? *He would never get father's approval now.* This thought took him by surprise, but it was so obvious, he wondered why he hadn't thought of it before. Men doffed their hats to him, odes had been written, and titled women asked him to marry their daughters. Yet, it was his father's approval he had wanted. As far back as he could remember, Reverend Oates had called him a dunce or a snotty-nosed fool, and had despised him for having convulsions.

When he'd moved into Whitehall Palace, his father had shown surprise at his sudden rise to fame. But, had he been proud? Closing his eyes, Titus realised he would never know the answer to that question.

CHAPTER SIXTY-TWO

Sound Plans

Charles lay asleep in his house at Newmarket. He'd arrived a few days earlier, having travelled down with his brother, and their retinue of attendants. He did not intend returning to London until the first of April, over a week away, and he welcomed the respite.

Charles and York were both entering horses and had teased each other about the superior quality of their own individual champions. So he could be at the stables before the races started, Charles had retired early.

The bedroom door crashed open and Charles startled awake.

York shouted, "Fire! Dear God, not again."

Charles pulled back the covers and stepped out of bed. Two attendants rushed over to dress him in his outdoor clothes.

He rubbed his eyes. "How bad is it, Jamie?"

"Bad! It has already taken hold."

As soon as his attendants had finished dressing him, Charles followed his brother out the room and raced down the stairs. The attendants followed behind, their faces ashen and their mouths agape.

As soon as he stepped out the front door, the noise and stench hit Charles, and it increased with every step he took. People rushed around with water pails, shouting orders as they went. The neighing and kicking of the panicked horses drew him on at a quicker pace.

The left area of the stables was ablaze and couldn't be entered, but the other entrances were still negotiable. Sparks, sprang up into the night air, and were carried and fanned by the wind to settle on nearby homes, hay bales and outhouses.

Charles and York removed their topcoats and set to work freeing the horses from the paddocks. When the horses were too distressed to be escorted out, they were sent away with a slap to their rumps.

People screamed, dogs barked, children cried and men bellowed orders. The elderly and infirm hobbled about, dazed and getting in the way of those trying to put the fire out.

As the sights and sounds crashed in on him, Charles recalled the Great Fire of '66. Then, he had worked with York for three solid days, trying to bring it under control. As they worked alongside his people, they had roused shocked faces into action and, when all seemed lost had joined the groups tearing down undamaged houses to prevent the fire from spreading.

Covered in soot, exhausted and hungry they had triumphed over the fire, but not before it had wiped out a huge part of London. For the next few days they had worked alongside the people, re-homing, feeding and calming those who had lost everything in the fire. The fire's spread had been quick and far reaching, burning down everything in its path including, food-stores, shops and churches.

Tonight they had been lucky – the fire had been brought under control. As long as the wind remained stable, Newmarket would be saved.

The following morning Charles learned a jockey had been smoking in a stable, and the fire had caught hold when he had emptied out his unfinished pipe. Half the town had been affected by the fire.

After bathing and eating Charles and York agreed there was no point remaining in Newmarket; the races had been cancelled. They set off at once for London and arrived back that evening.

Charles roared with pain. "Damn it! Hurry up! Struth, can't you leave it be?" A wound on his leg, which wouldn't heal, was being cleansed and dressed, and he hated it. Red faced, he gritted his teeth and cursed the attending physician.

"I have finished, Your Majesty, and will return tomorrow," the physician said and backed out the room. At the door he stopped and bowed.

"Damn it," Charles muttered and tried to raise himself off the chair. "What is it?" he asked Jenkins, the Secretary of State, who had stood to the side waiting to speak with him.

Jenkins coughed and stepped forward. "I have information of a very urgent nature Your Majesty, and need to speak with you in private."

"Sit down," Charles said and collapsed back onto the chair. He raised a hand and signalled for his attendants to leave. Two guards remained standing beside the door. "Bless you, but having this wound dressed sets off the gout in my feet and I cannot bear it, and it will take hours to settle again. I'm sure they do their best. Now what is it you wish to discuss? Pray tell me."

"Your Majesty, I have information of a failed plot on you and your brother's life. Unlike the Popish Plot, there is no reason to disbelieve this. We need to bring the Privy Council together."

Another plot on his life. Charles was bemused. "What plot, and how do you know of this?"

Jenkins told him all he knew. "I received a visit from a reliable source, who told me of a plot to assassinate you and your brother, as you travelled past Rye House on your return from Newmarket in April. The plot was foiled when you returned early, following the fire.

"A known Whig supporter approached me with information in return for a pardon. He is in financial difficulty, and the promise of a reward ensured the names of the conspirators were revealed to me. I'm afraid the list is a long one."

The following morning Monmouth rushed into the ante-chamber of his father's apartments and threw himself at Charles' feet. "Father, please. I knew nothing of any attempt on your life. I was present at talks against my Uncle, but believe me I would never allow anyone to harm you."

"If you mix with known Republicans and those against the Crown, then by associating with them you are party to their actions," Charles said, with a firm voice. "Rise from the ground. I have loved you all I could. I believe you would not plot against my life, but cannot countenance your actions in pursuing to further your own needs by mixing with my enemies. You will travel to Holland and never return to England."

"Father, I'll tell you all I know, but let me remain in London. I also want to see those who plotted against your life brought to trial. I'll name names and act as a witness against them."

By offering a pardon in exchange for information about the Rye House Plot, thirty eight leading Whig members and Republicans were named. Ten fled abroad, including John Locke. Eleven were imprisoned. Four were implicated but not brought to trial, including Monmouth. Two were sentenced to death, but pardoned. Eleven were executed, and the Earl of Essex cut his own throat in the Tower.

Charles did not distinguish between those who had plotted to assassinate or abduct him and those planning a rebellion against him. As far as he was concerned they all had to be removed.

With London cleansed of the main plotters and political opponents against him, and a strong message sent out to all would be plotters, Charles felt released from the pressures of governing his countries. He recalled James of York from Scotland, and allowed him to take his seat once again on the Privy Council.

Charles determined to spend more time at Windsor, relaxing and pursuing his interests. For the first time since his restoration he felt King of his Realm.

Part Ten: Game Over

1684

*'The Devil helps his servants for a season, but when
they get into a pinch, he leaves them in the lurch.'*

Sir Roger L'Estrange

CHAPTER SIXTY-THREE

The Petition

Elizabeth met with Mary Beatrice, Mrs Cellier and Castlemaine. Mary Beatrice had returned from Edinburgh and had no intention of returning there. They'd gathered together in her apartments to hear what Castlemaine had found out during his time in Spain.

"My visit to Valladolid proved most fruitful," Castlemaine informed them. "But I have to wait for a letter from the Rector of Salamanca confirming everything. How did no one notice Oates only spent five months in Spain? Dear God, he never even visited the University of Salamanca, let alone receive a Doctor of Divinity there. Doctor indeed, by all accounts he was asked to leave. The Fathers told me he had little grasp of Latin and performed poorly in his studies. And, William Bedloe visited him there. Yes, there's much to reveal. As soon as the letter arrives from Valladolid, I'll have it placed before the Privy Council."

Elizabeth contemplated what he had said. "I could never fathom how he received a doctorate."

"I always doubted it," Mary Beatrice said. "Salamanca's an esteemed University."

"So, now we wait," Elizabeth said.

The following week, they all met again in Mary Beatrice's apartments. Elizabeth leant forward on a chair beside a roaring fire and sobbed. Mary Beatrice stood with her arms around her, uttering soothing words.

Castlemaine paced the floor, red-faced and sweating. "I cannot take it in. We have to do something. We cannot let this continue."

Mrs Cellier retrieved a phial from her bag and brought it to Elizabeth. "Drink this it will settle you."

Elizabeth held up a hand, refusing the medicine. "Castlemaine's right. We need to take action."

Baron Petre had died. He'd been ill for some time and, fearing he would die in the Tower, sent a letter to Charles. L'Estrange published the letter, stating Petre had been forced to spend five years in the Tower under a false claim of plotting to harm the King. Now he was dying, and would be called to be judged in the next world before being allowed to prove his innocence in this one.

"The letter provoked public outrage," Castlemaine said. "But still Petre was left to die. I don't know what else we can do. Buckingham and Shaftesbury always managed to get out of the Tower."

Elizabeth startled at this comment. "Dear God, why didn't we think of this? Of course, they need a writ of habeas corpus."

"It worked well enough for Shaftesbury and Buckingham," Mrs Cellier said.

"Many times," Castlemaine added. "But, for a case of high treason. I need to think about this. . . Yes, I have it. The Catholic Lords should submit a petition *asking* for their cases to be brought to trial. They should inform the King's Bench they're ready to answer to the charges brought against them.

"Dear God, we've spent our efforts pushing to have their cases delayed, fearing the worst if they were brought to trial. But, most of the accusers are now dead. Shaftsbury's no longer pulling the strings of his marionettes. And, Titus Oates no longer wields the power he once did. It takes two witnesses to convict a person of high treason. I'll help the Lords draft out a petition asking for their cases to be brought to trial. The Privy Council will have to consider if there's sufficient evidence to keep them imprisoned. I'll start on this today."

The wait for the outcome of the petition was unbearable for Elizabeth. Unable to sleep, she lay in the dark and stared at the ceiling. She swung between shallow hope and deep despair. A glint of moonlight peeped through the shutters and reflected onto the roof. Was it a sign, an omen?

She had lived her life trying to do the right thing. She'd believed with all her heart that living a good life helped ensure an easy passage through it. Her parents had been good people, yet her mother had died, and her father had been imprisoned for fighting for his beliefs. What had made her think goodness led to justice? Should she have given up her Catholic faith to save her husband? Would things have been different if they'd both renounced their religion and taken on the ways of the Anglican Church? But there was no point in thinking such thoughts. Neither of them would have been able to turn their backs on their faith.

Today, Powis and the other Catholic Lord's petitions would be heard in the Commons. Elizabeth waited in Queen Catherine's withdrawing room for Castlemaine to return with the verdict.

Elizabeth's children waited with her. Winifred, Lucy and Anne sat on a settee with Mrs Cellier. William sat beside Frances and Mary, who had returned from Wales. Mary Beatrice sat close to Elizabeth, with an arm around her shoulder.

Despite the bright calico prints on the walls and the sunshine pouring in through the windows, a dark mood surrounded them. To help pass the time, they made small talk. Her children's fearful faces tugged at Elizabeth's heart. But, there was no point making false promises. The outcome remained uncertain. After all these years, could Powis now be released or sentenced to death?

Elizabeth worried at her pearl necklace and said a silent prayer. *Dear God, bring an end to my family's torment and bring us together again.*

Queen Catherine, poured tea for them and smiled at Elizabeth. "Six years ago I went on a trip with my Ladies. So I could attend a fair, my Ladies disguised us as village maidens. We set off on the back of a cart horse. I had such fun walking around and kept stopping to look at the pretty ribbons and fabrics on sale. Then I saw an archery stand. I adore archery, and could not resist watching."

Elizabeth couldn't imagine Queen Catherine doing such a thing, and looked at her with awe. She had heard tales of nobles dressing as paupers and mixing with commoners, but Queen Catherine?

"A crowd soon formed around me," Queen Catherine continued. "When whispers started I was their Queen, I retreated. It was unusual for me to do such a thing, but what fun I had."

"It sounded wonderful," Mary Beatrice said. "*Che so,* I've never had such a day out as you describe."

"It was wonderful," Catherine replied, as she continued to pour and hand out tea. "Now, my trip to the fair is a distant memory, as so many things become. At the time it felt like a most important occasion. But memories, good or bad, have a way of disappearing to be viewed later as if through a fog. Just as my day at the fair has become a distant memory, so too will Powis' time in the Tower."

The door swung open, and Castlemaine strode in, his face held a blank expression. Elizabeth jumped up and fingered the pearls around her neck. Mary Beatrice's stood up beside her and placed an arm around her shoulders. Elizabeth's legs felt as if they would give out beneath her. *Dear God, help me see this through.*

A figure appeared behind Castlemaine, and Elizabeth startled as the man walked towards her. She took in his pale and bearded face and her heart lurched.

"Powis! Dear God, Powis!" As Elizabeth ran into his open arms, chaos erupted around the room; shouts of 'Papa' and 'Powis' filled the air.

Elizabeth trembled as she held her husband close. Though he looked like Powis and sounded like Powis, he felt different. He even smelled different; the smell of the Tower clung to him. Her thoughts were stilled when Powis' lips met hers and their tears mingled. The brush of his warm breath on her skin comforted and soothed her.

"I missed you my darling," she whispered. "But now you have come home to me."

An hour later, Elizabeth travelled in the family carriage to 66 Lincoln's Inn Fields, the children followed behind them. As they clattered along, Elizabeth adjusted her fur-lined winter cloak and placed an arm around her husband's shoulder. Gazing out the window, she caught sight of the Tower in the distance and smiled. After five years, Powis was heading home.

As Queen Catherine had said, the memory of their time spent apart would fade. It might take time, but Powis would heal; they all would.

"I never thought I'd live to see this day," Powis said. "My only regret is that it took Petre's death for people to see sense." After a few minutes of sombre silence, Powis pulled a paper from his pocket and handed it to her.

Elizabeth scanned the fading pamphlet – the same one she'd given Powis on her first visit to see him in the Tower, advertising the play, 'She Would if She Could'.

As they laughed together, Elizabeth saw the gleam of the old Powis spark back into his eyes.

CHAPTER SIXTY-FOUR

Supping With The Devil

Sitting alone at a small wooden table in the Amsterdam Coffee House, Titus worked on his latest pamphlet. He'd grown bored of his usual comments and tried to think of something new to say to make people take notice again of his Popish Plot.

He wanted to implicate the King, and worked on wording that would make the biggest impact. As he dipped his pen in the ink, his heart pounded.

James of York is a Catholic and aligned to Catholic France. He is a traitor. The King is also a Catholic and supporter of his brother's intention to return England, Scotland and Ireland to Papist control.

After reading the pamphlet over, Titus nodded. Now all he had to do was add some evidence. *I overheard a conversation that implicates York in the Popish Plot.*

Mmm. Yes. Now, what could he have overheard? Looking out the window, Titus hoped inspiration would strike. He needed to cause an uproar that would prove beyond doubt that the King and his brother were involved in the Popish Plot. Once printed, he would have the pamphlets distributed as widely as possible to keep public interest in his Plot.

Dipping his pen back into the ink, Titus smacked his lips and bent his head forward, lost in concentration.

James of York addressed the Privy Council. "I SAID, I want Titus Oates arrested for treason. In referring to *me* as a traitor, surely he's gone beyond even your limits. He also accuses *your* King of treason, and yet you sit here doing nothing. Nay, the time has come for you to act."

Around the table, heads nodded in agreement.

"But, we have no just cause to charge Titus Oates with treason," a member said.

"We could charge him with sedition," a member sitting opposite York suggested.

"It is clear these words . . ." another member said, stabbing at the pamphlet with his fingers. "These words were written to stir rebellion against the King –"

"And the Government!" another member shouted. "I agree we should charge Titus Oates with sedition rather than treason. This pamphlet is a direct attack against His Majesty, and James of York as his successor. The aim is to incite public hostility against them."

"Have Titus Oates arrested and charged with sedition. It's not before time," York said.

In the Amsterdam Coffee House, Titus discussed his latest attack against James of York with a group of friends. "I told him, if you've supped with York, then I'll not sup with you. Nay, I'll not sup with anyone who has supped with the Devil. I was–"

Three armed guards marched to the table. "Titus Oates, you are charged with being a devisor of false news and horrible and false lies."

Titus scraped back the chair and stood. "Blaady Papists, the lot of you."

One of the guards cocked his pistol and pointed it towards him. The other two guards gripped him by his arms and dragged him out the Coffee House.

The following morning, Titus' cell was a hub of activity as men arrived with a small table, four chairs, a writing desk and a comfortable bed. His supporters also ensured he retained a good table and joined him in his cell for sumptuous meals and good wine.

When the order arrived for him to appear in front of the King's Bench to present his plea, in response to the charges against him, Titus ignored it.

A case of scandalum magnatum against Titus Oates was brought before the Court of the King's Bench. He didn't attend the enquiry, and no one spoke in his defence.

The Sheriff sighed and called the first witness for the Crown. Titus's Pamphlet denouncing the King and York was produced, and the Court Clerk read it out.

Afterwards, the jury huddled together for a few minutes before a spokesman presented their verdict. "We find Titus Oates guilty of *scandalum magnatum* against the King and James, Duke of York."

The Sheriff ordered Titus Oates to pay a fine of £100,000 in damages. He also ordered that he remain in prison until the fine was paid . . . in full.

Titus learned of the verdict when two guards entered his cell, to remove him to Newgate Prison. He was appalled to find himself sentenced to such a large sum. Unable to pay, he was to be taken to the common side of Newgate.

"I have friends! You are part of the Popish Plot! I'll see justice done! You cannot do this to me! I'll see you revenged!" Titus shouted as the guards led him out of his comfortable room.

Looking for an opportunity to escape, Titus waited until the guards dropped their attention and turned and ran. The guards gave chase and soon caught him. Pinning his arms behind his back, they marched him into Newgate and forced him onto the floor of a bleak cell. They manacled him and informed him he would be held until all of the £100,000 had been paid.

On hearing this, Titus baulked. For the first time, the gravity of the situation hit him, and he was terrified of what would happen. "I am not guilty!" he screamed.

"Be quiet!" one of the guards shouted. "Any more noise and 'yer shackles will be tightened.

"I have friends – Truth of the Popish Plot. I AM –"

"SILENCE! That's 'yer last warning," the guard roared back, and opened the door to leave.

Titus noticed the rosemary hanging on the outside of the door and snorted. "Rot 'em! Blaady gaol fever. 'Tis I who should be protected. 'Tis I who have to lie here surrounded by filth and vermin. Me. The Saviour of the Nation, I –"

"Shut up," a voice called from the next cell.

"Traitors," Titus muttered.

Epilogue

1685

'Justice will overtake fabricators of lies and false witnesses.'

Heraclitus Greek Philosopher

One Year later

When the door of his cell swung open, and two guards marched in, Titus stepped back and cowered against the wall.

"Whaat? Is it time?" he asked them, his voice trembling.

"Aye, and put 'yer best coat on," the bulkiest guard said and roared with laughter.

"'Yer to make 'yer first appearance. Now get a move on," the second guard said and gripped him by the arm.

As they marched him towards the waiting cart, Titus felt the sun on his face and screwed his eyes closed against the bright light. He'd been retried and imprisoned for perjury. Judge Jeffreys had presided, and called him a 'shame to mankind'. A letter had been submitted to the court from the University of Salamanca, in Spain, stating that he had not received a Doctor of Divinity there. He was also found guilty of a second count of perjury - in claiming to have attended a Jesuit Consult in London when he'd been at St Omer. Unable to pronounce a death penalty for perjury, Judge Jeffreys enforced a harsh punishment.

As the cart clattered along on the cobbles, Titus looked out at the milling throng. He lifted his shaking hands and frowned at his dirt-encrusted nails. He recalled riding through the same streets in his private carriage, dressed in his silk parson's gown. Tears formed in his eyes, and he brushed them away. He faced life in prison, but believed he would be released one day to be hailed again as the 'Saviour of the Nation'. He could see it clearly. He visualised the crowds clambering to touch his gown, shouting praise for him, listening with rapt attention to his every word.

♛

Elizabeth strolled through St James's Park, heading for Westminster Hall. She linked tighter into Powis' arm and let out a contented sigh; at the sight of their children walking in front of them. At last, she had her family close beside her again.

Twelve-year-old Winifred and fifteen-year-old Lucy walked arm and arm at the front. They were followed by eighteen-year-old Ann and twenty-year-old William. Frances and Mary, who had returned from Wales, followed behind them. Mary had waited until her father had been released to announce her betrothal. Elizabeth had birthed her last child but God willing, she might live to see her grandchildren born.

Reaching Westminster Hall, the family positioned themselves beside Castlemaine and Mrs Cellier, at the front of the crowd gathering outside. It was a warm afternoon, and the air smelled of roses and other summer blooms; from the carts selling flowers. As people crowded around them, Elizabeth remained linked into Powis' arm. He had his other arm wrapped around Winifred's shoulder.

Three ragged women jostled in front of them. When Elizabeth made to step back, the tallest woman fell against her. The smell of jasmine and spirit of musk on her skin took Elizabeth by surprise. Gazing into a pair of jet eyes, realisation dawned, and Elizabeth smiled as she recalled Queen Catherine's story of disguising herself and her ladies as village maidens so she could attend the fair. Fearing she might reveal Mary Beatrice's identity, Elizabeth hid her delighted surprise.

As more people arrived, the atmosphere grew jovial, and vendors shouted out their wares.

"Knives, combs or ink-horns!" a well-dressed young man called.

"Pastries, fresh cakes," cried a woman, carrying a basket in each arm.

It had been over a year since Powis' release, and their life had now taken on some semblance of order. At first, Elizabeth found it hard to rely on her husband to make decisions for her. Powis had also found this difficult, and his mood had dropped at the thought she no longer needed him. On Powis' return, the children hadn't seen him for five years. Through time, they'd learned to live with each other's ways again and, although it would never be as it was, family life had resumed.

One by one, the Popish Plot accusers had been brought to account. While undergoing a public whipping, Dangerfield had died from an injury he had received in a scuffle. Miles Prance received a pardon; it was evident he'd been forced into giving his evidence.

At Titus Oates retrial, Judge Jeffrey's stripped him of his clerical dress and sentenced him to be whipped through the streets of London. Five days a year, for the rest of his life, he would be tied to a cart and whipped from one city gate to another. Also, once a year he would be pilloried outside the gate of Westminster Hall, for people to throw rotten eggs and other waste at. Today was the first of those days, and Elizabeth couldn't contain her excitement as she waited for Titus Oates to arrive.

"I pray you never have to visit your husband in the Tower," she said to Winifred.

"God forbid I ever have to. Having Papa there was enough for my lifetime," Winifred replied.

A roar erupted from the crowd, and Elizabeth turned. The cart carrying Titus Oates had drawn up. When he was dragged out, the Herbert family heckled him. His chin was tucked into his chest, and his sunken eyes looked to the ground.

Elizabeth joined in with the crowd and jeered at the words written on his hat – *Titus Oates, convicted upon full evidence of two horrid perjuries.*

When the guards removed Oates' shackles, the crowd hissed, and a man held up a dead cat. When he was hauled over and placed into the pillory, the crowd pushed forward.

A man ran toward the pillory and shouted, "Perjurer! Hang him! No justice, rot in Hell!"

Opening a bag, Elizabeth drew out a rotten egg. "You've earned the right to throw the first one," she said and handed the egg to Powis.

Winifred tittered. "Mama, who *is* Titus Oates?"

Elizabeth linked back into Powis' arm. "Six years ago, Winifred, I asked the very same question. I now know that Titus Oates is no one . . . No one of any importance."

SOURCES

All characters, except for some servants and the astrologer, Bridgefield, are people who lived and held the roles in *Reign of the Marionettes* in 17th century Europe. Documented accounts were used to dramatise their lives and show how they might have experienced events at this time.

The period covered was one of great political and religious upheaval. Records are patchy and often contradictory, depending on who is doing the telling. Adding to the confusion, many documents were destroyed during the Great Fire of London in 1666.

With so many factions formed - with their spy and foreign networks, secret negotiations, clubs, conspiracies, plotting and propaganda - there is a great deal of confusion that required unpacking. There are notable authors who do this with greater rigour and insight than I could ever hope to, and I am indebted to their efforts and have drawn heavily on their work. Even after extensive reading, the only thing that is clear about this time is that nothing is certain. All mistakes are my own. These were the most useful sources:

Jacob Abbott, History of King Charles II of England. 1849 e-book.

Catharine Arnold, City of Sin. London and its Vices. Simon & Schuster 2011

David Brandon, Life in a 17th Century Coffee Shop. The History Press. 2007

Alan Brooke and David Brandon, Olde London Punishments. The History Press. 2010

REIGN OF THE MARIONETTES

Arthur Bryant, Samuel Pepys: The Years of Peril. Collins.1948.

Emily Cockayne, Hubbub: Filth, Noise and Stench in England. 1600-1770. Yale University Press. 2008

Barry Coward, The Stuart Age: England 1603-1714. Pearson Education Ltd. 2nd edition. 1994

M. A. Everett Green, F. H. Blackburne Daniell. (Eds.) Calendar of State Paper, Domestic Series, of the Reign of Charles II 1660-1685. GB. Public Record Office. Longman. 1860 Digitized 5th August 2010

Antonia Fraser, King Charles II. Orion Books. 2002

Tim Harris, London Crowds in the Reign of Charles I: Propaganda and Politics from the Restoration until the Exclusion Crisis. Cambridge University Press.1990.

Tim Harris, Restoration: Charles II and his Kingdoms 1660-1685. Penguin Books. 2006

T. B. Howell, A Complete Collection of State Trials and Proceedings for high treason and other crimes and misdemeanours from the earliest period to the year 1783 Volume X, 36. Charles II to 1 James I 1684-1685. T.C. Hansard. London

Geoffrey Howse, A History of London's Prisons. Wharncliffe Books. 2012

John Kenyon, The Popish Plot. Phoenix Press. 2000

Jane Lane, Titus Oates. Greenwood Press. 1971

John Locke, Memoirs relating to the life of Anthony, first Earl of Shaftesbury 1824. In John Locke 1632-1704. Includes some of Shaftesbury's letters. Kindle edition.

James Long, Ben Long, The Plot Against Pepys. Faber & Faber. 2007

William Lloyd, A sermon at the funeral of Sr. Edmund-Berry Godfrey. Printed by Tho. Newcomb.

Alan Marshall, The Strange Death of Edmund Godfrey. History Press. True Crime. 1999.

Alan Marshall, Intelligence and Espionage in the Reign of Charles II, 1660-1685. Cambridge University Press. 2003

John Miller, The Stuarts. Hambledon Continuum. London. 2004

Carola Oman, Mary of Modena. Hodder & Stoughton. 1962.

Liza Picard, Restoration London. Orion House. 1997

Jean Plaidy, The Merry Monarch's Wife: The Story of Catherine of Braganza. Crown Publishing, 1991

Jean Plaidy, The Loves of Charles II: The Stuart Saga. Rivers Press. 2005

John Pollock, The Popish Plot: A Study in the History of the Reign of Charles II. Reprinted Edition. Kessinger 2005

Linda Porter, Mary Tudor: The First Queen. Piatkus. 2007

Lord George Scott, Lucy Walter: Wife or Mistress. George G Harrap. London. 1947

John Wroughton, The Longman Companion to the Stuart Age. 1603-1714. Longman. 1997

Songs

A Ballad Upon The Popish Plot. Written by a Lady of Quality. Unknown author. Broadside ballad attributed to Elizabeth Herbert.

Packington's Pound. Broadside ballad and popular tune.

Restoration Dramas

Aphra Behn, The Forc'd Marriage or, The Jealous Bridegroom. 1670

George Etherege, The Man of Mode or, Sir Fopling Flutter. 1676

George Etherege, She Would If She Could. 1668

George Ruggle, Ignoramus.1615

Publications and Tracts

Mrs Elizabeth Cellier. Malice Defeated. 1680

Sir Roger L' Estrange, Citt and Bumpkin in a Dialogue Over a Pot of Ale, Concerning Matters of Religion and Government, in response to, 'Papists Plotting to Kill the King'. 1680

Marchmont Needham or, Marchamont Nedham. A Pacquet of Advices

449

and Animadversions sent from London to the men of Shaftesbury. 1676

Titus Oates. True and Exact Narrative of the Horrid Plot and Conspiracy of the Popish Party against the life of His Sacred Majesty the Government and the Protestant Religion. 1679.

Shaftesbury's (and possibly John Locke's) tracts. A Letter from a Person of Quality to his Friend in the Country, 1675. Two Seasonable Discourses concerning this present Parliament, 1675. An Appeal from the Country to the City, 1679.

London's Defiance to Rome. A Perfect Narrative of the Magnificent *Procession,* and Solemn Burning of the *Pope at Temple-Barr, November* 17th, 1679.

The trials are well documented and available online. They are, however, long, dry and stylistically written for the time. I used these as a basis to select and dramatise events using the characters.

I used the content of Edward Coleman's letters, but selected, reduced and reworded them to make them more readable.

Broadsides/broadsheets reporting the last dying words of people hanged are available for this period, and events are recorded in the Gazette. These were dramatised for the story and characters. The characters of Anne Jurejon and Amos Child are taken from the listings of hangings at Tyburn.

AUTHOR'S NOTE

The period covered in Reign of the Marionettes was a complex and difficult time with great political and religious unrest. Some figures switched allegiances many times. The situation in Scotland, Ireland, France and the Netherlands add to the complexities, and it is beyond the scope of these notes to do this justice.

Like his father, King Charles I, Charles II believed in the divine right of kings to rule without interference. In 1649, King Charles I was executed for treason against the people and Charles II fled into exile with his supporters. There followed a period with the Lord Protector and Puritan, Oliver Cromwell, until his death - Cromwell's son was regarded as an unworthy successor, and Charles II was restored.

Charles' Restoration Agreement was based on a tight control by Parliament - Charles was not to rule through any divine right, and Parliament would hold the purse strings. Despite a generous agreement, Parliament frequently gave Charles less funds; keeping him reliant on them. With no real political requirement as King, Charles was free to lead the life of a 'Merry Monarch'- with Parliament running the Country. During his enforced exile, Charles developed close friendships with many of his young, loyal supporters, such as Buckingham and Rochester, and they benefited from his return as King. The Restoration Court grew frivolous, licentious and bawdy. The theatres, which were closed during Cromwell's time, re-opened and 'Restoration Plays' replaced the staid

'Shakespearian Plays' from before. These new plays reflected topical issues and often mocked Charles' Court and Couriers.

The prologue in Reign of the Marionettes opens over a hundred years before the main events, with Queen Mary I, at Smithfield, London. The persecution of Protestants during her reign later earned her the name, Bloody Mary. During the 17th century, people still feared this happening again.

While Charles worked towards religious tolerance, his Parliament worked towards greater restrictions. It was illegal to practice mass or keep rosaries or missals. Practising Catholics were driven out of London and punished if they were caught. Despite such legislation, Protestants and Catholics mixed freely together on a day to day basis.

Despite fathering numerous bastards, Charles had no legitimate children - Queen Catherine was barren. Charles' brother, James, was his heir. The revelation of James of York's conversion and then his marriage to Mary Beatrice, a Catholic – followed by the discovery of Charles' secret treaty with Catholic France - prompted Shaftesbury and his supporters to set up in opposition to the Crown. At this time, England was engaged in the Anglo-Dutch war - in alliance with France against the Dutch. But, the majority of people were moving away from France to supporting the Protestant Dutch, and by 1678 a war with France seemed imminent.

It was against this turbulent background that Titus Oates appeared claiming to have uncovered a Papal plot to kill the King and replace him with his Catholic heir, James, Duke of York. Whether or not a Papal plot existed is unclear. It is possible a Protestant plot to replace York with

Charles' eldest bastard son, Monmouth, existed. Old Republicans may also have been plotting to remove Charles. It is also possible that all of these conspiracies were occurring simultaneously.

At a time when it was difficult to know who to trust, most of the nobility employed spies – Shaftesbury and Buckingham had links to both France and Holland. Coffee Houses became the source of many conspiracies, secret negotiations and intrigues - with separate ones for different factions. In addition, many of the Old Republicans who had intrigued the events for the removal of Charles' father, continued to plot in the background.

Edmund Berry Godfrey's death sparked the public hysteria that lead to Titus Oates' Popish Plot being taken as a reality. Theories and debates continue as to who murdered Godfrey and why. These include - Jesuits, Pembroke, Titus Oates, and Buckingham. It is possible Godfrey was not murdered at all but committed suicide and his death made to look like a murder. Alternatively, Godfrey may well have been murdered, either accidently or intentionally, to obtain the original of the narrative of the Popish Plot. After all this time it is unlikely the truth will ever be revealed. Numerous books and papers have been written on the subject of Godfrey's death, examining all of these theories, and more.

Many Protestants believed that the Great Fire of London, which seemed no more than an unfortunate accident, had been deliberately started by Papists to burn them out. Omens were taken seriously; with people watchful for signs of impending disaster or good fortune. The Civil War, the Plague and the Great Fire were taken as signs of approaching doom. John Gadbury was the main astrologer of the time - William Lilly had retired. Mrs Cellier's reading from the fictional character, Bridgefield, is loosely based on Lilly's documented prediction for Oliver Cromwell.

Elizabeth is presented in sources as a somewhat, motherly, matronly figure, and this was taken as the start point for her relationships with others. While there are some documented accounts of Elizabeth's father - he was a famous inventor - there is little account of Elizabeth and Powis' early lives. It is recorded that Powis was a particularly religious man who did not take a mistress.

The relationship between Elizabeth and Mary Beatrice is also not well documented. The developing relationship between them

is, therefore, fictional. There was, however, a close trust and bond between them. When Mary Beatrice was later forced into exile with James, Elizabeth and Powis fled to France with them, and Mary Beatrice's children were entrusted into Elizabeth's care.

A note about dates

During the 17th Century, England's Julian dates were ten days behind France's Gregorian dates. England and the Netherlands used the older Julian calendar OS (Old Style), while France used the Gregorian calendar, NS (New Style).

ACKNOWLEDGEMENTS

This novel was a long time in the making. Thanks to everyone who read and commented on drafts.

To Kenneth Greig for editing early drafts and helping with translations, and Emily Hakkinen, editor, thank you both. All errors are my own.

A special thanks to Carol Jeffries, for sharing her research and knowledge of the Stuarts.

To Douglas Debelak, thank you for supporting me through the final part of this journey.

Finally, thanks to my family and friends, for their unending patience and understanding.

Sheena

Macleod

Scotland,

UK

2016

70419079R00255

Made in the USA
Columbia, SC
06 May 2017